THE
REAPER
FOLLOWS

THE
REAPER
FOLLOWS

HEATHER GRAHAM

mira™

ISBN-13: 978-0-7783-6973-8

The Reaper Follows

Mira
22 Adelaide St. West, 41st Floor
Toronto, Ontario M5H 4E3, Canada
BookClubbish.com

Printed in U.S.A.

For Pierre Brown...

A friend who is always incredibly kind, optimistic—and a gift to the world!

Rides the Pale Horse

"And I looked, and behold a pale horse:
and his name that sat on him was Death, and Hell followed with him.
And power was given unto them over the fourth part of the earth,
to kill with sword, and with hunger, and with death, and with
the beasts of the earth."

PROLOGUE

Aidan

The day was warm and humid, but a light breeze stirred, creating just a slight ripple on the shimmering water and an occasional glint among the rich growth of trees and grass. But looking ahead, with the sun also casting dazzling bits of diamond reflections on the water, Aidan Cypress thought about the beauty of the region.

But it didn't alleviate his sense of dread.

They'd all been waiting.

And now it was possible the last shoe had dropped.

He had always loved his homeland, the Florida Everglades. There was an incredible sense of peace and majesty to be found here in the great sweeps of trees, hammocks, and saw grass prairies. Birds soaring high in colors that shamed a rainbow held sway over the skies, and the land and the water offered so much more in nature's bounty.

Despite the beauty of the great "river of grass," he knew dangers awaited the unwary and the vulnerable. Alligators basked in the sun on the embankments of the countless streams and ponds that continually moved throughout the tropical wetlands;

the area was home to extremely poisonous coral snakes, eastern diamondbacks, pygmy rattlers, and the cottonmouth.

He swatted at his cheek.

Of course, there were the mosquitoes and other flying pests like gnats that could drive one wild. But he'd been out with Jimmy Osceola in his flatboat many times and had almost become oblivious to the flying pests that could be far more annoying than a fear of lethal predators.

He also knew that once upon a time, it had been this great river of grass that had given his people sanctuary. In the early 1800s, peoples from Georgia had fled south: Upper Creeks, Lower Creeks, and many other Indigenous people. They all became known as Seminoles, or sometimes, Runaways. The Seminole Wars raged throughout the early 1800s, and many Indigenous people were rounded up and shipped out to reservations in the West. But in the end, approximately six hundred people survived in the Everglades, never surrendering. Sometimes they were known as the Undefeated, or the Unconquered. Those six hundred or so people eventually thrived and in time separated into their two main language groups, Hitachi and Muscogee. In the mid-twentieth century, they were finally recognized as the Seminole and Mikasuki Tribes of Florida.

Aidan grinned to himself. Times changed. Now his people were doing well. It didn't hurt that they'd purchased many of the Hard Rock properties, not the least of which was just in Hollywood near tribal offices, the stunning Guitar Hotel and the casino drawing thousands of people from across the world—not to mention, of course, the local population who just enjoyed a night or two away to experience the pools, the fabulous restaurants, and, naturally, the gaming.

He was glad Amy Larson and Hunter Forrest were there right now. A friend of his in casino management had arranged for a very special room for them. They really needed the break because the two of them had been on the case from the beginning, following the bizarre killings that had to do with the Book of Revelation—and the coming of the Apocalypse. He'd worked with Amy many times, and he loved her dearly as a friend. He'd met Hunter Forrest when crucified victims had been displayed just south of here, and he admired the man tremendously.

And with all that they had seen…

They deserved a break. One they might have expected to be cut short.

Because they'd all dreaded that despite the monsters taken down so far, more would be out there. And now…

He was resigned to the fact this had been bound to happen—the dreaded arrival of the pale horse, and whatever truly lay behind the devastation they'd been fighting.

The Everglades were truly a national treasure of nature, and the very wild beauty of the place invited those who loved the remote and austere elegance of the landscape and also those who wanted to make use of it.

"Pull in here," he called back to his friend Jimmy Osceola. They'd taken the flatboat rather than Jimmy's airboat so Aidan could watch the shoreline. Aidan worked for the FDLE—Florida Department of Law Enforcement—and he was proud of his expertise in the forensic field. But Jimmy was just a hell of a nice guy who loved people and loved being a tour guide in the Everglades.

Aidan didn't know what he was going to find, if anything. When whoever was really behind the Horsemen cases had begun, the killings had been shown in pure spectacle, victims hanged as if crucified and left to be discovered. Then there had been the ridiculous displays with dead gang members.

But these trends never repeated themselves. Still, one of Jimmy's customers had been convinced she'd seen something strange on the embankment, and so, when he'd finished the tour, he'd called Aidan. Just because a worried tourist had seen something that bothered her didn't necessarily mean there was anything wrong…

Except as he somehow knew inside, the fourth horseman was

still out there—and whoever was behind it all wanted something. Aidan's sixth sense warned him the pale horse would waste no time in arriving.

And as he had feared, this tourist had been right—there was something wrong. Very wrong.

Aidan hopped off the boat, motioning to Jimmy to stay behind, and walked slowly and carefully toward the flash of pale color he had seen against the intense green of the foliage. Jimmy was an amazing guy who loved his people, their culture, and the Everglades. He was not, however, in law enforcement.

And as he came closer, his heart seemed to freeze, and he hated his own instinct.

There was a hand sticking out from the ground with fingers outstretched as if they'd been reaching, trying desperately to dig out. Except that...

As he came nearer, he realized there was no way the hand might dig a body out of a grave.

The hand was attached to a ravaged forearm and nothing more.

A few feet away, half-covered by brush, was a foot with part of an ankle, and beyond that...

More. More chopped-up body parts—body parts belonging to more than one person. This was no leftover or regurgitated meal discarded by a predator. These parts had fallen out of one of the barrels entangled in a stretch of mangrove roots.

Only one barrel had fallen over.

He could see four more barrels. Perhaps there were additional barrels in the twisted and tangled undergrowth that proliferated in the area.

Carefully he inched forward; he could see what looked like a small figurine—a pale green horse—lying near the overturned barrel, but there was more. It appeared there was something twisted in the fingers protruding from the grass and roots and fallen leaves.

Slipping on gloves, he reached to keep his distance from the area of the crime scene until the medical examiners, photographers, the rest of his team, and the detectives and agents could arrive.

It was a torn scrap of paper, possibly secured by the person before death, and maybe unnoticed by the killer—or even purposely left to be discovered. He had to be careful with the paper; the elements had already played havoc with the dismembered corpses here.

Naturally, at the same time, his phone was ringing. Caller ID showed him Amy Larson, FDLE agent on loan to the FBI for the Horsemen cases, was on the line.

How the hell did she know already?

A sixth sense like his? Or...

"Aidan," she said before he could speak. "Any chatter, any anything? Mickey Hampton called and told me he opened a package at our office—it contained one of those plastic horses."

"A pale horse," Aidan said, swallowing. "Pale green, the color of death, of rot and decay. Amy, he's here. Our fourth horseman is at work already, out here once again in the Everglades."

"You found a body?" she asked.

Aidan looked around and winced.

"Definitely. Um, more than one."

"How many?"

"Amy, frankly, I have no idea. I'm just very afraid things may get a whole lot worse before...well, hopefully, before we all do our best to stop whatever Apocalypse is being planned, and..."

He broke off. As he'd spoken, he'd managed at last to read the faint writing on the scrap of paper he'd extricated from the fingers.

"'The Reaper Follows,'" Aidan said.

"Pardon?" Amy asked.

"Scrap of paper in a hand—"

"A dead man was holding a scrap of paper?"

Aidan shrugged, shaking his head.

"Aidan?" Amy pressed, concerned.

"A hand. Fingers attached to a hand and a forearm. Just get the hell out here, please! I'm pinging you the coordinates. And…"

Behind him, he felt a presence; Jimmy Osceola had stepped off the boat. And now Jimmy let out something of a twist between a startled choke and a scream.

"Oh my God, what—" Amy began.

"We're good—Jimmy just saw… Please, Amy, tell Hunter—all hands on deck. The Reaper isn't following—the Reaper is here."

1

Hunter Forrest was grim as he surveyed the scene at the coordinates Aidan had sent.

When the little plastic horse, the "pale horse," had shown up at FDLE, they'd known their respite was over. Whoever was making use of the biblical warning regarding the Apocalypse and the Four Horsemen who would bring it on wasn't going to stop until he, she, or they had played their game out to the very end.

They'd circumvented so much of the insanity already, Hunter thought. But now they were playing the finale—the endgame—without knowing what that game was intended to be.

Except, of course, that it would include the deaths of more innocents. As apparently it had already done.

A pale horse—pale green. The color of death and the rot and decay that followed.

Then again…

This was the Florida Everglades.

Where one could often find miles and miles—and miles—of nothing but waterways, saw grass, palms, and more natural flora and fauna. Where Miccosukee and Seminole tribal lands abutted state and federal lands.

There were no security cameras lurking around, just a few gators here and there.

No one to see the pale horse easily dispense pale, sickly green—dispense death.

In truth, they were looking at many colors here, mostly green already, but deep green, bright green—colors of life. And apparently these murders had been intended to stay hidden—for a time at least. All in all, they had discovered eight large oil drums filled with body parts. It was going to take a team of medical examiners to put them all together. It was truly horrendous, like a thousand-piece jigsaw puzzle, except this puzzle had been created from dismembered corpses.

The strange thing was they hadn't heard of any mass killings. And by the evidence they had ascertained so far, the victims hadn't been shot. And since they were in so many pieces, they had been left anywhere from a few days ago to a few weeks ago. The medical examiners on-site couldn't tell them much until they had time to try to piece the bodies together in a mass autopsy.

But so far, they hadn't found a bullet in any body part, nor had any cartridges or shells been discovered in the area.

"They weren't killed here," Amy Larson said.

Hunter turned to look at Amy, his partner and so much more, and wondered if he wasn't appearing to have a bit of green on his own face as she did. Despite the years he had spent in the service of law enforcement, this was one of the most horrendous crime scenes he had ever come across.

Even seasoned medical examiners were looking a bit green.

Just like the fourth, "pale" horse.

But Amy stood firmly and grimly, angry and determined. She was a beautiful woman, about five-ten in height, with sweeping, dark auburn hair and classic features. She usually tied her hair back when working and wore very professional-looking pantsuits—unless law enforcement was making use of her looks in any kind of an undercover operation. But a professional appearance took nothing away from her sculpted face or the emerald flash of her eyes.

She turned to him, frowning, one brow arched. "I hate to admit it, but I'm not feeling much like a hardened law enforcement officer at this moment. What? Do I look as…queasy as I feel?" she asked him.

"No. The green in your face just enhances the shade of your eyes," he told her.

"You look a little bit under the weather, too, you know."

"I'm human. And back to what we're seeing, I agree, they weren't killed here. They were murdered elsewhere and dumped here. This isn't going to be easy. We're going to need to have identities on these corpses to discover who they were and how they all wound up being here at the same site," he said.

Amy nodded as she looked around, shaking her head. "This is…so strange. We were meant to find the bodies eventually, I think. Why else leave a toy horse and note? But to chop human beings up like this and put them in barrels… I don't believe we were supposed to find them quite so quickly. The tourist was concerned because she saw a barrel had fallen over or a predator had knocked it over. And when we did find them, I don't think the killer wanted us finding out who they were."

"I agree on that, too. I think you're right about that," Hunter said.

"But!" another voice chimed in.

They turned to see their friend Aidan Cypress, forensic specialist, coming their way.

"But?" Amy queried, frowning.

"*But* while we may be missing a few fingers here and there— the wildlife around here does get hungry—we are going to have many. And it's likely we'll discover most of the identities between fingerprints and DNA."

Hunter studied Aidan and said thoughtfully, "We're on the pale horseman. With each of the others, there has been a leader—except we believe that these leaders have been following someone else."

"The horseman above the other horsemen?" Amy queried.

He nodded. "And I'm wondering... Okay, what I'm thinking is we'll have a fourth horseman—but expendable to whoever is really pulling the strings. All these things are meant to cause chaos, just like the Four Horsemen of the Apocalypse. This is loose, of course, because there are so many interpretations of the Book of Revelation. But bear with me. The First Horseman, riding the white horse—seen as Christ himself by many but seen as the Antichrist in later interpretations—came to create war and conquer. The Second Horseman, seated upon the red horse, had a great sword and was to go forth and slay men. The Third Horseman, riding the black horse, was given scales and talked about the price of food—and that was interpreted as someone bringing famine. The pale horseman rides along with the grave and brings death and an overall interpretation is the demise of a quarter of the population. But here's the thing—we've stopped the white, red, and black horse riders. And while they were clever, I'm going to go with either batshit crazy or maniacally brainwashed."

"And you think there's someone directing all the so-called horsemen," Amy said. She grimaced. "Someone who isn't batshit crazy."

"Right," Hunter agreed.

Aidan was nodding. Hunter arched a brow to him.

"You know, hungry big alligators will eat smaller alligators," Aidan said thoughtfully.

"What?" Amy asked, frowning.

"I got it. I think we're all three thinking that maybe...this leader of the pack may have been getting rid of baggage, those beneath him doing the dirty work *and* anyone who failed him or wasn't toeing his line closely enough," Hunter speculated.

"A theory. Possibly," Aidan said. "A toy horse was sent to the FDLE, and there's a toy horse here. We may discover that some of these people were failed followers, and some of them are victims who were simply getting in the way or causing trouble."

"Okay, at the beginning, I was called in on this specifically because of the cult involvement. And let's face it, we've taken down a few sadly deluded people," Hunter began.

"But this kind of planning isn't crazy, four horses until the Apocalypse—" Amy said.

"Tells us that there will, yes, be a fourth horseman—and then a someone over them, someone who has caused all this for a greater plan. And while he or she might have had a few crackpots—conspiracy theorists, whatever—in their employ, I don't believe the master puppeteer really believes in the Apocalypse or even the Bible or any other religious texts. This elongated path of death and destruction calls for something else, something deliberate," Hunter theorized.

He looked around at the scene again and shook his head. "We've all seen the power of a charismatic leader, especially a cult leader, someone who can truly convince others he—or she—knows the way to the afterlife in all good grace. It's often *mind-boggling* that the human mind can be so twisted and coerced. But brainwashing is very real. The puppeteer found people in different stages of loss, confusion, or personal trauma and belief to prey upon. Some are just those who..." His voice trailed for a minute.

He knew a lot about cults and was called upon when cult activity was suspected because he'd spent time in a cult as a boy. It had started out for the right reasons—his mother had been infuriated by her rich father's refusal to help those in need in any way. She had believed she was bringing his father, him, and herself to a better place of kindness and faith.

Only to discover that when rules weren't obeyed, kindness was the last thing on a cult leader's mind. And the cult concept was being used here. But he believed it was being used for a very specific reason.

"Hunter?" Amy said.

She was worried about him, and he smiled. "I'm just trying to figure out what the endgame in all this might be. What could someone want? Everything in this has been the same—death and destruction—but different. Bodies out here, bodies in a cave, gang killings, bodies displayed, and bodies hidden. Why?" He grimaced. "Going back to scores of great minds in our field—when crimes are committed, we look for motive, opportunity, and means. When the Behavioral Analysis Unit got started, they had to take a new look at motive when they dealt with killers like the Son of Sam—his motive was that a dog told him to kill. They interviewed and studied serial killers, trying to learn the reasons killers would select victims at random, victims who had done nothing to them. Anyway, I think we have both situations going on here—the follower 'horsemen,' some of whom do believe in what they're doing in a cult fashion, and then someone with a definite desire to make something happen."

"Like what, though?" Aidan asked.

"I don't know. And figuring that out might be the key," Hunter said.

They were all quiet for a minute.

"Hey!" Amy said, pointing to the score of officers, agents, forensic experts, and medical examiners carefully searching the area. "We're not alone in all this."

"No. But still, Amy, you are targeted," Aidan said grimly. "Amy, the horses are always sent to you or appear wherever you and Hunter may be."

"Hey, my friend, you've been with me at some of the most frightening twists in this thing, but as I said, we're not alone. I'm always careful. And I have you and Hunter and amazing teams behind me."

"I know," Aidan said. "And I know you won't sensibly back away from this."

"I can't," Amy told him. "And we're all only safe when we find the truth."

Hunter nodded. "I did spend time taking classes and working with some of the behavioral analysis agents, and I think we might bring someone in on this. I'm trying to put a finger on just who we might be looking for, but we all know that help can be just what we need, too."

"Well, I admit I've never been able to take any of those classes—trace evidence, blood spatter patterns...you name it. But no profiling. But! I think I can tell you a few things, and you can tell me a lot more," Aidan said. "The Everglades seems to be the prime location, so we may be looking for someone who is a Floridian or loves and knows Florida. Or at the least, we're looking for someone who has really studied the maps and the terrain. And I think it may be someone who even knows where all the boundaries are on tribal land, state land, and federal land. They know many of the waterways, and also where roads come close to waterways."

Hunter smiled grimly and nodded. "And someone who is a narcissist, convinced of their own power, so much so that taunting us along the way brings them extreme pleasure. Clues are spread about, but the real leader of all this is convinced they're superior to any of our efforts to come close to the truth. Yet we all believe that while we were supposed to find these bodies, we weren't supposed to have found them so quickly. I also believe the victims were dead before they were chopped to pieces. The horror of the situation—corpses in pieces, rotting and *green*—is something that is supposed to disarm us. A barrel fell over. We found these victims a little early. It may help, or it may not."

"Maybe law enforcement was supposed to have been on edge by the arrival of the pale horse at the FDLE office," Aidan said. "They would be desperately looking but having to take time to find the bodies. If the barrels had all remained tightly sealed, it would have been some time before they were noticed here, where they are."

"Still, for now, we wait for forensics and the medical examiners to tell us just who we have here and what clues there might be. I'm going to speak with Assistant Director Garza and find out if he doesn't have an agent from the BAU he thinks might be able to help on the profiling side. I don't think these barrels were brought through the roads. It would be a long way through rugged terrain to carry them out here. They were brought through the waterways," Amy said.

"And here's the thing—no security cameras are hidden in these trees," Aidan said. "There's nothing to catch on video, no facial recognition to be used." He wrinkled his face and said dryly, "Alligators and even the most beautiful birds don't make great witnesses."

"We need to work on the victimology," Hunter said.

"And we will get names for you," Aidan vowed.

His friend and coworker was angry, Hunter thought. And he didn't blame him. Some people found the Everglades to be a no-man's-land of heat, mosquitoes, and killer creatures. To Aidan, the area was a natural wonder, one that offered exquisite birds, tranquil waterways, and nature, all beautiful and hazardous at its best.

He understood. He wasn't from the area himself, having endured his own strange childhood. But he knew Amy loved an airboat ride and watching for the various storks to be seen along with the Florida panther, endangered and protected, and yet seen by a lucky few.

He knew such an area—treacherous to the unwary—had been used through the years as a dumping ground, but never on a scale such as this.

"Thanks, Aidan," he said. "I know you and your team will get whatever there is that can be gotten."

Aidan nodded and tried to smile. "So, how was the holiday?"

Amy laughed softly. "Not sure you can call so few days a holiday, but wow! Aidan, thank you. It was beautiful, wonderful! Incredible."

"I'll get you back there!" Aidan promised.

"Let me add to that. Thank you, thank you, thank you! It was great," Hunter emphasized. He noticed Amy was frowning, wandering toward something that wasn't really a trail, but more or less like animal tracks between saw grass and trees.

"Amy?"

"Be right back!" she promised. "I thought... I'm probably wrong. I'll be right back!"

There had been movement.

Of course, there could well be movement. Man wasn't the only creature to prowl through the Everglades. But...

Amy moved carefully, going inland, back toward the road, doubting she was going to stumble upon an alligator this far inland from the water, but it was possible. The danger that might be faced was more likely that of venomous snakes in this area.

And then again, possibly human snakes as well, she thought grimly.

But while the barrels had been there an indeterminate amount of time, they hadn't been left there in the trees by the water in the last hours or even the last days. Whoever had dumped them there was probably long gone.

And still...

She wasn't sure why whatever she had seen set off alarm bells. Birds caused leaves and branches to tremble. There were also the usual critters—alligators, snakes, frogs, lizards, and, coming increasingly to the north in the Everglades and along the Atlantic coast, crocodiles as well. Deer, rabbits, raccoons, and opossums. Near the water, river otters. In the water, manatees.

She saw a flash of dark blue through the intense green of the area.

None of the creatures she knew about wore garments in blue.

Someone was there. Someone moving quickly through the trees ahead of her.

She quickened her pace, still moving carefully, aware of patches of saw grass and watching the ground and low branches for creatures other than man as well.

"FDLE! Stop!" she commanded. She was just feet behind her quarry now.

She stopped. There was no movement. She waited, listening, hand moving toward the Glock in its holster.

Then a man stepped out before her wearing blue jeans and a blue shirt. He was young, perhaps twenty-five, tops, with long, rich dark hair and well-cut features.

He was wielding a gun.

Fine—she had one, too. But she didn't want to kill this man. He could be the lead they so desperately needed to what had happened here. She set her hand on her hip, hoping for conversation.

"It's you!" he said, his face filled strangely with recognition, surprise, and pleasure. As if he had just won the jackpot at a casino.

"It's me?" she said, hoping to keep him talking, to understand him, and to find a way for him to relinquish his weapon.

"I know who you are!"

"And who am I?" she asked.

"The beloved of the Antichrist!" he said.

She arched a brow. Not the answer she'd been expecting. But everything about him seemed real; he believed what he was saying.

"Um, honestly, I'm not even sure I know the Antichrist," she told him. "And what makes you think I'm his beloved?"

"Because I know you. I've seen your picture," he assured her.

"Where?"

"The Archangel showed it to me," he explained. "And it is you. I'm certain. And don't try anything on me. We were all warned you were beautiful, and you might try to seduce us and dissuade us, but...we all know what we must do."

"Okay, please, I promise you, I don't know the Antichrist. Please, let's start over. I'm Amy Larson. Who are you and what are you doing out here? I just wanted to talk to you—and you're aiming a gun at me," Amy said.

"You don't know who I am?" he asked, amused.

"No, and that would be why I'm asking you."

His smile deepened. "Angel."

"Your name is Angel. Angel…what?" she asked.

He started to laugh. "No, you really are blind, aren't you? I'm an angel, part of all the greater glory that will come!"

"Right," she murmured. "How about your earthly name?"

He smiled. "Amy, you must pay attention. Petty things of this flesh are unimportant. Take it like this—I am an angel. And I know who you are. And I know what disguise you've taken on while here on earth. Yes. You're Special Agent Amy Larson. Such a hotshot! And you think I won't shoot you—because you'll shoot me. Of course, I know you carry a gun. What you don't understand is I am a messenger angel, and my strength and power come from the pale horse! So, you see, I don't care if you shoot me. Because the greatest reward awaits me. Though, to be truthful, I do hope my shot disarms you first, and yours misses me. Because you see, you need to pay for all your sins."

"My sins? I'm sorry—you want to hurt me, kill me, and I have never killed an innocent, sir. It appears you have been involved in the deaths of many," Amy said. "Put your weapon down—"

"No, no, no. You are such a fool, bound by stupid laws, created by stupid people. I have merely joined with those who want to see the world for what it should be! Some are ready, so good that the heavens await them. And some must be sent to the pits below! I do what I am commanded by the grace of the Archangel, who leads us to our great reward in the hereafter. Not many are selected as I have been!"

He spoke the last part almost angrily.

"Well, I don't think many are as gullible as you are, I'm afraid.

Laws protect us all to go about our lives seeking happiness with-out harming others," Amy said.

He sniffed and shook his head. "You are so brainwashed."

"Think about what you're saying. I'm a friend to the Anti-christ—"

"You're his concubine!"

"Trust me, I am no one's concubine. And I'm begging you. You're so young! Don't throw your life away. Put your weapon down and—"

"Ah, well. I will have done my part! But…you were supposed to pay a greater price on this earth. Even you should be able to pay the needed death, suffer in the flesh that you may rise high above with the angels in the beauty that will be! Oh, so many must suffer here, but we are saving them, you idiot, and you are doing all you can to see that so many burn eternally in agony!"

"Drop it!" came a harsh voice.

She had her gun out in a flash, but it was unnecessary. Amy realized Hunter was with her, just a step behind her. Of course. When she hadn't returned quickly, he had headed after her. That's what a good partner would do in any case.

"Drop it now. I promise you, we both have great aim, and you'll be dead before your finger twitches," Hunter said evenly.

To Amy's astonishment, the man smiled.

"I have tried. I have tried and tried. You know, I might have honored her. Provided the blood and pain and death that would have allowed her peace and beauty. But now…"

"Drop the weapon," Hunter repeated quietly.

The man bowed down, as if to toss his gun on the ground. But he didn't. Rather, he aimed the gun at his own head.

"No!" Amy screamed. She had one chance, and she took it as she aimed for the young man's hand.

The sound of their bullets exploding seemed earth-shattering against the blanket of green that surrounded them.

2

The young man had managed to fire, and he fell to the ground. But Amy was pretty sure she'd somewhat deflected his aim, and he just might live.

She looked at Hunter, aware they were both dismayed. This man was obviously involved with what was going on and possibly a lead to others.

They raced to the young man, hunkering down by his side. Hunter instantly checked for a pulse and breath.

"Hunter?"

"He's alive. He's breathing…has a weak pulse. We've got to see about the bleeding. Put on your gloves and place your hand here for a minute. I'll rip a piece of shirt to press against his skull."

She nodded, placing her gloved hand as he directed. The bullet had skimmed his forehead. There was a surprising amount of blood. She hoped it was just because flesh had been torn—and not because the bullet had grazed too deeply.

It wasn't a pleasant feeling, and she winced inwardly as she did what was necessary.

Hunter was good and quick, pulling his shirt out and ripping up the tails of the garment, creating a bulk of fabric to press beneath Amy's hand.

"I'm going. I'll get someone—"

"I'm staunching the bleeding but...we've got it under control. It's a head wound. We'll need to see just how much damage he did to himself. I feel so bad. How...how can people be so...?" Amy began.

"Amy, that shot was perfect. Right now, he has a fighting chance. Yeah, and he looks like he's little more than a big kid just starting out on his adult life so how could he be so batshit crazy?" Hunter suggested. He shook his head. "Amy, even after my childhood, after all the years I've spent doing this...I'll never know. The human mind is a dense jungle, every mind different, and every mind subjected to everything that hits it through our years of development and beyond. We need help fast—"

She carefully set the material Hunter had given her around the young man's head to keep it steady with the wound pressed and removed her bloody gloves before pulling her phone out. "Calling Aidan—he's on scene. And the place is crawling with medical examiners who are physicians—"

Aidan answered her call. She explained briefly and promised to walk back along the poor animal trail she had taken so he could find her quickly.

"Of course. I'm going!"

She checked that the blood flow from the young man's head had been stopped before standing, ready to head back.

"Amy," Hunter said, and she paused.

"Just so you know... I know you were doing fine on your own—I have no doubt you could have shot him before his finger twitched if he'd come close to shooting you. But what you did... You might have given us what we need—and saved a life," Hunter assured her.

"Maybe. But, Hunter, like you said, I think he was just barely more than a kid, seeking something, clinging to something. A young life thrown away. I just wish there was a way that…"

"People wouldn't believe what they choose to believe, no matter what evidence exists to the contrary? Amy, that is so far beyond us."

"Right. I know that. I just mean that— I just wind up feeling so sad when I see someone so young and so deluded." She was backing away, ready to race through the trees, as they spoke.

"You're human," he called after her.

She nodded with a grim smile. "Thanks for that. All right, I'm on my way to lead Aidan and a doctor to our location. Be right back."

"Careful. We're still in—"

"I know!" she broke in. "A dangerous swamp, but it's my swamp, and really—a river of grass. I know all about the snakes in the grass, those that are real, and those who come in human form!"

Amy left him, carefully retracing her footsteps almost all the way back to the cordoned-off area where the barrels—including the one that had fallen over and distributed its tragic contents—still stood.

She saw Aidan had found an ME, one she knew, Dr. Bethany Rodriguez, a woman who worked with FDLE often. She was based in Orlando but Amy knew as well that from FDLE headquarters, in tandem with the FBI, medical examiners had been called on from both agencies and all around the state. She was an impressive woman who often seemed to learn more from the dead than they sometimes did from the living.

As she met up with Aidan and Dr. Rodriguez, she greeted them both, explaining quickly what had happened before leading them back the way she had come.

"I don't know. It may not have been enough," Amy said. "Of course, his hand is in bad shape and the bullet grazed his skull. But I'm hoping—"

"Hey, I don't get the living often," Dr. Rodriguez said. "I

will be doing my best to keep him that way. My assistants are right behind us coming along with a gurney."

"That's wonderful. Thank you," Amy said.

"And an ambulance is on the way. We had vehicles for the bodies or body parts, but now we need help and help fast."

"Dr. Rodriguez, what do you think?" Amy asked anxiously as they moved quickly through the terrain. "I was hoping to keep him from a direct shot into the head...well, hoping he'd drop the weapon, but—"

"Amy, it's amazing you kept him alive at all," Aidan assured her.

She smiled at Aidan. They had always been close. While she'd always loved her home state and the incredible if strange wilderness that covered over a million acres of the southern section of it, Aidan had taught her so much about the history, especially the history of his Native American people.

"Photographers had finished with the scene, but I caught one. He could be right behind us, too, though life takes precedence over forensic procedure," Aidan told her.

"And our victim is right ahead of us," Amy said.

"Curious. He was trying to kill himself but not you?" Dr. Rodriguez asked.

"He thought I was best friends—or more—with the Antichrist. He wanted to kill me, but Hunter reached us. There were two guns trained on him, so we'll both have to be debriefed on this. My weapon will go in... But at the time, he turned the gun on himself. Shooting it out of his hand seemed to be my only recourse."

"I can't begin to understand the brainwashing being done," Dr. Rodriguez said, shaking her head.

She had worked on many such cases.

Cases that included the dead who were victims of earlier horsemen, or horsewomen, as they had seen as well.

Amy shook her head. "Right ahead. This is...so disturbing. This one... Well, we watched him. He spoke so bizarrely, absolutely convinced of what he was saying. I guess that meant he would find his glory. Young, early twenties, I think. Totally... off the wall. He was telling us how we were ruining everything. We were the sinners, and we were keeping people from reaching their nirvana or their place of glory. When Hunter appeared and there were two guns trained on him while we told him to drop his weapon, he chose to turn it on himself."

"Amy, you did what you could," Aidan said firmly.

They heard footsteps behind them. Turning, Amy saw one of the FDLE photographers was coming up behind them along with two grim-looking men who had made their way through the junglelike growth with a gurney.

"I don't know what Hunter has done. We staunched the blood on his forehead, but his hand was a mess, too."

"We're here," Dr. Rodriguez said. "I will quickly see what I can do...give a preliminary prognosis, but he'll need a specialist as soon as possible. It won't be so easy from here, but our ambulance people are the best. Let's hope. It's your venue not mine, but it will be a bit before we get the other...bodies sorted out and offer identities for them. I'm sure you want to know who this injured man is. You've got gloves?"

Amy reached into her pocket and pulled out another pair of gloves and put them on. Amy showed the doctor her hands. She was always prepared.

"Right. Aidan?"

"Right along with you," Aidan said, showing his gloved hands.

"I didn't need to ask, did I?" Dr. Rodriguez murmured. "Let's get this fellow and get out of here!" she said.

"You know, as much as I love the Glades, I'm ready to head out," Aidan said.

Amy nodded and turned.

As she had expected, Hunter had spent the time doing his best to keep the young man alive; more of his shirt was ripped

off. The man's shattered hand was wrapped to keep the blood
flow down to the barest minimum.

Dr. Rodriguez knelt by the man, quickly taking his pulse,
listening to his breathing, and looking at Hunter's desperate
measures.

"Good job," she murmured.

"Thanks, but—"

"Will it be enough?" she said. "I don't know, but, Amy, his
bullet really did just graze the skull—it didn't pierce into it.
There's a chance." Dr. Rodriguez gave her a reassuring smile.
"Fellows, over here!" she called to the young men with the gurney.

They saw Bobby Dryer, the photographer, was taking shots,
but carefully. He knew how to get what he needed while not
getting in the way of the doctor or her assistants.

The injured man was quickly placed on the gurney.

And Dr. Rodriguez was calling back to them as she hurried
ahead to stay with the gurney and her living patient.

"I'll be in touch!" she promised.

And suddenly, Amy, Hunter, and Aidan were alone.

"One of us should go with him," Amy said.

"He's going to make it," Hunter said. "Right now, we'd just
be in the way. And I have his wallet—I sincerely doubt he'll
be conscious for a while. We need to get on whoever he is—"

"He just left," Amy said.

"But I have this," Hunter said, opening the wallet he'd had in
an evidence bag. "Elijah Thayer, twenty-three, Fort Lauderdale,
according to his driver's license. And there's a student ID here
as well. He goes to the local college. Twenty-three years old.
Most graduate at about twenty-two, but he might have started
late, or perhaps he was working on his master's degree. Anyway, it's a place to start."

"We'll try his address first," Amy murmured. "Looks like a

house, though. We'll need a warrant. I'll call Mickey Hampton and he can get right on it. Or..."

She paused, looking at Hunter.

She was actually with the Florida Department of Law Enforcement, but since she and Hunter had worked together when the first victims of the horsemen had been found, she was officially on loan to the FBI and, therefore, subject to Hunter's boss, FBI Assistant Director Charles Garza.

"Call Mickey—he may make things move fast in this state," Hunter said.

"Then you two can get moving," Aidan said. "I'm here. I'll take the evidence, give the area another once-over to see if he had anything with him, where he was going. You have his cell phone?"

"Locked," Hunter told him.

"Ah, but I know magicians who can unlock it," Aidan said. "Call Garza, get moving on the guy's home. Maybe there will be someone there."

"We will still need a warrant," Hunter murmured. "Amy."

"I'm on it!"

She called Mickey, who was the deputy commissioner of the FDLE; he promised he'd have something by the time she and Hunter made it back to the road and could drive out of the wilds.

Amy nodded at Aidan, heading out. But she paused and turned back, making sure that even under these circumstances, she'd shown her appreciation.

"Aidan, our room was incredible. We loved it. And our time out there was too short, but it was the best mini vacation ever!" she assured him.

"The best," Hunter agreed.

"Do it again!" he told them, grinning and turning to make sure he'd gone over every inch of ground.

"Hunter, did you get the—"

"Bullets. In one of the bags that I gave you!" Hunter reminded him.

Amy and Hunter started back through the foliage, making their way back to and around the initial crime scene and then through more rough terrain to reach Hunter's SUV, parked on the poor dirt road that was still laden with official vehicles.

"What time is it?" Amy murmured as they climbed inside.

"Time to stop the Apocalypse," Hunter said. "This... Amy, this must end. Fast. But as of yet, we don't even know what the hell is really going on."

"But we will," she promised him. "Hey, white horse, red horse, black horse—pale horse. Hunter, we harnessed three out of four. And now—"

"Now it's time to figure out what the hell is really going on," he said. He hit the button to start the ignition of the vehicle and turned to her. "Someone is playing for the big time. Someone who was ready to kill his own lieutenants or archangels rather than allow them to ever name him—or her. Or even them. This isn't real. That poor fellow—Elijah Thayer—he believed every word he was saying. Sinners had to die. And I'm sure the sinners who needed to die were identified for him, as in someone knows you're dangerous and wants you dead. Because that's the only way they could reach heaven or the clouds or sit with the angels. Someone who doesn't believe in anything is causing others to embrace a cult in which they truly think they're doing great and holy work."

"We all agree, Hunter, that someone is pulling strings for a reason—someone who most likely doesn't believe in any god in any form."

"And that's just it. What in hell is it all for?"

Amy looked at him and wished she had a decent answer. But she didn't.

"I don't know. But we have a great team behind us: agents, officers, forensic scientists, and psychologists! Hunter, trust me. We will stop it all!"

Her phone was ringing. She answered it, glancing at Hunter.

It was Mickey.

"We have our search warrant," she told Hunter.

"Damn, he's good!" Hunter said.

"He is. An FDLE agent will meet us at the address. So…"

"Back to civilization. And those who are not quite so civilized."

"Elijah Thayer," Amy mused aloud. "Young, nice-looking, he must have friends. What was in his past that could cause all this?"

"I honestly don't know in this case. I always thought I understood so much because of my mother. She was born with a silver spoon in her mouth, and she's the most giving and caring person I've ever known. I know my parents joined the community when I was a kid because she couldn't understand why her father had money—but didn't help others. It was all for a good reason until I found a dear friend dead. I know you know all this, but here's the thing—when my parents learned the truth about what went on, they were out. When they discovered the truth about the people they had admired, they knew they'd been wrong." He hesitated. "From everything I've learned, there were those in Jamestown who wanted to get out—but it was too late. Even now, I can't imagine that horror. And in this case, maybe some of the bodies in those barrels belonged to those who wanted to get out. But people often slip into something because at first it sounds so good, as if a leader truly loves people and wants equality and wonderful things for everyone. Sadly, it's often good people, caring people, who get sucked in and wind up going down the drainpipe."

"I can't imagine what you went through," Amy murmured.

He glanced quickly at her, smiling. "Not that much," he said quietly. "My parents are good people, they were great parents. And as you know, they saw the truth. We were damned lucky. We got to the FBI and we made it out—and others also made it out because of their courage."

"I know they're great people," she assured him, smiling. "They made you!"

"Aw, man! That was nice. What a great way to suck up," he teased.

She was glad they both smiled.

Because what lay ahead would be grim, she knew.

Her phone rang and she glanced at it quickly. Caller ID informed her that it was Dr. Bethany Rodriguez.

She answered it quickly.

"Dr. Rodriguez? Hello," she said, glancing at Hunter.

"Well, Special Agent Amy Larson," Dr. Rodriguez said, "you did save a life. Your disturbed young man is unconscious right now—necessary medication—but Dr. Merton, ER physician, got him stabilized, a specialist was called in, and, believe it or not, we're looking at little more than a concussion. The hand is another matter—extensive surgery. But the kid—sorry, to me anyone under thirty is a kid—is going to live."

"Thank you!" Amy said, breathing out a sigh of relief. "When do you think that we might see him?"

"It will be a few hours. And it's been a long day, but I imagine that under the circumstances, it will be about ten o'clock tonight. I've spoken with all the right people—Mickey also put through a call. It might be two or three hours...they will give you a heads-up."

"Thank you, thank you!" Amy said.

Bethany Rodriguez was silent for a minute. "Thank you. It was great to be part of saving a life. I don't usually have that opportunity when it comes to my work."

"Good things all the way around," Amy said softly. "Anyway, thank you again. We're headed to his house or his address. But we'll be at the hospital to see him as soon as possible."

When she ended the call, she looked at Hunter. "He's going to live!"

"I got that," Hunter said. "Now let's hope that he or his home can give us something."

Her phone rang. She glanced down. This time, it was Mickey.

"We're almost there," she told him quickly.

"Just letting you know it's all in order. The place is owned by long-distance landlords. Greg and Sydney Cafferty live in New York and rent out their place down here. They've been contacted, and we have their blessing to see whatever is in there. Find something."

"We'll try," Amy promised.

Mickey laughed softly. "Don't try—do!" he said. "Amy, we've got to stop this. You and Hunter have been on it. If anyone can figure out the lunacy behind it all…"

"We intend to," she promised.

"Get in there!" he said. "And keep me—"

"In the loop. And we'll be heading to the hospital after. Dr. Rodriguez says they'll let us in by ten."

"Late night. But then again, you did just have a vacation."

"Mickey!" she protested. "A vacation is usually a few weeks."

"Solve this and I promise you a month!"

He ended the call.

"We're all clear. Elijah Thayer doesn't own the place, but Mickey made sure the owners were aware of what's going on."

"Good. I hate it when someone shoots at you when you try to execute a warrant," Hunter said dryly. "And…voilà!"

They had arrived. And as Mickey had promised, agents from FDLE were waiting for them. It was time to execute their warrant.

The house, legally rented to Elijah Thayer, was a small ranch-style place. There was no fence in front, just a walkway to a little porch and the front door.

The agents, four of them to Hunter's surprise, were waiting on the street.

One of them stepped up, a man of about forty with a lean, muscular build.

"Hank!" Amy said, greeting the man.

Hank smiled at Amy and shook Hunter's hand.

"Amy and I have worked together before," the man said. "I'm Hank Bakersfield. I'll introduce you quickly to Larry Naughton, Cindy Smith, and Gerald Mason. Mickey wanted us all out here. He said we need to go through the place with a fine-tooth comb. He's anxious."

"Understandable," Hunter assured him, shaking hands all the way around. The FDLE agents were somber as they met him. Cindy Smith appeared to be fifty with steel-gray hair that matched her serious eyes. She'd probably been at it for a while. Naughton appeared to be young—late twenties—while Mason, like Cindy Smith, appeared to be older. They all greeted Amy, either having worked with her before or at least having met her.

"So…any activity here?" Hunter asked.

"None that we've seen. And there's only one name on the rental contract, so…place should be empty," Hank said.

"Warrant?" Hunter asked.

Hank lifted the paper he held in his hand.

"Let's do it. Are we prepared to break a door?" Hunter asked.

"We are," Hank assured him.

But they didn't have to break any doors down. As the six of them headed on the path toward the house, the front door opened.

A young woman, probably not yet twenty, was standing there, terrified.

She was, Hunter thought, college age, young, with long brown hair and a slim build.

Hank was still holding the warrant. "Miss, I'm—"

"I haven't done anything, I swear it!" she cried.

"We're not here because of you, but we are a joint task force with FDLE and the FBI," Hunter said. "I'm afraid that—"

"It's Elijah! Oh my God! He's been scaring me so much! What has he done? What has he done? I've been so afraid, I've been getting my things. I mean, when I met him, he was so great, and then…then he started going wacko. He kept telling me that everything was going to be all right, he would see to it

I sat among the angels… He said he was going to explain, but he had to check on a few things first and… I was packing! I was getting my things! I'm terrified of him now. He used to be the nicest, most gentle human being in the world! I must get out. I didn't do anything, I swear. Please…please…"

"Miss, please, calm down," Amy said. "We don't think you did anything at all. But we need your help."

"My help?" she said blankly. Then she continued, "What… what happened? Is Elijah…dead?"

"No, he's alive, but he's in the hospital. He suffered some injuries," Hunter told her.

"Then he could still come after me—"

"No. He won't come after you. He'll be facing charges," Amy assured her. "Let's start with this. I'm Amy Larson and this is Hunter Forrest. May we have your name?"

"Annabel. Annabel Escobar. I'm a junior at the university and Elijah…Elijah is just a year ahead of me. We met at a football game. School, you know. We just hit it off and…" She stopped speaking, looking a little panicked. "I was just here. I wasn't living here. I have a dorm room. I, uh, I mean, don't go and tell my parents I was living here. I'll call you all liars saying anything to get what you want. I mean, nobody trusts the FBI, and not cops anymore, either."

"We're not officers, we're agents at FDLE," Amy told her. "And we don't want to get you in any trouble with your parents. If it comes up—"

"Oh, they met Elijah, and thankfully, it was back when he was sane. There would be no surprise I'd been his friend, but my dad is old-fashioned. Go figure in this crazy day and age. But…" Her voice trailed. She winced, closing her eyes, and said softly, "And I'm so sorry. Come in. Do what you need to do. But I do need to finish packing up. No matter what was going on, I had decided I was getting out of here today."

"That's fine," Amy assured her. "We have a search warrant, but what we're looking for is not anything you would have. But—"

"Come in, come in—do whatever you need to do! My suitcase is on the bed. I was checking the bathroom and looking around. I didn't think I wanted to have to ask Elijah for anything back and… You know, it's like when you leave a hotel. One last look."

"That's okay. But we would sincerely appreciate it if you would take a few minutes to speak with us. We need to know everything about Elijah that we can."

"To hurt him?" Annabel whispered.

Hunter glanced at Amy. Annabel might be terrified of a crazy Elijah, but she still cared for the man who had once been kind and gentle.

Amy gave him a barely perceptible nod and said, "Annabel, we don't want to hurt him. We want to help him if we can. But he got mixed up with some strange people—"

"Strange people. Totally and completely whacked-out!" Annabel said.

"Some yes, and we believe they may have an agenda," Hunter told her.

"But if we just talk," Amy said gently, "we may learn a great deal about him. What can you tell us about his past?" She turned around, sweeping out an arm toward her fellow FDLE agents. "We'll let these guys get to work searching for a connection to whoever has been poisoning Elijah's mind. And you, Hunter, and I can sit and talk. We'll all do what we can to help Elijah."

Hank and the others gave her a nod and moved on into the house. Annabel still looked lost. Hunter smiled at her and gently took her elbow, indicating the sofa, where he led her to sit. Amy sat next to her while Hunter took the big easy chair across from her.

The FDLE agents moved through the kitchen, the dining room, and the bedroom. Annabel glanced at them uneasily, but Hunter didn't believe she thought they would find anything that was incriminating against her. She was simply in shock with the arrival of six law enforcement officers suddenly sweeping through her life.

"It's okay," Amy told her gently. "What we're trying very hard to do is find out who it is that changed Elijah so much, who is convincing him that crazy things are true."

"We want to help you, help others, and help Elijah, too," Hunter told her.

Annabel's face was still wrinkled in worry, but she gave her attention to Hunter. "I don't know how I can help. Elijah… Well, he didn't bring friends here. He'd be out, but he wouldn't tell me anything other than he'd met some great people, real people, those who were trying to make the world and life and even death better for everyone." She hesitated. "At first, I thought he was cheating on me, but he behaved so weirdly, swearing I was the only one he'd ever love. And I did love him! Poor Elijah— he still has scars on his back from where his father beat him."

Hunter glanced at Amy, and she gave him a slight nod. The analysts back at her headquarters were already working on the man's background.

They'd know the truth soon enough. But Hunter wasn't surprised. While it wasn't necessarily so, people who had suffered some form of abuse or unkindness in the past tended to be the ones seeking something good in life—and falling for what seemed like something wonderful at first.

Then they often learned there were rules.

And there was one punishment for breaking rules, and that punishment was death. Then again, there were those like Elijah Thayer who believed and continued to believe and were willing to take their own lives rather than hurt the elders or their cause.

"Did he ever talk about anyone?" Amy asked her.

She frowned. "Not really. I mean, I don't know how to make you understand this, but Elijah was good, he was the best. He said he was afraid to give money to beggars on the street, because they might use it for drugs—but he'd buy all kinds of ten-dollar gift certificates for restaurants and hand them out when he saw someone in trouble."

"Was he working? Where did he get his money for these certificates?" Hunter asked.

"I… He said he had some kind of fund. I don't think he was working—he was a student. I mean, I think I would have known if he was going to work. I have a part-time job in my department—I'm an art major and a student assistant—but as far as I know, he had money to go to school from his parents or something like that."

"The father who beat him was paying for his school?" Amy asked.

"I don't know—we didn't talk about his home life. He would just shake his head and say it hadn't been the best experience." She hesitated a minute. "I first saw the scars on his back when we slept together. And…like I said, he told me his life was good now. He loved me and loved being with me and… I don't know, but if the money is coming from his family, maybe on his dad's end, it was because he felt guilt," Annabel suggested.

"Annabel, we know this," Hunter said gently.

She shook her head. "Or… I don't know. Some people think corporal punishment is good for children, but… I don't know. I think it's possible his dad felt guilty, or even though he was abusive, he thought a college education was important."

"You never met any of his new friends," Hunter murmured. "You didn't find that to be curious?"

"School and work are a long, long day for me. And he was studying hard, too. And we valued our time alone together."

"But do you remember where he was or what the occasion was when he first began to change?" Amy asked her.

Annabel was thoughtful, and then she nodded and looked at Amy suddenly. "We went to a protest about a month ago—a legal protest. We'd never hurt anybody or even be destructive. News about it went through the school. We just wanted the world to be equal. Anyway…it was huge—cool, in a way, it was so…so American! No one was destructive. We were controlled, just chants and placards—we just let our opinion be known. No one was even arrested! But there was a time during it all when Elijah and I were apart. I mean, there were several hundred students—and professors—out there. And it wasn't weird that in all the movement, we got split up. But it was after that day he began to change. I didn't realize it until now but…that night, he talked about all the evil in the world. And he said it was time the world needed to start over. Evil people were ending the American dream. The Apocalypse was on the way. And even though it sounded terrible, the world needed to be cleaned out and begin again."

Hank had been in the bedroom. As he came out, he held a laptop in his hand. He lifted it and said, "Getting this to headquarters—we'll get the analysts tearing through it. He had to be in contact with people somehow. We've been over the whole place. No notepads. No safe, nothing under the bed, in the laundry…we've been through it all, but we'll send a forensic crew in next. We're heading out."

Hunter nodded. "Great. Ask them to find out about a protest on the campus about a month ago. Who were the organizers, all that."

"Got it," Hank said. He hesitated, waiting to see if there was more. And Hunter understood, but Amy rose to reassure him first.

"We're going to take care of Miss Escobar. We'll verify a protection protocol."

Hank nodded, looking relieved. Hunter thought he liked Amy's co-agent. The man was smart enough to realize that given what they were dealing with, if the right person knew that Elijah Thayer was alive and in police custody at the hospital, the young woman he had lived with might well be in danger.

And of course, Annabel Escobar frowned, realizing the same thing.

"Oh my God!" she breathed. "I… Oh no. Now I'm really scared!"

"We don't mean to frighten you," Amy assured her. "You may not be in danger at all. But you will have the protection of the Florida Department of Law Enforcement *and* the FBI."

"But how? I…I can't stay here! I want to go to the dorm, but I don't know how anyone could protect me. There are kids coming and going at all hours and… I am so scared. Oh, my sister warned me! She said I was an idiot and I'd go for the wrong guy."

"All right, we understand you want out of here," Amy told her. "And a dorm might be a bit difficult at this time. But we have safe houses where you'll have plenty of space and privacy—"

"But I'm in college!"

"An officer or agent can accompany you. I promise, we will do everything in our power to keep you safe—and living as normal a life as possible."

Annabel was holding her phone. She looked down at it and then up at the two of them.

"Oh my God!" she breathed in horror.

"Annabel, has something happened?" Hunter asked her.

"The news…the news flashed on my screen. They think there were twenty bodies found in the Everglades—or the body parts of twenty people! Not even an hour from here! Oh my God, oh my God! Please tell me Elijah didn't put those people in barrels, please, please…"

"We don't know how they got there yet. Elijah was out there, but we don't know if he had anything to do with killing the people who wound up in pieces in the barrels," Hunter assured her. He glanced at Amy. It was time to talk to Elijah himself.

She nodded and walked away for a minute to place a call.

"Where is Elijah from—not here, right?" Hunter asked.

Annabel shook her head. "He grew up in Cleveland. He told me once the city sometimes got a bad rap, but that it's a good city that has the Rock and Roll Hall of Fame and that made up for anything bad about it. But he loves the warmth and the water, and always said he was never leaving Florida again. I didn't push it, but I got the impression he didn't have family that he wanted to see again back in Cleveland."

"We have agents coming to escort you to a safe house, Annabel," Amy told the young woman after finishing her call. "One of them is Lucy Randall, and she's great, young, in her twenties—she'll go to your classes with you, and no one will ever know who she is. So...hopefully, your life will be nice and normal while we do our best to get to the bottom of this."

Annabel jumped to her feet, surprising Amy as she threw her arms around her. But Amy was quick on the take, and she hugged Annabel in return then stepped back to direct the young woman to get her things and get ready to leave.

Annabel nodded and headed to the bedroom. But she paused, turned back, and looked at them both.

"Thank you!" she whispered. She hesitated again and then said softly, "Tell Elijah I love him. Tell him to get normal again, and I'll be there for him."

She turned and slipped into the bedroom. As she did so, there was a knock on the door; it opened before either could reply. Instinct made Hunter reach to his holster, but before he could draw his gun, he could hear a woman call out, "FDLE. Amy?"

Amy smiled at Hunter. "It's Lucy—she was already on call. I talked to Mickey, and he has her coming out here because he... he's been around the block a few times. He knows we're headed out to talk to Elijah, and he figured—with all this going on— that Annabel might need guarding."

"Mickey is on it," Hunter acknowledged.

"Lucy, we're right here," Amy said.

The young woman entered the room along with a second agent, a man who looked about as young as she did. The two of them were either in their early twenties or hadn't aged in a few years.

"Well, as you can see, Amy, we're here. You know Theo, right?"

"We met at a briefing once," Amy said. "Lucy Randall, Theo Parker, this is Hunter Forrest, FBI. Annabel Escobar is in her room getting ready to leave with the two of you."

Hunter shook hands with them both. "Nice to meet you. And good call. You look like college students."

Lucy, with short dark hair to match her eyes, grinned. "I'm not that young, honestly. I'll be thirty on my next birthday. And hunky rockstar boy here is almost thirty-one. And it's a pleasure to meet you. Because this is an ongoing thing, they've tried hard to keep your names out of the media—but we know about you, Special Agent Hunter Forrest. You're famous among us!"

Hunter grinned. "What a way to put the pressure on, huh?" he said lightly. "Let's hope we can really bring this in, sooner rather than later. We'll leave Annabel in your care and get going. Elijah Thayer is conscious and ready to be seen. We are hoping we can get something from him."

"I'll just take Lucy in and introduce her to Annabel. I don't want to unnerve the girl more by having her come out to strangers," Amy said.

"Good call," Hunter said.

Amy and Lucy headed to the bedroom. Hunter looked at Theo Parker, nodding. "You guys really do look the part."

Theo nodded. "We've played it before—drug bust at a college south of here. We're honestly all grown up, and both of us were at the top of our classes, if you're worried."

"I wasn't worried," Hunter said. He laughed. "Just envious."

"I'm pretty sure you don't need to be envious of anyone," Theo said, grinning as well. "Anyway, I promise you, we'll keep good watch over Miss Escobar."

Amy and Lucy came out of the bedroom, followed by Annabel. She looked at them all nervously.

"You're going to be fine," Amy assured her. "These are my coworkers and friends. They will take good care of you."

"I believe you," Annabel said. "I'm just still so…"

"It's okay to be scared!" Lucy assured her. "That's natural under these circumstances."

"Well, let's head on out," Hunter said. As the others went out, he locked the door behind him. His SUV and another like it were parked on the street just feet from the house.

But as they walked to the cars, Hunter frowned. He saw a man standing just a house down, looking into a mailbox. Hunter wasn't sure what alerted him.

People often came home late from work or from a night out and checked their mail before going inside.

But he felt that something wasn't right. The man wasn't really looking at the mailbox. He was pretending to look at it. And there was a car parked directly by the mailbox.

The engine was running. The car was ready for someone to leap in and make a speedy escape.

No, it didn't seem right…

And it wasn't.

The man suddenly turned. He was wielding a gun. And he was aiming it at the group leaving the house, or more precisely, aiming at Annabel Escobar.

There was no choice.

"Get down!" Hunter shouted.

Amy threw herself at Annabel Escobar, bringing them both down to the grass. The other two agents fell low as well while drawing their weapons.

But there had been no time; Hunter got off a shot before the man could fire.

3

One of the most amazing things about Deputy Commissioner Mickey Hampton was his ability to move about the state of Florida at record speeds. Then again, he had his pilot's license, and he had just recently saved up enough to buy his own little Piper Cherokee. He had once assured Amy that the airplane was purchased at a more reasonable price than many a car on the market.

Therefore, she shouldn't have been surprised when he arrived at Elijah Thayer's rental house within an hour after the shooting.

Hunter, she knew, was disturbed. She knew how much he hated shooting, that he chose every possible negotiation tactic when he could.

But he would not let a victim be shot, nor would he sacrifice a fellow law enforcement officer.

And when the man taking aim at Annabel first went down, Annabel had been so hysterical, she had been everyone's focus of concern.

For seconds…

Then Hunter had hurried down the sidewalk to check on the man he had shot.

There was no hope. His aim had been true. Annabel's would-be killer was dead.

It was while Annabel was being convinced she'd be all right—since the only witness to her leaving was dead and she was in the company of two agents who were excellent shots themselves—that Mickey arrived in person.

"Sorry, any shootings by law enforcement—you know we need your weapons for everything to be cleared up and all the paperwork…"

"Amy's bullet and the one fired by Elijah Thayer against his own head are with Aidan Cypress already," Hunter assured him.

"Right, so, rather than let you children run around unarmed—" Mickey began.

He was interrupted by Hunter's laugh. "Mickey, you know we both have personal—and legal—backup weapons," Hunter reminded Mickey.

"Nevertheless, I know a day beginning with body parts in the Everglades and going on like this is not an easy one. As I said, I've been around the block. I'm here to accompany you to the hospital and to check on the police security setup for Elijah Thayer while you question the man. And we'll be staying at a local hotel." He appeared amused for a minute. "I understand you both have packed bags with you already?"

Hunter glanced at Amy, shaking his head.

"Whatever. Garza knows where we were, too," Hunter said, referring to Assistant Director Charles Garza, Hunter's supervisor and—since Amy was officially on loan to the FBI—technically Amy's director also, for the duration of the case. They'd never kept it a secret that they'd become more than partners. Since they were still employed by separate agencies, there was nothing unprofessional about it. Except that if the case wasn't as complicated and far-reaching as it had become, it was likely that their relationship would have kept them from working together in the field.

Mickey laughed. "And Aidan set it all up! Hey, it's lucky when one of your best friends has connections at one of the coolest hotels and casinos to be found anywhere." He suddenly grew somber. "I am so sorry the respite was so short. But these bodies in the Everglades…there were so many of them. Along with the pale horse. So much death and decay. Amy, you did speak with this Elijah Thayer before he shot himself and you shot up his hand."

"I did. And I'm not sure I've ever spoken with someone so disillusioned! The man has been convinced by someone that killing certain people is a way to the highest rungs on the ladder to heaven. Oh, and apparently I'm a concubine of the Antichrist," Amy told him.

Mickey smiled grimly. "I guess he doesn't mean Hunter."

"Hey, who knows?" Hunter asked. "In his eyes, maybe I am the Antichrist. This fellow is so brainwashed that it's tragic. And like many, he believes killing himself is better than failing—because the afterlife is the true reward. And alive…well, alive he might betray the great Archangel or whoever it is he sees as his leader. Oh, and Amy already has analysts researching a campus protest that happened about a month ago. That's when Annabel Escobar saw the change begin in Elijah. Sounds like it was all on the up-and-up—good things going on. But it seems he met someone at that protest who was a total radical but fit a bill of 'goodness' Elijah wanted to see."

"Your thinking is sound," Mickey agreed. "For now, I'm your company to the hospital. After, I'll direct you to our hotel. Sorry, it's kind of a cheap one, but you know we're on taxpayer money."

Amy smiled and indicated their car. It was the only one remaining after Lucy and Theo had whisked Annabel away at last, and the ME, his assistants, and the body had gone.

Even the police officers running crowd control were gone, as was the small, curious crowd that had gathered. Neighbors who had all fled when it had appeared the police might want to question them had trickled back to their homes.

"There's our chariot," she told Mickey. "How did you get

here? Whisked away by a twister like Dorothy and Toto and then dropped on the street?"

Mickey shook his head. "I landed at a little airport not far from here, and agents were quick to drop me off. I am all yours. And since it's now nearly midnight… Wait, it is tomorrow," he said. "But the hospital is expecting us. We're good to go."

Amy nodded and opened the car door, feeling a small sense of pleasure. Mickey had certainly been "around the block" as he had told them. He'd spent five years as a cop, earning a detective's shield, before he'd joined FDLE, where he had risen through the ranks to his current position. He was nearly sixty now, a man capable of being in control, of showing compassion along with tremendous strength. Amy didn't think there could be a better boss.

Hunter walked around to the driver's side.

As they drove, Mickey told them, "We have Elijah Thayer guarded with local cops in the hallways, and obviously he's on suicide watch. But I'm wondering if he'll give you anything at all. And we don't have an ID on the man who tried to shoot Annabel Escobar yet—no wallet, nothing on him except his Colt. Of course, we've got fingerprints and DNA, and I suspect we'll get something soon enough."

"I have a feeling he purposely didn't have any ID," Hunter noted. "He was on a suicide mission."

"So hard to fathom," Amy murmured.

"But people have been convinced of causes throughout history. World War II had kamikaze pilots. The terrorists aboard the planes that crashed into the Twin Towers. Convince someone that what they're doing is far superior to their own lives…"

"Well, we have Elijah Thayer. Amy, play him. If he thinks you're the devil's own concubine, you may be able to get him talking," Mickey said.

At the hospital, Mickey paved the way. But on the fifth floor, where Elijah Thayer had just been moved from intensive care, he nodded to the two of them and took a seat next to one of the police officers on duty.

"Have at him gently," he said, indicating that they should go on in.

They did so.

Elijah Thayer's eyes were closed. His right hand was in a massive bandage and his forehead was wrapped in gauze as well.

The young woman on suicide watch, who had been seated next to the bed, rose as she saw them enter.

She arched a brow at them, and Hunter told her quietly, "We'll be just a few minutes, but if you'd like to get some coffee or anything, we'll make sure that we're here until your return."

Elijah Thayer let out a groan and opened his eyes, a pained look on his face.

"I knew you would come," he said.

"Mr. Thayer, I don't know who told you what or convinced you of what, but seriously, you're a smart man! A good man, according to Annabel Escobar."

He stirred as if he would rise from the bed, but he couldn't quite make it.

"You saw Annabel?" he demanded. He looked as if he were about to cry. "You… Why? Annabel…Annabel is good, but she doesn't know yet, she won't understand—"

"It would have been better if she'd heard you committed suicide in the Everglades and were dead?" Hunter asked.

Elijah remained silent.

Amy sat next to him and held his hand. For a minute, she thought he would jerk away. After all, who wanted to hold hands with the Antichrist's concubine?

But he just went still, and she spoke gently but passionately to him.

"Mr. Thayer, Elijah. Annabel had such good things to say about you! You must have an incredibly kind and good heart. You never wanted an addict to have access to more drugs, but you wanted to see that people could eat. You kept gift cards to restaurants on you to give to those you saw on the street who were truly suffering, who needed food. I think you're a good person, a really good and decent human being. But I also think your soul is so good that you were looking for something greater out of the whole of humanity and, well, you fell hook, line, and sinker for someone who was playing you from the start."

He frowned, his head moving in denial, his eyes closed.

"Come on, Elijah. What were you doing out in the Everglades where we found you?" Hunter asked. "Did someone send you? I don't think you went out there to kill Amy. The idea of killing her came to you when she stumbled upon you, and that was because someone convinced you she was evil. Elijah, Amy has stopped all kinds of torture and murder. And if you look in your heart, you'll know that killing anyone is evil."

"No, no, no. You don't understand. Rewards come in the afterlife—everything here is like window dressing. Our lives can be as easily cast off as our clothing. But if you've been evil, only by truly suffering in this life can you hope for any redemption in the next," Elijah said.

"What happened on the day of the protest?" Amy demanded.

"I, uh... Most of the school was in on the protest," he murmured. "We wanted everything to be good and equal for everyone. It didn't matter where we came from, what color we were, or who we loved, none of it! Good people were just good people."

"We understand the protest was legal and controlled and for all good things," Amy said. "But something else happened to you that day."

"Nothing happened—"

"Who did you meet?" she asked.

He looked disturbed, angry. But he turned his stare hard on Amy and he said, "Yes, fine. You're right. That's when I started to learn the truth."

"What truth?" Amy asked.

"That it's coming and it's needed!" Elijah said.

"What's coming?" Hunter demanded. He surprised Elijah by adding, "The Apocalypse?"

Elijah turned to stare at Hunter. "Don't you understand? It's needed, and it's necessary. This world has gotten so out of hand! People have turned mean. Maybe when they had to sit home during the pandemic. Maybe they just sat there feeling trapped and afraid and alone—and because of that, they had to lash out. They turned mean, ready to hop on board with anything to argue, anyone to hate. But that was the beginning and now… Yes, many, many, many have to die. And we try so hard to bow before the Archangel who will orchestrate all that will come. If we let the evil souls suffer here on earth, we're saving them! There is greater glory. And… I could have been there and…" He broke off, staring hard at Amy again. "Don't you see?" he whispered. "I could have saved you!"

Amy shook her head, looking at him, squeezing his hand. "I don't know what you're hearing—and since we're talking about the Book of Revelation, I'm thinking you're a good guy who believes he's doing things by order of an archangel. But how did you miss the real message? I mean, I think you had it once—'Love thy neighbor as thyself.' Thy neighbor—not thy white neighbor, Black neighbor, Hispanic neighbor, gay neighbor, straight neighbor—just 'thy neighbor.' You were trying to do that, help anyone who was downtrodden—"

"Don't you understand?" Elijah protested. "No one is doing that anymore. All people do is fight. It's like no one can have their own opinion anymore. People are just in groups, pitted against one another. That's why it's so understandable that the Apocalypse has begun!"

"No," Amy said softly. "All that's happened is that a master puppeteer has been manipulating people and killing those who don't agree with him—or her."

Hunter spoke up, leaning forward. "Trust me, Elijah. I spent years as a kid in a cult with my parents. They didn't know we were being manipulated, not until we found a dear friend had been murdered. She was murdered because she dared to express her own opinion. Frankly, she realized she was being used. It was only because my parents saw this, and they were horrified to discover the truth, that we got out. Right now, Elijah, we can help you get out. We can give you your life back. We can get you into witness protection. And you can see Annabel and tell her goodbye if you like. Tell her you still care about her. You're young, you're bright—and you are good! Let us give you all of that back. Because all you have right now is a lie."

"I don't… I mean…listen to me, please. It makes sense. Have you ever seen people so contentious? Artificial intelligence is taking over. I mean, seriously, try to log in on a few sites. A robot asks *you* if you're a robot! Plagues and famine are sweeping over the world, war is crazy and… Tell me it doesn't seem as if we've all sinned to the nth degree and that the world doesn't deserve to be wiped out!"

Amy glanced at Hunter, almost smiling.

Well, he had a point; but in reality, the world had always been in trouble. Mass communication systems were now just letting people vent on a major scale.

And it also allowed for someone to accrue followers on a grand scale as well.

"Elijah, if you're so convinced you've been told the truth, why won't you tell us who got you started on this journey?" Hunter asked.

Elijah Thayer looked at him as if he'd clearly lost his mind. "You want me to reveal the spirit who brought me to the light so that this Antichrist's creature can go out and kill him?"

"No. The supposed creature of the Antichrist saved your life," Hunter reminded him. "We don't want to kill anyone."

Elijah frowned.

Amy glanced at Hunter, arching a brow. Maybe Elijah didn't know that her shooting his hand had kept him from his goal of suicide.

"Your hand," Hunter said. "See how it's bandaged? The very good human being here shot your hand to save your life."

Elijah let out a sound of tremendous aggravation. "I would have sat high with the angels!"

"No. You'd have been a failure. You'd have killed yourself for nothing. And if you hadn't killed yourself, your so-called angel minions would have killed you. Like they tried to kill Annabel," Hunter said.

"What?"

"We visited Annabel like we told you," Amy explained. "And when we were leaving, a man tried to kill her."

"No, no… Annabel. Is she all right?" he asked anxiously.

"Someone was afraid you'd told Annabel something, and she was targeted," Hunter said flatly.

"Annabel is good, she's the best. She didn't do anything or know anything—" Elijah began.

"But this great Archangel of yours doesn't give a rat's ass," Hunter said matter-of-factly. "Look, trust me, you're done with them. Of course, now we need to know about the barrels—"

"I didn't put the bodies in those barrels!" Elijah protested.

"Maybe not. But you knew they were there," Amy said.

"How did you know to be there—and why were you lurking and watching?" Hunter asked.

"I was just… I was just supposed to monitor activity," Elijah informed them. "I swear. That's why… Well, I've seen pictures. Everyone seeking the higher plane knows that there are evil, evil beings wearing the guises of normal human beings. She is one—she is a succubus, a creature of the Antichrist, we've all been told! So…when I saw her, I knew I needed to shoot her, at least get her out of this disguise she's been wearing."

"Elijah," Amy said, wincing and shaking her head. "I am not an evil creature. I swear it. You have been so deceived!"

There was a tap on the window. Looking up, Amy saw Mickey was motioning to her.

She glanced at Hunter. He nodded. They couldn't both leave Elijah's side—not when he was on suicide watch. But they automatically knew Hunter would stay with Elijah while she stepped out to find out what Mickey had learned.

"Anything yet?" Mickey asked her when she was out in the hallway.

Amy shook her head. "But I think we are getting to him."

He nodded, glancing at his watch. "Almost two in the morning, but…as we know, crime doesn't run on a nine-to-five schedule. Still, we're all going to need some sleep. I'll get a night crew moving on things."

"We're fine—"

"And I want you to stay that way. Come on, Amy, we all know we have to eat right, sleep right, and keep fit in order to be worth anything. And this—"

"I swear, when we finish here, we'll sleep!" she promised.

"You bet. Because you'll be escorting me to the hotel where we're all staying."

"Right, Mickey. I got it. But you called me out here—"

"We've gotten several identifications for the victims in the barrels," he told her. "All sent to your emails. But they came from all walks of life: male, female, young, old. But here's the only common denominator. Three of the six people we've identified were on an online chat group. They called themselves the Commonsense Party. I went through the threads on the site—it's not private. People are invited to join, but there is an administrator. He or she warns there won't be any negativity, and all opinions are welcome, but no badgering or name-calling."

"Do you think it's a front for something else?" Amy asked him.

"I don't know what to think so far. There hasn't been enough time yet to dig deep enough."

"But—"

"Ask our friend in there if he knows anything about this on-line chat group," Mickey said.

"All right. You said three out of the six. What about the other three?"

"One came back to a false identity—trace led back to a Glen Bolden who died twenty years ago. But whoever the hell this is, he managed to get his fingerprints down as a dead man's. Maybe he was collecting social security. As good as the combined analysts of the FDLE and the FBI might be, like I said, we need more time.

"Another victim, Shelly Jenkins, had an arrest record and time served for a drug rap. The third had an arrest for assault, Val Nickerson. She was in a bar fight five years ago. She left a patron with a scar across her entire face from a broken beer bottle."

"Three clean people and three with records," Amy murmured. "Maybe we've had it right from the beginning. Someone was cleaning their house. The good ones who were beginning to question, and the dirty minions who failed to perform as commanded?" Amy suggested.

Mickey nodded. "See what you can get."

She nodded and headed back into Elijah Thayer's hospital room.

He had been speaking to Hunter. And while Amy didn't know what they'd been saying, she was glad to hear there was something different about Elijah's voice—as if he just might be starting to realize he'd been fooled.

But he wanted to deny it.

No one ever wanted to believe they'd fallen deep into a rabbit hole that led to nothing but more darkness.

"Hey," Hunter said, "Elijah and I are doing okay here. I told him about me, about growing up, and about my mom, mainly.

She was such an incredibly sweet person against all odds. Any-way…"

"Elijah," Amy said, retaking her seat where she'd been by his side before, "this is important. Have you ever heard of some-thing called the Commonsense Party?"

She had surprised him.

"Um, uh, yes. I've, uh, heard of it."

"Do you hate the people involved with it?" she asked.

"No! They're all about good things. They want people to talk. They want people to compromise and to learn to work to-gether. They're…they're the only hope against the Apocalypse. Well, them and people like them."

"Do you know that so far, three members of the Common-sense Party were found among all the body parts in those bar-rels in the Everglades? I really don't believe you put them there, Elijah. You don't seem to have the personality for random or senseless premeditated murder—or for chopping up bodies. But someone did ask you to watch what was going on. Apparently, police activity in the area drew someone's attention, and you just needed to report back to your superiors. Honestly, I believe you are too decent a person, and I really hope you get the chance to be one again in the future," Amy told him.

"I already told you I didn't kill anyone. I was watching what was going on. And you have to be wrong. There's no reason that members of the Commonsense Party would be in those barrels. I mean, unless… Well, there are gangs in South and Central Florida, you know," Elijah reminded them earnestly.

"Right," Hunter said. "But if a gang had put those barrels in the Everglades, no one would have asked you to see what was going on, right?" Hunter asked. "Don't you see—you've been taken. And if you just give us a chance to reach your contact, we can give you more proof that whoever has been telling you all this…well, it isn't to save anyone. It isn't to reach the angels.

It's for something entirely personal and greedy, and people are dying by the scores for nothing."

His voice had grown passionate. Amy was afraid at first that he might have pushed Elijah against a wall where he'd fight back.

But Hunter had evidently studied Elijah, and he'd pegged him right.

"Colin," Elijah said.

"Colin? That's the name of your contact?" Hunter asked him. Elijah nodded.

"Last name?" Amy asked softly.

He shook his head. "We… I don't know. It never seemed necessary. But Colin was fascinated by the Commonsense Party. He loved reading the posts—and the idea for compromise on a bunch of our major issues that people would put out there. He would never hurt anyone who chatted on that site or met—"

"Met? The group met?" Hunter asked.

"All over the place. Come on, think about it—do you know how many people are just sick of the constant fighting? Of the idea that you're in this camp or that camp, and no one allows anyone else an opinion or is willing to listen and compromise? The Commonsense Party isn't a real party, but people love to meet in person and talk, and it's so cool. I've only been to one meeting, but strangers meet and become friends. And they just have a good time and listen, and…they shouldn't be dead!" he whispered. "They…they should have been able to rise without any punishment!"

"Maybe, just maybe, someone has really been lying to you. And murder is just wrong. And kindness—like you were practicing—is really what's important," Amy suggested.

He was quiet. "Colin. I just know Colin," he whispered. He shook his head. "Go on the site, link up. They have meetings all over the country. They'll have another one here, somewhere, Miami-Dade, Broward, or Palm Beach County. I…" He stopped speaking, just shaking his head. "Maybe I should have died!"

"Elijah Thayer, no. You have a lifetime ahead of you," Amy said gently. "You have just been enlisted and were charged with only watching the site. You didn't kill me or Hunter—and thankfully, you didn't kill yourself. Live. We will protect you. Just as we're protecting Annabel Escobar. And in time, you can just be you, a smart student, and a kind student, helping those without food. I swear to you, I am not sleeping with the Antichrist. All we want is good for people—and to stop those who want to hurt others."

He didn't look at her, but his eyes welled with tears as he stared straight ahead and frowned.

They might have reached him.

The door opened and closed. The young woman on suicide watch had returned. She smiled and lifted a cup of coffee.

"How's my patient?"

"Doing well," Hunter said. He leaned toward Elijah and said, "You're going to fight, right? Fight for life. Fight for good things."

Elijah Thayer nodded, but still looked perplexed. Somehow, they had broken through. They could still lose him, of course. But they'd made him think. And with all the cops outside his room, the doctors and nurses on staff, and the therapist looking over him, he had a chance.

"Will you come back?" he asked as they rose.

"Of course," Hunter assured him.

"Will you...maybe see if there's any way Annabel can come see me?"

"We'll certainly see if she'll come in. I know she cares about you deeply," Amy assured him.

And at last, they were out of the room. Mickey was waiting for them, silent, expecting them to speak.

"He met some guy named Colin at the protest," Amy said.

"And apparently, he—and Colin—know all about the Commonsense Party. The group gets together online and chats *and* gets together in person. I think we need to get involved—" Hunter began.

"I'll have our techs all over it. The night crew can start, and we might have something by tomorrow. Or later today. Right now, you are going to the hotel, and you're going to get me there, and we're all going to get some sleep!"

"That's a deal," Hunter agreed.

"Oh, you bet," Amy told him.

They left the hospital, Mickey nodding to the officers who were on duty on the floor, watching over their patient. They were in the SUV when Hunter asked Mickey, "Did we find out anything about the man I shot?"

Mickey shook his head. "Night crew techs will be working on that, too. Please! We must—I do mean *must*—function at the full level of our abilities. Tonight, let's get some sleep and put our trust in others. While you are among the best, you're not the only agents working for the FBI or even FDLE. Teamwork, remember?" Mickey asked.

"I am all for it!" Amy assured him. "All for it!"

Mickey told them there was nothing luxurious about their accommodations that night, but there was certainly nothing wrong with them, either. Amy liked the hotel chain; their amenities included coffeepots and microwaves in the room, which beat a fancy lobby or surroundings in her book. But Mickey had known that, and he looked amused as they checked in.

"You're being a jerk," Amy assured him, grinning, and she was not afraid of speaking lightly even if Mickey was the big, *big* boss. While other people in his position might easily sit behind a desk and always send others out, when a situation warranted, he immediately stepped out into the field.

"No, I just knew where you guys had been staying. A room that brought you directly into a nice and luxurious pool," Mickey told her. "Oh, they do have one here. And even a hot tub. Not that it matters. I doubt we'll have the time. Although that would be nice in my book, but…"

They had reached the third floor, where their rooms were located. Mickey shrugged and told them, "Good night!"

"Good night, Mickey," Hunter said, opening the door to the room he and Amy would be taking.

Once inside, Amy left her roller bag just inside the door and collapsed on the bed. "Oh my God! I could have only a floor somewhere and would still be able to sleep tonight!"

Hunter laughed softly. "You called your boss a jerk."

"He was being a jerk. And he's Mickey…he's great. I love him. Hey! You're pretty casual with him, too."

"He's not *my* boss, and I didn't call him a jerk," Hunter said lightly.

"But Mickey is…amazing," she murmured. "And he didn't just become the boss by accident—he worked for years in the field. I mean like for over twenty years. So he knows what is needed, and he steps in when Florida is being used! The Everglades are being used. Not that it hasn't happened before—swamps in Georgia and Alabama and Louisiana have also received their fair share of bodies and evil deeds. But…shower. I need a shower."

She said the words, but she didn't move. She noted dimly that Hunter was already on his computer.

She closed her eyes for a moment.

And sleep claimed her.

Hunter had seldom seen Amy fall sleep so quickly and so deeply, but he was glad to see she was out—and he was eager to be that way himself.

But he had become determined to do some research on his own though he knew many of the young technical analysts at both FBI and FDLE headquarters were on it and were probably much better at delving into secrets behind the web than he was.

And there was no trick to logging in to the Commonsense

Party website. The website quickly explained there was no such thing as the Commonsense Party, but rather it was a forum for news without bias. It was a place where those interested in civil discourse could come. The rules were written regarding name-calling and personal attacks. All civil voices were welcome, all civilly stated views and opinions were welcome, and suggestions for compromise on those issues that were explosive elsewhere were more than welcome.

The administrator identified himself only as John Common Sense.

As Hunter read, he frowned and wondered how anyone on the site might have angered any other user. Apparently, writing anything that went against the "civil" code as explained in the rules was simply and quickly removed. Of course, that suggested John Common Sense might have been several people since one administrator couldn't always be awake.

He realized he had spent another hour researching and forced himself to close the computer, aware it would still take him time to get to sleep.

Because he would be wondering what anyone associated with the site might have done to bring about the murder and dismemberment of so many people.

But then again...

White horse, red horse, black horse...

So far, everything had been a play for power or riches, doing nothing but preying upon others—some so brainwashed they needed serious mental care and others just...just caught up in the violence or vengeance against a wrong, either perceived or real.

But he sighed as he closed the computer. The bathroom light had been on, and he turned it off before crawling into his side of the bed. He noticed Amy hadn't even taken her shoes off; he smiled as he removed them from her feet.

She barely stirred. But as he lay down, she curled naturally against him, resting her head on his chest and slipping an arm around his waist.

And he was glad for the warmth and the comfort. As always, such a simple touch, a human touch, her touch, one of love, helped to ease the stress and violence and length of the day.

He breathed in the scent of her hair, pulled her closer and thought dryly about how they'd been called today from their own little piece of earthly nirvana, the wonderful room that opened onto the pool, and beds that were as comfortable as could be imagined.

But the bed never mattered. The place never mattered. Humanity—and love—were always where she was.

He managed to sleep. But even as a child, or perhaps because of his circumstances as a child, he'd never slept deeply. He awoke at the slightest sound, even at so much as a whisper.

But Amy didn't wake up whispering.

She awoke distressed.

"Oh, yuck! Oh, man, I never meant to fall asleep without a shower! Oh, after the day, after everything we touched, after everything around us!"

Hunter was up on his elbows and watched her with amusement.

"Hunter!" she murmured, turning to him. "You let me… Oh. Wait. You didn't take a shower, either."

"Amy, you just lay down and passed out."

"You could have woken me. Oh, wait! Hmm," she murmured, suddenly smiling and shaking her head. "You were on the computer. No concept of sex, which of course, yuck! Seriously, after that day, we really needed showers!"

"Maybe we should shower now."

"Oh, we will shower now!" she said. "But it must be late and—"

"We're going to head to the hospital to see Elijah Thayer again. We'll check on Annabel Escobar and make sure she's okay and being cared for. And we're going to start investigating the victims from the barrels who have been identified. But others are working. We're okay."

Amy leaped out of bed and headed for the bathroom while shedding her clothing as she went.

He rose more slowly, grinned, and was ready to follow.

But his phone was ringing. He glanced down at it.

Mickey Hampton was already up and moving. He might have tried Amy's phone first, but it was still tucked into her shoulder bag, and she wouldn't have felt it vibrate.

"Mickey?" he said.

"Glad you're up. We need to get moving. I'm downstairs at their little breakfast area by the hotel entrance. Come on down and join me as soon as you can."

"Sure. Of course."

"We've got something. A living, breathing human being who is one of the directors for an upcoming Commonsense Party meeting."

"Okay. Great. We'll be as quick as possible."

"No messing around, huh?"

That could have been taken many ways.

Hunter decided simply to answer politely.

"We'll be right down."

He ended the call and headed to the bathroom door.

"Mickey is waiting for us," he called.

"What? Already?"

"Well, it's almost eleven. He's down in the breakfast area, though I doubt there's any breakfast."

"All right, I'm almost out, but you need to get in here…"

"Not with you in there."

"What?"

"You're too tempting! And I said we'd be right down, and, um, that we wouldn't mess around."

"What? You said that!"

The water went off, and Amy, wet and beautiful and wrapped in a towel, appeared at the door and stared at him in horror.

"Hey, he said, and I quote, 'No messing around.' I told him we wouldn't mess around!"

She stepped around him and gave him a shove. "Get in there! I'm going to head straight down without you. Argh…seriously!"

"Hey, we couldn't see each other in this way at all if we were technically employed by the same agency and on the same team. I take us as a win…even if the morning is going a wee bit awkwardly," he told her.

"Argh!" she murmured as she hurried to dress and get ready.

Laughing, he headed in for his shower. And he was fast; but true to her word, Amy had already gone downstairs. He followed, grinning at first and then growing more somber.

It was going to be another long day. He knew the horseman on the pale horse had only just begun.

4

As it happened, meeting with Perry Carson turned out to be their first business of the day. They didn't take Mickey anywhere. He had a car delivered by an agent, and he was going to spend the majority of the morning at autopsy and working on the wave of information himself.

Perry Carson, a man who proclaimed himself to be an Independent, held a good job as an investment banker, and according to the information drawn up by their techs, he was happily married, had been for nearly thirty years, and was the father of two college-age children who were both attending universities out of state.

He was meeting with them during his lunch hour at a pleasant downtown restaurant in Clewiston, which turned out to be a good thing for Hunter and Amy since the breakfast bar had indeed been shut down by the time they'd reached the hotel lobby. They opted for salads and coffee—lots of coffee.

"I'm happy to meet with anyone about my participation in the conversations on the Commonsense Party website!" he told them. Then he shook his head. "And I'm saddened and can't begin to figure out why anyone would hurt anyone on the site. Whatever happened, it had to have had something to do with another facet of their lives. We are the most reasonable and peace-loving people you are ever going to come across."

"Maybe being peace-loving isn't considered a good thing by someone," Amy suggested. She pulled out her notepad, looked at him across the table, and read names to him. "Katherine Parsons, Winston MacGregor, and Eduardo Mercado. Have you met any of them personally?"

Perry Carson stared back at her in disbelief. "I... Yes."

"How did you meet them, sir?" Hunter asked.

"We had a barbecue down at a park in Hollywood. There were fifty or so of us there, all meeting for the first time though we'd conversed often on the website. Katherine was... She was a great-grandmother, a beautiful, feisty little lady of eighty-two. And Winston... Winston was retired, too, and gave all his free time to working with the sound system at his church. Eduardo Mercado was another wonderful man, in his forties, an attorney, a man who did a lot of work pro bono for those who were destitute and in trouble. These were all not just good, decent people—they were amazing people. I mean, I only met them at the barbecue, but I looked everyone up—not just social media, but I looked people up when they came on the site through every means available. Not that we turn people down if they have a record. I just want to know," the man told them.

Amy knew Perry Carson was in his early fifties. He had good features, outstanding posture, and a headful of hair that had naturally turned to a platinum color rather than gray. His eyes were dark and earnest, the same as his expression as he stared from one of them to the other, trying to make sense of what he was hearing.

"I heard about the bodies in barrels in the Everglades," he said. "But I can't imagine any of these people having done anything that would cause someone to...to kill them! Are you sure?

I mean, from what I understand, they found *pieces* of bodies. Maybe they were wrong in their identifications. I just… No. They couldn't have wound up in those barrels!"

"I'm sorry, Mr. Carson," Hunter said. "Please, trust me. The people working on this with both the state and federal agencies are very, very good. They have identified the remains by fingerprints and DNA. Trust me, sir, we're doing everything we can to—"

"Have you spoken to the families?" the man interrupted.

"Not personally. We were…"

"You were trying to see if we had some nutjob political thing going on? If someone on the site might have done this? Don't you understand? It's all about getting along, expressing opinions, listening when we have different—"

"Sir," Hunter interrupted, "trust me. I went to the site. I believe you. I find it incredibly commendable. But maybe there is someone out there who doesn't want people to get along, who has a different, more radical agenda in one way or another. Was there anyone like that you might have come across? I mean, I think you are John Common Sense."

The man hesitated and shrugged. "I'm one of three people who are John Common Sense. My wife, Julie, is another. And our friend Sarah Layton is the last. As moderators, we do take off anything that's ugly—and yes, it happens. When you're reasonable, there's always someone who wants to shake you out of it. But… I never saw anything that would suggest someone would get violent!"

"Nothing on the web disappears forever," Amy said.

"We'll need access to your computers," Hunter told him.

"Right, but…"

"I know what you're trying to do is good," Hunter assured him. "And we don't want to harass anyone. But we know at least twenty people were killed, and we're following every lead. We need to know about those people who got hateful. Sir, we know three of the people who were killed were part of this— wanting to be reasonable."

Perry Carson suddenly looked as if he wanted to cry. He shook his head but said, "Of course. I thought we were doing such a good thing. I have a friend who is a political analyst. He interviews people on the street. He has told me most Americans are reasonable and want the same things. Most think it's wrong to shove everyone in a shoebox, and the mass media and social media cause all the whacked-out things a few people cling to. They're just loud people. I never thought this forum could... Oh God."

"Sir!" Amy said softly. "Never blame yourself for the evil done by others. We'll send a few of our analysts for the computers. Just say the site is down for maintenance. We'll get everything back to you as soon as possible."

"Of course, of course. My computer is at my house, my wife is at home, and I'll have Sarah bring her computer to my house. I'm assuming you want them now, or I could gather—"

"That's fine. I need your home and business addresses," Hunter said.

Perry Carson drew an old-fashioned notepad from his pocket and started writing. As he did so, their waitress came by asking if they'd like anything else. Hunter thanked her and asked for the check.

"I can get that," Perry Carson said.

"No, it's our meeting and we'll pay," Hunter told him. "But thank you. Thank you for your help."

Hunter paid the check, noting Amy was already texting the information to Mickey so he would get the computers picked up and put into the hands of their tech analysts.

As they prepared to leave, Perry Carson turned to them and said passionately, "Please! Find whoever did this! Those were good people, sweet people, the best. Others came to them for help, others needing more, to understand..."

"One more thing," Amy said. "Do you know of a man named Colin?"

"Colin? Yeah. He was at the barbecue."

"Do you know his last name?" Amy asked.

"I… No. But he's been in several of our chats. Always as nice as can be. Maybe you can find him through the computers."

"A description?" Hunter asked.

"Oh, he's a good-looking man. Not a kid—I'd say he's in his midforties, but just a touch of gray in his hair. He's about six-one, maybe one hundred and ninety pounds…fit. Nice face, great features, and better smile. Oh, he's one of the good guys, talks reasonably in the chats… No. No, no, no. Colin couldn't swat a fly, much less…chop someone up!"

Hunter smiled, nodding. "We're just hoping maybe he can help us," he said. "But we do need to find him. We'll have a sketch artist come by your office, if that's okay with you."

"Do I have a choice?"

"You can come into the closest FBI or FDLE office instead," Amy offered.

"No, fine… It's not going to be easy today, but I need to try to work and… I'll announce immediately that the site is down for maintenance. Whenever. It would be easier for me if the sketch artist came to my office."

"We'll do anything we can to make things easy," Amy promised.

"Thank you," Perry Carson said. "And…get them. Who… Oh God. Please, get them justice. Get them justice. No, no, no, if you can and you find the bastards who did this, shoot them!"

He walked on out of the restaurant. Amy and Hunter followed.

As they did so, Hunter's phone was ringing.

So was Amy's.

He arched a brow to her as they both answered.

"Mickey," Amy whispered.

"Garza," Hunter told her.

"Hunter, this thing is growing. They just found more bodies. These weren't in barrels—they were left on an embankment. Still federal land in the Everglades, but this time abutting

Miccosukee land. We have FDLE and Miccosukee police out there now. It's a good hour south of you by the time you get out there, but Aidan has his friend Jimmy Osceola waiting to get you down there as quickly as possible by airboat. The site isn't easily accessible by any of the roads or even the farm roads or animal trails. We have plenty of people on it, mainly forensic, but under the circumstances, you need to see every site."

"Right," Hunter said, glancing at Amy. The look she gave him assured him she was getting the same information from Mickey Hampton.

"How many?" he asked.

"Eight. We think. It can be tough in the Everglades these days. They estimate a hundred thousand python and boas are out there now, eating up the food supply, so when an alligator sees an easy meal..."

"Gotcha. Thanks. We're on the way."

"And FYI, as Amy will be learning, Mickey is calling a task force meeting. All local authorities, rangers, Miccosukee and Seminole police. There are too many dead. Too many from too many walks of life."

"We're on our way."

"One more thing."

"What's that?"

"They found another toy horse, pale green, along with the bodies."

"Right."

"Someone is truly arrogant and amused they're keeping us running around like dogs chasing their tails. We need to prove them wrong."

"Yes, sir."

He ended his call as Amy ended hers.

"I feel bad for Jimmy Osceola," Amy said. "He's just a nice guy running a tour boat business, but he keeps becoming involved in the Apocalypse."

"Jimmy is a nice guy. And he wants to help. This hurts every-one—and in his own way, he's as determined as we are. This is his land—even the federal and state part—because he loves it. And it's being used as a dumping ground."

Amy nodded. "So, we've been given our orders. At least I always did love a good airboat ride."

"Yeah. It's just, uh…"

"Where we're going," she said. "But I guess we'd better hurry. They'll want to get the bodies out of there quickly. This kind of thing…"

"Is like a dinner bell?" he suggested.

She shuddered slightly. "Well, that's one way to put it. But at the last scene, there were enough people running around so the creatures stayed away. That was smart. So…"

"Onward!" he said.

Jimmy Osceola had nothing to do with law enforcement. He ran tours, and he was an operator who had five stars on every travel site out there. He could talk about history, flora, and fauna. He could explain geography in a way Amy knew she never could, and he had a wonderful sense of showmanship.

But when they met up with him where the road brought them into the closest meeting area for a vehicle and an airboat, he looked grim.

He greeted Amy with a quick hug and shook Hunter's hand and then ushered them onto the airboat. "Conversation is kind of difficult on this thing," he called out as he started the motor.

"True!" Amy shouted in return.

"One thing," Hunter called above the roar of the boat. "Did you—"

"Nope. Not this time. The bodies were found by tourists who were visiting Miami. They'd gone out to the Miccosukee Casino, and then they crossed over from Shark Valley, went on to the village, and then to the state park. The Everglades is so strange.

Of course, we're in Miccosukee reservation land here, but just north, we're in Seminole tribal land. In between we have state and federal land as well as private property. Sugarcane is still a big thing down here, and we still have big cattle ranches. I'll be honest, as well as I know these many, many miles, I wasn't sure myself just where we were.

"The couple are hikers—they stumbled upon the bodies. Somehow, they got a cell signal through, and a ranger got out there. Then reps from both the Miccosukee and Seminole police arrived, and they called in the feds. In this case, it was a good thing because all hands on deck are needed." He hesitated and shrugged. "Aidan was called out, and he called Mickey and then me. He said you two needed to be out there. You were lead on the case. But—"

"He's calling a meeting. Everyone who can be there will be there, and he'll create a task force," Amy finished.

"Yes," Jimmy told them. Then he ceased speaking as the airboat whirred them southward and to the west.

Eventually, the airboat slowed, and Jimmy moved it to the embankment. "I can get you back to your car if that's the call."

"Thank you," Hunter told him.

Amy was glad she'd opted for something casual that morning including boots and long pants. Of course, her pants were immediately soaked as she hopped off and sank into the muck, but she hurried to the harder ground of the hammock.

Jimmy had brought them close. They went quickly to the site where the bodies lay strewed in various positions. None of the bodies had been hacked up. They were all still in one piece. Medical examiners were already on the scene along with a park ranger and representatives from both tribal police stations.

"Hunter Forrest!" a man called.

Amy hadn't seen him before, but he had apparently been briefed. He greeted Hunter with a handshake and turned to her. "Special Agent Amy Larson, I'm Eric Dayton, FBI. I've worked a few cases with Hunter before, and Hunter suggested to Garza that maybe you could use a profiler."

"Good to meet you," Amy told him. "Do we know what we have here?"

"No purses on the women—three of them are women—and no wallets on the men. The medical examiners were just waiting for you to see the scene as it was discovered. They're going to take the bodies. Due to the circumstances, they're taking them to Broward. We're working this as a federal case. But for the moment..." He turned to introduce the others. "Howard Billie, Seminole police, Josh Otter, Miccosukee police, and Jay Sebring, ranger and first one out here."

They all shook hands, greeting one another; as they did so, Amy saw Aidan Cypress approaching them holding an evidence bag.

He had collected another of the pale green toy horses.

"It's the calling card," he said.

"Well, we do know we're looking at the same killer or killers, or possibly an organization."

"But under one great archangel," Eric Dayton said. "We've been speaking with our fellow law enforcement. We're grateful we've got involvement from everyone down here, because I think we're going to discover we'll be finding more—and more—victims. They'll be strewed all over the Everglades, perhaps with the perpetrators purposely using federal, state, and tribal lands in the hope of creating confusion and anger and maybe even dissension. They miscalculated."

"They already tried once with the last horseman," Howard Billie said. He was a tall man, striking in his stature, in his early forties, with his dark hair tied back in a ponytail. He shook his head. "But they left weapons popular among Western tribes, not at all common during any part of our history. Apparently, they know we're different tribes, but they missed the history that we were all Seminoles until the tribes were distinctly recognized in the mid-1900s. Somehow, they don't realize times have changed drastically, and rangers are friends with cops—and we all love the Everglades and will not accuse each other of these things."

"We will do anything in our power—report anything," Josh Otter said vehemently. He was a younger man, perhaps in his late twenties, but steady, well-built, and determined. "I think while we're looking at state and federal land so far as dumping sites, the first was near Seminole land, and here we are near Miccosukee land. But I don't believe—"

"No," Amy assured him. She shook her head. "We don't know what the game is with the dump sites. Perhaps they're trying to create friction between all factions, state, federal, and tribal. This is being done for an endgame we haven't yet figured out—but with help, we know we will get there. We've gotten the three horsemen this main leader or archangel or whatever they have their followers call them has used as their pawns."

"More like bishops or even queens," Aidan suggested dryly.

"Rooks, bishops, queens—we've gotten them. There's a fourth working this—and the Archangel is over them. We're doing everything we can to trace the victimology, and we've been given the name of a man who may have been involved. We have just his first name, but we've got a sketch artist on it. I think we're close to turning a man we discovered at the first site—observing—who probably was used just as a pawn," Amy told them. "We'll be getting all the information we have out to every agency. Every bit will go out as soon as we have it."

"We will stop this!" Aidan said determinedly. "And if someone is trying to create dissension down here, well, the Third Seminole War ended in 1858—and we get along fine with each other and the old white settlers."

"Bingo," Howard Billie said. He shrugged. "We've a pack of casinos doing great all over the state. I have white friends who say the gambling establishments have been the true revenge of the Florida tribes. Personally, I'm just thankful they've provided us with good income. And maybe they don't realize that not all tribal members live on tribal lands or work for the tribes. Aidan is a top-notch forensic expert working for the FDLE."

"Thanks. I try to do my best," Aidan said. "And on this…"

"Aidan, you are the best," Amy assured him. "And we are all determined, and we will all work together straight across the Everglades."

"And this person is not associated with the tribes. They may not even be associated with the state of Florida," Eric said. "From what I've seen, researching, catching up with the Horsemen case, this is someone looking for a power gain by making others look ineffectual. I know this team won't let them do it. But…"

"It may take time, but we can't afford time—more and more people will die," Amy said.

"With a team, we can move fast," Hunter said. "Thank you, one and all. And the MEs are waiting. Amy?"

She hesitated. It had been a while now since the first discovery of the bodies. Still, she couldn't help but wonder if an observer hadn't been sent to this scene as well.

"Where is the couple who called this in?" she asked. "They might have seen someone else in the area, though it doesn't sound as if the bodies were left here in the last hours."

"One of the MEs said he believed the bodies had been there since last night," Aidan said. "But they have been dead different amounts of time. That's just a preliminary report based on what they've seen so far, of course."

"And the couple?"

"We let them head back to the ranger station," Josh Otter told her. "They wanted away from the scene as quickly as possible. They wanted out of the Everglades and out of the state, but I asked them to stay. Naturally, I asked for their ID's."

"Thanks. Can one of you call the station and ask them to stay just a little longer? I know the MEs were waiting on us, and I don't want them to wait any longer. We won't be long—we aren't forensic experts or MEs. We will be quick," Hunter said.

"Sure thing," Jay Sebring assured them.

Hunter thanked him and the others and indicated they walk quickly to the bodies. An FDLE photographer was there, assuring them he had it all secured on video as well as stills. They thanked him and observed the bodies where they had been left.

Placed, Amy thought.

They hadn't been displayed as earlier victims of the Apocalypse had been, but they had been left about three feet apart from each other, some on their sides, some flat on their backs, and all with their feet toward the water.

"Cause of death?" Hunter asked, turning to one of the medical examiners silently waiting for their inspection.

"The young woman's hair is covering it there, but a bullet through the forehead. The man at the end was stabbed, and the knife caught several major organs. We believe two of them were poisoned. We need to get them to autopsy."

"Of course, of course, but no identifications as yet?" Amy asked.

"We'll be doing our best," the ME said solemnly. He was an older man, gray-haired, wrinkled, and straight as a poker. "We're going north with the bodies—we'll be working with our fellows and keeping all information in a dedicated file."

Hunter thanked him.

There was nothing else they could do at the site.

Three of the victims were women. One, with the bullet through her forehead, couldn't have been more than midtwenties. Another was thin and appeared to be in her sixties, and she looked as peaceful as if she might have been sleeping. The third woman was perhaps in her forties, and the blood that covered her clothing suggested she was one of the stabbing victims.

The five male bodies were as diverse, two appearing to be young, two in their forties or fifties, and one who might have been seventy. The young men were bloodied, the middle-aged men had been shot—again with bullets right to the brain—and the elderly man appeared completely peaceful.

Amy realized Eric had joined them and was standing quietly at the edge of the scene.

"Eric?" Hunter asked quietly.

"This was a cleanup. Hunter, I believe you two have a sound theory on what is happening. The problem is that with what we have now, I can only agree something big is behind all this. I just don't begin to have a finger on what it is yet. However, I do think this person is using everything that has happened in the world to further their agenda. We had a pandemic and in some areas that caused hunger because people couldn't get food, because fields were left forgotten. And then we had war shake the world. Well, of course, we all know war is always going on somewhere all the time."

"All right, let's go speak with the couple who found the bodies," Amy said.

But as she spoke, Jay Sebring came toward them, frowning. "We called in to the ranger station. One of my colleagues went back with them—I know they were there. But they're gone already. I guess...well, finding something like this had to have been unnerving."

"We'll need to find them," Hunter said. "You have copies of their ID's?"

"Right," Josh Otter said. "I'll get them to you now." He pulled out his phone.

Aidan spoke up. "Josh, I'm connecting all of us. We're going to make sure we all share everything with each other. Whatever is going on, this person is making use of the entire Everglades—and we don't know where he'll strike next."

"Gotcha."

Aidan was a brilliant tech. In a minute, he had a mass text going out that included their entire group as well as Mickey Hampton and Charles Garza.

But even after copies of the couple's ID's arrived in their texts, Aidan looked up, frowning.

"They were fake," he said.

"What?" Josh asked.

"They gave us fake ID's. That couple didn't exist! No such people are listed at the address they gave. In fact, it would be on the edge of the Gulf of Mexico if the address they gave even existed."

"Ah, hell, I should have seen that!" Jay Sebring said, angry with himself.

"And I saw those ID's, too," Josh said, equally disturbed.

"It's not your fault," Hunter assured them quickly. "Your first concern was eight bodies on the embankment. Are the pictures on the licenses good images of the couple?"

"They are," Jay said.

"Yep," Josh seconded.

"We'll get their images out on everyone's radar right away," Hunter said. He looked at Amy.

"We have a person of interest in the hospital," Amy said. "He's a pawn in this, but he gave us a name—and we're getting an image of the person from a sketch artist anytime now. Since we can't do anything here, we're going to get Jimmy Osceola to take us back."

"We're all connected. And I'm not sure how far they might have gotten," Josh said. "I'm willing to bet they headed for Naples. It's the first place they could really mingle with people and hope to stay hidden."

"Do you know what they were driving?" Amy asked.

Jay Sebring shook his head. "But I can find out." He turned aside and made a call. They watched as his face twisted into a frown before he thanked the person on the other end of the call and turned back to them.

"Did you find out?" Hunter asked.

"Yeah. I found out. And it doesn't matter anymore."

"What? Why?" Eric asked.

"Because the driver decided to play chicken with a two-ton truck on the road into Naples. The trucker survived, but the couple...they were killed on impact. The strange thing is they did it at a light, and the entire thing was caught on a traffic cam. There is no way the trucker was at fault. The car drove straight into him at seventy miles an hour while he was stopped at a red light!"

Amy looked at Hunter.

"You're not surprised!" Jay said. "Who would do that? Who would opt to die that way? It had to have been horrible!"

"One of our brainwashed people. Someone convinced that by doing so, they bought themselves a place high up with the angels," Amy said quietly.

"We're looking for someone extremely charismatic," Eric said. "But not just one person."

"We're dealing with the horseman riding the pale horse, and the orchestrator of the Apocalypse," Hunter said.

Eric nodded. "Exactly."

"But these bodies… It looks like the people were all murdered, but in different ways at different times. Did the couple who supposedly 'discovered' them…bring them here?"

"I doubt it," Hunter said. "They were the follow-up—the ones sent in to make sure we did discover them. They were the observers sent to make sure they were found before too many predators in the wild got to them. But no matter how minor their involvement, their great Archangel doesn't want them to be questioned as they might give away some information. And so, they die quickly, before the great Apocalypse, and then sit among the angels."

"So we have no clues and nothing left," Jay said bitterly.

"We have one clue," Amy said. "One man. We're going to go back and see him again. We have agents questioning everyone involved with the victims we've identified so far. This great Archangel is too arrogant. Between us all, we will find him," she said quietly.

"Our tribes and our agencies will be all over it," Josh said quietly. "They think they know the Everglades?" He looked at Howard Billie. "Whoever it is, they don't know the Everglades the way we know it!"

5

"I could listen to Jimmy Osceola forever, I think," Hunter murmured.

They were back to the SUV and headed to the hospital.

"His history is amazing. I mean, the man goes back to fourteen thousand years ago, not so much the written history, but the artifacts discovered that belonged to those long-ago peoples. Not that my Florida history is great—"

"You're not a Floridian," Amy reminded him.

"You know everything Jimmy Osceola knows?" he asked.

She smiled. "A lot of it. I had a few great history teachers in high school and college. But I always love listening to Jimmy, too. I also love history, especially local history, and Jimmy is the best. He tells you what's in the books, and then his opinion of things. Without his opinion, I find two things to be reasonable. One, while his namesake was not executed by the American government, Osceola was betrayed. He was taken prisoner under a flag of truce. Two, the Native Americans in the state were betrayed several times. They mainly fled south from Georgia—most were Upper or Lower Creeks, two language groups. And many slaves also escaped their owners to join with the Native Americans who fled south from persecution. The Seminole sided with the British during the War of 1812, and most people believe the First Seminole War began in 1817. Florida was still a Spanish possession at the time. Many scholars believe the Seminole War was a factor in Spain ceding Florida to the US in the Transcontinental Treaty of 1819."

"Whoa, hmm," Hunter said, flashing Amy a quick smile.

"The Second Seminole War was waged from 1835 through 1842. The US wanted the Seminoles to move west of the Mississippi. First, they'd been pushed to the center of the state from the panhandle. Then, when the Indian Removal Act was passed in 1830, the government came after them, and there are many Seminole tribesmen and women in Oklahoma. The Third Seminole War took place from 1855 to 1858, arose when the American government went after them to move west again. But it's estimated that only about two hundred to six hundred or so escaped into the depths of the Everglades. They didn't gain tribal recognition until 1957. And since they were from two language groups, the Miccosukee gained tribal recognition in 1962."

"Well, you're as good as Jimmy Osceola," Hunter told her.

"Oh no, Jimmy, as you know, can tell you so much more! The skirmishes that still occurred, the way that they lived. I mean, you've been deep in the Everglades. I think the nature to be found there is amazing—but I've never been desperately trying to survive among snakes, alligators, and more mosquitoes than one can imagine. They are remarkable people. Of course, Jimmy really made me laugh one day because a lady who was fascinated by his stories asked him what he did for fast food. She was a little perplexed when he told her he usually ordered a pizza."

"Ah! Well, time changes for all of us. Aidan doesn't live on any of the reservations, does he?"

Amy shook her head. "You don't have to live on a reservation to be a member of the tribe. But Jimmy does, as is his choice."

"No, I think I knew that."

"You should have!" she said, but she was smiling. "Jimmy Osceola's home is on the Big Cypress Reservation. There's a great museum there, and a boardwalk path that is really, *really* nice!"

"We'll go," he said softly. "When we can, we'll go."

"I would love to bring you!" She was still smiling, but her smile faded quickly as her phone began to ring. She glanced at it, answered it, and listened gravely to the voice at the other end.

Mickey Hampton, he thought. And he was right.

She ended the call. "So, apparently, Elijah has been asking for us—and for Annabel. Mickey has spoken to Annabel. Mickey— along with two other FDLE agents—will be bringing Annabel to the hospital to see Elijah."

"Let's hope that will help us."

"Let's hope it helps. Of course, if she hadn't wanted to come, no one would have forced her. But she agreed quickly, Mickey said, because she's convinced Elijah is a good person, and he can…he can be swayed from being crazy. She's convinced he didn't kill anyone, and I think she's right. The people sent in are pawns in this chess game, as we've said, and they're just supposed to report back."

"Or they're just to kill themselves if they're caught," Hunter said dryly.

Amy shook her head and looked forward. "I don't think anyone could convince me that my reward would come by driving into a two-ton truck at seventy miles an hour."

"No, but it is pretty amazing just what someone can do to the human mind. By the way, Eric is on his way up here. He's going to study everything we have so far and try to give us a better idea of what we're looking for."

"That's great," Amy murmured. "As far as Elijah is concerned, I think our biggest help is going to be Annabel."

"Quite possibly," Hunter agreed.

They arrived at the hospital. Checking in with the agents on guard, they were assured the day had been quiet. No one had tried to get near Elijah.

"Then again," Hunter murmured to Amy, "there was no media about. No one knows yet that he didn't succeed in killing himself."

"They know he didn't report in," Amy reminded him.

Hunter nodded. "But the media just knows about bodies in the Everglades. Whoever he was supposed to report to might think he was among the bodies."

"True."

"There you are!" Elijah said, rising slightly in his bed as he saw them enter.

Another young woman was on suicide watch. She smiled as she saw the two of them.

"Elijah has been waiting for you," she told them.

"And here we are. Sorry we're so late," Hunter said. "Miss, if you'd like coffee…"

"I would love coffee!" she said. "In fact—"

"Go ahead and have a meal. We're expecting more company," Amy said.

"That sounds great. Thank you."

She slipped from the room, and Elijah looked at Amy and whispered, "Annabel is coming? Really?"

"Annabel is coming. Really," she assured him.

He closed his eyes and leaned back.

"She doesn't hate me?"

"She doesn't hate you. She says you were misguided. Our term, of course, is *brainwashed*," Hunter said, "and we might not have known what a good guy you are if it wasn't for Annabel."

He closed his eyes, winced, and shook his head.

"You have to understand, there was something about Colin…"

"We have someone working with a sketch artist to get a good image of him, but we might have you do the same. And our computer techs are trying to trace him. How many times did you see Colin after the day of the protest?" Hunter asked him.

"Five or six," he said, shrugging.

"Where did you see him? His house?"

"Oh no, no. We always met in public places like restaurants and cafés."

"Do you remember where you met him last?" Amy asked.

"Oh, yeah. In Broward County, um, a place in Davie. A Little Bit of Heaven Café. Fitting, right?" he asked dryly.

Amy glanced at Hunter. It seemed their witness had come full circle. If he had realized on his own that he'd been taken as a patsy, he'd made tremendous progress.

"Do you remember when?" Hunter asked.

"Yeah. The day before yesterday." He hesitated, looking pained. "I was told the sinners had been released, their souls were free, and they had repented and suffered here on earth, and I needed to make sure that they..."

"What?" Amy asked.

"That they hadn't been discovered yet. But they had been. And I couldn't slip away quickly enough. Colin had warned me that...that if I was found, the authorities would think I was a murderer—and I'd be in jail and I'd never find my way to the angels. The Archangel was counting on me. That's what he told me. But now..."

His voice trailed.

"Elijah, how did you know me when you saw me? You said the Archangel showed you pictures?" Amy asked.

"Colin has them on his phone."

"What kind of pictures?"

"All kinds. He has you at a pool, walking in a parking lot..."

Hunter turned to look at Amy.

Colin had been following them!

"Excuse me a minute," Amy said.

Hunter knew she was calling it in to find out if there were any traffic cams or if the restaurant had a security camera—or if they could find any security footage from their last days of vacation that might show them who had been taking pictures of Amy.

She was being targeted.

But they knew that.

Just as he knew the only way for Amy to ever be safe was for them to solve the mystery of the Archangel.

"I don't… I believed everything he said," Elijah told them as he shook his head in bewilderment again. "When I woke up this morning…I couldn't accept I had believed everything he had said." He paused, looking at Amy. "You saved my life," he said softly.

"And I am so glad you lived," she assured him. "Elijah, you may be our way of putting an end to all this."

"I hope so," he whispered. "Some of it made sense. A pandemic. People starving. The war, those poor people in Ukraine… and the war causing so many to starve. It made sense when he spoke to me, when we were sitting together, and I…"

"Have the doctors spoken with you?" Hunter asked, thinking they should have spoken to one of Elijah's doctors first themselves.

Elijah nodded. "He said something about my blood testing positive for hallucinogens, but I wasn't with Colin all the time. I mean, why didn't I have moments when…? I don't know. When I was away from him, when I might have…" He paused, then continued dryly, "Seen the light!"

"He probably knew how to keep you dosed. When you left him—" Amy began.

"How did he get it into me?" Elijah asked.

"You met him at cafés and restaurants, you said. Easy enough for him to dose whatever you were drinking or eating."

"I don't think I killed anyone. I just believed the other sinners had been cleansed," he said worriedly. "But… I think I would have shot you!" he told Amy miserably.

"It's okay—you didn't," Amy said.

"I'm still going to go to prison, aren't I? And I deserve it."

"You're a cooperating witness," Amy told Elijah.

"Keep helping us. We'll keep you safe, and we'll do everything we can with the attorney general. I don't think you need to be afraid of prison time, but—"

"I do need to be afraid of Colin and the Archangel!" he said.

Hunter glanced at his phone as it and Amy's phone pinged simultaneously.

The timing was perfect. They had just received copies of the sketch artist's rendering of the man that had been seen at the Commonsense Party barbecue.

He showed the image to Elijah.

"Is that Colin?"

"Wow. Yeah. That's an amazing likeness. Yeah. How…?"

"He's shown up elsewhere," Hunter said simply.

"Charming wherever, I'm sure! He's not old…maybe thirty-eight, tops. Good-looking, sandy hair, bright eyes…nice face. Women seemed to like him instantly… Not just women, though. He had a way about him. He was nice to everyone. Had a great smile. And he liked everyone. He was controlled at the protest, warning others to be determined but legal. Someone told him I gave out gift certificates to those who were down-and-out and… I guess he singled me out from that."

"And you talked to him then?"

"Yes, and I was an idiot. He gave me a bottle of water. It was probably tainted, right?"

"Probably," Amy agreed. "But the thing is…your system has probably been completely cleaned out now. You're going to be okay."

As if in honor of her words, there was a light rap at the door.

Hunter saw Mickey Hampton had arrived.

With Annabel.

Either the fact that Annabel had come was truly amazing and the best thing on earth, or Elijah was truly an amazing actor.

The tears that spilled from his eyes were either real or award worthy.

But everything about this man's involvement now appeared to have a reason—hallucinogens. If someone was on such a high, it was possible to see almost anything.

And come to believe what was seen.

Mickey made a motion. Hunter and Amy both said goodbye, but Hunter didn't think Elijah heard him.

Annabel had gone straight to him with a sob and carefully embraced him where he lay in his bed.

"Wait," Amy said.

Hunter turned to look at her.

"The suicide watch therapists and nurses are all vetted by us before they come in here to work. No one—not even Annabel—stays with him alone. Go see Mickey. I'll be in the chair."

"All right," he said. "I'll talk to Mickey."

If he had to bet, he'd wager the emotion Elijah was showing and what he was saying was truth—but while he might work on instinct, he didn't bet on human lives.

And Annabel seemed as good as Mary Poppins. But he didn't know her, and he didn't know if she did have some hidden involvement.

He stepped out alone to see Mickey.

"Hallucinogens," Mickey said. "Doc said he showed a span of use that goes right back to the time when he went to that protest—and met with our mysterious Colin. I'm hoping he's not too mysterious anymore. We have a BOLO out on him with every conceivable agency. They're also putting the image through facial recognition hoping we'll get an identity. Amy really saved this fellow—his bullet just grazed his head. Bruised the skull when he might have exploded half of it." Mickey shook his head in wonder. "They're going to release him in another few days."

"He has to be protected," Hunter said.

"He might still face charges."

"We can't put him into a jail or the prison system. Not until this is over. Not until we have Colin and whoever is behind Colin."

Mickey looked at him and nodded slowly. "Feel free to wait until his keeper returns—then I'll expect you at headquarters. We have a task force meeting scheduled and we need all hands on deck. Including our tech and analyst teams—FBI and FDLE. The media is running wild with this. Garza told me he got a call from the White House. Too much information has gotten out, and you know how social media can take off. Our average citizen is beginning to fear the Apocalypse is nigh."

Hunter frowned. "How? We don't give out information on active investigations. How would anyone know about the little toy horses?"

"Well, there's another mystery for you," Mickey said. "I believe our Archangel has been dropping tips to select outlets around the country. Seriously, these last murders have occurred—or at least the bodies have been found—in Florida. But this many dead... It has become a national concern."

"How are we doing on identifying the dead?" Hunter asked. "We plan a trip to the morgue after your task meeting."

"It's slow work, but they're getting names down bit by bit. The task force meeting is in an hour." He glanced at his watch. "I'm heading over now. If you want to get Amy—"

"She won't leave Elijah alone. Not even with Annabel. And with the speed at which things are going on, I think she's right. We can't trust anyone."

Mickey nodded. "I'll get an officer in there." He turned to one of the uniformed officers in the hall. "Can you man the room until Elijah's person returns?"

"Yes, sir," the officer said, heading in. Hunter could see Amy was on the phone, but as she finished the call, she thanked the officer and came out of the room.

"Task force time. I need you there," Mickey said.

"Right," Amy replied. "I didn't like leaving Elijah with any-one without someone else physically in the room."

"I hope you're wrong, but that's a good call," Mickey said. "And the phone call?"

"I just heard from Aidan. He works with a young woman, Sabrina, an amazing tech analyst."

"Naturally, I know about Sabrina," Mickey said. "And?"

"She was able to get the real identities for the couple who discovered the bodies in the Everglades—and later drove into the truck. She said it was a piece of cake. She used facial recog-nition, and they both had records. Lorena and Oscar Morrison. They did time for drugs, but they didn't have anything for use of force, resisting arrest, or anything violent. But here's what she discovered that's interesting. They were both part of another web group—this one big on law and order. She hasn't had time to study much yet, but the group supports a politician named Frank Hamilton. Hamilton is big on police presence during protests, on raising fines for traffic violations, and the like. He has an ad out on social media—according to Sabrina, it's a good one and he's charming. Like the Commonsense Party people, he wants to talk, he wants opinions. He believes we agree with each other on major issues, and we must have someone at the helm who can remind us of that."

"Interesting, two groups all about fairness—and their people wind up dead or taking their own lives. Yes, of course, after the meeting we will find this man," Mickey said. He looked at Hunter. "Garza will be at the meeting—we'll sync our next moves. So, let's head out."

They did so; Mickey had a car and driver waiting for him.

Hunter and Amy headed for their SUV. As they drove out, Amy said, "It's strange. As far as I know, Perry Carson isn't run-ning for anything. He's an investment banker, and apparently good at what he does. We know this Frank Hamilton is a politician who wants law and order. Both men sound like they're trying to be reasonable in a world of dissension. So..."

"So why do their people wind up dead?" Hunter asked.

"It doesn't make sense."

"Well, either it doesn't make sense—or it makes perfect sense," Hunter said. "Let's get to that meeting and then find out what we can about Frank Hamilton."

"There's a plan," Amy murmured.

They arrived at the meeting. Hunter quickly noted Mickey Hampton and Garza had coordinated, and they had gotten a hell of a group together. FBI, FDLE, representatives from county police from Lake Okeechobee on down and across the state, rangers, police, and council members from both the Seminole and Miccosukee Tribes.

The powers that be were determined they cover all 1.5 million acres of the Everglades.

Charles Garza and Mickey Hampton took the floor, addressing the large group they had gathered. While the bodies had been found in the Everglades, the four horsemen had ranged far and wide, but it was apparent Florida was being used as a dumping ground.

"Despite the many deaths we're looking at," Garza said, "the strongest weapon being used is mind control. To that end, recently we discovered that the pawns being used to commit murders or perform sacrifices have also been pushed to mental deterioration with hallucinogens. We're studying victimology and the contacts, habits, and lives of the victims, but we have very little else to go on. So far, the grand leader referred to as the Archangel has used their followers, creating leaders including the functioning head for the crimes that have come before, those of the white, red, and black horsemen. We believe, with profiling assistance from the behavioral unit and through the simple common sense and theories of our lead detectives, that this is the so-called Archangel's final, pale horse assault—and whatever their Apocalypse is supposed to culminate in when the pale horse finishes his work.

"We're looking for someone charismatic. Someone capable of fitting in just about anywhere, of breaking into conversations with strangers just like one of the guys—or girls. Someone who is not threatening in any way.but puts forth a demeanor of friendship along with confidence, intelligence, and stability. But in general law enforcement, I don't think he will be caught in the act of carrying out any of the crimes. Rather he will keep pawns out there—like the couple who called to announce the recent bodies in the Everglades. They were more than ready to sacrifice themselves rather than give away their horsemen. What I'm asking of everyone is vigilance. We all know how thick, dense, dark, and isolated places in the Everglades can be. But none of us believes the Archangel's killing spree has stopped.

"We need everyone to be aware of what has happened, and what we need to be looking for—and how we stop it before this person does get to their final goal. More, we need to stop the killing. The victims thus far have been those who have done jail or prison time for past crimes—and those who look as innocent as a fairy godmother. We need you out there watching for people who don't belong. The person who is out there not to bird-watch, not to head for any of the camping grounds, but those who are looking for specific dump sites to fit the bill," Mickey said. "Stop anyone who looks out of place, and even those who look like they're just hiking. Have a chat. And watch for boats, cars, conveyances that might be bringing out more bodies. I'm afraid that's a solid possibility."

Mickey rubbed a hand across his face. "We're all being used, and I know none of us likes it. We need real teamwork on this. Everyone watching the best that they can because not only is a spectacular natural habitat being used, but the horsemen, angels—killers—are tormenting us, laughing at us, and think they can do anything and not get caught. Between us we can change that."

Mickey looked through the crowd, finding Hunter and signaling to him. "Special Agents Forrest, FBI, and Larson, FDLE, have been on this from the beginning. They've taken down three of the horsemen. Forrest is a specialist in cult investigations, and he'll give you an idea of how these people work."

Amy stood by as Hunter addressed the group. "Cult leaders generally offer something incredibly good that draws people who have had losses in life. They go after adults who might have been abused in their youth in one way or another, those who feel they've been wronged, or they've watched too much that has gone wrong in the world, and they're offering something better—something purer. This is taking it a step further. He's looking for those who want to see an end to arguments, the kind of people who donate to the needy. Simply, those who would always help an old lady across the street. He paints a picture of nirvana. And in this go-around, drugs and hallucinogens have been added into the mix, easily convincing the followers that those they are supposed to kill are truly monsters, and that the only hope they have of redemption is by suffering here on earth before going on to a chance at a greater reward. On the other hand, as we've seen in the victimology, he's going after those who have done time for previous crimes. The Archangel recruited lieutenants as his horsemen, and each made use of cult tactics, gangs, and anything at hand. But the ante has been upped here. We're coming close to something. What we need is help stopping anything even remotely suspicious in and around the Everglades. And these followers are so brainwashed, they'll die before they surrender. Do your best to bring anyone suspicious in alive. When they have been drugged, they can come around after their systems are cleaned out."

Amy thought Hunter spoke well, but it still surprised her his words were followed by such silence. Usually such a meeting created endless questions.

"They will have to make a mistake. There are miles and miles and miles of wilderness and tangled waterways," one of the officers said. "But we will get them. We report anything, right?"

Mickey nodded to Hunter, then spoke again. "Yes, report anything, no matter how minor. Please, report to me immediately and I'll see that the information gets where it needs to be. Special Agents Forrest and Larson have been working hard— and we'll team up with Special Agent Eric Dayton, one of the FBI's superior profilers, Detective Howard Billie of the Seminole police, who works with the FBI Safe Trails Task Force, and Josh Otter, representing the Miccosukee Tribe. Aidan Cypress is lead on forensics and is working with Sabrina Martinez. You've all been sent contact numbers. With everyone's help, we will solve this, and I know that not one of us will stop until we do. We thank you for your attention and…let's all get out there!"

Naturally, the questions began, and Mickey and Charles Garza answered everything. The room was filled with screens depicting the crime scenes and information on what they had gathered.

"What about relatives of the victims?" someone asked.

"We've been sending out agents. Thus far, nothing has created a red flag. We don't believe any relatives or close friends are involved. As you can see, we are now investigating two websites. One promoting civil discourse among all parties and another one dedicated to a politician who is also running on a moderate, work-together agenda. We're investigating any lead."

The meeting broke up. Amy saw many friends in the room, officers and agents she had worked with before. She was able to greet a few friends and coworkers, but then Hunter was at her side.

"We're free to go?" she asked.

He nodded and she turned to head out, but they stopped at

the door when she saw Aidan and Sabrina standing together, watching them solemnly.

"Sabrina, I'm not sure you've met Hunter," she said. "Formally, anyway. Hunter Forrest. Hunter, this is our most amazing tech analyst and researcher, Sabrina Martinez."

Sabrina was one of the most beautiful women Amy had ever known. Her eyes were almost gold. Her hair was a long, rich, thick black. And her facial features were well-set and strong.

"Sabrina, great to meet you. I've heard nothing but rave reviews regarding your work," Hunter told her.

Sabrina smiled. "Likewise. I'm still working the web, and I do think a lot of the answers—or at least the leads—may be found there."

One of the officers excused himself and walked by them, speaking briefly to Sabrina in Spanish. She replied and quickly shrugged to Hunter, saying, "I'm a member of the Seminole Tribe, like Aidan, but my dad is half Cuban and half German American. Hey, it's South Florida. We're a heck of a mix."

"We're a great mix!" Amy assured her, grinning. "And we're headed out on your lead right now, to stop in on the politician, Frank Hamilton. The couple who—"

"The couple who ran into the truck were supporting him," Sabrina said.

"Sabrina and I have both studied the chats on these sites," Aidan said, "and I can't begin to understand how they could have resorted to this kind of violence. They're both so moderate and reasonable, and the only people who are blocked are those who go in furious about something or are hateful or belligerent in their speech. We're digging up web addresses to find out more about those who have been kicked off, but…it's confusing as all hell. Most of the people being really hateful have all kinds of encryptions surrounding anything they do, so it's a dig."

"Keep digging, and we appreciate it!" Amy said.

Aidan frowned. "And you be careful, Amy! You should be sitting this one out—"

"As a target. No, thank you," Amy told him. "I am willing to bet we're all targets, so we all need to catch this person or persons."

"We're heading back to work right now," Sabrina assured her.

"Thank you. And we'll find out just how real Frank Hamilton is," Hunter told her.

They left and hurried to get to the SUV. A few people were leaving but most were staying, and now asking all kinds of questions about the current case and past horsemen and what were the ways a needle could be found in the giant haystack of the Everglades.

In the vehicle Hunter was quiet. Amy glanced at him and said, "Hunter, we have every agency on guard and on tap. Whoever is doing this is so arrogant that he or she or they will have to make a mistake. The meeting was good, and both Mickey and Charles Garza are still there working with reps from all our agencies."

He nodded. "I know. And I think they will start finding some of the people involved. I'm just afraid they'll find more pawns. Whoever is really the head of this is careful and determined to let others take the fall while convincing them heaven and the high place among the angels will be their reward for trying to save others. Add a few hallucinogens to the deal…"

"Hunter, if this job was easy, everyone would do it," she said.

He nodded and glanced at the vehicle's GPS screen. "Well, we're almost there. That's interesting. Sabrina's research showed it's Hamilton's home—and his campaign headquarters. This guy must not need lots of contributions—it's all mansions and horse farms out here."

"You know, being rich doesn't make you a bad person," Amy reminded him.

He smiled. "No. It depends on how you happened to get rich."

She winced inwardly, remembering it was his mother's anger

with her father failing to help others with his wealth that had caused him and his family to spend years in a commune.

"Hey, not to worry. I know a lot of rich people who are great. And this guy may be, too."

The house was an estate, complete with security gates. But the gates were open, and with a shrug Hunter drove on in.

There were at least ten cars parked in the massive horseshoe driveway.

"Campaign workers?" Amy wondered aloud. "There's a big garage, so I'm assuming his family's cars are in there."

"One way to find out," he said dryly.

They headed to the door, but they didn't need to knock; the door was open.

Hunter looked at Amy with a frown. They drew their weapons and pushed the door inward and stepped in.

The entryway opened to a massive room with doors to the left and a sweeping stairway to the right. The room was littered with desks.

And bodies. At least ten of them, men and women, looking as if they'd risen from their desks to crash down in sleep.

She prayed they were just sleeping.

People lay strewed atop the shimmering hardwood.

Amy took out her phone and hit her speed dial for Mickey as they moved carefully into the room. Hunter dropped down by the first body.

"She has a pulse! Tell Mickey," he whispered as instinct and training took over.

"Ambulances and paramedics are already on the way along with a backup squad," she told him, speaking just as softly.

He moved to the next body; again, he found a weak pulse. Amy was checking on the man nearest the young woman he checked next.

"Alive!" he said.

"Thank God!" she murmured. "And help is on the way, but we need to check the house. Whoever did this—"

"May still be here," he said softly.

He nodded toward the stairs. She gave him a nod in return and walked to the doors to the left.

The first door led to a dining room, almost as massive as the living room or gallery where they had entered.

There was no one in the dining room, moving or not. But another door led from the dining room toward the back of the house.

The first room she encountered was a well-appointed pantry and cupboard, one that offered a dumbwaiter to the floor above and painted shelving with glass doors that were spotless.

But there was no one in the pantry.

She kept going, then carefully opened the next door. It led to the kitchen.

And there she saw someone at last, a figure in a dark sweat suit, complete with hoodie. He had been standing at the sink.

He heard her, turned, and took a shot. She ducked back and his bullet flew into the door frame.

She swung around, shouting, "FDLE! Throw down your weapon—"

But he fired again and flew to the back door. He fired shot after shot as he raced out the back.

Shouting for Hunter, Amy took off after him.

6

Hunter was in a child's room when he heard the first gunshot.

He'd already discovered there was no child to be found, not under the bed, and not inside the closet, when he heard the crack of the handgun.

"Amy!" he shouted, hoping she could hear him. The house was a good seven to ten thousand square feet in its expanse.

She did. His heart began to beat again when he heard her shout back.

"He's running! Out the back."

Hunter tore down the stairs, taking care not to step on the people on the floor, torn between leaving them in the house...

And getting his hands on whoever had done this to them while praying it was just a narcotic or hallucinogen that could be cleaned from their systems.

The back door was open. Amy was gone, far across the road, leaping over a fence that led into nothingness.

This far west...

The house itself bordered the Everglades. The population continued to grow in the land of sunshine, and developers pushed farther and farther west.

Amy disappeared into a wealth of foliage behind the property. He hurried after her, leaping the fence as well, tearing into the dense growth of trees and shrubs that lay behind.

He heard sirens as he continued to follow at breakneck speed, and he had to have faith that backup and the medical team would go right in.

And hopefully ascertain what had happened.

He burst through a trail and came to an instant halt, having encountered a waterway. One with a huge adult male alligator basking on the edge.

He didn't see Amy. But neither, thankfully, did he see a gator struggling with a human body, trying to drown his victim or already consuming it.

He decided not to shout her name as he wondered if they had run parallel with the water—or if they had decided to cross it.

A man on the run might well have done the latter while hoping to lose his pursuer.

"Ah, hell!" he muttered to himself. Because he knew Amy. She would have pursued him into and across the water. She wasn't an idiot and had no desire to be a prehistoric creature's dinner, but if the animal was calm and she could move without making waves, he knew she would do it.

He started into the water, but a cry from his left suddenly alerted him to the fact that at least someone had gone in that direction. He tore along the embankment, searching across the water as he ran. The tail end of the grand yards for the west Broward mansion ended and became unclaimed wilderness in this direction, too.

But he heard the cry again and then a young, panicked voice desperately saying, "No, no, no, you don't understand. I didn't do anything. I was going to get out and call for help!"

He hurried around a giant banyan and saw Amy cuffing a young man. He was maybe somewhere between eighteen and twenty-one with long, shaggy brown hair and a lean face.

He certainly didn't appear to be the brains behind any operation. Not that the young couldn't be brilliant or violent, but the look in his eyes belied such a possibility.

"Why did you run?" Amy demanded.

"Because something was wrong, and I didn't do it. I didn't do it, I swear, but I heard you, and I was scared. I didn't know you were cops—"

"Agents," Hunter said pleasantly.

"Agents, whatever. I mean, I came to pick up my mom and everyone was on the floor… I tried to wake her up, but she wouldn't wake up. I came into the kitchen to get water and then heard you walking around and turned and there you were and… I was scared! I didn't know what had happened!"

"Hmm," Amy murmured and glanced at Hunter.

"Could be. Who is your mom?"

"Angie Jamison. She's like best friends with Aubrey Hamilton—you know, the big guy's wife. I mean, he will win the next election! He's so cool, cooler than any of the main party people, that's for sure. I mean, he's all about fairness and… Hey, I even love the guy. His wife is great, and my mom works on the campaign. And I even volunteer sometimes. I do flyers and… You're arresting me? You're really arresting me?"

"What's your name?" Amy asked.

"Rory. Rory Jamison. I swear—"

"Rory Jamison, you shot at me."

"I thought you were whoever hurt all those people!" he protested.

"What were you doing at a campaign headquarters with a gun?" Hunter asked.

"There have been threats! People who don't want people to be reasonable. Like Hamilton. The man says that we don't defund the police, we ferret out the bad ones. We respect everyone. We're all human beings. There are lots of people who don't like that, and my mom told me they were picking up some nasty stuff on the web page and… Oh, I know how to shoot, it's all legal. I am so sorry, I was scared, I was terrified!"

"What were you doing in the kitchen? Why didn't you call 911?" Amy asked.

"I was going to… I dropped my phone in there somewhere. But my mom! I mean everyone, but… My mom is an amazing lady. I thought that if I could get some water out of the kitchen, I could wake my mom up!"

"We have to check out your story," Hunter told him. "And you can hear all the cop cars and ambulances. Let's go see what was done to that group and hope they are all still breathing."

"I just came to get my mom!" Rory said.

"Hey," Amy told him. "What you're saying rings true. Right now—"

"Oh my God, yes! We have to get back there. She has to be alive…she has to be alive—"

"Everyone we checked was still breathing," Hunter assured him.

Amy was looking at him. He knew she meant to let Rory out of the cuffs.

"Where's his weapon?" Hunter asked her.

She indicated her waistband and he nodded.

"Listen, Rory Jamison, I'm going to take off your cuffs. I'm pretty sure that's the only way we'll get back over the fence. But if you pull anything, I will not hesitate—"

"To shoot. I know, I know. If you're really the cops—agents— good guys, then I swear, I don't want to do anything bad. I only want to see if my mom is okay!" Rory promised.

Amy took his cuffs off and nodded in the direction of the house.

"Walk ahead."

He did so. Amy looked at Hunter and gave him a question- ing grimace.

He shrugged and they followed the young man back through the green and humid terrain. At the fence he hesitated.

"Special Agent Larson will go over the fence, and then you. I'll bring up the rear," Hunter said.

Amy easily climbed over the fence, followed by the young man. Hunter kept an eye on him while he scaled the fence himself.

As they headed back for the house he shouted, "FBI!"

He was surprised to see Aidan come to the rear door. "Headed out right after you. Figured if this politician guy was innocent, he wouldn't mind a little prying into one of the campaign computers. I thought it might give us something. But we got the call and..."

He broke off with a frown as he saw Rory Jamison.

"This is Rory Jamison. His mom is in there."

"I need to get to her!" Rory said.

"Paramedics are in there now. You can't get in the way—"

"Please!" Rory begged.

"Come with me," Aidan said sternly. "If they're working on her, you know they need their space. We'll get you with her as soon as possible."

But as they walked back through the kitchen, pantry, and dining room to the living room or campaign headquarters, they saw the victims had all been loaded onto gurneys—the last was headed out. Police had filled the room as well.

One of the officers came over to them, glancing at Aidan and then asking, "Sergeant Kevin Williams here. Agents Forrest and Larson?"

"Hunter Forrest, Amy Larson," Hunter said. "What do you know—"

"We haven't found anyone else in the house or the environs." He arched a brow, indicating Rory. "But this young man?"

"He came to pick up his mother. Angie Jamison. He was afraid we were whoever did this," Amy explained quickly.

"Where is my mom?" Rory asked anxiously. "Oh my God, she isn't..."

"No one is dead. Yet," the sergeant said, wincing. "Aidan, maybe you can explain or at least say something more scientific."

"Obviously, we need to analyze, but basically, I think they were given sedatives. And it was in the water and the coffee. So that's why some are in worse shape than others," Aidan explained. "I'm not a doc or a medic—we'll know more when they get to the hospital."

"Oh no, oh no, oh no!" Rory said, shaking his head. "My mom loves coffee!"

"Kid, kid, the paramedics think they'll all be okay. The paramedics don't think those people were intended to die. Maybe someone wanted to steal something, or..."

Even as he spoke, they heard a commotion. Someone was trying to enter the house, and one of the police officers was trying to hold her back.

Hunter studied the woman, thinking she looked familiar. Then he knew—he had seen pictures in the brief bits of news he got on his phone and when they had downtime.

She was Aubrey Hamilton, wife of the politician and owner of the house, Frank Hamilton. She was well- but not extravagantly dressed in a simple skirt suit and low heels. Her brown hair was neatly cut short and curled around her face—a face that was now bright red and awash with tears.

"My husband, my baby, where is my family?" she cried.

"Excuse me," Aidan said. "I'll take this."

"We'll follow," Hunter said.

"Oh, come on! My mom isn't important?" Rory cried.

Amy stopped, took him by the shoulders, glanced at the sergeant, and said, "Listen, Rory, most of the ambulances have taken off, I think. But the officers will take you to the hospital. But believe this—you'd best be there when we get there. You understand?"

Rory frowned and looked back with a severe and determined expression. "You will find me there. I didn't do anything. And

I will want to know what happened just the same as you, more than you—because that is my mother, and she is just as good a person as any politician!"

Amy gave him and the sergeant a curt nod and followed Hunter as he made his way to the door.

Aidan now had his arm gently around the woman as he spoke quietly, explaining that someone had drugged and sedated everyone in the house; but they had been found quickly, and they were all on the way to the hospital.

"Even Marc? He's only ten! Oh my God, in his little body. I've got to get there, I've got to get to the hospital!"

Hunter looked at Aidan and frowned. He and Amy had moved so quickly through the place that neither of them had noticed if Frank Hamilton was among those on the floor. He might well have been.

But a ten-year-old?

He thought about the room he had been in when he heard the shot Rory had fired at Amy.

"Mrs. Hamilton," Aidan said, "your husband is on the way to the hospital with the other campaign workers. But we didn't find a child in the house. Could Marc be with a relative or a friend?"

"No! He was upstairs playing when I ran out to the printers. He helps a lot down here, but he was upstairs playing a video game. Everyone here watched out for him. His dad was here. No! I didn't have anyone pick him up, he… Oh God!" She burst into tears; Aidan attempted to comfort her and assure her the police and the FBI would be on the search immediately. They would find Marc.

So that was it.

The perpetrator hadn't come to commit mass murder.

Just to kidnap a child. To what end?

Aidan glanced at him. Hunter stepped forward. "Mrs. Hamilton, I need your most recent picture of your son. We'll get an Amber Alert out immediately, and as Aidan said, we'll have police and FBI and FDLE agents combing the state and beyond until we find him."

She tried to nod and began to fumble with her purse. "I have a hard copy of his school picture," she managed to say. She produced the photo and tears poured from her eyes like a geyser before she collapsed.

Hunter was able to catch her, and one of the EMTs saw and quickly came to help. "Get her in an ambulance and to the hospital, please. And then make sure she's all right so she can be there with her husband. We'll get someone from social services over there, and we'll be right behind you."

The EMT nodded. A strong fellow, he picked her up easily while calling for another gurney. Amy was already on the phone alerting Mickey.

He held the photo of Marc Hamilton.

She quickly snapped a picture with her phone and forwarded it on to Mickey.

"My team is on the way," Aidan told them. "We will lift every print, find footprints. I'll search the kid's room and see if I can find a lead."

"We'll head to the hospital," Amy said.

"The hospital. Shouldn't you be looking for Marc Hamilton?" Aidan asked.

Hunter nodded. "But by going to the hospital, we may find a direction in which to look."

"Of course," Aidan murmured.

"Aidan, anything that you find—"

"You bet. You'll know right away. The folks at the hospital, after taking blood, will know better what to tell you about how this was done."

"Right."

"Sabrina is scouring everything to do with Frank Hamilton. Apparently, he's an Independent, but a front-runner for a stab at becoming an Independent president. Of the US. We're looking for anyone out to stop him from taking his moderate agenda with a will to listen and compromise and becoming the front-runner in the election."

"And she's good," Hunter murmured. "Get your team on any tire tracks, especially where it looks like someone might have pulled out quickly. We need to know where the drugs came from, how they got into the water and the coffee. I'm hoping someone comes to quickly—and hoping they have some idea of how they were all drugged."

"Collecting water bottles, cups, the coffee machine…on it," Aidan promised.

They departed at last, leaving Sergeant Williams in charge and coordinating with all the state and local authorities who would arrive.

Along with the media.

They saw a half dozen news vans arrive as they drove away.

"Should we go back?" Amy asked.

"I think Sergeant Williams will say what we would have."

"'No comment, the case is under investigation'?"

He nodded. "And they'll close up the house and retreat inside—by the time they're done, the media might have given up."

"Hunter, this seems like a really intricate scheme to kidnap a ten-year-old."

"Yes."

"To what end? A bargaining chip? To try to make Frank Hamilton not run for office?"

"Possibly. You saw Aubrey Hamilton. She will give up any-thing for that child."

"A good mother. So…we should be getting closer. But we keep getting further away," Amy said.

"No. Come on, you know Aidan is the best. He and Sabrina can find things on the web in places we don't even know exist.

They'll give us a lead, and maybe once he's conscious again, Frank Hamilton himself will be able to help us."

"That's the logical assumption, isn't it?" Amy murmured.

He glanced her way. "Someone doesn't want him running."

"Is he that good, is he that far ahead?" She winced. "One of my first instructors—way back at the police academy—really drilled it into us that we were to serve the law—we weren't political. I heard it again when I became FDLE. We serve the law—we don't make it. And I guess... I need to be more involved in my, uh, personal space, I think. When we see pictures, I recognize people—but I really haven't... Well, I need to do a lot more research on the world at large—and not just the bad guy I'm after at any given minute."

Hunter smiled. She might not realize she paid attention, but she did—or else she was one of those people who innately respected her fellow human beings from all walks of life. But it was true that while all manner of things were going on, they'd been focused on the Four Horsemen case recently. In the few times they were off...to be fair, to stay sane, they had done nothing but try to find pleasure and peace with one another.

"We're doing exactly what we're supposed to be doing," he assured her.

She looked over at him, arching a brow.

"Hey, Major, okay! We have to stop the Apocalypse."

She nodded. "But now...hmm. The Archangel or someone has drawn us in. I'm not sure how, but I do believe with my whole heart that kidnapping that poor child is part of the whole thing."

He nodded.

"I'm with you. Let's hope Frank Hamilton is going to come through it all okay, and he'll be able to give us something."

"Here's hoping!"

They were disappointed. The doctors informed them Frank Hamilton was receiving the best care they could give, but he had been heavily drugged with several different substances. They were flushing his system. His wife was sitting at his bedside, but it would be hours before he was awake and aware enough to carry on any kind of a conversation.

Dr. Ottoman was a serious middle-aged man who kept his charts in front of him as he spoke to them.

"And Aubrey Hamilton? She had collapsed—"

"The trauma. She's okay. She's sitting with him—and as you know, we're already crawling with police and FDLE and FBI. All are making sure none of your possible witnesses receives any attention they're not due to receive."

"And do we have a list of the substances that were in these people—with suggestions on how they were received?" Amy asked.

He let out a sigh. "Fentanyl, but thankfully, not enough in the mixture to cause death. That's a real win for us. Trazodone and hydroxyzine, and the one that really did it, xylazine. The last is not approved for human beings—it's a tranquilizer used in large animals like horses and cows."

"Veterinary supply," Hunter murmured. "We'll get on a list of any missing animal tranquilizers around the state. Other drugs—"

"Yeah. We all know. They're all available on the streets. There's no questioning how anyone was able to acquire it, but then again, some of the most addictive stuff out there is legal, and there are good uses for it. There are those who abuse it," Ottoman said. "But this may be helpful—Marty Benson, Frank Hamilton's right-hand man, has come to and is lucid. We plan on keeping him overnight for observation, and quite honestly, those who have opened their eyes or mumbled something seem to be happy to be at the hospital. It's safer here. Anyway, Mr. Benson is there in room 503, sitting up, and he even ate a little. He's still on a saline drip but coming along. Maybe he can help you."

"Thank you," Amy told the doctor. "As far as how this got into people—"

"Someone made a call about the water—seems like this strange cocktail was ingested. And of course, those who ingested the most are the worst," Ottoman told them. "The EMTs brought in some of the water bottles. I buy that brand, and I promise, it doesn't usually come with sedatives. But they don't use that water in coffee. From what I understand, tap water is good enough at the campaign headquarters. Somehow, we believe, it was in the coffee, too."

Hunter nodded gravely. "If Mr. Benson can give us an idea on what was happening before they all passed out one by one, it will help with the investigation."

They thanked him and headed for Marty Benson's room, nodding to the police officers who were on duty along the way.

Marty Benson was sitting up in his bed just staring straight ahead. He turned to look when they entered his room. He was probably the perfect campaign manager, old enough to give an impression of authority, young enough to have a good-looking quality about him. His face was classical with strong cheekbones, a firm chin, deep blue eyes, and sandy hair, which was plentiful but neatly cut.

He arched a brow when they came in, smiling and wincing at the same time.

"Police?" he asked politely.

"Agents," Hunter said.

"Amy Larson, FDLE, and Hunter Forrest, FBI," Amy said as she went around to the other side of the bed. "How are you? The doctors believe everyone will be all right, but it's going to take time to clean the drug cocktail out of some."

"I heard. It was my first question!" he told them, shaking his head. "I don't get it. I don't get anything that happened. Frank Hamilton is truly one of the best men I have ever met, and Aubrey, she's just as good, and even their kid, Marc, is great. He catches any bugs that fly in so he can let them free! But I did tell Frank we needed security. I mean, he made his home our campaign headquarters. We were always welcome—anyone who volunteered with him was welcome. And this was… Man, it was just bizarre! Everything was fine. We were all in the main room. Frank was going to practice a speech on all of us. He was always willing to listen and he looked for criticism, saying it was better to get it from us than find out he'd done something stupid later. Anyway…we saw Angie drop. Frank and I looked at one another. And then I saw him go down like a ton of bricks, and I started moving toward him, but…man, it was like a black shadow just swept over my mind! I…I don't know what happened, how the hell it happened!"

"It was in the water—" Hunter began.

"We know. What we're hoping you can tell us is how it got in the water. And more importantly, do you know where Marc Hamilton went?" Amy queried.

Marty Benson shook his head, frowning. "The kid wasn't there? He'd been downstairs, but we were all busy. I guess we were boring him, so he went up to play his video game, at least that's what he said. Oh no. Frank and Aubrey…they love that kid so much! He's everything to both of them. He can't be missing!"

"All right, as his campaign manager, do you know how the water gets to the house?" Hunter asked.

"Frank has it delivered by the case every week," Marty told them.

"From where?"

"The grocery store just down the street. There's just one grocery store in the immediate area. And they've been delivering cases of water, bags of coffee, sugar, sweetener, cream…snacks, doughnuts, group food, and whatever from the time we started the campaign. Nothing like this has ever happened."

"Who goes out to get the groceries and bring them in? Does someone walk them into the kitchen?"

Benson shook his head. "The delivery service leaves it outside, piles it all up on the little porch right by the door, and we take it in when we're ready. They notify both me and Frank when it gets there, and we grab whoever is around to bring everything in." He paused again, shaking his head. "That's the thing about Frank. He doesn't expect servants to run around doing everything. Oh, don't get me wrong. He has a lawn service and housekeeping staff, but he will always pitch in to do any manual labor himself or help others when they need help. This…"

He broke off as he frowned and turned to them. "You can't find Marc? Do you think he got scared when he saw everybody out on the floor and ran away?"

"No, I'm afraid we think someone sedated your entire crew so they could take Marc," Amy said flatly. "As far as the threats you've gotten lately, did Frank take any of them seriously?"

"Shouldn't you be out looking for Marc?" he asked anxiously.

"Trust me, sir, we will be—but we were desperately hoping to get a lead from you. Dozens of officers and agents are out on the road. Well, in truth," Amy said sweetly, "there's an Amber Alert out and really, every law enforcement officer of any kind in the state is looking for Marc."

He nodded. "That's good. That kid… He's a good kid. And like I said, he is everything in the world to Frank and Aubrey."

"All right," Hunter said. "The water was delivered from the store just as always. Was that today?"

"Last night, I think. I wasn't the one to bring it in. In fact, I left last night at about five—early for me—but Frank insisted I go out with a few friends from college. He said I'd been working too much. When they wake up, one of the volunteers will know."

"Okay, what about the threats you've been getting?"

Benson shook his head. "None were…specific. I mean, stuff like, 'Take a stand, ass! The world will get you if you don't!' or 'You're a fish, Hamilton, swimming in both directions, promising nothing! Fish get eaten!' And Frank said there was no way to advocate compromise and civil discourse without someone who liked to fight cutting you down. He didn't take any of them seriously. He said politicians were supposed to serve the people. They were supposed to be approachable. That they might stand for one thing or another, but they should always listen to the other side. And I think his policy has been really attractive to a lot of people. I mean a lot of people. He has a chance at the polls. But I wish he'd let me talk him into getting some security!"

"You could have had a school of snipers on duty, but if the water was tainted before it got to the house, it wouldn't have done any good," Amy noted. "We'll be investigating the grocery store and the delivery service, and our tech team is on it. Criminals always make mistakes. We'll find something."

"I just wish!" Benson said, pursing his lips and shaking his head again. He glanced at Hunter. "Sorry. I mean no disrespect. But there are unsolved murder cases all over the country. And there have been serial killers—some that we know of—at it for years and years. But on this... You have to find Marc. He is a really good kid."

Amy smiled at him. "Thank you." She handed him a card; it had her number on it and Hunter's. And as a precaution, it also had a phone number that went directly into Mickey's office.

"We hope you feel better," Hunter said. "We'll probably need to speak with you again, so—"

"Trust me," Benson said, grinning. "I will not be leaving town. My loyalty lies with Frank Hamilton, and I will be here supporting him through this and all else."

They thanked him and left the room.

"Do we stay? Think anyone else has come to?"

"I think we should come back. Someone would have notified us if anyone could speak now. And this is a child abduction. We all know that's a ticking bomb, and time is everything. It's *time* we do get out there and try to find Marc Hamilton," Hunter told Amy. "We'd have been called if anyone had made a ransom demand. This is about something else."

"But we didn't get anything helpful from Marty Benson except the store and the drivers need to be checked out. I...I think we need to find out the names of the delivery personnel and the grocery personnel—"

"That needs to be done, but we'll get other people on that," Hunter said.

"So...?"

"So, we're going to work with Aidan and Sabrina. We're going to find out who wrote the threats. Except..." He stopped speaking, just shaking his head.

"What?" Amy asked him.

"We need to see all the threats, and we need to get Aidan and Sabrina and their team analyzing and tracing them all. The computers have gone in, so I figure that they're already on it. And there's an Amber Alert out. I must admit, I'm not sure how to start—except by going back to the house, checking the kid's room, and figuring out how someone got in and out with him. I seriously believe the only plan here was the child abduction. An elaborate child abduction," Hunter determined.

"Perpetrated," Amy continued, "by someone who knew just how many people would be in that house—and knew that the way to get to the kid was to find a method to knock them all out at the same time. That was risky. What if someone in there didn't have water or coffee? Then they wouldn't have been out," Amy said.

"True. The plan was risky. Which suggests it might have been carried out by someone who was supposed to be around—which, since Hamilton is such a believer in an open format and an open house, could have been just about anyone. But the risk paid off. And still..."

"Still?"

"I don't know. It's just so strange."

"Do you think our mysterious Colin might have been part of this?" Amy asked.

"I don't know. But there's another place we might learn about the more violent radicals out there, maybe something else that might point us in the right direction."

"Something or someone? You're talking about Perry Carson, administrator for the Commonsense Party website?" Amy suggested.

He nodded. "I am. Except we have all the computers where the threats and users might be found. So..."

"Aidan will still be at Frank Hamilton's home headquarters."

"But Sabrina wasn't there. She's bright and has a great sensibility of what lies between the lines. I'm going to give her a call."

"Let's check on Rory!" Amy said. "He's either guilty or the first witness at the scene."

"Right," Hunter agreed. He stopped one of the nurses in the hallway to ask her about Angie Jamison and Rory.

"She's still asleep, but she's coming along okay, pulse good, and she's breathing easily. He's sitting at her side. Oh, and he told me he wasn't leaving. I brought him a pillow and blanket so he can sleep on the chair that stretches out. Of course, you know how many officers and agents are on duty here."

He thanked her.

"Now I'll call Sabrina," he said.

He never got a chance to do so.

Amy's phone was ringing.

"Aidan," she said, answering the call, listening with a frown.

She ended the call and looked at him. "He wants us back. He thinks he found drag marks in a few places, and he talked to the man who knows the Everglades like few others."

He smiled. "Jimmy Osceola?"

"And Jimmy told him there are a few old shacks out there, ramshackle—"

"Amy, I know what they are."

"Well, he thinks whoever took the kid might have used an old trick—and stuffed him into one of those old ramshackle places. For now, at least!" she said softly.

He nodded, heading down the hallway, walking fast. Amy was moving quickly to keep up.

"Hey!" she whispered. "I'll drive!"

He laughed softly. "Sorry. Now we have a direction! And I want to get on it as quickly as humanly possible."

"Agreed. But I'll still drive!"

7

It didn't take much time to get back to the Hamilton house and headquarters. Aidan was waiting for them in front when they arrived, and to their surprise Jimmy Osceola was there, too. Amy was glad. There was no one who knew the entire south of the state the way that Jimmy did.

"You know about these abandoned shelters, right?" Jimmy asked.

Amy nodded, remembering their last horseman.

"Only too well," she assured him. "But before any of all this started, when I was a kid, my dad had lots of friends who liked to come out to go fishing. And hunting. Mainly, they just spent time together and shot up beer cans. The shelters were prohibited a long time ago, and still—"

"A lot of them remain, mostly in the most tangled and remote areas, as you know. But Jimmy thinks there are about three of them in back—between this waterway and the next," Aidan told them.

Jimmy pointed to the rear of the place. "The waterway beyond here is accessible from far to the south as well. I take that waterway a lot when I have people who really want to see the scope of the Everglades. From here, though..."

"Yeah. We need to walk across that shallow waterway," Amy said, making a face. "It's cool. I wore my boots."

"I didn't," Hunter said. "But what the hell. A pair of shoes to maybe find that poor kid? I'm all in. Let's head on out."

Aidan still had a team working in the house, and Sergeant Williams remained as well. He nodded to them as they passed through, and Amy knew Aidan had already described their purpose.

They hurried through the large, manicured lawn to the fence Rory had hopped over earlier when she had followed him. One by one they went over.

She looked at the water briefly before starting through it.

"You checked this out? You sure it's shallow?" she asked Jimmy.

"Yep. Two feet at the deepest," Jimmy said.

"At least our big basking male alligator has moved on," Hunter commented.

"The big males can be tough if they're threatened. But nothing is as fierce as a female if you mess with her nest!" Jimmy warned. "Honestly, you can see those guys. But watch out for snakes."

"Thanks. I'm feeling better and better," Hunter said dryly.

But Amy knew Hunter. And he was already walking through the shallow waterway and well on his way to the other side.

She followed, moving quickly. Aidan and Jimmy were at her side.

"We'll move west. You can move north?" Hunter suggested.

"Not to argue but put one of us with each of you. We just know it better," Aidan said.

"Works for me because that is something I definitely won't argue," Hunter told him.

"How about Jimmy and I go west," Amy suggested. "And you two—"

"North," Hunter said.

"And believe it or not, because of all these very expensive homes, you will get cell service even in the thicket," Aidan said. "We can try shouting if we need help, but the cell phones will work."

They all nodded and split up. Amy lowered her head as she smiled. She knew that in any circumstance, Hunter would keep his head.

And he'd been in the dense green of the Everglades many times now.

But it made good, solid sense the way they had split!

Jimmy led the way. "You have an idea of where we're going?" she asked him.

"There are two leftover shacks this way, one to the north. Of course, we can search all three of them and find nothing—"

"But Aidan thinks the kid was dragged out."

"I do, too. Aidan called me when he found what he's darned sure are drag marks. He thinks whoever took the kid knocked him out, too. And then the kid might have gotten heavy, and he had to get him over the fence. Even with evidence a theory can be wrong, but since the Amber Alert is out, since pictures of the kid are up everywhere, and he hasn't been spotted, well…"

"It makes sense he disappeared before he could be seen. And if he was knocked out, the sedation might not have lasted long. And whoever took him might have thought he'd be seen trying to get him to a hotel room or a house. The kid isn't stupid from what I hear. He would have put up a fuss. Anyway…"

They plowed on through.

Jimmy knew how to follow animal trails, which kept them out of big sweeps of saw grass. The tree growth was heavy, and with the sun lowering in the sky, the deep green of the Everglades seemed very dark.

But finally, Jimmy pointed about a hundred yards ahead.

"There! I knew there was one near here in this direction. See?

The waterway I sometimes take is through there just a football field away!"

"And the shack?"

"Look hard. Fungus has taken over, of course, but you can see the brown of the wood if you look hard enough. Come on. We'll be there in five."

He was right. Of course, it wasn't easy going. Ground vines caught her feet now and then. She almost tripped when she wasn't looking, but Jimmy was there to catch her.

"Just another fifty feet!" he said.

When they approached the old decaying hunter's shack, they both stopped dead.

It was supposed to be abandoned.

Nature was supposed to be taking over such dwellings.

This one had a brand-new padlock on the door.

"He's there!" Jimmy said.

"And let's just pray he's alive. Jimmy, how are we going to break the lock?"

"We're not," he said. "I'm going to help you through that broken-out window. And I'll be right behind you."

She was glad. Her heart was beating a little too quickly. It was bad enough finding adults dead—she didn't want to find a ten-year-old boy had died.

But she wasn't going to, she determined.

A padlock wasn't needed to prevent a corpse from escaping.

"Come on, Jimmy. Quickly! Get me in there!"

"Hunter?"

Hunter had come to a dead stop. Aidan called to him, wondering why he would do so when they were on such a determined search.

But he had a good reason.

"Sorry," he said lightly, grimacing at Aidan. "Eastern diamondback, heading across the path. I figured I'd give it the right-of-way."

"Good call. A lot of cops would have just shot it."

"Hey, don't judge. If it had come in my direction, I might have done so. It's gone…moved off into the grass over there."

"That's why even I hate walking through shallow water," Aidan told him. "When I was a kid, I was playing with a friend in one of the canals, and he got bit by a Florida cottonmouth. Kid was in the hospital for a week and he was lucky he lived. We were small, the snake was big. The coral snake is really our worst, but it just about has to get you between the fingers…not much of a jaw. Anyway…"

"We're after a different kind of snake. He's gone—let's keep going."

Aidan gave him a grim smile. "You do all right out here. A lot of nonnatives to the area just think it's a hot, humid, and creepy place with nothing."

"I like creatures, even the creepy ones," Hunter said lightly.

"Yeah, well, we've got a new one, you know."

"Pythons and boas that have multiplied like rabbits," Hunter said. "I can see how it happened. People buy a big snake—then as it passes six feet, they realize they made a mistake. But they don't want to be inhumane and kill it, so they bring it out to the wilderness and let it go. And suddenly there are eggs everywhere and more snakes than anyone can handle."

"Let's hope we don't run into one."

"If a python embraces you, my friend, no matter how I like to see wildlife be wild, I will shoot it."

"Don't miss and shoot me. Hey, there's one of the abandoned shacks Jimmy was talking about just ahead around a hundred feet."

They both paused, then nodded to one another. Aidan was forensics but he also carried a weapon in the field. He drew his gun quietly as Hunter went for his Glock.

With nods of understanding, they moved around the shack in opposite directions. Windows were gone, weather having most likely taken them out through the years. It was easy enough to approach carefully with the trees and brush as shields and come up to the opposite windows.

At some point in time it had been a nice, if small, dwelling. The remnants of a brick chimney stretched out in a crumbling manner at the roof. The little building didn't appear to be more than a one-room dwelling, but a spigot suggested it had once had running water and an outdoor shower.

Hunter carefully flattened against the outer wall and looked in. There was no one inside, but the place did offer furniture—outdoor furniture, the kind bought at any home store for a patio—inside.

The rain in Florida often came heavy. Whoever was making use of the old place hadn't bothered to refit windows, but the waterproof furniture offered chairs and tables for whoever frequented the little place.

"Clear!" Hunter called.

"Clear," Aidan returned from the other side.

Hunter walked around to the front and pushed in the decaying remnants of the door. Lawn chairs surrounded a plastic-topped table. In the not-too-distant past, though it hadn't been cold in quite a while, someone had burned a fire in the hearth. Then again on a wet night when the temperature did dip a bit, it could cause a chill.

"This is the weirdest combination of rustic and cared-for I think I've ever seen," Aidan said, looking around.

Hunter barely heard him. There was something on the table, and he walked over to see what it might be. A little plastic piece. He didn't touch it; it was small, but that didn't mean it might not provide a partial print.

"Hunter?" Aidan asked.

He grimaced and indicated the piece to Aidan.

It was another of the little plastic horses. The pale horse sat among empty paper cups, plates, and plastic dinnerware as if someone had idly been playing with it as they ate and conversed.

The settings had been for three people.

"Don't touch anything," Aidan begged.

"I know that," Hunter assured him.

"I need a team out here and my kit," Aidan said. He had pulled out his phone, but he hesitated. "Wait, there's still a kid out here somewhere. This is the only shack remaining in this vicinity so we can hope Jimmy and Amy are finding something. This can wait. A kid can't. We should turn back and help them."

"Call it in, get a team out here, and we'll move on," Hunter said. "But this is your purview, Aidan. I can go and you can stay—"

"When there's a kid out there? Unless you are ordering me not to go, I'm with you. Oh, wait, you can't. I'm still FDLE, not even on loan, just part of the task force."

"Aidan, it wouldn't occur to me to order you to do anything," Hunter assured him. "So let's get it called in and..."

He broke off, frowning.

And he quickly answered the call.

"Glass, Amy, be careful!" Jimmy warned.

The windows were high; Jimmy was giving her a hike up. But there had been glass in them once, and of course, when they had broken or shattered through time and weather, shards had remained.

"I'm all right. I'm using my jacket to protect my hands," she assured him.

He had her up, and she was glad she'd thought to use her jacket. She might have caused herself some serious harm.

But she was in position, and she could see into the dilapidated old cabin. It was stark, bare. But there was a darkness against the far wall, a form...

"Jimmy, give me another push!" she said.

He hiked her higher. She got the hold she needed and crawled as cautiously as she could through the window frame, trying to be so careful as she allowed herself to fall to the floor within. She rushed to the shadow she'd seen, because she was convinced it was the missing child.

She found a pile of blankets and was riddled with disappointment. But she pulled away the top blanket and stopped for a split second, totally frozen.

They had found him.

She snapped quickly out of her state of being immobile, calling his name and checking for a pulse, for breath.

He was breathing. He wasn't conscious, but he was breathing.

"Jimmy, get someone out here, fast! He's here. We need to get him to the hospital as quickly as possible. He's nonresponsive but he's breathing! Call Mickey for the EMTs to get out here and then get Aidan and Hunter!"

"Got it!" Jimmy assured her.

It was dark in the room, but she unwrapped her hands and searched in her jacket pocket for her penlight.

The room, other than for the child and the blanket, was truly empty. There was dust and dirt everywhere. There was no way to try to make the child—seated and leaned against the wall—any more comfortable. She wanted to get him out of the room. But they had nothing with them that could break the bolt on the door, and lifting him through the windows with their jagged shards of glass could be dangerous.

She figured she could lean against the wall herself and lean him down into her lap. But she needn't have worried. She heard a tremendous thud against the door.

She was grateful when the boy in her lap responded with a jerk.

There was another thud, then another.

And then Jimmy Osceola managed to shatter the old wood.

What remained of the late-afternoon sun came flooding into the space, and Jimmy was with her.

"Might as well stay as you are, though. There is nowhere outside to take him," Jimmy told her. "But Aidan and Hunter are on their way, and there are still cops and members of the forensic team at the house. As soon as there are EMTs, they'll get them out here."

"No, no!" Amy argued. "We can carry him at least halfway back, get him to help as soon as possible. Staying here is just…"

"You think someone may be hanging around here?" Jimmy asked.

"I don't know. I don't know if whoever planned this expected anyone would know about these old shacks, but, Jimmy, at the two body dump sites, people were there watching. Well, I mean the couple who 'found' the bodies didn't get them there, and our young man coming around, Elijah, was sent to see what was going on. So I expect it might have been the same and… we can't risk this boy, Jimmy. We can't risk Marc. We just can't! The poor kid is only ten years old."

Jimmy nodded. "I can carry him. I was thinking if he's hurt, if he has any broken bones—"

"I don't think so, I really don't. I think his abductor managed to knock him out—he gave Marc something pretty strong, because he's alive and breathing but his pulse is…faint. Jimmy—"

"Got it," Jimmy said. He reached down and easily picked up the ten-year-old boy and headed out of the shack through the shattered door.

Amy quickly rose to follow him.

"Wait! I've got to go first. Jimmy, I'm armed. We didn't see anyone, and there might not be anyone out there, but…"

"Go. I guess you're not the worst tracker."

"Thanks!"

She wasn't the best tracker, either, but she did have a good memory—she knew the different twists and turns they had taken to get to the shack. Of course, now she was moving more slowly and taking care to search the foliage all around her.

"Are you okay?" she asked, pausing for a second.

Jimmy nodded and she smiled. Jimmy spent his life outside on his various boats, but he was naturally a fit man, and carrying the child didn't seem to be much of a burden for him.

But after a few more steps, she paused again. She heard something.

Someone was in the brush near them. She lifted a hand so that Jimmy would know to stop.

But then she heard Hunter's voice, calling her name.

"Amy?"

She let out her pent-up breath and answered him quickly. "It's us!"

A second later, he and Aidan appeared in the brush before them. Hunter hurried forward, looking worriedly at the boy in Jimmy's arms. He automatically checked for the boy's pulse and let out a sigh of relief. "Sorry, had to—"

"Yeah, yeah," Jimmy said. "Hey, you want to take over for a minute?" Jimmy suggested.

Hunter grinned and carefully took the boy from him.

"Let's move, we're getting closer to the house," Aidan said. "The EMTs are getting close, but I'm afraid that without one of us, they won't find their way out here. Once we get Marc to the medical personnel, I'll get some of my people out to the cabins—"

He broke off as they heard a whistling through the branches and the grass.

"Down!" Hunter shouted, falling to his knees with the boy.

Jimmy was down with him instantly, taking Marc back from him as Hunter and Amy both drew their weapons while they kept low and silent in the denseness of the brush.

Then there was nothing. No sound. A second bullet didn't come flying through the trees. There was no sound of rustling in the grass or brush.

Amy looked at Hunter. He lifted a hand. They needed to stay down and silent and listen longer.

They then heard a shout that brought relief.

Mickey Hampton was there again.

"FBI! FBI! Whoever you are, wherever you are, drop your weapon!"

Amy moved against a large cypress tree to shield herself as she shouted in return, "Mickey, we're here. Moving toward you now!"

"And we're nearly to you!" he cried back. "Take care—we're not alone out here."

"We know!"

Of course, by then, she'd advertised their position. But Mickey appeared through the brush in just a minute and he wasn't alone. He was surrounded by officers and agents, FDLE and Seminole police. Ten in all were moving carefully, armed and ready.

"Marc has to get to the hospital!" Amy said.

"We're on it. Jimmy, you keep the boy in your arms. Hunter—"

"Yep, Amy and I will join the guard group. Thanks, all of you!" Hunter said.

Of course, the trails weren't really trails. It was almost impossible to create the kind of human shield they might have done elsewhere. But whoever had been watching in the Everglades, whoever had taken the shot, had apparently determined not to go against a force of their size. There were no further incidents as they made their way back to the house.

EMTs were there, getting ready to hike gear over the fence. Mickey shouted to them they had the boy; he just needed the hospital as quickly as possible.

Hunter hurried forward to help Jimmy get Marc over the fence.

Amy ran up to join them as she holstered her weapon. "Please, I need to go with him!" she said.

"Of course. But only one," the young EMT said. "Anyone else can follow—"

"I'm going back into the brush with these guys," Hunter told her. "I'll meet you back at the hospital."

She nodded. She felt responsible for the boy, no matter how good the medical care the med techs could give him.

Marc was already on a gurney when she crawled over the fence and joined the EMTs. One was on the phone talking with one of the doctors who had handled the other cases and was receiving instructions. As soon as they'd gotten through the house and to the ambulance, the one EMT began setting Marc up with an IV drip.

"Saline," the young man told her. "Doc says most important thing is to get his system cleaned out of whatever he's got in it. I'm going to take blood samples so they'll be ready the minute we get there, though it seems it's been the same cocktail in each person we have in the hospital already, just in different doses."

"Thank you," Amy murmured. She sat by the gurney just down from the EMT who worked over the young boy. Marc Hamilton's eyes were closed. His brown hair curled around a cherubic face. He was a ten-year-old, and she couldn't begin to imagine his parents' distress.

She glanced at the EMT, a focused young man, probably about twenty-five, serious and painstaking in all that he did as he cared for the child.

Amy just sat there, reaching for and holding the little boy's hand.

She glanced at the EMT.

"He's going to make it," the young man promised softly.

She gave him a weak smile. But he was telling her the truth. It seemed like the longest drive in history, but as they neared the hospital, she was suddenly rewarded for being there.

Marc's eyes opened a crack, and he squeezed her hand as his eyes closed again. And while it seemed he had passed out again, there was something different in the way his little hand rested in hers. There might have been greater warmth, maybe even a touch of movement, but she believed the child really had a fighting chance.

As they drove into the ER section for ambulances, the EMT told Amy, "We'll take him in. You don't need to worry—the hospital is still crawling with cops and agents. Maybe you could go and tell his mother you have him here, and she can see him as soon as the doctors give him the proper care. She can come down to the ER if she likes."

"Wait! Can't I stay with him until she comes down?" Amy asked.

"I…I don't know. That will be up to the doctors."

It might be up to the doctors, but Amy wasn't leaving him. The hospital had been alerted, of course, and the doctor she had met earlier, Dr. Ottoman, was already on his way out to meet them.

"I'm staying with him for now," Amy said flatly.

"As you wish. We can send someone to let his mom and dad know."

"Frank Hamilton is awake?" Amy asked.

"Still groggy, but he's getting better by the hour."

"Thank you!" Amy breathed.

"Just, uh—"

"Stay out of the way. I can do that," Amy assured him.

She glanced at her phone, tempted to call Hunter. But if they'd found anyone or anything, he would have called her.

She wasn't sure why, but she didn't want to leave Marc's side, not until his mom was with him at least.

The ER had numerous beds that were curtained off and only three little rooms.

Marc was taken to one of the rooms. It was easy enough for her to stay against the far wall completely out of the way.

Finally, Dr. Ottoman and the ER doctor working with him

finished their consultation. The nurse had the right mixture of antidotes going through Marc's IV.

Dr. Ottoman told her she was welcome to take a seat next to the bed.

"Where did you find the boy? His mother should be down shortly. I hated not telling her the minute we had him in here, but I felt it more beneficial to the patient that he be settled first. We may be changing some of this up when the lab gets back to us, but he should be coming to fairly quickly now. Even the most heavily dosed of the campaign staff are starting to come around."

"Thank you so much, Dr. Ottoman."

He nodded and left her. She glanced at her phone, but she hadn't missed any calls.

Holding Marc's hand again, she closed her eyes, knowing she just needed to be patient. She was hungry and she was tired, but the day wasn't over yet. Still, sitting there it was all right just to shut her eyes...

She heard the door opening and she turned quickly, ready to give her seat up to Marc's mom. But it wasn't his mother who had come—it was Frank Hamilton's campaign manager, Marty Benson.

"You're better!" she said. He was dressed in a handsome suit and looked as if nothing had happened to him at all.

He nodded. "I've been released. I was lucky today. I'm usually the one swilling coffee as if there was no tomorrow, but I was running around this morning and just had one cup."

"Well, it's good to see you up and about."

"Thank you. I'd just signed my discharge papers when I heard Marc had been found and was here. And you're in here, with him. Thank you, thank you! I heard you were the one who found Marc. Amazing, wonderful!" Marty said. "His mom is on her way down, and Frank is beside himself because they don't want him up yet. The docs promised him that they would bring Marc up to be in the bed next to his. That's the only thing keep-

ing Frank down. Well, Miss Special Agent Amy Larson, from
the little bit I've heard, you really are a miracle worker. You
found him out in the wilderness?"

"It took teamwork, and we know some awesome people who
know things when we don't," Amy said. "But whoever took
Marc brought him out to one of the old shacks that was out-
lawed a bunch of years back. We have forensic crews out there
now, and our people—federal and state—are very good. We
will get answers."

"Of course. And again, thank you. I can't imagine what might
have happened... Never mind, don't even want to think that
way."

"Marc!"

Amy turned quickly to see Aubrey Hamilton, in a wheelchair
accompanied by a nurse, coming through the door.

She saw Marc and flew to her feet, almost causing the chair
to knock over the young nurse who had brought her down.
She catapulted to the bed, almost falling on top of her son but
catching herself to stand over him and encompass him in a hug.

She held him for a long moment before she turned to look
at Amy with tears in her eyes. "Thank you, thank you, thank
you! I could never, ever, in a thousand years thank you enough!"

"Finding him was gratification enough, Mrs. Hamilton,"
Amy assured her, "and it wasn't just me. We have a friend who is
a Seminole guide, and he had the idea of where we should look.
It was a team that went out to find him. We're very grateful!"

"I'm going to just get this out of the way," the nurse murmured as she backed out with the wheelchair. "I believe you
are fine here—"

"Yes, thank you!" Marty assured her and she smiled briefly
and made her exit.

Amy stood, ready to leave the chair next to the bed for Aubrey.
As she did so, she was startled to hear her name called weakly.

Marc's eyes were open, and he was clinging to his mother but looking at her. She wondered how he knew her name, but then she knew the human brain was complex. He'd probably heard her called by name when he was in and out of consciousness.

She leaned over and squeezed his hand. "Hey, little man! It's wonderful to see you awake!"

He gave her a weak smile. "I…I was so scared!"

"Who did this, Marc? Who took you into the back of your home…into the wild part?" she asked.

He shook his head. "I was sleeping. I woke up and couldn't move, I was just so scared, I didn't know where I was, I…I know you were there. Amy, you made the darkness go away."

"I'm so glad. You don't remember anything, anything at all?"

"I was playing my video game. I kind of woke up, and it was green and dark, and I was so scared and then I don't remember and then…"

"It's okay, it's okay," Amy assured him. She glanced at Aubrey Hamilton.

"I will not be leaving him!" Aubrey whispered. "He's awake. They'll be transferring him up to Frank's room. The doctor said he thinks Frank and I can be discharged by tomorrow." She paused, looking at Marty Benson. "Oh, Marty, you were right! We need security. Why don't people just want to try to get along? Frank never says a bad word about an opponent. He doesn't disparage anyone's ideas. His campaign is like his life, always fair, seeking good and compromise!"

"Aubrey, Aubrey," Marty said gently, "we will get things changed in the future. Frank will understand now. I know he will. We'll be very careful, and now all the millions of people who support him are up in arms, determined they'll be on the lookout for anything dangerous in any of the messages on the chat site and…we're going to be okay. We're going to take this as a warning, and we'll be super careful in the future!"

"Maybe," Aubrey murmured. "No campaign is worth my

son!" she whispered. "And now I'm afraid to return to my own home!"

"I'm good, Mom. Honest!" Marc said. "And I love our home. But I'm scared, too."

"We'll have you protected in the future," Amy promised. Of course, it wasn't her place to make such promises, but she knew Mickey and she knew Charles Garza.

Hamilton's family would be protected from now on.

"I'm going to find the doctor and see about getting you and Marc moved up with your husband," Amy told Aubrey. She offered a nod to Marty, who was looking concerned and perhaps baffled with himself—she had a feeling the man seldom felt helpless. Hurrying out, she found Dr. Ottoman at the desk, going through a file, but he quickly turned and gave her a questioning look as she approached.

"The boy is awake?"

"He is, thanks. And, Doctor—"

"I'll escort him and his mom up myself right now," Dr. Ottoman said. "We're only two beds to a room, but I think Aubrey is doing well enough for a discharge. She's going to be with her child all night as a patient or a visitor. She can have the pull-out chair while her husband and son are in their hospital beds." He paused, looking at Amy. "If there's anything… Well, we have your boss on speed dial. And I have never felt quite so safe at work. You have good people here. Must be boring on hospital guard duty like this, but I don't see any of them who aren't alert and on the job."

"That's good to hear. Thank you," Amy told him. "And since all is well, I'm going to head out now and rejoin my team, whatever they're up to."

"Of course. We will be vigilant!" he promised.

She smiled. "I am deeply impressed by the care you give your patients. Thank you, sir."

She turned and walked out the ER doors, calling Mickey

as she did so. She'd come in the ambulance with Marc, so she needed a ride back. On a day like today, she didn't feel comfortable calling a rideshare.

Mickey was on another line; his assistant told Amy he was sending out a surprise driver for her, and she'd be happy.

"A surprise?" she murmured.

"You know him. He's there right now."

Amy frowned and stepped out of the automatic doors to look for a waiting car.

And then she smiled.

It was Mickey himself.

Hunter knew there had to have been someone out there, watching, when they brought Marc back to the house and the waiting ambulance.

Now there were at least twenty officers and agents prowling the foliage, along with himself, Aidan, and Jimmy.

Knowing how many armed and angry men and women were on their trail, they might well have taken the fastest possible route out of the denseness of the hammock.

"Think he's gone?" Aidan asked as he moved just behind him.

Hunter paused, then shook his head. "No. Succeed—or commit suicide. That seems to be the Archangel's mantra. Whoever was here—whoever fired that shot—is still here."

He had barely spoken before he frowned. He could hear a voice, someone speaking softly but quickly.

"Two people?" Aidan asked in a whisper.

Hunter stopped to listen closely.

"Just one speaking...around that clump of brush by the big cypress..."

"I'll take right."

"I'm going around left," Hunter said.

He would go by all legal measures and protocol, but he wasn't going to mess around. Amy had made the right move with Elijah.

If this person had a gun, Hunter was going to shoot it out of their hand if they didn't drop it immediately.

He rounded the corner. And found the speaker.

It was a young woman. She had long brown hair, wore no makeup, and was dressed in khakis in almost military style. She had a gun, but it was at her side, and she was talking and gesturing wildly, as if she was indeed speaking to someone else.

But there was no one there.

Hunter strode straight for her and kicked the gun far to his right—where Aidan, just coming around from behind, quickly picked it up.

The young woman stood up, smiled, and stared at them as if they were ants on the ground and she was something far greater.

"It's time! The sun will collide with the moon. The pale horseman has come among us, and he will protect us and sweep us up to the clouds. I can see them! Can't you see them? They are there, riding the clouds. Oh, it's so beautiful and it doesn't matter if it's you first or me first...the time has come!"

He realized that she was thin, almost bone thin, as if she'd been malnourished for a long time. Her eyes were blue, huge in her face, and she looked at Hunter as if every word she spoke was truth.

"Miss, I'm sorry, but—"

"It's happening! Can't you feel it? The sun and the moon, the burst of light will be amazing. The angels will fill the clouds with a brilliant light, and we will drift up and up and up..."

She suddenly stopped speaking and frowned. "The boy... Oh my God, the boy—"

Then she stared at Hunter with absolute horror and reached down, desperately searching for the gun she'd had.

Hunter moved forward to catch her by the shoulders, spin her around, and get cuffs on her as quickly—and gently—as possible.

"No!" she shrieked. "I have to die, I have to die!"

"No, actually, you don't," Hunter told her.

"What the hell is she on? And...is this a mistake or what? You'd leave someone in this state to look after a hostage?"

The girl tried to run past Hunter. He caught her and she screamed, "I won't sit with the angels, I will burn and burn... I have failed!"

Hunter gave her a gentle shake. "No. You have been duped. Now..."

She burst into tears.

"Let's just get her back. Maybe the doctors can help her," Aidan said.

Hunter nodded, but the girl fell to the ground. Shaking his head, he lifted her up and over his shoulder, bearing the brunt of her fury as she slammed her cuffed fists against his back.

"Let's move fast," he suggested dryly as he turned to start the walk back to the rear of the Hamilton house.

And as he did so, he was almost thrown back when the landscape before him suddenly seemed to explode and fire enveloped the trees and brush, turning green to brilliant shades of red and yellow.

"It's come!" the girl shrieked. "The Apocalypse is here!"

8

Amy shouldn't have been surprised to see Mickey except he usually spent time in his office—handling the many cases and agents beneath him.

"You really are hands-on in this case!" she told him.

"Yeah, well, FBI may have the lead and I'm fine with that, but it's my state that's being used as a dumping ground. It's all happening so fast. There are new leads we wind up with before we can follow up on our old leads. By the way, your boy Elijah is doing well. Doc said they might be able to release him in a day or two, but we need to keep him protected, and he can still face federal and state charges."

"He's come around well, Mickey. He's given us most of what we have. I don't want him charged. I want him protected."

"May not be up to you. We are looking at a lot of dead."

"He didn't kill them, Mickey. His job was just to see what was going on when someone got wind the bodies in the barrels had been found. And the drugs in his system! Mickey—"

"This Colin person found him and persuaded him he was

going to have to join some kind of a revolution. We still don't know just what his participation was."

"Mickey, he's not the person we're looking for."

"No. The person we're looking for orchestrated the murders. I doubt if they ever got their hands dirty in any way. They just found that if you combine old-time charisma, cult mentality, and some damned good hallucinogens, you can make anyone do just about anything. But it doesn't mean whoever wielded a knife or a gun or other weapon isn't going to be charged."

"Seriously, I think Elijah—"

Mickey interrupted her with a laugh. "What? Are you going to be his defense attorney? Our responsibility is justice for the dead."

"I know that. But, Mickey, justice…"

"And while you and Hunter have been pursuing the new leads as they pop up like popcorn, I've had crews interviewing family, friends, everyone and anyone we can think of. And still, the only thing we have is that it's like a twenty-eighty split. Good people, some religious, some not, comprising eighty percent of the dead, and petty criminals being about twenty percent of the dead with just a few in there who have served time for assault or more serious charges. Every agent has made a report, and they're all being sent to you and Hunter. There are no visible red flags. And the only thing they all have in common is chat sites on the web—supporters of Frank Hamilton and folks who love the conversation at that Commonsense Party website."

"Someone is trying to shut down the moderates. Someone has an agenda. I believe there's a plan to turn people against one another with greater vengeance. And the thing is, Mickey, that's not the majority. Most people want to raise their families and be happy. It's just fringe elements who want to see chaos. Should be easy to discover, especially when we have pros like Aidan and Sabrina and—"

"Trust me, Garza and an FBI team have been looking at Hamilton's opponents, searching the web, every kind of social media known to man. Some wacky people, even some violent people, but nothing on this scale. They're loud, they're vocal—but they tend to be loud and vocal on social media, they try to make the news to make their points, but nothing like this."

"The Archangel's plan. Who are they, and just what is that plan?" she murmured.

Mickey's phone was ringing. He pressed the button on his car that answered it. "You're on speaker, Hunter. I've got Amy with me, on my way out to you."

"Stay at the house. Someone has started a fire out here. We've got great teams of firefighters from the region here, but the expanse of glades to the west of the Hamilton house are burning with a vengeance."

"Hunter, you guys are—"

"We're all fine. And we found the woman who fired the shot. She's not so fine. She gives new meaning to the term *unstable*. Don't come closer than the house. Aidan, Jimmy, and I should be out by the time you get here with our new…friend. We have medical waiting, too. Watch out for the smoke—it's getting bad."

Hunter rang off.

"And now a fire," Mickey said. He glanced her way. "Thankfully, we have some of the best firefighters known to man down here, thanks to idiots who leave campfires burning and guests with cigarettes. Of course, controlled fires are set upon occasion. But this is getting worse and worse."

"We need to find out what the plan is!" Amy said softly.

They were nearing the Hamilton house, and Hunter had been right; the smoke was getting heavier. While the estates out here were far apart, she could see neighbors of the Hamilton family were out in their long driveways watching worriedly.

"I don't see flames," Amy murmured.

"They might have gotten it under control. I wonder…"

"What?"

"I'm wondering if the poor kid was supposed to die in the fire or if the fire was something that came about to create more havoc or burn up evidence," Mickey said.

"Maybe Hunter's unstable-lady can tell us something," Amy suggested hopefully.

As they reached the house, she saw an ambulance was in front. Hunter, Jimmy, and Aidan had returned with the woman they'd found who had fired the shot earlier; she was already strapped to a gurney.

As they exited Mickey's car in front, Amy could hear her shouting.

"The flames! The flames must burn, the world must be cleansed in fire lest the fires of Hell engulf us all. You will damn us all! Please, please, please, let me burn here lest I suffer what will come. I want to be among the clouds. I failed… I failed. I must redeem myself. Watch the sky, the blackness is beginning to consume us—"

"Honey, night is coming and the sky is filled with smoke," an EMT told her, shaking his head.

Mickey hurried over to the ambulance to speak with the EMT. Amy joined Hunter, Jimmy, and Aidan, arching a brow as she reached them.

"I am not sure I get this at all," Hunter told her. "She had a gun, she fired that shot. Maybe she was supposed to kill whoever came for the kid, but I'm not at all sure how any great master-mind would have left her. I don't know what the hell she's on, but she's higher than a kite."

"We should go back to the hospital and find out—" Amy began.

But Mickey interrupted her. "No!" he said flatly. "You two are going back to the hotel for the night. I just spoke to the EMTs. That kind of crazy? They're going to need the night to bring her down from whatever she's on. Elijah is fine in the hospital. Annabel hasn't left his side. We still have law enforcement all over the place. The Hamilton family is together—we have everyone who was in that house and drugged under guard. We've also had people out to the grocery store, and we've questioned the delivery drivers. Whatever happened came from inside the house. And as you know, forensics has been at it all day. There's nothing else you can do right now. And I can't stand sleepy, cranky agents who just may get so tired they make mistakes. Go. Now. That's an order."

Hunter grinned at him. "I am kind of all for dinner and sleep, but—"

"Right. You're FBI. I can't order you. But Garza can. And he'll be calling shortly, as in—now."

Hunter's phone was indeed ringing. And it was Garza on the other end. Amy could tell because Hunter was nodding and grinning.

"Yes, I heard about this call. And yes, sir, we live to obey."

"Like hell," Mickey muttered, but he was grinning, too.

Amy turned to Aidan. "I don't know how to thank you and Jimmy—"

"Hey, the day has been its own thanks." He glanced at Mickey. "Notice the boss didn't order me to take off—"

Mickey interrupted him with a groan. "Home, Aidan, go home. And, Jimmy Osceola—you went above and beyond for us. Thank you. Get some food, go to sleep."

Jimmy laughed. "I'm going to do those things but not in that order. I feel like a doused firepit. I'll shower, eat, and go home. But…"

"Jimmy," Mickey said, "you earned it. We'll keep you up on what's happening every step of the way."

"I'm getting her out of here before she tries to hop in the ambulance with crazy lady," Hunter said, setting his arm around Amy's shoulders. He looked at her questioningly.

"Not fighting you!" she promised him.

"Dinner," he said.

"Naw, I'm with Jimmy. Shower. To the hotel, sir. And pronto!"

They broke off, Mickey heading back to watch and making a call as the ambulance got ready to leave.

"Imagine the poor staff at the hospital," Amy said as they walked out to the SUV. "Not that operations and sick people aren't enough, but now…working with the fear that something might happen there despite the place crawling with law enforcement."

"We all make our choices in life," Hunter reminded her.

"Right. We took oaths, but the nurses are just hoping to help save lives, not risk their own."

"Let's have faith in our people, huh?"

She smiled and nodded.

"Amy, you saved a kid's life today. You have to take the win."

"I know! And I'm happy. I just…"

"We're all frustrated and on edge. But I realized a half hour ago, we haven't eaten in a long, long time. I say showers, room service…"

"And sleep?" she teased.

He shrugged. "Well, if you make it, maybe a little exercise."

"Hey!"

He laughed. "There is no way in hell I would have bothered you when you were out like a light. But tonight—"

"I wasn't even with you out by the fire, and I can smell the smoke on myself. No worries. I won't be plopping on the bed. Yuck. Shower first."

He was smiling as he stared at the road. But his smile faded and he was silent.

"Hunter?"

"I'm just frustrated."

"I didn't save the kid by myself. And you guys saved a deluded lady who would have died in that fire since, apparently, she didn't start it. She was with you when the first flames went up?"

He nodded.

"Like you told me, Hunter. Take the win!" she said softly.

"You're right. The win. Hot water. Room service." He glanced her way again, his smile returning. "You," he said softly.

She reached over and squeezed his hand. "Yep, for better or worse, you got me."

"We should make it official," he reminded her.

"Yes, but not in the middle of—"

"The Apocalypse? What better time?" he asked.

She laughed. "I want my mom and my dad. And your parents are still in the witness protection program, but they can be friends of the family. We'll have a pack of agents there and maybe some marshals, too, so..."

"I got it, I got it. You want the frills."

"No. You know me. I don't want frills, though frills are nice. I want the people we care about."

"Ah, well, that can work. Then again, we could run to a courthouse and have a big party for all those people later."

Amy nodded, smiling. "We could. As long as, of course, we outlive the Apocalypse."

"Okay. Come on. You know. Shake it off for the night. We won't be any good tomorrow—and as this situation deepens—unless we can keep ourselves sane."

"And sex will keep us sane?" she asked, grinning.

"Total sanity? Maybe not. But it will definitely help," Hunter said.

Amy laughed softly.

"Because there are good things in life," Hunter said.

"Like sex."

"And you," he said softly.

Amy looked down, smiling. There were many reasons she felt the way she did about Hunter. He'd started off in a rough position in life.

He'd grown into a man whose strength always allowed for empathy and compassion; his sense of honor was keen, as was his sense of humor.

Like her, he could be determined and relentless.

He'd seen the horrible, the heinous, and the depraved.

And yet he knew how and when to appreciate every moment in life that was a blue sky with a brilliant sun shining.

"Well, will it bring sanity?" she pondered. "Who knows. But we can give it a try."

They reached the hotel. And while they headed straight for the bathroom and Amy hit the shower spray first, they both brought their service weapons in with them, leaving them on the backstop for the commode—close enough to grab quickly in the shower.

So far, other than the strange episode with Elijah, nothing had been done against either of them.

But then again, Elijah had talked about the fact Amy's picture was out there as a concubine for the Antichrist.

Hunter's image was probably out there, too. Maybe he was just supposed to be a demon.

That meant being careful—no matter what the time or where they were.

And then equally...

There was nothing like the deliciousness of hot water to wash away the dirt, grime, smoke, and humidity of the day they'd been through. Nothing like the feel of suds in that hot water and mist being sluiced over flesh and the body heat that awoke while they touched one another, laughed, and kissed with the incredible feel of the hours washing away.

They made it out of the shower, dried, and headed back into the bedroom—pausing first to grab their guns and set them on one of the bedside tables.

They fell into the softness of the bed and the cleanliness of the sheets and teased, talked, laughed, grew serious...

Made love.

And later, staring up at the ceiling, Amy smiled, thinking he was right. The amazing things in the world that could be so beautiful made what they did more important than ever.

Hunter groaned softly. "I'm hungry."

"Again?"

He laughed. "I meant for food! Room service menu!"

"Oh!"

"I need to find my phone, scan the menu—"

"Or we can pick up the bedside phone, hit Room Service, and order a couple of burgers and fries."

"That'll work."

He ordered the food and they grabbed the hotel robes out of the closet to open the door for their meals, which came quickly, and naturally the case came back up in conversation as they ate.

"Sabrina," Amy said.

"Sabrina?"

"You and I both know how important being in the field is, but this... We need desperately to trace whatever is going on with the web. Probably the dark web," Amy said. "Aidan is great, but his expertise is with physical evidence. But Sabrina is—computers! There are different kinds of people showing up as victims—those cleaner than Mary Poppins, and those with records. So, some are being talked into a reward greater than life. Some are being recruited with an earthly reward to do bad things. But...how? Okay, we have what happened at Frank Hamilton's house and his son's kidnapping. We found the boy before any kind of a ransom demand came in—"

"The boy was left to die in the fire," Hunter said quietly. "The door had a chain and a padlock on it. The kid couldn't just leave if he'd gotten the nerve up to do so."

Amy was quiet for a minute.

"Who does things like that to a child?"

"As we've theorized—someone with a plan in which kids are nothing but collateral damage."

Amy nodded. "And he was knocked out, too, so he's not going to be able to help us by identifying anyone."

"We still need to find the elusive Colin. Tomorrow morning,

we'll head in to work with Aidan and Sabrina and find out what we can on the web. Get people studying every bit of exchange on the Commonsense website—and find out who might have been sending Frank Hamilton hate messages. And for now..."

"I'm going to push the tray out into the hall. The smell of old food just isn't that great to sleep by," Amy said.

She did so, turned out the light, dropped her robe, and crawled back into the bed, curling up against Hunter, who lay staring up at the ceiling. He slipped an arm around her and rested in silence a few minutes and then murmured quietly, "I'm hungry."

"We just ate."

"Different hunger this time," he teased.

She laughed.

The day could be trying.

But nights together could remind them they fought what was bad and cruel for all that was good and beautiful.

"Well, we've found that among the dead in both the barrels and on the embankment, there are those who were involved in either supporting Frank Hamilton as a candidate, or people who considered themselves members of the Commonsense Party—in the web chat at any rate. You already know that," Sabrina told Hunter and Amy as they stood by her desk and computer at headquarters. "But," she said, looking at them both, "there's something else curious I found. Some of those who died, sadly some in their twenties or thirties—oh, sorry, not being offensive to older people but at least they got to live some—belonged to something called the Real Church of the People. I'd never heard of it, but apparently there's a congregation in west Broward County—not at all far from the place where we found the barrels."

She was hitting keys on her computer and sending images up on one of the office's large screens. "There," she said, displaying a building that was apparently fairly new, but it was built in an old Mediterranean style. It might have been a large house or a hall for any number of different groups. But there was no cross sitting high atop it, neither was there any indication it might have been a temple.

"I mean," Sabrina continued, "you can see it's hard to tell it's even a church. There are no announcements about the time for services or anything. In other words, you'd have to know it was a church to go to it!"

"So, the congregation is selected," Hunter murmured. "From a community. What's near there?"

"A few housing developments, most of them ten to fifteen years old, carved out of the eastern edge of the Everglades," Amy said, studying the building. "I've driven by. Sabrina, you're right—I had no clue it was a church. The area has some nice homes on one-acre lots, and it also has some larger properties where the owners keep horses. And there are riding trails at one of the large parks nearby."

"Well, the pastor there is a Reverend MacDowell," Sabrina told them. "Reverend Benjamin MacDowell. He was ordained online."

"I think we should pay him a visit," Hunter told Amy.

"Commiserate with him, of course, on the loss of his parishioners," Amy said. "Sabrina, can you send me a list—"

"Already emailed to you. One man found on the embankment—Angus Slattery—was a member of the congregation, as were two of the victims pieced together at the morgue," Sabrina said. "And two people who are alive, to the best of my knowledge, have names that coincide with those chatting on the site for the Commonsense Party and commenting on a campaign site for Frank Hamilton. Maynard Gilby—Commonsense—and Justin Abernathy, a fan of Frank Hamilton."

"Well, maybe we can find Maynard and Justin," Hunter said. "We've got one stop to make first," he reminded Amy.

"The hospital," she said.

"The hospital," he agreed. He looked at Sabrina. "Do we have a name for unstable-lady yet?"

Sabrina nodded. "Carole Spinner. In your email, too."

"I didn't see it yet," Amy murmured.

"Done while you were on your way here," Sabrina told them. "Oh, when you head to the church, Aidan would like to accompany you. No warrant, of course, but he thinks there might be trash somewhere he could pick up or that… I don't know. He wants to go with you." She grimaced. "Aidan is like…like he has special instinct or mental powers or something when it comes to trace evidence. I'm the computer girl."

"A very brilliant computer girl," Hunter assured her.

Sabrina indicated the room where several techs and analysts were working. "Thank you. But trust me—as they say, it takes a village."

Amy laughed softly. "A few villages on this case!" she said.

"And as far as making sure we bring Aidan, no problem," Hunter assured her. "We'll call from the hospital so that we can meet up."

They left headquarters. As they drove to the hospital, Amy looked at him and said, "Where do we start? Now we've got Frank Hamilton, Aubrey, and Marc. We still have Elijah there. And now—"

"Now we get to see unstable-lady," Hunter agreed.

"You do know that our calling her unstable-lady is entirely crude and not something we should do in public," Amy told him.

"I do know and… I just feel ill for the poor thing. I don't think I have ever seen anyone quite so disillusioned, and I don't know the term, but…sick?"

"We'll see. I'm willing to bet there were a pack of hallucinogens in her, too."

"Most probably," Hunter agreed. "So, shall we start with her?"

"We need to start somewhere," Amy said.

"And that is true," Hunter agreed.

As they walked down the hallway, he noted the officers and agents in the hallway. He wondered what effect it was having on the hospital staff—sometimes, there might be one patient in a hospital being guarded, maybe even two. But now...

There might be as many law enforcement officers here as there were certain medical personnel. But as they neared the room where Carole Spinner was being treated, one of the local police officers, a tall young woman with a serious demeanor, stepped toward them, shaking her head.

"She's just started screaming several times. And when either one of us or a nurse or doctor steps in, she rants and raves that she must be let go, that we'll all rot and burn in Hell, we're not seeing what must be, we need to die now to avoid burning for eternity."

Hunter nodded. "I'm assuming they found—"

"Heavy psychedelics, but they've been cleaning her out all night and... I guess it takes time, but I wanted to warn you... Oh! You're the agents who found her."

"Hunter found her," Amy said. "And, well, we've met. I don't think we'll be long, and hopefully she will improve."

"I mean, can she really believe everything she's saying?" the young woman asked. "You would have thought I went in to check on her with devil horns sprouting out of my head!"

"It's impossible to know, for me anyway," Hunter told her. "But I do know people often believe what they want to believe. Anyway..."

"I'm sorry, please, see your witness!" the young policewoman said, stepping back.

He and Amy nodded to her and went on into Carole Spinner's room. He wasn't surprised to see she was being held down on the bed with restraints. And as they entered, she started screaming again, but this time her cries were different.

"Kill me, kill me, kill me, let me die!" she shouted.

"Ms. Spinner," he said gently. "You don't want to die."

"But I do!" she said, her voice suddenly a whisper.

Amy walked to the side of the bed, gently placing a hand on top of hers.

"You want to die because you believe you failed the Archangel," she said softly. "But you didn't. You managed to save the life of a child. The angels in heaven are singing with happiness. They weep every time that a child dies."

To Hunter's surprise, Carole Spinner was silent for a minute.

"But I failed!" she whispered again.

"No," Amy said. "You need to rest—you need to heal. There are strange things in your system, in the physical realm. Please, rest, just rest. Try to sleep."

"But…it's been coming. You don't know. It started with World War II!" she told Amy earnestly.

"World War II has been over for decades," Amy reminded her.

"Well, that's what we're supposed to think," Carole said, nodding very seriously at Amy. "You see, he's still out there, too."

"Who is still out there?" Amy asked her. She glanced at Hunter, arching a brow. He gave her a nod; she should continue the conversation.

"Adolph Hitler," Carole said seriously.

"I don't think that's possible—" Amy began.

"No, no, no. He was the beginning of the end. And he knew that even though he might have the best technology, even the best couldn't win if thousands upon thousands were coming at you with rocks. So he made deals with Spain and Switzerland not to attack them. And then, when all was failing on that campaign, he escaped through tunnels leaving his look-alike in the bunker. And when he made his way to Spain, he had a plane waiting to take him to South America. You see, he had a deal with Satan. And he's down there now, commanding his minions among men to infiltrate others, and that's why the Archangel knows they must die, and assigns us to see to it and…we are still rewarded for trying, but when we fail, we must die."

"Who told you all this?" Amy asked her.

"Well, one of the angels, of course."

"Who was this angel?" Amy asked her.

"On earth? He's called Colin. And he's beautiful. He's a beautiful and beloved servant of the Archangel, and if I can just die now... Well, I will sit honored with those who have served the great Archangel in the clouds and fields of beauty!"

"Does Colin have a last name on earth?" Amy asked.

"He doesn't need one. He is just...Colin." She let out a soft sigh. "If you wish to serve, just find him. All you need to do is find Colin...and maybe you won't fail him, maybe you will have a chance to sit in beauty with all the angels and the great Archangel when the coming Apocalypse explodes upon the earth!"

Amy smiled at her and gently patted her hand. "Carole, please, you must rest now. My friends here, the doctors and the nurses, want you to be well. And when you've rested and you're well, we can talk again. You can tell me more."

"You have a chance!" Carole told her. She whispered, "You must get away from him!"

"From...?"

"Him!" Carole whispered, indicating Hunter with a nod. "He's... Well, you can't see them, but I can. He's a demon. You must get away from him!"

Hunter said nothing, keeping his distance.

"Carole, rest, please, rest—and we can talk again!"

Amy brought a finger to her lips, as if the two of them were in a conspiracy. "We're going to go. I'll take him away from here," she said softly. "But we can talk tomorrow and you can tell me more."

She turned and walked out of the room. Hunter looked at Carole. It was so strange but her eyes were already closing.

She seemed to be at peace.

Hunter stepped out of the room, meeting Amy again in the hallway.

Amy grimaced. "So, now I'm not so bad, but you're a demon."

"You think?" he asked her.

She grinned. "Only sometimes. Seriously, Hunter, I won't really feed into this, but I think when the doctors have her system cleaned out a little more, I may be able to learn more from her. And maybe we can even get her to explain how we might meet this mysterious Colin."

"Colin has pictures of you he gives out so people will know you're the Antichrist's vixen," he reminded her.

"Ah, but I can change my appearance. It might be a bit harder to change yours! Anyway, it's a thought. Now..."

"Elijah? Or Frank Hamilton and family?"

"Let's check on the Hamilton family. I'm still so grateful about Marc! And maybe we can talk Frank Hamilton into giving a speech or a rally, or something like the protest that brought Elijah out—an event where Colin might arrive... I mean, come on, he has lost a few minions lately."

They headed to the room where the Hamilton family was being observed and guarded. When they arrived, Marty Benson, looking distraught, was just leaving the room.

"Hey!" he said, seeing Hunter and Amy.

"What's wrong?" Amy asked him quickly.

He shook his head, glancing back at the hospital room. "Frank...Frank is awake and aware and lucid and...he doesn't want to run anymore! He thinks he brought horror down on his wife and child and... He's the best thing in the world! He needs to keep up his campaign. Seriously, without men like him, the Apocalypse may really be upon us!"

9

"Mr. Benson, right now, Frank Hamilton is still reeling from what has happened, I'm certain," Amy said, setting a gentle hand on the man's arm.

"I think he's decided," Marty said, wincing and shaking his head.

"Well, time will tell. I wouldn't do anything drastic now," Hunter said. "As Amy just said, this is the day after his son was found as part of a game piece in an attack. I think he'd face any danger for himself, but he's naturally worried for his child. And if he really wants out, that's his option. But let us talk to him. Maybe he'll change his mind."

"I...I need breakfast, coffee, something, though, with what was done, I'm afraid to have a drink of water!" Marty said. "I just... I mean, here's a guy who is strong enough to have his opinions, and strong enough to respect the opinions of others as well. A man who knows compromise—oh, and knows that most people actually agree on most major issues with just a bit of that compromise. He... Ah, man. We need him."

"I think you're okay to have the water in the hospital," Hunter told him. "Coffee and food, too."

"Right. I'm going. I, uh, I'll be back if you need me."

"Mr. Benson, have you thought of any way that all this possibly happened? Is there anyone working on the campaign who may not be the real thing? Who might have infiltrated just to cause this very reaction?"

"I vet people," he said. "That's just it—I can't begin to imagine how this happened. That's what is so upsetting. If we can't figure it out, I'm afraid we will lose him."

With a grimace, he headed away at last. Amy glanced at Hunter.

"We can't force him to stay in the race or hold any kind of a rally," Amy said.

"No, we can't. But…he may be in danger even if he drops out. Or worse—his family could remain in danger. I think it's important he realize that."

"Hunter, we can't just use a man when his family may be in danger."

"I don't intend to, Amy. I'm not making that up, and I'm not saying it because we need him, though we do. But if this has happened to him, whoever did it may be afraid he'll return to wanting to show the world that talking like adults instead of name-calling like children is the better way to get things done, maybe the only way to get things done."

Amy nodded slowly. "All right."

They nodded their thanks to the agent on duty at the door and stepped into the room. Aubrey Hamilton had drawn the hospital chair/bed so that she could sit or sleep between her husband and her child. She rose as they entered.

Frank Hamilton was sitting up in his bed. Marc was asleep, a sweet smile curved into his lips as if his dreams were good.

"How are you doing?" Hunter asked, posing the question to both Aubrey and Frank.

"My health seems to be just fine," Aubrey said.

"And as you can see, I… Well, I'm cognizant, awake, aware, angry, frightened…" Frank told them. "I saw you ran into Marty in the hall. I know he's upset, but I feel I should run away, take my family to Antarctica or maybe Mars."

"Mr. Hamilton, we must find out who is doing this," Hunter told him.

Frank didn't seem to hear. He looked at Amy. "You saved my son. I could not, in a million years, express my gratitude, our gratitude. I may have said that before. I'm sorry. My mind is still…or my memory, or… I mean, thankfully, they say I will be just fine. It will take some rest and a lot more of this saline stuff rinsing me out—kind of like a lot of suds coming out of clothing during the rinse cycle on a washing machine, as one doctor explained to me." He offered them a weak smile.

Amy smiled in return. "I love kids, Mr. Hamilton. I was incredibly grateful to find Marc. Your gratitude is sweet, but it's also my—"

"It's your job, I know. But I have a feeling you put yourself at risk. But we've been talking. I guess I can't go to Antarctica, but I…I need to become nothing more than an average private citizen. I thought I could offer something good, an alternative to a massive divide, but…"

"You still can, sir," Hunter said. "But here's the problem. We must find out who did this. If we don't, you and your family might well remain in serious danger, whether you stay in the spotlight or try to hide from it."

"I never even felt the need for security," Frank murmured. "Trusting—or flat-out stupid. I'm thinking the latter right now."

"Sir, I'm afraid anyone in the public eye may fall prey to any number of fanatics out there," Hunter told him. "It doesn't mean that trusting is stupid—it just means you are truly a man of the people. And I seriously don't think situations like this arrive often." He hesitated, glancing over at Amy.

"Mr. Hamilton—" Amy began.

"Frank, please. I'm a man of the people," he said lightly.

"Frank, I am so afraid Hunter's right. We need to find out how to get to the bottom of what happened, the truth of the situation," Amy said.

They were surprised when Aubrey Hamilton spoke up. "Frank, they need our help. And we're going to give it to them," she said.

"Aubrey!" Frank said, looking miserable as he turned his attention to his wife. "Honey, please, I can't possibly put you and Marc in a bad position again!"

"You can't get us out of one—unless we find out what happened," Aubrey told him. "Frank, I will not spend the rest of my life looking over my shoulder—or being afraid to eat or drink anything! These people have already proven they will give their lives for us, give their lives to protect us. The least we can do is step up and help in any way we can."

Frank grimaced and then smiled weakly at Hunter. "The real boss has spoken. I'm just… My boy, our son. I would do anything to keep him safe."

"I'm going to suggest we keep you in a safe house when you leave here—a place where you'll be protected by agents at all times, where any food coming in will be tested and acquired through our people. But—"

"There's always a 'but,'" Frank murmured.

"Frank!" Aubrey chastised.

Her husband smiled. "Okay, let's hear it."

"We want you to have a press conference or rally—something where your followers can come," Hunter said.

"What?" he asked incredulously.

"Oh, Frank!" Aubrey said, shaking her head. "They'll be there with us. I imagine Agents Larson and Forrest will be at your side—ready to stop a bullet."

"And Aubrey and Marc can be safely away, guarded throughout," Amy promised.

Frank didn't have a chance to say anything. Marc stirred on the bed and woke up, rubbing his eyes. He saw Hunter and Amy were in the room and he smiled and said, "Hi!"

"How are you feeling, buddy?" Hunter asked.

"Great! I was so sleepy, and now... I feel great!"

"He has a bit of a cough," Aubrey said.

"The fire," Amy murmured.

"I think I kinda almost remember," Marc said.

"As long as you're okay now!" Amy said.

The boy smiled and crawled out of bed and ran over to offer her a shy hug. Amy hugged him in return.

"So, I'll get hold of my people—" Frank began.

"No," Hunter said.

"No? How will I pull this off?" Frank asked.

Hunter hesitated. "Frank, someone involved with your campaign—no matter how carefully you vetted people—might have been involved in this. Let us make some plans. Don't tell anyone what we're thinking yet, not until plans have been set into motion. Please, not your campaign manager, not your longest worker, no one. Please. I'm begging you," he said at last.

"Don't go against a word he said!" Aubrey said. "Frank, I've never been so frightened for myself, and worse, for our boy. These people are why we're alive." She glanced at Marc, who was still clinging to Amy. "They are why I even care that I'm still alive!" she said softly.

"As you wish," Frank said. "So, I had said—"

"I know. Marty Benson was incredibly upset you were thinking of stepping out of the race. Just tell him you need to get your head cleared, you think you're right, but you haven't decided what you're going to do yet," Hunter told him.

"Well, as I said," Frank told them lightly, "Aubrey is the real power. I bow to her judgment—which has seriously proven to be pretty good over the years." He grinned at his wife.

Aubrey stood and walked over to her husband, leaning down

to put her arms around him and plant a kiss on his forehead. Then she walked around and put her arms around her son, gently smoothing back his hair.

"I think these guys need to go, sweetie. They're very busy people."

"You are going to come back, right?" Marc asked.

"You bet, buddy!" Amy assured him. "We want to see you all well with that cough gone, too. You bet we'll be back!"

They said their goodbyes to Frank, Aubrey, and Marc, then left the room. Amy smiled when they stepped into the hallway, greeting a man of about fifty who was standing close to the door.

"Hey, Lyle!" she said. Turning to Hunter, she introduced him. "Special Agent Hunter Forrest, meet Special Agent Lyle Comer, FDLE. Lyle, Hunter, Hunter, Lyle."

"Good to meet you," Lyle said, shaking Hunter's hand.

"Likewise," Hunter told him. "You're on guard duty here?"

"Along with two local cops—right down there," he said, pointing down the hallway. "Amy, I heard that this was connected to your Horsemen case. And…" He broke off, shrugging with a grimace and then a smile. "I'm a huge fan of Frank Hamilton. He reminds me in a strange way of Walter Cronkite."

"Walter Cronkite? Um, he was a news anchor years ago, right?" Amy asked.

Lyle Comer laughed. "Yes, children, that's right. My dad was a huge fan of Cronkite. Thing is, when he told the news, it wasn't skewed. It was just the news. Dad always said that Cronkite's manner of reporting the news was stoic—he gave the facts with no emotion. The only time Dad remembered Cronkite showing emotion while on the job was the day of JFK's assassination. Which really makes me admire the hell out of Frank Hamilton. It's not that he doesn't have opinions—he does. But he is more than willing, always, to listen to other opinions. That's why this is so stunning. But I asked for this detail. I won't let a soul near him. Trust me. I talked to Mickey and handpicked our people with him."

He looked at Hunter. "Don't get me wrong! Mickey runs a tight ship. All our people are good. I just wanted those who I knew would never doze on the job, and those who question everything. In short, I just wanted to tell you both someone would have to riddle me and others with an AK-47 to get us to step away."

"Thanks, Lyle," Amy said.

"Any closer?"

"Maybe by percentages of inches," Amy said. "And thank you. We just need to—"

"Yeah, I heard you already saw our deranged woman. The doctors have sworn she'll be more rational tomorrow except I have a feeling her rational is different from most. Now, I stepped in to check on Elijah Thayer, and he seems to be doing extremely well. Oh, his girlfriend has been there and she's quite lovely, too."

"He's been a help to us," Hunter said.

"We have an agenda today," Amy said. "So—"

"Didn't mean to stop you. Just wanted to say hey," he told her.

Amy smiled at him. "Thanks. And hopefully we'll see this thing through to the end."

"That's not a 'hopefully.' We will," Lyle said with assurance.

They left him in the hall and Hunter looked at Amy.

"I worked a kidnapping with Lyle and my old partner, John Schultz, years ago. We were lucky. The kidnappers just weren't that bright, and we traced their burner phones. John and I went for the kid and the man holding him while Lyle picked up the fellow who came for the ransom. If only all cases went so well."

"Elijah may well be the one who helps break this."

"I'm not sure what else he can tell us."

"How to draw out his friend Colin," Hunter said.

Amy looked at him with surprise but nodded. "All right, then!"

They entered Elijah's room and saw Annabel was indeed at his side, holding his hand, reading to him.

Hunter wondered at first if it might be a religious text or something regarding conspiracies or cults.

It wasn't. Annabel was reading a Jack Reacher novel out loud.

"Hey!" Elijah said, pushing to a sitting position as he saw them enter.

Annabel greeted them as well, closing the book.

"She's better than any audio book reader I've ever heard! And," Elijah added, "she can hold my hand and read at the same time—except, of course, when she has to turn a page."

"That sounds great," Hunter told him, "no pun intended."

"He's doing well but the doctors said he's staying here until they're certain he's well. And I think they're keeping him because it's easier to guard him here," Annabel said.

"I'm sure that might have something to do with it. We have a number of safe houses—especially because you have every police force in the south of the state, FDLE, and FBI on it. They're probably making arrangements," Hunter assured her. "We'll check on things with our bosses and let you know what's up tomorrow—if one of them doesn't tell you by then."

"We're really okay. The hospital chair isn't a bad bed at all," Annabel assured them.

"Good. We're glad to hear you're doing well," Amy said.

"I…" Elijah started speaking and then seemed to struggle for words. "I am so lucky!" he whispered. "I almost killed you, almost killed myself, and you stopped me. I realized just how much life and—" he paused again, looking at Annabel "—life and love mean to me!" he whispered.

"We're very glad you're alive. We have another question for you," Hunter told him.

"Anything I can answer, I will," Elijah promised.

"You were at a protest when you met the man who introduced

himself to you as Colin. We've gotten a pretty good sketch of him, but how exactly did you meet him?" Amy asked.

"At the protest, hmm… Annabel and I were apart for a bit, both walking, we had signs, and I think…I think I was just yelling and chanting. Others were yelling and chanting, too, but I can be really loud—"

"Oh, dear Lord, can he!" Annabel interrupted.

"And he came up to me. I guess I was the loudest in the crowd. Like I've told you, it was a good protest. We were all totally law-abiding. But we were shouting."

"And he came to you? How?" Amy asked.

"I had my sign up—I was shouting. Those signs get heavy. We finished a chant, I turned around, and he was there."

"And you think he found you because you were loud?"

Elijah nodded. "He was like, hmm, a cool dude, patting me on the back, commending me on the way I handled myself. Then he said we should sneak away, have coffee, and he started talking. We agreed to meet again. But when I talked to him, he started warning me. All the things we were protesting had to do with the coming of the Apocalypse. And I…I started seeing things. The things he described to me. Angels, looking down, weeping, talking… And when I looked at him, I suddenly knew he was an angel."

He took a breath. "Now I know I was chock-full of hallucinogens. But when he was talking to me, I could see things. I could really see things. And I thought he was being nice, always having coffee or water, a soda, even a beer once, for me when he saw me. Of course, I now realize when I drank whatever it was, I was consuming stuff that would make me see what he was telling me. And then I began to believe in everything he was saying."

"Maybe he had stalked Elijah!" Annabel said. "Maybe he'd seen him give food to the needy, seen that he would—"

"Be a great patsy?" Elijah cut in a little bitterly.

"No," Annabel said firmly, "you were such a good person, you would want to help others, even if that meant watching the police or agents in the woods. And if you believe in good, you'd also believe in bad, and therefore Special Agent Amy Larson might really be evil!"

"He showed pictures," Amy said. "Of me? And anyone else?"

Elijah nodded. He pointed at Hunter. "But his picture of Agent Forrest wasn't clear—he shot it in a crowd somewhere sometime, I guess. But he got you in a restaurant, sitting, smiling," he told Amy. "Oh, and he told me to be careful. He said you were really beautiful and you would try to seduce me and then my soul would be damned forever." He stopped speaking and looked at Hunter. "I believe you are supposed to be the Antichrist."

"Thank you," Hunter told him. "But when he met you—"

"It was never at a public place where people were close together. I mean, there would be people. We'd be at a park or something, but always somewhere that wasn't well populated. Park benches— Oh, one day I went all the way out to the beach in Fort Lauderdale. He told me to take an Uber. I did. Maybe he didn't want me arrested for causing a wreck."

"Thank you, Elijah!" Hunter told him, before glancing at Amy. The man's story didn't exactly line up with what they'd been told before, but it gave them enough.

"Thank you both," Amy said. She grimaced. "We have to go to church."

"Church?" Elijah looked concerned. "You're not going to—"

"I like regular churches, usually. You know, the kind where they talk about Good Samaritans and loving thy neighbor and all that," Hunter said. "We don't know about this one."

"Be careful!" Elijah warned. "They can..."

"Forewarned is being prepared," Hunter assured him. "Thanks to you, we'll be very careful. We'll see you tomorrow."

"I think they're moving me," Elijah said. "Some guy who must be important but told me to just call him Mickey came by. He said I wasn't being arrested—yet. Maybe not at all. Maybe they'd make a deal and I'd just have probation—"

"And maybe nothing at all!" Annabel whispered.

"But they'd see to it we were both safe," Elijah said.

"Well, Mickey would know. He's my boss," Amy told them. "Anyway, wherever you are, we'll be checking up on you. Take care."

As they were leaving his room, Amy was drawing her phone out. "Calling Aidan," she told him. "He's—"

"Right in front of us in the hall," Hunter told her.

Aidan was walking toward them. "You don't mind, right?" he asked.

"Hell, no," Hunter assured him. "We have no idea what we'll find, but from what we know, the place is a bit weird. A secret congregation? With dead members? We want to find out what we can."

"And I am with you," Aidan assured them.

They left the hospital. Amy glanced at Hunter as he drove and then back at Aidan. He thought she might be determining whether to speak or not since they weren't alone. But she apparently decided to plunge in.

"Hunter, you want to set up an event with Frank Hamilton because you think our mystery man, Colin, will come to see what's going on. But we have a sketch of Colin, so we have an idea of what he's going to look like. But as we know, Colin shows our pictures to his converts and tells him we're pure evil. Now—"

"I know what you're going to say, Amy. Disguises. Give yourself dark hair, glasses, maybe nose putty."

"But you think he'll see through them," Amy said.

"Not if you have my help," Aidan said from the back.

Hunter glanced at him in the rearview mirror. "Are you going to change my DNA?"

"No, I'm going to bring Sabrina in on it. She's spent a lot of time at conventions for comics, special effects, pop culture. It's kind of her thing," Aidan offered.

"Oh!" Amy said, surprised.

Aidan leaned forward from the back. "Um, yeah. I just went

to a workshop on special effects with her. Oh, she loves what she does and she is truly the best. She can cull traffic cams and find license plates, run facial recognition, you name it—but she likes to play dress-up at Halloween. She's into pop culture. And I have a great time with her and—"

"Oh, wow!" Amy said. "You two are…"

"Nothing official," Aidan assured her.

Amy flashed a smile at Hunter. "She's gorgeous! I'm so happy for you."

"But seriously," Aidan argued, "nothing is official. Yeah, I'm, uh, yeah. But—"

"Hey, our lips are sealed!" Hunter assured him. "And I'm going to surprise you both. I think we'll be happy to take any help we can get from Sabrina, but I wasn't going to argue with Amy. We need to find Colin. If we can find Colin, we can find out what's going on behind all this."

"'I'm your Huckleberry!'" Aidan told them. "When do you plan to do this?"

"I need to run it by Mickey Hampton and Charles Garza, but my plan is to get Frank Hamilton to give a news conference, and at his conference, he's going to say he's undeterred. It's always a fringe element that's the loudest, and what the American people want, what they can agree upon and what they can compromise on, is bigger than they are. He isn't giving up."

"Is that…real?" Aidan asked.

"Maybe not," Hunter admitted. "But I think he knows if we don't stop whoever is doing this, he may not be safe anywhere once he's not under guard from law enforcement. He'll be ready to play the game for that, if for nothing else."

"He may still give up his campaign?" Aidan asked.

Hunter shook his head. "I don't know. But the fact that his son was taken… Well, you can imagine he doesn't want the boy in danger again. But on the other hand, his wife is pretty fierce, so at this time, I guess it's all up in the air."

"But she doesn't want to spend her life hiding," Amy told him.

"Hmm. So now—besides stopping Armageddon, the Apocalypse, and the end of the world as we know it—we must find a way to get to the head of the snake so a decent man can run for office?" Aidan asked.

Hunter grinned. "Yeah, something like that."

"There—you can barely see it. There's the road ahead that twists through the trees and goes by the community and the church," Amy said.

"Yep, I see it ahead," Hunter told her. He glanced back at Aidan. "We're going in as nicely as humanly possible, just giving them our condolences on the members they lost."

"Of course," Aidan said. "Come on, I'm the nicest guy in the world."

"Right. You can't grab his hands for epithelial cells, right?"

"I'd have nothing to compare them to at the moment," Aidan assured him.

They passed large estates and two horse ranches, fields of grass, a forested area, more estates, and then Hunter saw the building that was the church ahead of them. He pulled into the small parking lot and glanced at Amy and Aidan.

"Let's do it," Amy said.

They exited the vehicle. As they approached what looked like the front door to another of the estates in the area, the door opened.

A man emerged. He was in his late twenties or early thirties, pleasant-looking with dark hair and light eyes, and a leanly sculpted face. He was dressed as if he were a father in a Catholic or Episcopal church, and yet they knew this wasn't a house of worship for either denomination.

"Hello, friends," he said, greeting them. "You're not from the neighborhood. Of course, we are a bit off the beaten path. We are glad to see anyone interested in worshipping, so you are welcome. How can I help you?"

"Sir, how do we address you?" Amy asked him pleasantly.

"Reverend MacDowell, Reverend Benjamin—or just Ben, if you like!" he assured them.

"Reverend Ben," Hunter said, "I'm Hunter Forrest, and with me are Amy Larson and Aidan Cypress. I'm afraid we're here with bad news."

"You are police?"

"FDLE and FBI," Hunter told him.

Reverend Ben nodded and winced. "I have been so afraid I would be receiving bad news. The news is full of the many dead recently found in the Everglades—many near us—too near us. We've been praying here, but we know sometimes the Divine Power has plans that do not coincide with our own. We pray for ourselves then, that we may find peace, because we know our brothers and sisters rest and find peace with the angels. We haven't seen Brother Angus in weeks, and we've been worried sick as well for Brothers Herman Needleman and Samuel Houseman. They are—they have been—killed. How? Who did it?"

"We don't know, Reverend," Amy said. "We were hoping that you could help us."

"How?"

"Were they at discord with anyone here? Were there fights over land, wives, girlfriends, money, anything at all that might point us in the right direction?"

Ben MacDowell shook his head. "No. They were not killed by other members of the congregation! Look around you. We have land, we have plenty. And my parishioners do not covet one another's wives. There's absolutely no reason anyone here would hurt anyone else here! We are about love and obedience to God's will."

"Of course, just as it should be," Hunter said politely.

"I would love to see your church!" Aidan said.

"Then you are welcome, sir. You are…" he began curiously.

"Seminole," Aidan told him, smiling pleasantly. "We derive from the Muscogee Tribe, so our traditional beliefs are similar.

Many of us adhere to other religious affiliations as well. I am an open book, Reverend, always ready to learn!"

"Well, of course, you must come in. We're a bit different. We have a choir and a pulpit and an altar. The rear of the church is our mausoleum—members stay with the church even after death. You are welcome. Come in."

He indicated the door, ushering them in.

"Reverend," Amy said, "there are members of your church who have been on websites where those who were found among the dead also visited. Maynard Gilby and Justin Abernathy."

He cocked his head in a question as he looked at her. "I'm afraid I'm a spiritual adviser, and not a man to police what websites my congregation visit."

"But these men…have you seen them? We have addresses from their licenses, but we thought we'd see you first," Hunter said, following Aidan into the church.

Once inside, it did have a more traditional look.

But there was one thing a bit different about it. Behind the altar, the rear wall was concrete—as Reverend Ben had told them, the back was a mausoleum. A typical-looking mausoleum wall—except it was directly behind the altar. Where the concrete ended, there were doors on either side of the mausoleum wall.

"Death is a part of life," the reverend told them. "And love never dies. We honor our dead in this way."

"Oh. Interesting, different," Aidan said politely.

Amy was wandering down toward the altar—raised slightly on a dais—and on to the mausoleum area.

"Please! The area behind the altar is for clergy only," the reverend called.

But before Amy could respond, a shrieking scream tore through the church. There was a thudding sound against one of the doors, and another scream, one that seemed to shake the very foundation of the church.

10

Amy went tearing toward the door, ripping it open. Someone was fleeing across the grassy area at the rear of the church, an area set with picnic tables here and there, a few shade trees, and an outdoor podium.

That someone wasn't fleeing quickly, and turned out to be dragging a screaming woman behind them. Amy was close behind, drawing her Glock, and yet she knew she wouldn't shoot. She stood a good chance of killing or injuring the woman.

But the community had been built on the far western side of the massive built-up areas of Florida's east coast. The Everglades stretched beyond the manicured section of land that had been claimed from wilderness by the church and the entrepreneurs of the housing district.

She tried to see and to reason even as she ran.

The abductor was big and powerful, or so it appeared. He was a man who could throw the woman over his shoulder and run fast while carrying his burden. She could see little of him; he was dressed in black and wore a black hood along with a mask that would have done Darth Vader proud.

"Stop! FDLE! Stop!" she commanded.

Of course, her words went unheeded.

She heard footsteps on her tail. Hunter. He was coming close behind her as they raced across the line from manicured lawn to dense, twisted foliage.

Amy plunged after the man and his screaming burden. Except now the screams were fading.

But while her suspect might have run into the depths of the Everglades via some unknown trail, he now seemed to be confused as he zigged and zagged. Of course, some of that was the only way to travel through such territory, but the man appeared to be lost in the confusion of trees, vines, brush, and thick, rich grasses. And Amy knew what she was doing might have been foolish; she wasn't wearing boots, just her low-heeled black shoes. She had been aware all of her life of the dangers on such ground that could prey upon the unwary.

"Stop! FBI! Stop!" Hunter shouted from behind her.

They heard another scream.

This time, it came from the man. And Amy could dimly see through the foliage that he'd apparently tripped or fallen over something and had gone down. She could see his head, and then she couldn't.

"Hunter!" she called.

"I see!"

They made their way through the growth, arriving at the place where the man had fallen. There had been a break in the foliage; a slim, shallow canal twisted through the wilderness. And just across from where the man lay fallen half in the water and half out, an ankle having been caught by a tangled tree root, was a large gator, a really good-sized creature at least twelve feet in length.

Amy stood still, as did Hunter. They were both armed. And if you aimed for the brain, you could kill an alligator with a Glock.

The alligator wasn't doing anything. Just basking on the embankment.

The masked figure on the ground still had his arms around the young woman he had seized, who now lay unconscious. He turned toward Amy and Hunter, aware they were there.

"Shoot it! Kill it!" he whispered.

"Not all that easy," Amy explained. "Of course, he is just sitting there, but if I don't get him right in the eye or pierce the hide to take out the brain... Well, he could charge."

"I think it might be a she," Hunter said. "And there might be a nest somewhere around here. *She* could charge."

The big man in the mask seemed to be weeping. "Please! I don't care about me. You have to save Samantha!"

"Save Samantha?" Amy asked quietly, keeping an eye on the alligator. The creature remained just basking. Of course, grown humans weren't the customary dish for a hungry gator. People usually wound up in trouble with the creatures because they walked small pets by waterways where the creatures might be seeking a bite-size meal.

Amy wasn't particularly in love with the creatures; she just didn't like the idea of putting down an animal that wasn't doing anything wrong.

Of course, human life would always outweigh such a thought, but...

"You're referring to the young woman you dragged screaming from the church?" Hunter asked.

"I'm referring to my daughter!" the man said. "You don't know what was happening. Samantha is my daughter, and I came to save her!"

Amy glanced at Hunter, surprised and somehow certain the man was telling the truth.

"Your aim is still top-notch, right?" Hunter asked Amy.

"Great. A life-or-death test?" she asked him.

"I don't want to try to kill it for nothing," Hunter said. He grinned. "Maybe he has a score of friends nearby."

She almost smiled. Alligators were not pack animals. The

gator's "friends" would most likely *not* be coming after them. But she knew what he wanted: he was going to tread carefully through the tangled roots at the edge of the narrow waterway and free the man and the girl. If he did so carefully enough, the creature would just sit there quietly, biding its time.

And if they fired...

They could miss.

She didn't watch Hunter as he went about his determined effort. She kept her eyes on the creature basking in dead stillness on the embankment. Peripheral vision assured her he was moving quietly, warning the man in low tones to keep quiet as he extricated his ankle from the tangle of roots and vines.

He had the man standing carefully, and he was carrying the girl himself as he indicated a path that would take them back into the trees.

Amy slowly backed away, reaching the three of them at the area that resembled a trail since they'd all crashed through it already.

Hunter was speaking in a calm, controlled voice, but then...

Hunter's past had stayed with him. It hadn't twisted him; it had made him a better man.

"There is no choice. We will not leave your daughter here. We will take you both to our headquarters. We have a man back at the church, one of our crime scene investigators. And our vehicle is there."

"He'll take her—he'll try to take her!" the man claimed. He'd shed his mask and cowl; Amy saw he was about fifty with short graying hair, dark eyes, and a desperate look on his face. He was at least six-four and well muscled, but he was offering no threat at all. He simply looked desperate.

"Okay, I'm FBI Special Agent Hunter Forrest, Amy is Special Agent Larson, FDLE, and Aidan Cypress is also FDLE. He is certified to carry as well. You have the three of us—no one will take your child. But we must get back," Hunter said. "We can't endlessly roam around in the wild of the Everglades. We need a vehicle. I don't know what your plan was—"

"Wait, wait," the man said. "Please, listen to me." He paused, taking a deep breath. "My name is Harvey Russell and Samantha is my sixteen-year-old daughter. I swear to you, I am a rational human being. I own an art gallery in Fort Lauderdale. Samantha met this man at a protest and—"

"Colin?" Amy asked. "Did she ever mention him by name? Was his name Colin?"

The man went dead white, eyeing them fearfully.

"You're, um, not—"

"No, we are not friends or even acquaintances of Colin," Amy quickly assured him. "His name has come up before."

"Yes, that was the name she gave her new 'friend.' She talked about meeting this man named Colin and how amazing he was. And I don't know what he did to her, but the next thing I knew, she thought her mother and I were…misguided, misinformed, pathetic people—that we didn't understand anything about the world. We didn't see what was coming, and she'd pray for us. I sent her to her room, I…"

Harvey Russell stopped, his face wrinkled with care and concern. "She went out the window! I didn't know she was going to run away, but she left my wife a note saying she loved us so much, and she would speak with the angels and save us. She was just gone, but…I tracked her on the phone. I found out about the church. The reverend told me she wasn't there, but I knew her phone was. And maybe it was stupid, but I thought my only hope was to kidnap her and get her out of there and get her to a hospital because she just wasn't right. I did have a plan. And I didn't walk from Fort Lauderdale—I have a car. I was trying to get away with her. I ran wildly, but I can show you where there's an old road. There was a sugarcane plantation out here once. I can take you to my car. Please, please, Samantha needs help. And I can't go back to that place!"

Hunter looked at Amy. Their SUV and—more seriously—Aidan were back at the church.

"I'll call Aidan."

"I have the key to the car, which has keyless entry, but…I'm here, so the car won't start."

"I can call Aidan and Mickey. He'll see Aidan is picked up."

Hunter didn't look happy. Technically, Aidan wasn't a field agent. And he'd already put his life in danger on the Four Horsemen case.

But Amy knew Aidan well; if they jeopardized an innocent life on his behalf, he wouldn't be happy at all.

"Trust me, Aidan is armed, he's smart, and he knows how to watch out for himself," Amy assured Hunter. "Please, call Mickey—I'll call Aidan."

She dialed Aidan. She could hear him speaking in a cool, casual manner just before he answered the phone.

"Just keep smiling," she told Aidan. "Tell him we're still looking for whoever ran into the Everglades from the back of the church. We'll be out there to get you and the car as soon as possible," Amy said.

"I'm fine. The reverend has no idea who was out back. He told me they were a small community and most of his parishioners came from the area. He didn't know who was screaming and hopes you can find the man and the girl. She might have been running to the church for help. Though he can't figure out how she might have gotten there. He is worried—the area behind the church is wild. Most of the homes have barbed wire on their back fences—too close to gator land. He hopes desperately you don't run into anything. You two, be careful out there. I know, I know, I know you know what to look out for, but you're not in a state park. It's really the wilds in this area, once you leave the new housing districts," Aidan said.

"Gotcha," Amy murmured.

"We're having a great conversation here. I didn't mean to

take so much of the reverend's time, but he said it's fine. He has nothing going until tonight. I'll see you when I see you," Aidan assured her.

As they ended the call, Amy heard him speaking to the reverend and saying, "They lost whoever they were after. They'll keep looking for a while. And I'm so sorry—"

"No, no, I'll tell you about more of the signs!" she heard the reverend reply, just before the phone went dead.

Aidan was playing it out beautifully. He'd be a fountain of knowledge for them once they were able to reach him again. And from his words, it seemed there was something off—way off—about the good reverend himself and the church.

Aidan was being told about "the signs." The signs of the Apocalypse?

Hunter looked back at her. "Aidan is good," she assured him.

He nodded. "Mickey has agents going back out there, and they'll move quickly. They'll get Aidan, and we'll head back for the car when we can."

"Thank you, thank you!" Russell told them. "Thank you. Please…it's really not that far!"

"Yes, let's move quickly," Hunter said. But he paused, looking down at the girl in his arms. "What happened to her, though? She was screaming and shrieking. Her breathing and pulse are normal, but I thought it would be a good idea to hold off on questions until we were farther out of the swamp."

"I don't know, I don't know!" Russell said. "She was wild, fighting me. She thought I was a monster. Although, even if she had recognized me, I'm not sure her reaction would have changed!"

"No, I believe she's been on some pretty heavy drugs," Hunter said.

"She never did drugs! She was a good kid with great grades. She wanted to go to the Harvard School of Medicine."

"No, we believe she was given drugs," Hunter clarified. "Let's get her to the hospital. Then we'd appreciate it if you'd come into our headquarters and tell us everything you know."

They started walking again with Russell in the lead, and Hunter still carrying Samantha. The girl appeared to be sleeping peacefully in his arms. Maybe that was for the best.

But they had almost made their way to the road Russell had told them about when Amy realized that no matter how pleasantly the reverend was speaking to Aidan, he knew something had happened.

Reverend Ben might have told Aidan he had no idea who the girl was, but he most probably did. And if he knew who she was, he might know as well that one of her parents or a relative had come to rescue her.

Amy held back a bit and put a call through to Mickey herself, speaking softly as she gave him the man's name; they needed an agent watching his house—watching out for his wife and anyone else who might be in her home.

Mickey agreed and assured her he would see to it.

"Is this Reverend Ben the Archangel?" Mickey asked.

"I don't know. But he is in on this. He is preaching the same brand of the Apocalypse we've heard before. In fact, he's giving Aidan an explanation of the world to come right now."

"Agents are near the church. They'll get Aidan out of there safely," Mickey told her. "And the hospital has been alerted. No sense going anywhere else when we're already covering that location with law enforcement."

"Thank you!" she whispered.

They reached the road. Or something that still resembled a road. What had been fields of sugarcane had been reclaimed by the dense vegetation that marked the heartlands of the Everglades, the great ecosystem that covered so much of the peninsula and stretched through the inlands to the central part of the state.

As they made their way to the car, she saw Hunter glance at

her. She gave him a nod; Harvey Russell might appear to be sincere, a man with a true and desperate story.

But she would sit in back with the girl; Russell would drive. Hunter would be in front to seize the wheel at any point if necessary and she would keep an eye on him if he offered violence in any way, ready to react from behind the man.

They reached his vehicle, a Jeep, and crawled in as planned. Russell explained he'd been with a client years before who had thought about purchasing land that bordered the area; because of that, he'd known about the road.

"As you can imagine, it won't come up in your GPS," Russell said dryly. "But we can twist back onto the main roads soon, go through a bit of a canal, and hop on the turnpike."

Amy looked down at the girl who was stretched out in the back with her head resting in her lap. She was breathing fine. She looked like she was simply having an afternoon nap. She was a pretty girl with long dark hair and a sweet face. Her father had said she was a good student who wanted to go to Harvard.

How had she been so...subverted?

The vehicle bounced as they went through a shallow canal, moved onto a small street, out onto a main street, and then onto the turnpike.

Her phone rang and she saw it was Mickey.

"Aidan is safe with agents. We also have two agents keeping an eye on the church and the neighborhood."

"We're going to get Samantha Russell to the hospital. Then—"

"I'll meet you there. We're going to need something. I want to bring that internet-ordained preacher in—but until I get more on him, we need to observe. I don't know how they've managed this—other than plying people with drugs. But when we make arrests, they must be sound and they must stick like glue."

"Thank you, Mickey. And—"

She hesitated. She didn't want Harvey Russell to know she was worried about his family. Because no matter what Reverend Ben had said to Aidan, he'd known exactly who had been doing the screaming when Amy had run after the "abductor" and into the Glades.

"No problem finding a Fort Lauderdale address for Harvey Russell. We're watching the home, too. So far, so good."

"Thanks, Mickey," Amy said softly.

She ended the call and leaned back and closed her eyes for a minute. Every step in this case seemed to take them down a deeper and more twisted path. It seemed to stretch everywhere.

She didn't think the reverend was the Archangel calling all the shots. Too obvious. But he might be the fourth horseman.

They reached the hospital and Hunter instructed Harvey Russell to drive straight to the emergency entrance; their arrival was expected.

He appeared frightened again as hospital personnel rushed out to bring Samantha in.

Hunter placed a gentle hand on his arm. "Mr. Russell, let's get the car parked, and we'll head to the waiting room. There's nothing we can do here but be in the way. Your daughter is breathing well, and her pulse is strong. She's going to be all right."

"My wife!" the man said suddenly. "I need to call my wife. I can't believe I haven't done so yet. She needs to be here. She wants to be here. She…she knew what I was doing, and she must be worried sick and…"

"That's fine. Call her," Amy told him.

He frowned suddenly, looking from Hunter to Amy. "No. No, no, no. Does this have anything to do with what's been going on? How stupid of me, of course. All the bodies that have been found. They were going to kill her! They were going to kill my Samantha!"

"That's not necessarily true—" Amy said.

"You were out there! You went to see that crazy preacher in that whacked-out church!"

"Mr. Russell, please, calm down, and call your wife. She needs to know you and your daughter are safe," Hunter told him.

"My wife! What if they knew—" Russell began.

"Sir! Agents are watching your house. Your wife is safe," Amy said. "We need to move the car, get it parked. Samantha is in the best of hands. Let them work with her, and then you can go in and see her—see your daughter on her way back to health."

"You know," Hunter said. "I'll take the car out of here. They need this area. Amy, why don't you and Mr. Russell go into the ER waiting room? He can call his wife, let her know there are agents at her home, and they can follow her here."

"Yes, please!" Russell said.

Hunter reached for the keys, and Harvey Russell handed them over. He was on the phone as Amy led him through the entrance and steered him toward the ER waiting room.

When he ended his call, he looked at her, almost smiling and shaking his head.

"You didn't want to scare me. But we are in danger, aren't we? We took something from these crazy people. My daughter was in danger, but when we took her back, we put targets on ourselves as well."

"I'll be honest with you, Mr. Russell. We're still investigating everything that is going on. You may not be in danger, but it's always best to take precautions."

"I have a business to run. Of course, I have managers, people who can pick up for me, but I can't afford not to work. Should I be afraid of anyone who walks into my business? I'm no idiot— I have an alarm system on my house, but…"

He had such a sad and hopeless look on his face, Amy wished she could really assure him.

She couldn't reply at all because she saw Mickey Hampton walk into the waiting room.

"Amy?" Mickey said.

She smiled. "Mr. Russell, this gentleman is my boss, Mickey

Hampton—if anyone has the information you need, it's Mickey. Of course, Mickey is going to need anything you can tell him. Anything at all."

"They tried to take my baby girl!" Russell whispered to Mickey. "And yeah, I was an idiot dressed up like a big black bear and I went to get her, but..."

"Sir, we understand," Mickey said. "Sit with me. Amy will stop at the desk, and we'll see that you are able to be with your daughter as soon as possible. Please rest assured. Now, sit down with me, and we will talk."

Harvey Russell nodded and started toward a set of chairs with Mickey. But he stopped, looking back at Amy.

"You even saved us from an alligator!" he said.

Mickey arched a brow and looked at Amy. "You're alligator wrestling now?" he asked lightly.

"Hell, no," she said. "I just know how to stare at them and make sure they're not coming after me. Anyway... Mr. Russell, we're just grateful you and Samantha are going to be okay. Please, we can use anything!"

She left him sitting with Mickey and hurried to the ER desk to point out Harvey Russell and Mickey so that the nurses knew to check on the young woman and keep her father informed.

By then, Hunter had gotten Russell's vehicle parked and come in himself. He nodded to Mickey and looked at Amy and said, "I think we should have a chat with Elijah again."

"Elijah? He's told us everything—"

"No, no, I'm not doubting him. But I want to know if he heard anything about a church, a pastor, anything going on down at the development."

"All right. Sounds good. I'll tell Mickey what we're doing."

She left him waiting and hurriedly told Mickey they'd be there; they were just going to get some coffee.

That was a lie, but one Mickey understood. She didn't want Harvey Russell becoming unnerved and panicky again if he knew how many others under the thumb of the Horsemen craze were in the hospital as well.

They hurried upstairs. New officers and agents were on duty, but they quickly flashed their credentials and hurried to Elijah's room.

Annabel remained with him. She was asleep, lying in the chair. Elijah was awake, watching a sitcom rerun on the television.

He smiled, surprised, but pleasantly it seemed, to see them walking in.

"You two never catch a break, do you?" he asked. "Are you ever off?"

"Long enough to sleep," Hunter assured him. "You look good."

"I feel good. I feel better than I have in…weeks," Elijah told them. He smiled, looking toward Annabel. "I am the luckiest man in the world." He looked at Amy. "You didn't kill me, and you didn't let me kill myself. And I have this unbelievable, loving woman in my life. What is not to be grateful for and feel good about?" He didn't expect an answer, but rather grinned at Hunter and Amy. "Then you're lucky people, too. No, no, don't get me wrong. So professional in all ways, but…you look at each other and communicate. I can tell. You're lucky. Well, of course, you deal with the depravity of the world, and that has to be hard as hell, but…anyway. Sorry, shouldn't have spoken."

"Elijah, it's all right," Amy assured him, smiling, glancing at Hunter. "Do you mind that we're here to try to dig deeper into your mind and memory?"

"Not at all. If you asked me to hand you my mind on a silver platter, I'd try to figure out a way to do it!" he assured her.

"Nothing quite so serious. In all your conversations about the Archangel, angels, demons, and the Antichrist, did this Colin person ever mention a church?" Amy asked.

Elijah frowned thoughtfully. "He talked about the one true church all the time. I know I thought he was referring to a real place at the time, but when my mind started clearing, I started to think maybe he was talking about something that was ethereal."

"What did he say about it?" Hunter asked.

"Oh, he promised me he was going to take me there. It was a place where we would all learn our roles in what we were to do to prepare for the Apocalypse." He frowned. "Did you find something about a church?"

"Maybe. We don't know," Amy told him. "Please, anything else he said, ethereal or otherwise?"

Again, Elijah frowned, thoughtful.

"Colin said it was in the wilderness and that… I began to think he meant a wilderness of clouds or the like. That great rewards stretched beyond the church, because the wilderness taught us all obedience and humility. And for some who learned and honored the will of the Archangel, there were earthly pleasures to know before the end of the flesh. When he talked… I just listened. I saw things. I know now the drug cocktail he managed to get into me allowed me to see all kinds of things. I still don't know because I never fulfilled my earthly duty to obey, to observe, to report back, and to kill those who needed to die before they sinned so badly they could not be saved when the Apocalypse came. Please believe me, I would tell you anything I possibly could. I am grateful. If I need to go to jail, I'll still be grateful, because I'm alive and because I've learned what is important in that life I'm so lucky to be living." He glanced at Annabel, and then gave them his attention again. "Ask me anything at any time, and so help me God, I will try in any way!"

"Thank you!" Hunter told him. "We appreciate that. And we will be back, of course. For now, you're a witness, and one who must be protected."

"Thank you—and hey! Take off. Did you know that…you know…you usually both look so put together? Tonight, hmm, you're kind of messy-looking."

"We've been running around the wilderness," Hunter said dryly. "We'll see you later then, and thanks!"

They left Elijah's hospital room. In the hallway, Amy asked Hunter, "What do you think about what he was telling us—something beyond the church?"

"Earthly pleasures. You know what that usually means?" Hunter replied, arching a brow.

"Earthly pleasures? Food. Comfort? Sex?" she asked in return.

He nodded. "Beyond the church. Amy, I think there's something back there not too far from the church, but maybe deeper into the area than we went today."

"Something like a cabin or a shack or...hmm. Like one of the cabins where we found Marc Hamilton?" she asked.

"Something free enough from decay that it has a solid door and a padlock. It may be extremely difficult—even impossible—to prove that an ordained minister of any kind is preaching to his congregation that they must commit murder to survive the Apocalypse. But if he has kidnapped—or lured and seduced through one of his cocktails of drugs—more women, especially ones as young as sixteen for his 'earthly pleasures,' we can arrest him on that. And I don't think any judge out there would grant him bail."

"You're right," Amy said.

Her phone was buzzing. Mickey.

She answered it quickly.

"You might want to come back down. The doctors have said Samantha Russell will be fine. Like the rest, she needs her system cleaned out. She's in and out of consciousness right now and babbling a little when she opens her eyes."

"On our way!" Amy promised.

When they arrived back down at the ER, they found Samantha was in one of the few rooms that had walls and a closing door.

Mickey was in the hallway waiting for them. Through the

window, they could see Harvey Russell was there as well as a slim woman of about fifty who appeared to be his wife.

"Go in now," Mickey said. "They're sedating her—she'll sleep soon. But she is babbling. And something might make more sense to you than it does to me."

They went in. Harvey Russell turned quickly, and then introduced them to his wife, who was seated next to their daughter and holding her hand. Tears streaked her face, and she greeted them with a tearful thanks. Hunter quickly assured her they were grateful, too.

"She's been talking?" Amy asked.

Harvey nodded. "Stuff that makes no sense!"

They waited a minute, looking at Samantha. She still looked as if she slept in perfect peace. But then she tossed suddenly, as if she was uncomfortable, and began to babble.

"I will never be a handmaiden... I must be... I don't want to be... But in the end in, yes, in the end, and it is soon, then I will find my reward. I will be on the right arm of the Archangel and I will be honored above all if I obey and if I learn humility and to serve. I will never be, I don't want to be, I must be..."

Her words trailed and she suddenly looked as if she slept deeply again.

"What do you think she is talking about?" Harvey Russell asked them. "It's as if she's fighting within her own mind!"

"She probably is, because as you said, she was a good person," Amy said gently.

"But what does that mean?" Mrs. Russell asked.

"We don't know yet," Amy said. "I promise we won't stop until we do know what it means."

Hunter was holding on to her arm. "We'll leave you alone with your daughter. We'll see you tomorrow. And get some rest yourselves. There will be guards protecting you through the day and night, I promise."

They headed out of the room, running into Mickey almost immediately.

"Well? Did you listen long enough?" he asked.

"I think there's a cabin, shack, or something out back behind the church. And I think they're brainwashing, drugging, and kidnapping young girls to perhaps bribe, reward, or coerce others to their will. And I'm sorry to believe when they tire of them, when they're ready for something new, they kill the victims, but first making them believe they're going to a reward in heaven," Hunter told him.

Mickey nodded. "Hopefully tomorrow this girl can give us something that will allow us to arrest the reverend and put an end to his mockery of a church. And we'll get agents out—"

"No. Not tomorrow! Tonight!" Amy said.

"Amy," Mickey argued. "It's almost dark. We need to—"

"No, no, no, Mickey! I'm very afraid the good old Reverend Ben knows we're onto him. And if so, if there is a cabin where Samantha was slated to go as a handmaiden, he and his lackeys might go out there tonight and kill them all before disappearing themselves. Mickey, we need a small army in high hiking boots. Please, we need to get out there!"

"Amy, it's dangerous enough by day," Hunter reminded her. "But—"

"But?" she demanded.

Hunter turned to Mickey. "But she's right. We need a small army. And we need it tonight."

11

Mickey had made a good point.

Running around in one of the wildest sections of the great river of grass in the dark was not one of the things Amy would want to do frequently. But the good thing was Aidan had insisted on coming—and with good cause. And when their group of two dozen searchers had split up, Mickey and Garza had called out their best investigators and matched them with local and Seminole and Miccosukee police. While federal agents could make an arrest on tribal lands, the local police could not. The land behind the church wasn't part of tribal land, and they didn't expect to wander onto tribal land, but many of the Native American police were as knowledgeable as Aidan.

And like the federal and state authorities, they wanted what was going on stopped. Neither Mickey nor Garza had liked the idea of Jimmy being with the group in what could be a dangerous situation. They never liked civilians involved, but Jimmy was so proficient in moving about and knowledgeable regarding the terrain that they had been convinced to let him accompany them. After all, he'd already worked his way in when he helped to save the life of a child.

Of course, Jimmy couldn't make arrests at all anywhere, but they weren't worried about making arrests that night. They were seeking to save lives or rescue runaways and kidnapping victims. He knew what he was doing. He might not have frequented that section of their wilderness, but he knew the geography and geology in an amazing way. Jimmy Osceola was with Hunter on the grid that the group had created, and Amy was with Aidan. Another twenty officers and agents were also working on the grid, hopefully allowing them to cover the ground behind the church for several miles.

The Everglades.

Amy had loved the strange distinction of the area being a World Heritage Site, unique in that it was the meeting place of temperate North America and the tropical Caribbean. But she could see dozens of different trees she couldn't identify along with shrubs and flowers she had no idea about.

"Duck potato," Aidan said.

"What?"

"I have not seen a patch in a while." He shone his light down for her. "That pretty white flower is called a duck potato. Seriously. Ducks like them a lot."

"Cool," Amy said. "Duck potato. I love it!"

"Hey. Potatoes are cool. Apopka, Florida. A city named after 'potato eating people.' Potatoes get around."

"Like us, huh?" Amy asked. "We're like potatoes?"

Aidan laughed. "We seem to be getting around. And doing all right. I'm proud of you. Wilderness girl! You've got your light trained carefully, watching out for predators, snakes, and other dangers, and you aren't freaking out when a mosquito buzzes by. Ah, yeah, I forget you've already been held—oh, hmm, with me—captive in one of those old shacks being prepared to be a sacrifice."

Amy smiled and nodded. "I could almost be a guide myself. No, not at all. The best I could do on any guidebook would be a short foreword—'Hey, it's really a cool place if you get the best guide.' Hmm. And maybe another foreword? 'A guide to the sick mind'? Nope, but… Hunter is good at that. And now we have a profiler, a mind-hunter, with us, working on what kind of narcissist could conceive of all this."

"I'll tell you what—I wish they could just bring that reverend in on something. I understand the law—I do. But…wow. I listened as if I believed every word he was saying to me, and some of it is believable enough that I can see how people can get sucked in. We've had events that can coincide with prophesies. War—I don't remember when someone wasn't at war. Disease—COVID certainly qualifies. Several countries and areas were facing famine at the time, including South Sudan, Nigeria, and Yemen. The predictors can be seen as truly biblical."

"Hmm," Amy murmured.

"What?"

"I was thinking of something my dad used to say."

"Which was?"

"Something like, there was nothing wrong with most of the religions in the world, it was what men—as in mankind—chose to do with them."

"Good call. Most of the time, religion teaches us to be good to one another, to be kind, and to be decent. Somehow, people do manage to twist that."

"And Reverend Ben?"

"He didn't go overboard. He was pointing out the things I was just saying, that the world has been in a sorry place, and that many of the things happening aligned with the warnings in the Book of Revelation."

Amy smiled. "This one was from my mom—she isn't fond of the Old Testament. She thinks half the population would be stoned if we were back in the day!"

"Hmm. Florida. We could use coconuts instead," Aidan told her. He stopped walking for a minute to look back at her. "Amy, I know that man is not a man who is truly of any church. He's pure evil, and he's scary evil because he manages it all with a smile and a lot of charm. He acts as if he truly loves the Bible and his fellow man. I hope to hell we find someone—someone alive—who will give us what we need to arrest him."

"We'll do it right. And Mickey has people watching so he can't just disappear."

They'd been walking for about an hour, and their last communal check-in call had been a few minutes back right at 3:00 a.m. Hunter and Jimmy had come across one of the old hunting shacks in the area, but it had been almost completely reclaimed by nature, and Jimmy suggested that if there was one, there might well be more in the area.

"My mom told me when she was a kid, there were all kinds of shacks down here," Amy said. "Hunting shacks where her dad and his friends really came out and shot up beer cans. Some really did hunt gators. I know people still get in on the Great Florida Python Challenge."

"The pythons and other constrictors are a major challenge—one we haven't solved yet," Aidan said. "And I think it probably all started by people thinking they were being humane. They couldn't keep the pet snake once they realized just how big it was going to get, so they figured they'd let it go in a great environment. But they eat everything and destroy the natural food chain, and while they're not water snakes, it's amazing how those things move. Down in the Keys if they go far enough south, there's a danger they could wipe out the deer."

"Adorable little creatures," Amy murmured, wincing as she just managed to avoid tripping over a root in her path. "Hey! I've never seen a Florida panther in the wild. Have you?"

"Twice. I was with Jimmy. I might have missed it otherwise.

And it looks like the Florida panther has a chance of coming back. Anyway… Amy! Stop."

She did, going dead still, listening. Nothing. After a minute, she looked at Aidan, arching a brow.

"Amy, I swear I heard something. Like someone…crying."

"Okay, so, let's just stand here another minute and…"

She stopped whispering. She suddenly heard it, too. Soft, so soft…

She couldn't fathom the direction. The almost unheard sobbing seemed a part of the whisper of the breeze and chirp of insects.

But it was a sob. And there was someone out there.

"Aidan?"

He was still another minute. "To our left. Sorry, we need to find something through that field of saw grass. Otherwise—as prepared as we are in denim clothing and high boots—we'll wind up ripped to shreds."

"Hey, I'll follow you," Amy told him.

And she did. Aidan was now determined. They walked forward another fifty feet until he found a footpath.

"Someone came through here," he told Amy.

"Let's go."

They made their way forward, and then Aidan lifted his hand indicating they needed to stop again.

They heard the soft sobbing and then words.

"I have to do it. I have to do it. I will die! No… I will burn."

Aidan indicated they needed to move through a very poor trail to their left. They were walking through a hardwood hammock, an elevation of just a few inches, but it provided for a growth of trees that blanketed the area they were trying to travel through, cocoplum, mahogany… Amy wasn't even sure of what else might be in the tangle. But they crawled through carefully and finally glimpsed a small moonlit clearing in the distance.

With a shack to the rear of it. One with a solid door that had a padlock on it—just like the old shack in which they had found Marc Hamilton.

Amy got on her radio, certain that was going to beat cell phone communication where they were. She reached the group with one swipe of the screen.

"We've got something."

She gave the phone to Aidan, who gave them the approximate coordinates.

"Wait for backup," Mickey said over the radio.

But the sobs now were loud and desperate.

"No danger," she said quickly. "Hostages just locked in."

She didn't know if that was true or not. And she knew Aidan was aware she was lying. But she also knew Aidan didn't plan on waiting, either.

She clicked off her radio before anyone could speak again.

"We need to find her—I'm so afraid that she's about to take her own life."

"I'm with you," Aidan told her.

He crawled over a sprawling root and reached a hand back to help her.

Amy accepted, and for a minute, from her vantage point, she could see they would be at the clearing in a matter of minutes.

She paused, looking around.

"Aidan, it has a solid door and a padlock."

"Through the windows again," he told her.

"They may have gotten panes for this one—"

"And I see a really fine branch to break through glass right there, waiting for me—serendipity!" Aidan said.

She smiled as he wrested the branch from the ground. And silently, they started forward again.

Hunter never had a chance to reply to Amy or Mickey, because the radio communication ended as quickly as it had begun.

And he knew Amy. She wasn't waiting for anyone. But then

again, she wasn't a fool—she was probably right. If she had found a secret cabin where captives were being kept, she would reason that at best, there was one person watching over those being held. And with the mind games being played here, many may not even believe they were hostages and were toys for the great Archangel and his lieutenants.

Disposable toys.

Those who disagreed with the dictates of such a leader were quickly disposed of—in barrels, perhaps, or simply dumped.

Like the bodies he and Jimmy had just discovered.

They had belonged to three young women, now in various stages of decomposition, various stages of remains. Nature and swamp creatures had taken their toll. One was barely a torso, neck, and head. One was minus just a forearm while the other was missing a leg from the left side of her body and a foot from the right side.

"You didn't say anything on the radio," Jimmy pointed out, appearing sick as he stared at the remains.

"I'll call back—they were gone before I could speak. And I think we may be closest. I'd like to back up Amy and Aidan. We'll send coordinates, let them know these victims can't be helped. They need forensics and a medical examiner," he told Jimmy. He was back on the radio giving their position and stating they were heading to give assistance to Amy and Aidan.

Before he finished the call, he saw Jimmy was already moving.

He was glad to leave the bodies behind.

And yet, as he started to follow Jimmy, Hunter paused for a minute, looking around, wincing inwardly and wondering if there might not be more cabins out there that had been refitted for the purpose of holding hostages—or willing participants—seeking heaven through obedience to the Archangel and his closest associates.

"Hunter?"

"Right behind you," Hunter promised.

Jimmy was amazing. He seemed to have GPS embedded in his body. They moved quickly; he hesitated only briefly in certain places, seeking the best paths through the terrain.

"Almost there," he assured Hunter. "We weren't more than a half a mile apart. It's just that a half mile out here—"

"Is a long half mile," Hunter agreed. "But— Jimmy!"

Jimmy Osceola had paused, frowning, staring straight ahead. He beckoned to Hunter, and Hunter moved toward him, looking through the trees as Jimmy pointed something out.

Hunter saw it at last. Something reflecting off Jimmy's light. Pale in the gleam.

There was a person standing not far from them. Just standing there, saying nothing, doing nothing.

Hunter drew his Glock, indicated that Jimmy needed to be behind him, and he carefully made his way toward the person standing like a statue in the middle of the Everglades.

It felt like déjà vu.

The old rustic cabin was in the midst of a very small clearing, but even there, the grass grew long. There was a path that led to the door, probably the only door for such a small place. There were windows, but they had been covered by plywood. Aidan glanced at Amy.

"Hmm, not glass," he murmured.

"Not glass. But—"

"My trusty branch will get us through. Just—"

She pulled her Glock from its holster. "Be prepared."

He nodded and murmured, "Something about that suddenly made me want to whistle Disney tunes. Anyway…"

He started forward and she followed, turning as she did so, checking the trees and brush all around them. But no one appeared and there were no sounds, no whisper in the trees as if someone moved, nothing out of the ordinary.

They reached the shack. The windows were high, but Aidan

gave her a nod; he could get the leverage to do what was needed. And he was strong. Stronger than Amy had realized.

It took him one massive thrust with his hardwood branch and the plywood bucked and fell inward.

They heard screams from inside.

"It's here!"

"The Apocalypse!"

"Dear God, it's happening!"

"Amy!" Aidan cried, but she was already at his side, ready for him to hike her up so she could crawl through the window.

For a split second she feared an attack from panicked people, and she didn't want to hurt anyone. She desperately didn't want to hurt anyone who had already been hurt enough, having been abused and used.

But she needn't have feared. Very little moonlight made its way into the cabin, but she could see there were five people in the cabin, and they were all huddled back against the far wall.

"It's okay!" Amy said quickly, holstering her Glock. "It's okay, there is no Apocalypse, I'm here to help you."

One woman stepped forward. She—like the others—was dressed in a simple, unbleached cotton sheath. Short-sleeved, baggy, and knee-length.

She wore no shoes.

Barefoot would be no way to escape the Everglades.

"We...we don't need help. We're the chosen ones. We are here by design because we await the great coming of the Arch-angel, and then our turn among the angels."

I am getting so damned tired of hearing that! Amy thought.

But she didn't speak the words out loud.

"Well, I'm afraid that's not true. There are so many things I'm going to be sorry to tell you, but first—who was crying?"

"Crying?" The young woman, a blonde of about seventeen, who had apparently been chosen to be their spokeswoman, appeared to be truly confused.

"Someone was crying, and we were afraid that... Well, she sounded as if she might have hurt herself."

The blonde shook her head. "No one in here was crying. We care for one another—"

"Locked in this cabin?"

Suddenly, a brunette stepped forward. "That is confusing, Sandra," she told the blonde. "Why do they make sure we're locked in?"

"They don't lock us in, they lock others out," the blonde, now identified as Sandra, told her.

"That would put the lock on the wrong side of the door, right?" Amy said.

At that point, Aidan, who had hiked himself up, landed on the floor as he jumped down from the window.

They might be disagreeing with each other, but the blonde and brunette suddenly huddled together, screaming, looking at Aidan.

"No, no, no," Amy said quickly. "He's my friend. He's come with me to help."

"We don't need help! Don't you understand, we serve will-ingly—"

"I don't!"

A third young woman had spoken. She had long, long tangled sandy hair and big brown eyes and she looked at Amy earnestly. "I...I'm here because I'm terrified of...of what will happen to me if I disagree with anyone. I could wind up..." She paused, glancing at Sandra. Then she turned to Amy and Aidan and said, "I could wind up like Alexie—they took her out, and she never came back."

"She...she's with the angels," Sandra said. "We all get our turn, our place here to serve on earth, and then our time with eternal rewards!"

Amy didn't get to react or to assure the young woman—there was suddenly a barrage of gunfire coming at the shack.

Someone had a high-powered weapon and was pouring rounds at them.

"Get down!" Amy commanded, and she and Aidan both jumped instinctively into action, bringing the closest young woman to the floor and crawling to get the others. When they were flat on the floor, Amy crawled back to the area of the window where Aidan had broken the plywood.

Aidan was across from her, and they waited for one barrage to end before moving close enough to fire wildly in return.

But how long could they hold out, both armed with only their Glocks?

They would never have enough rounds, except that...

"Cease firing!" a voice exploded over a loudspeaker. "FBI, FDLE! Cease fire."

She didn't see what happened next.

The barrage of gunfire returned, followed by another.

And then there was a shuffling outside, and Amy heard her name called. "Amy! Are you in there? Are you and Aidan in there?"

"Yes! We're here!" she shouted. "With five young women—all are okay."

She realized she knew the voice. It was Special Agent Lyle Comer, and he and others were outside as the backup Mickey had sent.

A second later, there was a horrific bang—causing the five women to scream—and the door crashed in.

Special Agent Comer stepped into the room, followed by two others. The girl who had told Amy she was terrified cried out with delight and raced forward into Lyle's arms. He blinked, surprised by the reception. But the FBI agent from the Behavioral Analysis Unit was right behind, and he gently reached for the young woman and assured her she was all right and help was waiting outside the door.

Sandra, the blonde, still protested.

"No…oh no, no, no!" she told them, looking sincerely distressed. "We can't rise to heaven if you take us away. Those who do not obey, those who do not serve…we will burn forever and ever and ever and we… Oh, please! Shoot me!" she said suddenly. "It's a sin to take our own lives, but if we are sacrificed to the horrid regime of the disbelievers here on earth, we can still—"

Another brunette suddenly spoke up. "That's a crock of shit! Can't you see anything—even now? We were locked in—others were not locked out. And we're being used, horribly, and I…I was terrified, too," she told Amy. "Because Lana was right—when you protest, you disappear."

"We are here to help you," Amy assured her. She glanced at Lyle Comer and asked him, "Do we have any medical assistance on hand?"

He smiled and nodded. "Mickey called out the works. And a medical examiner."

"A medical examiner? But the girls are…"

"The fellow shooting at you and us is dead," he told her. "The ME is out there with her assistants. She'll see to him, and we'll get these ladies out of here and to the hospital. You can call it quits for the night."

"But—" Amy protested.

"No! No!" Sandra cried. "I need to be dead, too!"

Another of the agents had come in and Lyle turned to him. "She'll need to be on suicide watch."

"She drank the Kool-Aid," the brunette said. "Well, it's in the water they bring us. The water…when you drink it, you see the angels. But a few of us decided to try not drinking the water and…"

"Forensics is going to have a field day here," Aidan said. "So, Amy, you did it. We did it. We found them, and now we can be done and pass it all on!"

"Yeah, Mickey said you might be a problem, that you would argue, but also that you had to sleep and were to go back to the hotel," Lyle Comer told her. He was smiling. "I've worked with you before, so I know…"

"I'm fine, I'll go back to the hotel. But I'm curious about the man who was shooting at us. Do we know him?"

"Get the girls out," he said quietly to an agent behind him. And despite her protests, even Sandra was escorted out of the cabin and down the trail they had taken earlier.

Lyle turned back to Amy. "The shooter is this way."

Amy and Aidan followed him and then paused, standing in the grassy clearing, looking down at the dead man. He had been taken out with a single bullet to the head. His arms remained around the high-powered automatic rifle he'd used to riddle the cabin with bullets.

A medical examiner was down by him—as was Sabrina.

"Sabrina!" Aidan said.

She smiled and lifted the equipment she'd been carrying. "Fingerprints," she said. "He's in the system from a year or so ago. Drunk and disorderly. Vince Ricardo. I'll be heading back to work up everything we have on him."

Aidan looked at Amy. "Have you seen him before?"

She shook her head. Then she frowned and said, "Wait!"

Lyle Comer looked at her and asked softly, "Um, wait—why?"

"We need to know if Reverend Ben MacDowell is involved with this. He needs to be picked up as soon as possible," Amy said.

"Did any of the young women tell you he forced them out here?" Lyle asked.

"I didn't ask them yet," she told him.

"Right. Okay, let's get them to stop. Because agents are still watching his so-called church. They can go right in if we have anything."

"Perfect," Aidan murmured.

"Agents, hold!" Lyle called out to the group under his command for the operation.

Amy hurried toward them. The young women were apart now, each with one of the agents.

"How did you get out here?" she asked them. "Who brought you here?"

There was silence for a minute and then the brunette stepped forward. "Colin... Colin brought me out."

"Were you at the church? Did Reverend MacDowell have anything to do with this?"

"Well, we came to the church through Colin. Reverend Mac-Dowell said...we were blessed, and yes, we could serve."

"We're not going to straighten this out here, but I'd like to know. All of you came here through this man Colin?" she asked.

"I believed at first!" another of the young women, a petite redhead, said, glancing at her escorting agent and then at Amy. "You have to understand how real it all seems...maybe how real it all is, just not as...not as they claim it to be. Colin is a biblical scholar. He is wonderful, gentle, sweet, tries to help others all the time, and then, when you're with him, you suddenly see it as if the entire thing is like a movie showing before your eyes. Then when you're with him, you feel safe, and you try to tell others like family and friends, but they can't see it. And then you feel you must be with Colin to survive, and then he brings you to the church and you meet Reverend MacDowell. You can see even more clearly that this world is of the flesh, but the next world is created of light and clouds and beauty. You can sit among the angels if you only see what is happening and prepare..."

"And you were preparing in the cabin?" Amy asked. "How?"

The young woman closed her eyes. "Serving the angels in their human forms."

"Was Reverend MacDowell one of those angels?" Amy asked.

She shrugged. "They came in masks. They claimed the angels themselves hated their human forms because they were weak and needy, but like all who wished to celebrate the ecstasy of the next world, they were to serve here, trying to save everyone they could. They needed help. They needed us. I...I don't know any faces."

"In other words, you were seduced into being raped," Amy said flatly.

The young woman hung her head.

"It's not your fault!" Amy told her. "Don't you ever feel that any of this was your fault! These agents are going to bring you to a hospital. You'll be cared for. They'll find your family and friends and see to it—"

"No! No!" The blonde who had so recently asked to die was protesting. "You don't understand! Once we've been chosen, they'll find us. And if we betray them..."

"They'll kill you," Amy finished for her. "Don't worry— you will be kept guarded and no one will get to you. And I can promise you that none of us will stop until we know you'll be safe and you can live your own lives again!"

"Thank you!" one of them whispered.

"No. Thank you!" Amy said. "Just...just take care of yourselves. I'll see you again," she promised and hurried back to Lyle and Aidan with her radio already out.

"Mickey! Pick him up—pick up that parasite at the church, Reverend MacDowell!"

"I'll send them in," Mickey promised. "And, Amy, I am ordering you and Aidan—"

"I know. I know. I didn't argue."

"Well, it's all right if you wait just a bit. Hunter and Jimmy are onto something—they were headed for your location. Hang tight!"

As he said the words, she heard a piercing scream reach them from the dense trees to the rear of the shack.

12

Hunter had put a call through to Mickey, letting him know he wasn't sure what they were looking at, but they were close enough to the cabin for him to have heard the gunshots and commotion.

But the person standing in the woods had been oblivious to those sounds. She'd just suddenly let out a scream of anguish loud enough to wake the dead.

He didn't need his Glock. As he moved closer, he noticed it was only the young woman, now crying softly. And she held something in her hand, and she appeared to be vigorously maneuvering it against herself.

He moved closer.

He saw that it was a sharp, jagged piece of a branch she was vehemently working against her wrist. He couldn't worry about frightening her; he couldn't worry about taking her by surprise. He simply sprang forward, sweeping his arms around her and catching the bloodied piece of branch and throwing it far from her person.

She screamed and cried and fought him. But there was very little fight left in her. She was strangely dressed, in a loose blouse-like thing, taupe in color.

Her feet were bare, and her sandy hair was unbrushed. He thought that maybe she'd been wandering in the wilderness for some time…how long, he didn't know. But she had no strength whatever; after her screams of surprise and innate fear, she simply let him hold her as she sobbed.

Then she managed to speak.

"You don't understand, I couldn't do it. I still want to sit with the angels. Please, torture me, kill me, I was failing even at that. I want to rise above during the Apocalypse. I want to reach the heavens. I tried and I tried… I'm a horrible coward. Forgive me for that!"

"Miss," Hunter said quickly. "My name is Hunter Forrest, I'm with the FBI, and I'm out here with my friend Jimmy Osceola. We want to help you. Please, let us help you. There is no reason to kill yourself, and we don't want to kill you or torture you or hurt you in any way. We want to help you."

Her sobs continued. "We were told you might try to take us, dissuade us from the true path. I know the Apocalypse is coming, and I can't… I tried… I can't… No, no, no, I am doomed!"

Jimmy had reached him by then, and he hunkered down in front of her. "Miss! Please believe me. We want to help you. You are young and everything is in front of you. None of what you've been told is true. You are a beautiful young woman, and I am willing to bet you're a good human being, and you care for others. I know there are those out there who care for you. Where are your parents?" he asked her.

She had gone limp in Hunter's arms. He smiled at Jimmy and nodded, encouraging him to keep talking. And Jimmy did. He talked about the beauty of the world, and he said the world itself must love her very much. She had been wandering here, and she hadn't been hurt. And there was no reason, no reason at all, that she should hurt herself.

"But…we must prove we can serve and obey!" she whispered.

"No," Hunter said softly. "You are an individual and we are

subject to laws. And if you wish to be subject to others, remember this—we're taught to be kind to others and to forgive, even to forgive ourselves. And you…you've hesitated because you know, deep down, it's a sin to take your own life. You know what was being done to you was wrong. Anything you were told about serving and the Apocalypse is because someone was using you. I can tell you're a strong person, a good person, and you were coerced down here because you are such a good person. You wanted to believe that goodness was on the horizon and that you could help others!"

"No, I don't know. I don't… I don't know!" she whispered.

Suddenly, she went entirely limp and passed out in his arms. He checked for her pulse, and it was faint but present. Her arm was bleeding; he looked at Jimmy, who rose, ripped his shirt, and wrapped it around the arm where she had been attempting to reach her veins with the jagged branch.

"Is she…?"

"She's breathing and she has a pulse," Hunter assured him. "There's medical help just ahead at the cabin. Mickey gathered the troops and was sending them in. Let's just—"

He heard a rustling and swung around, adjusting the weight of the young woman to draw and take aim. But he heard Amy's voice, heard her calling his name.

"Hunter!"

"I'm here and Jimmy is here. We need medics!" he called in return. "But I have her. We can get to you!"

He nodded to Jimmy, and they started onward again toward the old ramshackle cabin and met up with Amy just feet from the cabin.

"Oh no, is she—"

"She's alive," he said.

The place was spilling with people: medics, the medical examiner, and a host of agents—FDLE and FBI—who were escorting young women into cars while a forensic team was busy now working under Aidan's supervision.

But Aidan saw him and excused himself to come to Hunter and the young woman.

"She was out there?" he asked.

"Crying, thinking she needed to kill herself, not wanting to kill herself. She was afraid of us and wanting us to kill her at the same time," Hunter said. "I've seen some serious brainwashing in my day, but—"

"This brainwashing is enhanced by an expert at creating drug cocktails, hallucinogens, and downers to make people pass out when they're not being useful. I'm not an MD. I don't know how it's being managed—and maybe half the bodies we're finding were practice rounds where his cocktails did kill. The MEs are still working on it. The drugs can be the groundwork for other deaths from heart or respiratory failure or even neuro incidents. So...anyway, thank God this one is alive, as were the others we found in the cabin."

"We weren't so lucky," Jimmy said.

"There were dead bodies in the woods, about half a mile to the northwest," Hunter explained. "We were headed to meet you. Mickey was sending people to retrieve them."

The look on Jimmy's face told Hunter he was seeing the bodies as they'd discovered them again in his mind.

But he said nothing.

"We need to get her to the medics, call in a report, and trust in teamwork," Aidan said.

He had barely finished speaking when Lyle came forward, nodding and telling them, "I'll get her over to the medics to get her out to an ambulance."

"Thank you," Amy said.

Lyle nodded and grimaced to their group. "I now have orders to send you to your beds for the night. There are cars back through here. As soon as you're ready, an agent will get you through to the dirt road and then on out of here."

"Great, Lyle, thanks," Hunter said, delivering his human burden to the medics who came up right behind the FDLE agent, carrying a stretcher.

"Man, I hope they have good psychiatric care at that hospital," Jimmy murmured.

"Oh, trust me, between Mickey and Garza, they'll see to it," Hunter assured him.

"And…we just keep finding more and more pathetic people," Aidan said, shaking his head.

"But tonight, we managed to avoid what worried Amy so desperately," Hunter said. "We found the shack, and we got them out."

She nodded. "I'm just curious…"

"About?" Hunter asked.

"The man who attacked the cabin and was killed… Was he sent out here to take care of them tonight? Did he think we were getting too close and the girls would talk?" Amy mulled.

"Possibly. Did they talk?" Hunter asked. "And who was the dead man? Reverend Ben?"

Amy shook her head. "Probably his lackey."

"Vince Ricardo—he had a record for drunk and disorderly," Aidan said.

"The perfect person to be drawn in. So beyond all else, this Archangel likes to supply his lieutenants—angels in human form—with earthly entertainment," Hunter said.

"They mentioned whoever this person Colin is again. Maybe he *is* the Archangel. Hunter, we got enough. They were going to go in and arrest him."

"It's time for us to head back," Hunter said. "Amy, it takes a team. In this case, several teams. They'll handle things from here. We've got to let it go for the night. The women will need medical help before they can rationally help us in turn. And others are going to bring in the good reverend. He's a better suspect to me than our mysterious Colin. The fellow meeting everyone seems to be very young, from the images we've come up with. I take nothing away from youth, yet I can't help but feel someone a little older—more world-weary and aware of the system, drugs, and more—is behind all this. We need a regroup time."

"Sabrina was out here—brought her kit. That's how we got the fingerprints," Aidan said.

"She's been a massive part of all this," Hunter acknowledged. "She found the church. Anyway, try not to dream about the Archangel. Amy, let's get out of here."

"I'll get you a guide out," Lyle told them.

Hunter shook his head, placing a hand on Jimmy's shoulder. "We've got our own, thanks! We came down in our SUV, we'll be fine getting these guys to their places, and then heading on back to the hotel. I'll let Mickey know."

"I will lead us on out," Jimmy said.

They didn't talk as they made their way back through the woods to the patch of rough dirt road which was as far as they dared bring the cars. But as they neared the SUV, Hunter stepped back, just nodding to Amy, and telling her, "Checking in with Garza."

Of course, he realized it was getting close to six in the morning— but he was sure Garza had been up all night as well.

And he probably had been because he answered his phone immediately.

"Letting you know, some were saved, a few bodies have been there for a while, and we're leaving the living to the medical personnel and the MEs for the dead. And we got enough to go after MacDowell. Agents were out there—"

"I've been in contact with Mickey all night," Garza told him, interrupting. "I don't believe you've been informed yet about the latest."

"The latest? We just walked away from the old shack or cabin or whatever you want to call those old hunting lodges."

"Well, this didn't have to do with the hunting cabins," Garza said. "They went in. They were on that church all damned day, even video surveillance from the front. But when they went in, the good reverend was gone. They are tearing the place apart. He couldn't have disappeared into a tunnel—not there, the water level wouldn't allow it. But he's gone. They crawled through the back…there was no sign of him. He might have disappeared as soon as Aidan was picked up—aware he needed to start worrying about the girl who screamed, and everything we might find by looking for her. He's just disappeared."

"Human beings don't just disappear," Hunter said.

"No. You'll find him, and you'll find Colin. And find out what the hell is going on. One of them may well be the Archangel."

"No. But one of them will lead us to the Archangel," he said, and he was as certain as his tone.

He decided he wasn't telling Amy yet.

Not until they'd gotten some sleep.

And just how far could the man get when an entire state of law enforcement was determined to bring him down?

He wouldn't get away.

The question was, just how long was it going to be before they found him?

Driving back with Jimmy and Aidan in the SUV proved to be interesting. He knew Amy had studied a great deal of Florida history but she'd grown up in the state. He was far more familiar with the western area of the country.

As they drove, Hunter glanced back at the two and asked, "So, what does the word *Seminole* mean? If I've got it right, the tribe moved down from northern areas…?"

"Starting in the 1700s," Jimmy told him, "Upper and Lower Creek Tribes started coming down from Georgia and Alabama. The squeeze was beginning. Oh, and in truth, the Lower Creek were also trying to shake the dominance of the Upper Creek. At that time, Spain held Florida, and they wanted to keep the natives around—we made a nice buffer against the British. Then from 1763 to 1783, Florida was held by the British. Around 1770, we became known as Seminole, Runaway, or you know, sometimes, Wild People. All the natives in Florida more or less fell into the one category. So anyway, in 1817 the first of the three Seminole Wars began. Andrew Jackson invaded what was then still Spanish Florida, and we went deeper and deeper into the Everglades."

"Then," Amy said, twisting around to smile at Jimmy, "came the Indian Removal Act of 1830. And the Second Seminole War, and while the Seminole people won many major battles against the US, thousands were shipped west to Oklahoma. And in 1837, the US did something that none of us would condone today—they captured the great warrior Osceola, in the midst of a truce. There were congressmen at the time who were even furious, calling it 'one of the most disgraceful acts in American military history.'"

"And there's a whole creepy story about that!" Aidan said. "The US didn't execute Osceola, but he died of disease while being held. Supposedly, his doctor, Dr. Weedon, cared for him—they were friends, but for some reason he thought it would be a good thing to remove his head to study and to display in his drugstore."

"The story goes," Amy said, "he put the head on his kids' bedpost at night if they misbehaved, then left it to his son-in-law—another doctor—who also thought it was creepy to use the head of a dead chief to make his kids behave. It was in his office when it burned down. But it makes a great ghost story at various places. He was held for a time at the Castillo in St. Augustine, and the ghost tour guides like to tell their groups that Osceola can sometimes be seen walking the grounds looking for his lost head."

"Yeah, thanks, Amy—great history here!" Jimmy told her.

"Sorry! None of the latter part of that may be true. Another form of history says Weedon gave it to a man named Mott who kept it in a 'cabinet of heads,' and after that no one knows."

"Hey, you know the old Dutch up in the Hudson Valley have their headless horseman—we might as well have a good headless story, too, huh?" Aidan teased.

"Amy?" Jimmy teased.

"Sorry, sorry! Okay, around 1855, settlers began to encroach on the Seminole again, and what was known as the Third Seminole War began. More and more people were sent west. But three to six hundred remained deep in the Everglades, the only people never to surrender, the Unconquered! Because in 1858, the United States announced the end of hostilities against the Seminole," Amy concluded.

"Yeah, and we kind of lay low until the end of the 1900s, finally trading, selling crafts and all that. Then in 1957, we voted in a tribal constitution and established the federally recognized Seminole Tribe of Florida," Jimmy said. "And then…drumroll! We discovered gaming!"

"Eh, Jimmy! We're also the only tribe in America who never signed a peace treaty," Aidan told Hunter. "Well, with our brothers. The Miccosukee Tribe was recognized in 1962. Historically, not so long ago. About a third of Seminole people speak Muscogee or Creek, while many, like the Miccosukee, speak Creek or Mikasuki. We're close, by heritage, many by birth, but we have been recognized as separate tribes. We have reservations all over the state, and most people live in nice houses in housing tracts while some still live on what were old family camping grounds. We're still very proud of our native chickees."

Hunter smiled. It had been quite a history lesson. Also, a lesson in the fact that people were people—and it was great to be proud of one's background while respecting and accepting all others.

It was also amazing to have Jimmy, who knew the terrain so exceedingly well, and Aidan, so expert in so many ways, as determined as he and Amy were to discover the truth—and to end the horror that was taking place. The dead had so far been found on federal land and state land, but they all knew they might wind up anywhere within the great river of grass. But it didn't matter where they were found—the facts of what was happening were enough to sadden and infuriate them all.

He hadn't realized how far they had come, because it had been fun to listen to them chat about truth and fiction, tell the facts and stories, and tease one another.

Back at headquarters, he left Jimmy and Aidan at their cars and turned around.

"Should we check in?" Amy asked Hunter. "It is day again."

"A day when we're going to be the night crew. No. I promised Mickey I'd get you back to get some sleep, and Garza reminded me that while we may be on point on this, we have amazing teams behind us guarding people and talking to those we never get the time to interview."

He wasn't going to tell her about Reverend Ben MacDowell being missing.

Not until they'd had some sleep.

Because they just couldn't spend any more hours trailing through brush and swamps.

"No. We're going to sleep."

To his surprise, she didn't argue. She leaned back in the seat. By the time they reached their hotel, she was out. He parked, smiled, came around, and went to lift her out of the car. Of course, she awoke, cradled in his arms for a minute, and then squirmed to be set down.

And when they reached the room, she didn't just crash down again. She shed her clothing on the way to the shower and, as always, kept her Glock near her on the rear of the commode.

Sleep. They needed sleep.

But he joined her in the shower. And it was amazing how beautifully peaceful a spill of hot water in a field of mist could be.

Also...

How strangely exhilarating.

She wound up giggling. Playing with soap.

They became very—very—clean.

Falling into bed was much the same. The clean, cool sheets were sweet, inviting them to close their eyes, find rest from the day and the night that had become one.

And still the warmth of one another…

They made love. And then crashed into deep, sweet slumber.

And it wasn't until he felt Amy stir hours later, seeking her phone, that he awoke himself. And then both peace and excitement were at an end.

She was going to discover Reverend Ben MacDowell was on the loose—right when they had what they needed to place him under arrest.

"No!" Amy told Mickey over the phone. "They knew there was an entry to the depths of the Glades right behind the church. Why—"

"Amy! We had FBI and FDLE staking out the place, front and back. How the hell he escaped is something they've been investigating all day. And his picture is out everywhere. The news has been given the story and there is no way that—"

"We still can't even get Colin!" she said.

"That's in the works," he reminded her.

"But—"

"Amy, Frank Hamilton is out of the hospital. He and his family are in one of our safe houses, and he's grateful to be there and completely cooperative. Hunter said something to him the other day that has made him willing to do what's necessary to try to draw this Colin out. Again, we have images of him out everywhere."

"How can we keep him safe?" Amy murmured. "These people get drugs into everything."

"Mainly water, Amy."

"But we haven't discovered how he got the hallucinogens in the water at Frank Hamilton's the day Marc was kidnapped," Amy said.

Mickey was quiet for a minute.

"Mickey?" Amy said.

"Let's face it—someone who was in that house was guilty. But the house itself was searched after everyone was rushed to the hospital. Whoever had the drugs had them fully distributed into the water and coffee supplies—"

"Wait! Someone else *was* there. Whoever kidnapped Marc!" she said.

"Yes. But I don't think the drugging and kidnapping were crimes that were carried out by one person. We're keeping an eye on everyone, Amy—everyone who was in that house. Now, of course…thank God for the FBI. Because on our own, even with local assistance, we'd be spread too thin to protect all the young women, Elijah, Marty Benson, Hamilton and his family…"

"We must protect them. These people, this person, the frickin' Archangel! He seems able to get to anyone and we—"

"Amy, if you get too frustrated, I'm going to need to—"

"Okay, okay, I'm calm. And you know I must stay on this case, Mickey, I'm the one receiving the horses!"

"And you're the one targeted by this person or these people, too."

"Which means I need to be there. But…"

"But what?" Mickey asked her.

"When we get this thing going, I don't want to be at the rally as me. I want to see if Colin might come after me—or if I see him, I can go after him. If I can get him to trust me, I may be able to learn a great deal more about what is going on."

Mickey was quiet. "You're not to go anywhere with him. And you can pretend to drink something when you're with him, but—"

"Mickey! I'm not an idiot."

"No, and you're not a bad actress. But it will need to be played very, very carefully. You'll need to make sure your backup is solid as solid can be. You'll wear a mic—you'll be in contact."

"If I can find him, and if I can look different enough yet still natural."

"Somehow, I have faith. But we need to make sure that Frank Hamilton is fully on board with this plan. He is protected to the nth degree. I'm working on the venue. Of course, the state will help with that. I want it at a park in western Broward, close to Miccosukee and Seminole land so we have all our friends. You and Hunter get over to see Frank Hamilton."

"What about the women we found last night?" Amy asked.

"Amy, teamwork. I'm going to have our agent, Lyle Comer, and the FBI profiler, Eric Dayton, speaking with all of them today. Or with what's left of today. It's almost three. You and Hunter need to get over to see Frank Hamilton. He's our most important player. Oh, he's agreed to do a press release. He's written a speech. I've read it and approved it."

"He's going to speak and be seen on camera? So he's going to keep his campaign going?"

"As far as we know, he hasn't made any decisions. And I believe his campaign manager, Marty Benson, will be right there. Maybe when he gives his speech, his passion for creating a world in which civil speech and compromise rule may get him back into it. And maybe he'll have decided we're in a world where nothing he can do can stop some in power from squabbling like teenagers. I don't know—I just know he's going to help us, and that's what we need."

"All right," Amy said. "No problem. I really like him and his wife, and of course, I've a truly soft spot when it comes to Marc. But I'm telling you, that Reverend Ben MacDowell—"

"Amy, people who know the terrain are out there. We will find him."

"Right. We'll see Frank as soon as we can," she promised, ending the call and looking at Hunter.

She smiled. He had just finished a call as well. Mickey had given her the orders—even though she was officially still on loan to the FBI, and Charles Garza had just done the same with Hunter.

"We have our marching orders," Amy said.

Hunter nodded. "But coffee! I need coffee."

"Me, too. But we'd better hurry on out—we'll grab it to go."

They dressed quickly, and though it took her about five minutes to be ready, Amy paused, looking at her reflection.

Change. She needed to…change.

Dark, dark hair, maybe, and colored contacts…maybe a haircut, too? And younger clothing. Then maybe…

Hunter was behind her. He slipped his arms around her.

"If we do this thing where you try to draw out the mysterious Colin who recruits the young and beautiful, you pay attention to every word said in your ear and know it won't just be me behind you—a team will be there. And—no matter where you think you might get—you swear not to ditch your phone, your earpiece, or your mic."

"Hey! I don't have a death wish!" she assured him. She turned into his arms. "I promise! But I think it's something that might get us somewhere. And we may do all this—and our Colin may not show."

"And that's true. It's an elaborate plan, but…otherwise, we keep getting the little heads of a hydra and finding the bodies of those who disobeyed or failed!"

She nodded. "So, coffee for the road."

They did stop long enough at the restaurant downstairs to grab their coffees to go. Hunter suggested bagels, too; as he did so, his phone rang, and he excused himself.

"We don't need food!" he told her, ending his call. "Aubrey Hamilton has ordered a late lunch or early dinner and… Well, Frank has really agreed to do this."

"Sounds good to me," Amy said.

The safe house where Hamilton and his family were being kept was gated. It was one that allowed for no entry unless it was opened from within, and the gate was electrified as well.

Despite that, Amy could see there were cars just off the property edges—and an agent in plain clothes was seated on the porch reading a book with his legs stretched, just as if he was enjoying a beautiful blue Florida day when the sun was halfway down its journey to night.

The agent knew who they were and hit a button that allowed them in the gate. He smiled and indicated they should go on in.

"They're waiting for you," the young agent told them. "Hamilton wants to practice his speech on you."

"News people here yet?" Hunter asked him.

"No, we're recording without townsfolk. Then we'll let it out to various media. That's the way the bosses called it," he said with a shrug. "They don't want anyone—anyone at all, outside of law enforcement—knowing where the Hamilton family is now."

"Probably a good call," Amy said, thanking him and heading in.

They'd done a nice job getting a comfortable safe house for the Hamiltons. A door opened as they approached and Frank Hamilton himself stood there.

"Don't worry!" he told him. "I had a visual on you—my family is here. I obey every rule I've been given. Look before you leap. Man, this has been hard on me! I'm so accustomed to trusting people. I never wanted to believe in so much…hate."

"Sir, you do have to be careful to the ends of the earth!" Amy told him. "But I don't think you're wrong. After years in this, I still believe most human beings are decent people. Maybe you could remind them all of that!"

He grinned. "I intend to! That's why I wanted you to listen first."

"Our pleasure," Hunter assured him.

"Come in, come in!" Hamilton said. "We've got a buffet set up in the dining room—all brought in by the FBI!"

The entry led to a large and well-appointed room with tile flooring and comfortable, contemporary furnishings. Amy noted the room was rigged with cameras. If anything went wrong, it would be known immediately.

But she didn't think anything would happen to Hamilton or his family here. The Archangel was too clever to take chances. They knew how to be patient. And they knew how to use their lieutenants to seduce and charm and drug innocents into trouble to keep law enforcement running around.

Sabrina was there, hurrying over to meet them as they walked through to the dining room.

"Hey, Aidan told me you were out all night and into the morning. I'm glad you're here!" She lowered her voice. "Hamilton is only comfortable when you're around. He trusts you!"

"That's great," Hunter murmured.

They were all smiling as they entered the dining room. Aubrey and Marc were there, and Marc instantly ran over to give Amy a hug. She was a natural. She hugged him back, smiling, ruffling his hair, and telling him how good it was to see them.

"So, Sabrina," Hunter began.

"I'm doing the filming," she told him. "I was going to start earlier, but he really wanted to practice his speech on you, and Mickey wasn't going to wake you up until he figured you'd had enough sleep."

"Well, that was polite," Amy murmured. "But unnecessary!"

"Hey, come get a plate and I'll practice while you're eating!" Frank Hamilton told them.

Hunter saw Marty Benson come in from the kitchen. He smiled and nodded as if telling them he was glad to see them.

"All right!" Hunter said. He looked at Amy. They often got so busy working they forgot food—but this was work and food.

Aubrey insisted on walking them along the buffet, getting their plates, and then glasses of tea to drink. When they were seated, Marty Benson told Frank, "Hey, Frank, it's a great speech. I know you're thinking of not going back, but if it will help…"

"If it will help, I want to help," Frank said. "So!"

He stood at the head of the table, his notes in his hand and a smile on his face. He waved as if he was in front of the camera or a crowd, and began, "Friends, as you may or may not know, my home and campaign were attacked—my son was kidnapped by members of a strange group of people who claim to be working for the angels, trying to save souls from the Apocalypse. Thanks to the diligence of law enforcement, my son was returned to me. But as the media has shown you, this group is killing innocent people indiscriminately and leaving their bodies to be discovered in our precious and unique Florida Everglades. Please, think about this when you go to vote. If not for me, remember, please, vote for decency and civility, total equality, and total respect. And please, vote for someone who can talk to others, listen to others, and compromise. And, remember this—every group, every profession, every religion, every you-name-it out there has members who don't belong, members who don't understand common respect and decency for all.

"But I promise you this! We don't want to lose our police, our law enforcement. We want to learn how to cull out and remove those who abuse power, who abuse their badges in any way. I could not thank the police and state and federal agents more. Also, you need to know—we were attacked with a strange combination of drugs. Don't take a drink from strangers, and beware of anyone warning you the Apocalypse is coming. One day, maybe a thousand years from now, it will come, but sadly the warnings in the Book of Revelation have come again and again through the years, and there is no reason now to hurt others or ever to hurt yourselves! Thank you!"

Hunter and Amy clapped, as did the others.

"That was great. An explanation about all that's being speculated in the media and a warning," Hunter said.

"And it's you!" Aubrey said proudly.

"Then I'm good to go!" Frank told Sabrina.

"I've got the equipment set up in the office area here. Let's do it!" Sabrina said.

"And I'm good now! Eat—please enjoy the food!" Frank

Hamilton told them, hurrying to follow Sabrina out to the office to film his speech.

Marc asked Amy to play tic-tac-toe with him on his tablet. Amy naturally agreed, and Aubrey was drawn along with the two. Marty Benson came and took a seat across from Hunter.

He shook his head sadly and spoke a little above a whisper. "He won't do it. He's still saying he won't run. He won't risk his family again."

"That's going to be his choice," Hunter said.

"I know, but...what a platform. And I don't think he knows just how many people love him."

"Maybe not," Hunter said. He wondered what Benson was going to think about the event Mickey had talked Hamilton into doing while swearing he wouldn't mention it to anyone, not his closest friends, not his manager—not anyone.

Well, it would happen soon enough.

His phone rang, and he was glad to excuse himself to answer it.

Garza.

"All went well there?"

"Sabrina is getting it all down right now."

"Excellent. So. Time to head back to the wilds," Garza told him.

"Um, lots of wilds down here," Hunter reminded him.

"Head back to the area of the church. Call Aidan as you get down there. He may have you parking out there on the same dirt road where vehicles could find their closest access last night."

"But, Garza—" Hunter began, wondering just what more they could do in the wilderness by the church.

"No wild-goose chase," Garza promised him. "Aidan found something—and he is convinced he's on the trail of the good Reverend Benjamin MacDowell. And I want you with him."

13

"I must admit, I thought someone just hadn't been on the ball," Amy told Aidan when they met up with him.

Aidan was back in the area of the shack where they'd found the young women—and where one of Reverend Ben's parishioners had died while trying to prevent them from helping the women.

Aidan shook his head, smiling. "I have more faith in my fellow human beings."

"Oh, I didn't mean—" Amy began to protest, but Aidan laughingly interrupted her.

"It was a disappearing act. The land level here is way too low for a basement. As is much of the state. We have basements, but only if someone has built the land up first. When we're in the south, though, we do have what I call the almost-hills of Ocala. And you've got Britton Hill, the state's high point, 345 feet. Sorry, I digress. Here, though, we're way too close to the water level. But the church was built on pilings. There were no tunnels MacDowell could have used to escape. But I also knew the man couldn't just disappear. It took me forever. I came straight back here after about five hours of sleep. But since the agents and

officers out here swore they watched the front and the back—
and I knew a human being couldn't just disappear—I was determined. No tunnels—impossible. But that didn't mean there
might not be a crawl space. I finally found it—underneath the
altar. All he had to do was slip under the altar and come out
the side by the massive stand of trees, slide into the trees, move
like the snake he is, and…reach the back. No one was looking
for him to find a way over the fence, and when you look far
enough to the left of the property at the back of the house, even
the fence is half-hidden by trees. So… I followed his path. And
he was so proud of his disappearing act, he didn't do much to
hide his trail. There was rain this morning, so he left footprints
until he came here…found it not to his liking, and moved on."

"Did he leave clues or a trail going forward?" Hunter asked
him.

"That I'm still researching. And I can use some help."

"We want to help!" Amy assured him. "But you know that—"

"We're not going to analyze blood spatter or search for trace
evidence," Aidan assured them, grinning as he looked from Amy
to Hunter. "I'm going to show you his prints as they approached
this place, and we're all going to take anything that looks like
an animal trail or even a crawl through to an animal trail and
follow where he led. He came here because he wanted to see
what was going on. And I am sure he watched and he bided his
time. The forensic crew finished up here by noon. The tape remains, but a man like Reverend Ben would know if there were
still vehicles or officers in the area. He wouldn't have minded
keeping watch for a while, because he'd know everyone would
believe he had managed to disappear—and might be as far away
as somewhere in the northeast by now if he had a lackey with
a private plane."

"You don't think, Aidan, that he might have—"

"Yes, he might have a vehicle somewhere, but his picture is
everywhere. I think he's lying low because he knows something

else will happen that will divert attention from him and give him a better opportunity to escape to a place far, far away—maybe as far as a Pacific island. What do you two think?"

Amy looked at Hunter. "If I was guessing, I would lie as low as possible right now. He would know FDLE, highway patrol, local cops, and FBI could only patrol the roads with a fine-tooth comb so long. He is clever—he would wait. I think."

Hunter nodded. "All right. So, Aidan..."

"Come on," he told them.

They'd been standing in the cabin with the now broken window. It was so empty. The women had been left poor cots and nothing more.

No blankets, sheets, or pillows.

Just pallets to lie on.

"No food or anything here," Amy commented. "How long could he hold out without dying of hunger and thirst?"

"I have a feeling this man will know what water is safe to drink out here." He grinned. "You forget—my people learned to live out here very well as they escaped the encroaching settlers by moving deeper and deeper into the Glades."

"Okay, true," Amy said, smiling.

"But that was before computers, cell phones, regular phones, grocery delivery...even TV and electricity," Aidan said, grinning. "Still, I have a feeling this man knows what he's doing out here. Maybe he was a Boy Scout before he went online to get ordained for this Apocalypse thing. And if he isn't the Archangel, maybe he even believes half his own rhetoric. Anyway..."

"Let's see the prints we're supposed to be finding. Hey, wouldn't it be a good idea to get dogs out here?"

"He would hear them. We're going to need to do this quietly," Aidan said.

"All right. But Amy and I just walked here—"

"His prints are different and deep enough. You'll see. Follow me."

They did. Once they were out of the cabin, Aidan directed them to a very narrow path—somewhat broadened by the human traffic of the night before—that led from the rear of the church. "This is how I know he came here," Aidan said. "His feet are larger than yours, Amy, but smaller than yours, Hunter. He's wearing rubber-soled boots, much like what you have on, but you can see the tread is different. Also, look for bits of fabric or even hair. You can get snagged on a lot of the branches out here."

"Got it," Hunter said.

Amy nodded. "I think I need to look closer than Aidan, but I can see the differences. I'm not sure all the paths will be damp enough, and when there is a lot of brush on the ground..."

Aidan smiled. "You're going to be fine."

"Shouldn't you have asked Mickey to send a team back out—" Amy began, but Aidan interrupted her again quickly.

"I know you and Hunter know how to move—without sounding like a stampede. Hunter, you and Jimmy found more bodies last night. Not that far from here. I believe there's another of their human stash houses somewhere near here."

"Great—let's see if the footprints from the shack may lead in that direction."

They did. Hunter led the way to the animal trail he and Jimmy had followed the night before, and Aidan hunkered low to study the ground.

He looked up at the two of them. "We don't need to divide and conquer. This is the path he took, Hunter, though I don't believe it will lead directly to the bodies." He hesitated a minute and then shrugged. "They weren't left far from an embankment. I wasn't there, but I saw the crime scene photos that were taken before the bodies were moved to the morgue. I believe in that case, they were left where they were left because the killer—or killers—believed they'd be consumed by alligators, vultures, other creatures, and insects."

"They didn't need to be found," Hunter said thoughtfully.

"Sabrina found the online connection regarding some of the dead with the church. I'm not so sure that was supposed to be discovered, either, because whatever the grand scheme might be, someone was being entertained by convincing young women they needed to serve the angels in their earthly forms," Aidan said.

"And you may well be right—except some weren't all so happy. Sometimes, all the drugs in the world won't mess with a moral code you've been taught through your lifetime," Amy said softly. "Let's find this monster. Hopefully," she said.

"Be positive," Hunter responded.

She smiled. "I think Aidan should lead."

"I will not argue with that," Hunter assured her.

Aidan moved ahead.

"You know, we really need to stop doing this once night is falling!" she said.

"Best time to move furtively," Aidan said.

"And I'm sure all the coral snakes and their friends know that, too!" she told him.

But they still had some daylight, and they were all equipped with their flashlights. But in the denseness of the trees, darkness could be overwhelming. They passed a massive field of saw grass, skirted the embankment of a mangrove swamp, and paused as Aidan searched the ground again.

"Yes!" he whispered.

"Just ahead and to the left," Hunter said. "That's where we found the bodies."

"Then the old shack is near here, somewhere. And Reverend Ben would know that..." Aidan began.

"That the recent inhabitants were dead—since he's quite possibly the one who killed them?" Hunter asked.

"Right," Aidan said simply. He paused again, hunkering down. Amy and Hunter waited. Aidan searched in a few directions and then nodded to an angle just to the east.

He started walking and they followed again.

Amy was between the two men on a very narrow, overgrown path. She paused, careful not to catch her foot on a vine, and then looked up.

"Aidan!" she whispered.

He stopped. She almost plowed into him.

"It's there!" she whispered. "Aidan, you knew it was going to be there."

"I theorized," he murmured, looking back at Hunter. "How do you want to play this?"

"Let's get a little closer," Hunter suggested.

They moved slowly forward.

"The footprints led here," Hunter said. "And you believe he's still in there?"

"I do," Aidan told him. "So, do we barge in with guns out, sneak around, or...?"

"This one has the windows boarded as well. It's just plywood, but we can't see anything unless we break through it."

"Just...barge in?" Amy suggested.

"He's probably armed, but if he doesn't know we're coming, we should be able to take him. He won't be expecting us," Hunter said. "We could wait forever for him to come out, and it's starting to get very dark, so..."

"Wait!" Amy said.

"What?" Hunter asked.

"The other shacks had padlocks on the doors. Can you see if there is such a thing on this one?"

"There won't be—not if Reverend Ben is inside," Hunter said.

"Of course," she murmured. "But..."

"First one will check and give a sign to the others," Hunter said. "We should move."

"Yeah, I don't really feel like sleeping out here—even if my ancestors did," Aidan said dryly. "So, which—"

"Amy left, Aidan right, I'll take center and shatter the door.

Careful moving up—one at a time, quietly. The good thing is that while we can't see in, it might be darned hard for him to see out."

The sky wasn't fully dark, but the moon was up, and the stars were beginning to dot the sky. Amy winced, thinking it was an oddly beautiful night.

Aidan silently moved first as he made his way through the last of the trees, then to the sparse clearing, an area still overgrown but devoid of any trees that might hide his approach.

He went flat against the wall, studied the door, and turned to sign to them.

There was no padlock on the door. Of course, there wouldn't be. Not if Aidan's theory was correct and Reverend Ben was using the place as his hideout.

Hunter glanced at her, nodding.

Amy followed Aidan, quietly stepping through the last of their cover, then sprinting toward the shack and taking her position.

Then they joined Hunter right in front of the door. He nodded to the two of them, aimed his Glock, and took a step back, gathering his strength and stance to give the door such a solid kick that it shattered inward.

And he was there.

This shack was different, outfitted with a cot and a massive upholstered chair.

The Reverend Benjamin MacDowell sat in the chair, not quite as unprepared as they had thought; he had a gun on the armrest and reached for it as they burst in.

"Don't do it!" Hunter warned.

But MacDowell went for it. Hunter blasted him in the arm, and he screamed as his bones shattered and the gun went flying across the floor.

"You're under arrest!" Hunter told him.

Then MacDowell went a little crazy, screaming and crying at the same time. "You have no authority over me! Only the

Archangel has authority. And you will learn that, you will learn that sinners such as yourselves must truly pay. Just as I am in pain now, you will suffer with far greater agony as, bit by bit, your flesh is torn, and your blood is shed, and you burn and burn and burn and…"

"What a crock!" Hunter said.

Still wincing with pain and half sobbing, the man also began to laugh. "But it's good, right, so good, such a line, and so many believe it! There is no hereafter, there is only this. And when the old Archangel has his way, I will be freed—and you will pay for this heinous injury you have done to me!" he announced.

"What?" Amy demanded, stepping closer but—despite his injury—keeping her Glock trained on him. "You don't even believe there is a hereafter?"

"What an idiot! And all those people, so many people!" He laughed and sobbed harder, not able to speak again for several seconds. "They believe you are a whore—or a special whore— the thing of the Antichrist. And you—Mr. Special Agent Hunter Forrest—you don't rate being the Antichrist. They don't know the Antichrist's earthly presence—they just know she needs to suffer, suffer, suffer. And you will suffer because the Archangel is the smartest, most cunning, intelligent, and capable human being—"

"And you'll tell us who they are," Hunter said flatly.

"No, never."

"If it makes the difference between lethal injection and life?" Aidan asked.

"I will never stay in jail! Besides, I can't tell you. I don't know who he is. He is smart enough to keep his identity entirely secret. So you see, you could torture me again and again, and it would do you no good. Except, of course, you can't torture me. You're the good lawman. Now, him—and that handmaiden there to the devil—I think they'd like to rip my eyes out right now. Oh, she's so indignant about what was done to the other whores—"

"Children! Almost all of them shy of their eighteenth birth-days!" Amy snapped. "The only way you can feel powerful is by drugging poor deluded girls who are looking for something good in life. To get you! Oh, vomit!"

"Police brutality!" he suddenly raged. "You're letting me bleed to death. I will tell all of this in court. You will be in trouble. But it won't matter if I go to jail."

"If it won't matter, why do people kill themselves, fearing they've failed?" Aidan asked him.

Again, he started to laugh, his laughter catching on a sob now and then. "They are nothing! They are worthless! Let them die thinking there's something greater! I'm a man of importance. I fulfilled a wonderful assignment for him, and I will be rewarded! Oh, sorry, not with angels, just here on earth. But so help me, you'd better fix my arm!"

Hunter strode over to him, pulling him up by his good arm. "We'll get you to medical attention. That's something you should have thought about, drawing on an armed agent when you were in the middle of the wilderness."

"Do something! Brutality, brutality! You will all be out, agents, cops. You'll all be gone, and he will see to it his people rule, and they will rule with force! I will be fine, you wait and see. Oh, I can't wait for the day—and it is coming!"

Amy walked to the cot, took the sheet off it, and ripped it into a form of bandage, joining Hunter by Benjamin MacDow-ell and looking at his arm. A bone was broken, she thought, so she was careful as she wound her improvised bandaging around it. Aidan helped without being asked, finding a slat from the shattered door that could serve as a splint.

As she worked on his arm she demanded, "Who is Colin and where the hell is he?"

Again, he just laughed. "I don't know!"

"Yes, you do. Colin brought those young women to you," Amy said. "The ones you kept—and the ones you killed."

"To me? I don't know anything about those young women."

"Really?" Hunter said. "Hmm. There's this thing called DNA. And they'll be doing rape kits on all those poor young things you brutalized."

"I did nothing!" he raged. "You'll never get Colin. But I don't know him, I did nothing!"

"DNA," Amy said simply.

Between her and Aidan, they had the blood stopped; the arm, though in an awkward position, was splinted so that bone didn't rub on bone.

"Well, whatever happens in the future, tonight you're going to jail."

Amy looked at him. So far, all the victims—and Elijah and the horribly drugged young woman who Hunter had caught right before the fire—had been brought to the same hospital.

But they didn't think either Elijah or "unstable-lady" had killed anyone.

And they knew MacDowell was, at the very least, guilty of kidnapping and rape.

"They have medical care—in fact, it's just great. The federal government will pick up the tab. We'll take him to the federal facility closest to the hospital," Hunter said. "We'll put a call through to Mickey and Garza."

"I'm on that!" Aidan assured them, stepping out ahead as the two of them dragged Benjamin MacDowell to the door.

He ranted and spewed vile promises the entire way, sobbing and intermittently laughing, assuring them he'd beat them in court, but that wouldn't matter. If he went to jail, it wouldn't be for long.

"Not true. Maybe the needle, maybe you'll rot in a federal prison for life," Hunter assured him.

Slowly, slowly, slowly, and painfully, half dragging, half leading MacDowell over the terrain, they made their way at last to the car.

But when they reached the road, they discovered they were about to be relieved of their burden.

Apparently, Mickey and/or Garza had sent out an ambulance along with a pair of agents.

As soon as Benjamin MacDowell saw them, he began to scream in pain while blurting out his accusations.

"I did nothing, nothing at all! They burst in on me and they shot me. I was surrendering to whatever crazy thing they had in their heads, and they just shot me. They tortured me, they left me bleeding and in agony!" he ranted. "They had no right, I offered them nothing but peace and goodness. I rescued those who were down and out and on the streets! They had no right, no right, no right! I want a lawyer. I want a lawyer now!"

"Wow," one of the agents said, "and here we thought you might want some medical care first!"

Amy wondered if she was growing paranoid, but she couldn't help but wonder if they were real—if they worked for the FBI, or if…

If they were also minions of the Archangel.

"Good to see you, Hunter," one of them got in.

"You, too, Ezra. You can take over the care of the prisoner," Hunter replied.

Amy lowered her head, smiling slightly. Hunter knew them. They were good.

"Special Agent Amy Larson, good to meet you. Though I wish we were in better circumstances! Aidan Cypress, we've heard you're a magic man, and I think you've proven it tonight," Ezra said. "Oh, Hunter, Amy, Aidan, my partner here is Special Agent Armand Lester, and we promise you, we won't be letting him out of sight! Oh, Amy, sorry, my last name is Smithson."

Amy nodded in acknowledgment to the introduction. It was about all that she could do.

MacDowell was still fighting and screaming.

"You'll pay, you will all pay, I will not forget! You will pay, you will pay..."

"Buddy, you want your arm treated or not?" Ezra asked as he and Armand got into the ambulance and strapped MacDowell down before turning him over to the medics who had come.

"Brutality! Brutality, brutality! You wait, you will pay and then you will pay again and again and again!" MacDowell raged.

"Don't worry—I'll be riding with them," Ezra promised. "Oh, from Mickey Hampton and Charles Garza. Please get some sleep while it's night. Important you're rested and alert tomorrow!"

Amy looked at Hunter.

Did that mean Mickey and Garza had spoken with Frank Hamilton?

Was the rally being planned, and...?

Once it was planned, how did a man like Frank Hamilton keep it from his campaign personnel before it happened? Because it still seemed someone working on that campaign had to have gotten the drugs into the water and coffee.

She lifted a hand and waved to the driver, then the ambulance carrying MacDowell and Ezra Smithson and Armand Lester pulled away.

When they were gone, Aidan turned to Hunter and Amy.

"I heard Frank Hamilton sent out a message to the media—it's being shown on cable and network TV all over the country. And apparently, he's loved but not by fanatics on either side. But his message has made a huge impression. And his warning to people! Maybe it will help," he said. "Forgot to tell you earlier that I pulled it up on my phone. Good job, guys."

"We didn't have anything to do with it, really," Hunter told him. "He wrote the speech. And the thing about him is he seems like the real deal."

"He does," Aidan agreed, but he frowned, looking at Hunter.

"And you're thinking he's so good he can't be for real?" Amy asked.

"It occurred to me. It's probably occurred to all of us at one time or another. We can't help it due to the nature of the way we live and work. I hope he's real. I like him," Aidan said.

"And," Amy said thoughtfully, "if people are actually being careful, it will make it easier for me to find the mysterious Colin. It will be more difficult for him to find someone who is either disenfranchised or ready to believe in the Apocalypse or..."

"It could help," Aidan agreed. "Anyway, we'll all find out tomorrow." He laughed. "I'm definitely putting in for overtime! Anyway, my car is just down there—"

"We can drive you to your car," Hunter told him.

"It's fifty feet—"

"Yeah, yeah, and it's been a long day for all of us. Get in!" Amy told him.

They dropped Aidan at his car. As they did so, Amy rolled her window down and called to him.

"Aidan!"

"Yeah?"

"Thank you! You are incredible. I wanted him locked up so badly!" she said.

Aidan smiled. "Yeah. Me, too. Good night. He won't be charming, coercing, or forcing anyone else into anything, ever again!"

Amy smiled and waved. She leaned back in her seat.

"You're actually smiling and almost resting," Hunter said.

She turned to him. "I think we really took a demon off the street."

"Yes. Now," Hunter said, "we just have to find Satan himself!"

14

Mickey and Garza were working together in a completely coordinated way, Hunter thought. Somewhat unusual, because once the FBI stepped in on something, they were happy for local help, but always took the lead.

Hunter awoke after a surprisingly good night—a somewhat normal night. They reached the hotel by nine, had dinner sent up by nine thirty, laughed their way through the shower and into bed, and savored every moment until sleep. They'd lain together talking for a while, with Amy telling him she did want to be married in a church.

"After all this?" he had asked her.

"Marriage by a justice of the peace or a clerk or notary public is a contract," she'd told him. "Love isn't just a contract, although contracts protect families and children, widows and widowers." She'd rolled over to crawl up on his chest, looking down at him seriously. "I still believe in God, in the beauty of the earth and people!" She smiled. "And sometimes, I know that He—or She—believes in us! Okay, so the people we care about, a church...and then the honeymoon!"

"And where would you like to go? Ireland, Scotland, Norway, or somewhere more exotic like Transylvania?"

She laughed. "I love Ireland, Scotland, and Norway. And I'd love to get to Transylvania. But no, I love beaches. Maybe some great resort somewhere—a reasonable one, of course, since we're government employees—but with a private wave pool, sunshine, room service—"

And he'd interrupted her, laughing. "Hmm. We are government employees. I'll talk to Aidan again about one of those incredibly special rooms we were asked so rudely to leave!"

And so they'd laughed and the night had been good. But he had been left to wonder what they were going to do when the case ended, when she was based in Orlando, Florida, and his main office was back in DC.

For the moment, none of that mattered. He'd awakened to the summons from Garza for them both to head straight to headquarters. As they'd gotten ready, he'd found himself stopping; they'd had the TV on for background noise and the news came on.

"It's not just Florida!" he'd said as Amy came to stand behind him, resting her hands on his shoulders as they watched.

Police were investigating, but there had been no arrests so far in three mass murders discovered in the wee hours of the morning—eight bodies near Yellowstone National Park, four near Bar Harbor, Maine, and seven just outside of Savannah, Georgia.

No details were currently being given out. Next of kin needed to be notified, and of course, the incidents remained under investigation. However, hotlines were available for people with any information, which the police in each jurisdiction would greatly appreciate. In Maine, a reward had been raised for information leading to the arrest of the guilty and it was expected that other rewards would soon be announced. The anchor ended the news piece with the information that the FBI would be coming in to assist due to the mass nature of the killings.

"I know why we're going to headquarters," he muttered.

"Are Mickey and Garza planning on sending us off to investigate?" Amy wondered. "And if so, which location? Is this all... part of the same plan? It is, don't you think? And whoever this is wants us scuttling all about. It's all part of the Archangel's great Apocalypse plan."

"I agree," he said. "Let's move—and find out what Mickey and Garza are thinking. Because it sounded to me last night as if we're ready to go with Frank Hamilton's public appearance— if so, we need to be there."

"Well, I think it's going to depend," Amy said.

"On what?"

"On whether or not little pale horses were found along with any of the bodies."

He nodded. "Still...this thing needs to be played through to the end."

They left the hotel and drove to headquarters, arriving right before eight only to discover Mickey and Garza were there already, deep in conversation in the office.

Amy tapped on the window, and both men looked up and beckoned them on in.

"Take your seats," Garza told them from behind his desk. "I'm going to assume you know what's happened around the country?"

"We saw the news," Hunter said.

"Were there any little horses found at the sites?" Amy asked, frowning.

"Yes. But more than horses," Garza told them.

"There was a piece of paper stuffed into the mouth of one of the dead men," Mickey said. "There was a picture on it, Amy. A picture of you and just two words—'Satan's concubine.' Of course, the paper is being analyzed, they're looking for prints, DNA...but we know that whoever is doing this is smart enough to make sure gloves are worn... There's got to be a mistake made somewhere, but the mistake that will get us to the end of this thing hasn't been made yet."

"Amy," Garza said, "we're offering you the opportunity to get off the case—with the full protection of the state of Florida and the federal government."

Hunter watched Amy give them a grim smile and shake her head. "You're not forcing me off, are you?"

Mickey and Garza looked at each other and then at her, shaking their heads. "No. But the offer of protection stands," Mickey said.

She leaned forward, speaking earnestly. "I believe I'm in a similar position to the one Frank Hamilton is in. We're both in danger until this thing comes to an end. I also believe my involvement in the case is something that is annoying whoever this Archangel is. He—she or they—wants to taunt us all as evidenced by all the little toy horses we've received. And sure, I think someone would love to see me tortured and dead, but I also believe I'm working with the finest team of law enforcement to be found anywhere, and at some point I may just be the key to all this being solved."

Again, Mickey and Garza looked at one another.

"Hunter, you're all right with this?" Mickey asked.

"I'm not Amy's boss," he said. "She's an intelligent and capable agent, and I respect her right to make her own decisions. I also believe she's key to putting an end to all these atrocities. Is she in danger? Yes. But we're all in danger every day we go out there. And neither she nor many, many others will be safe until this situation ends and the Archangel finally rots in prison."

"Call me bloodthirsty, I hope he gets the needle," Garza said. "This person could be dangerous from anywhere. Oh, person or persons. But I had a long talk last night with our profiler, Eric Dayton, and we pulled in others from the DC offices. The general conception is that there is one—just one—man at the head of all this. And we all know the game. Others are drawn in by two main concepts—fear and greed. Except, in this case, it often begins with preying upon the good and naive, then adding drugs to the format. All right. We're all aware of the latest circumstances."

"Are you sending us—" Amy began.

"No," Garza insisted. "We're not sending you to any of the sites, not now. Because we do have our planned live speech going on this evening. In about thirty minutes, the media will be announcing that Frank Hamilton will be addressing any who want to hear him speak about the things that have been going on—and how he plans to run for better things in the future."

"Is that enough time for people to make plans to hear him?" Hunter asked.

"We don't care," Garza said. "We only want one person to arrive. Our mysterious Colin. After the arrest last night, Eric Dayton spent hours with Reverend Benjamin MacDowell. In that instance, we were looking at coercion through greed. The Archangel saw to it he got a supposed church, and he had young women delivered to him on a regular basis. He had money, drugs for himself—and power. But Eric is convinced he really doesn't know who the Archangel is."

"But he does know who Colin is. Colin delivered the girls," Hunter said.

"Yes," Garza said. "But all he knows is what we know. He finally got so tired speaking with Eric, he agreed the picture of Colin done by our sketch artist is a good likeness. Eric doesn't have a last name that MacDowell knows, nor an address."

"You don't need to worry about MacDowell being back on the streets. That man did make mistakes. His DNA is all over the shack, the girls—and three of the dead," Mickey said.

"At least he's off the streets," Amy murmured. "What time is the speech, rally, whatever we're calling it?"

"He is a heck of a politician," Garza said. "Sent out a well-spoken notice on social media a few minutes ago, and the media all over is picking it up. The speech is tonight at the state park. We've been working on logistics for a while now. Plenty of room for our vans with cameras, everyone will be connected, and room for protection for Hamilton. We are not bringing his family out. They'll remain guarded at the safe house. There's space for conversation. Amy, we're not sure—"

"I am," Amy assured him. "But…did we get anything else from the young women who were taken from the shack?"

Mickey shook his head. "Even the young woman who was so convinced they were doing what was required of them to prepare for the Apocalypse has come around. According to the doctors, they pretty much got their hands on her just in time. The number of drugs in her system was beginning to play havoc with her organs. But she's calmed down and still can't tell us anything the others didn't. They met a man named Colin. Next, he took them to church so they could survive with the angels. There were others who came out to the cabins, but in the dark they never knew who, and it was only a few men."

"Let's really hope Colin is out there. But if anyone in Frank Hamilton's campaign knows about the setup, and they were guilty of spiking the water and coffee…" Amy began.

"No one. No one at all knows this is a setup. I spoke long and hard with the man—he insisted he tell his campaign manager and staff and I said definitely not. I believe he's an honest man," Garza said.

"Unless he was the one who did this himself," Hunter suggested quietly.

"Do you believe that?" Garza asked him.

"No. But I don't ignore the possibility, either," Hunter said.

"All right, then. We're having signs made up for the two of you. You know, the kind carried at rallies supporting the best in mankind, demanding people learn to behave civilly. Obviously, you'll need to separate. Hunter, there will be five of you assigned just to see that Amy isn't shot in the middle of the crowd or drawn away somewhere. We'll have FDLE and FBI as human shields for Frank Hamilton, all in their vests, of course—but the agents in the crowd are going to be responsible for seeing to it that no fanatics with guns are anywhere close. Also, water to the park will be delivered by the FBI," he added. "We have taken every possible precaution. Local law enforcement is aware and ready to engage. We have spent hours on this and we believe we have covered every base."

"Time to get ready," Amy said, rising.

Hunter stood, too. "You have a makeup artist in mind?" he asked. "Sabrina could help."

"She could, but I was thinking of someone else."

"Yeah, who?"

"Me!"

"Okay. Hmm. Not that I don't have faith in you, but I think Sabrina might add a few good touches that are necessary under the dangerous circumstances."

"If you insist. Still, we need a drugstore," Amy reassured him.

"Amy," Mickey said. "We have people who work with the undercover team—"

"Come on, Mickey!" Amy said, smiling. "I've worked undercover. Undercover work really requires you take on a persona more than a changed appearance, because you have to live whatever look you choose every day and make it real. Honestly, I've thought about this, and I know what I'm doing. And I agreed, Sabrina can help. But I know what to buy for her, really."

"A wig," Garza murmured. "That can—"

"Fall off. Trust me! I know what I'm going to do. I've been planning this," she assured them. "Hunter?"

"Onward, if that's all for now," Hunter said to Mickey and Garza.

But before they could leave, there was a tap at the door.

It was Aidan, and Mickey motioned to him he should come on in.

"First, of course, we've now been analyzing responses to Frank

Hamilton's message about his speech tonight. And the response is overwhelming. The man is admired from near and far. People who are wishing they lived closer, people proclaiming he's the answer to all the hatred in the world. We've only found a few negative responses, and we're tracking them down now."

"Good. We'll have agents out as soon as you've gotten anything for us."

"The whole team is working, sir—we will have information shortly. But that's not why I'm here."

"Oh?" Mickey asked.

"I want to be out there tonight—I want to be at the rally."

"Technically, Aidan, you're off at night, you know," Mickey reminded him.

Aidan shook his head. "I want to carry my Glock in and be part of the team. Please. I've been in the field many times now and—"

"Aidan, stop," Mickey said.

"But, sir—"

"Aidan, yes, you may be part of the team," Mickey told him.

"Oh, great, thank you!" Aidan said. He glanced at Hunter and Amy.

"Glad to have you there," Hunter assured him. He looked at Mickey, shaking his head. "This is all going with the speed of a bullet. We went out to the church. I'm sure we'd have been informed if anything important had been learned. But what about the woman who was in the woods—who shot at us right before the fire started after Amy and Aidan found Hamilton's boy?"

"Nothing," Mickey said quietly. "Nothing at all. It's as if someone erased her memory. She doesn't even remember being in the woods, and she doesn't know her name. We have people working with her—she's on suicide watch."

Hunter shook his head again. "I wonder if she's ever going to be all right. Okay. So. We're going to head out. Going to the drugstore," he added dryly.

They left. Amy was quiet. Thoughtful.

"You don't have to do this," he told her.

"No, no, I want to do this. I want to be everywhere, that's the problem. I'd like to speak with Elijah again, I'd like to make sure Aubrey and Marc Hamilton are okay, I want to…"

"To head to Yellowstone?" he asked.

"That one is really on the back burner. I want to guarantee Frank Hamilton won't wind up a casualty, and we know we can never give out guarantees and promises."

"Amy, we work with incredible people," he reminded her.

"What about a sniper?" she asked.

"If I know Garza, he's thoroughly judged the area and made sure there's nowhere anywhere near Hamilton where a sniper could get into a position to take a shot. And there will be metal detectors. The FBI will be the only people handling the water—which, if I know Garza, is being brought in by agents from the northwest of the state, not from any local markets."

"Okay, so…hair dye!"

"She's going to want a few funky colors. A few streaks here and there."

They headed from headquarters toward a drugstore Amy knew, one that offered an entire beauty supply section.

"Okay, hmm," Amy said. "I've aways thought pitch-black hair with a few blues in it would be cool!"

"I'm only along for the ride," he said.

"Don't be. You find me the dye I'll need for the blue streaks. I'm going for the makeup. I'm going with a darker shade of base and maybe some blue shadows… Grab the hair color. I'll work on the rest."

"Uh, all right."

Amy headed into one of the makeup aisles, picking up pieces here and there while he walked along rows of hair color.

He hadn't ever chosen a color from a box before, but he figured it couldn't be too hard.

Of course, he didn't know if he'd find what she wanted, but

she'd sent him on the mission so he did his best. Dark. Dark, dark, dark was what she wanted. He knew nothing about the brands.

That meant…

He looked for something blue—a bit harder for him than any regular color, but he found something that advertised streaking and figured that had to be what she wanted.

Amy was already headed for the checkout. He joined her.

"You know, it's early," he told her. "How long is your transformation going to take?"

"Maybe an hour or so," she told him. "With Sabrina on it, it will be fast."

"We can't fly anywhere with the time we have, but if you want to stop by and see Elijah or the Hamilton family, maybe see how things are going over there—"

"Hunter!" she said. "Brilliant. First, I'd like to check on the Hamilton family. Then, Mickey will have talked to Sabrina, and between us, we'll do our best at transformation, and then we'll see Elijah."

"After the transformation."

"He's still in the hospital and under guard for his own protection. They haven't moved him yet. And since he knows he needs the protection, he's not saying anything like arrest me or let me go. He has no computer or cell phone, so he won't be telling anybody about anything. So?"

"Annabel will be there. And she has a cell phone and comes and goes."

"I don't think she 'goes.' We can check, but I'm willing to bet she's stayed with him the entire time since we brought her to him."

"Okay. But I honestly believe Elijah has told us everything he can."

"It's not that—I believe he has, too. But I want to know if he attracted Colin by doing anything special or unusual."

"Okay, time to check on the Hamilton family," Hunter agreed. "That must be done first."

"Agreed."

They paid for Amy's makeover items and headed out to the SUV and drove on to the Hamilton safe house.

Again there was a different agent on guard. This one was dressed casually in shorts and a tank top and sat on the porch pretending to soak in the warm air with a baseball cap covering his eyes.

He saw them immediately and stood, pretending they were just friends coming to see him.

They walked through the gate and to the house, and Frank Hamilton let them in, pleased—nervous—and ready to welcome them.

"Well, it's out there, everyone knows," he said.

"And you're still sure you want to do this?" Amy asked him.

Marty Benson came out from the kitchen, shaking his head. "I'm just not so sure this is wise. I've been advising Frank against doing this—"

Aubrey, following him out, argued against Marty's point. "Marty, please! Frank knows what he's doing, the FBI and the Florida law enforcement people would never put him into danger."

"They are putting him into danger!" Marty said worriedly.

"Marty!" Aubrey continued. "People need to see that good men will not be put down according to the whim of tyrants! I have faith in these people—you must, too!"

Frank looked at Marty. "Okay, my friend, I love you for caring so much. But you've gotten out of here a few times. No one is trying to kill you or threatening your family. We don't want to live like this for the rest of our lives. And we don't want this for others. Oh my God! The news today. It was here, and now it's everywhere. That's the way of tyrants, of people with a God complex. They don't stop, Marty—they don't stop unless they're forced to stop."

"We want you to know we'll be there and we've made sure if anyone goes near you, they will quickly—and quietly—be escorted away," Hunter said.

Frank actually managed to smile at that. "Well, when I speak to a crowd, people are near me."

Hunter grinned in return. "Metal detectors will be used extensively, and I promise you, the crowd is peppered with agents. Marty, we will be watching like hawks."

"Of course, of course, it's just that men like Frank don't come along all that often," Marty said.

They hadn't noticed Marc at first, peeking around the door frame from the dining room.

"Marc!" Amy said.

He ran to her, and immediately huddled against her. He was ten—old enough to know something was going on, something that was contentious.

"Marc!"

Amy unwound herself and stooped down to be on a level with him. "Everything is going to be okay. Dad is going to be out for a while, but your mom will be here. We'll see to it that he comes home safe and sound. You were so brave out in that shack, Marc! So amazing. And we need you to keep being brave for a while. You have to watch out for your mom tonight. Can you do that?"

He nodded. Aubrey reached out for him, and he raced over to his mother.

"We're going to be fine," Aubrey said determinedly. "It's not just our lives. It's the lives of so, so many others if this situation keeps going on!"

"You people are the best," Hunter said. "We've got to get going—we just wanted to check in on you and make sure you were feeling all right about everything."

"I'm not," Marty said.

"And I'm sorry!" Amy said, wincing. "But at this moment—"

"Yeah, yeah, I'm not the one who matters. But I'll be there. Ready to throw myself in front of this man—his ethics cannot be lost!"

"And they won't be," Hunter said. "So, we'll see you there."

They left the safe house.

Amy looked at him, questioning something in his expression.

"I don't know. I'm not so sure I like all of this myself. I can't help but think someone in Hamilton's campaign circle is…"

"The Archangel?" Amy queried.

"I don't know. But I'd like to get into their computers again."

"Hunter, the computers were torn apart by our analysts—both our analysts. Anything even slightly out of the ordinary was checked and rechecked."

"I know. But we don't know what's gone on since then."

"We can have a team go over and see if anything has come into or out of the house," Amy said.

He nodded. "We can do that. In fact…" He grimaced.

"You're driving. I'll do the talking," she said.

And as she had promised, she put through a call to Mickey, who liked the idea of a check right before the speech.

"On their way," she assured Hunter.

They reached the hotel. He smiled, noting a few young field agents he'd worked with before. One agent was pretending to be on the phone by his car in the parking lot; another was in the lobby drinking coffee.

"Mickey is watching out for you," he told her.

"I'm going to be fine!" she promised. "And I'm about to become a few years younger with fetching, funky hair!"

"I can't wait," he said dryly. "Meanwhile—"

"You're taking a nap?" she suggested.

"Sure. Right."

She laughed at him. Of course, she knew he would be doing anything but.

She just might get away with it, Amy thought.

Adding the blue streaks to her hair—a cosplay touch of fun and edge—did make a remarkable change in her look even while her hair was dripping wet. Sabrina, who had applied the blue, grinned. Amy halfway dried it, then paused, cutting little wisps of hair around her face rather than bangs, hoping she might have a greater look of naivete with the softer hairstyle.

She thought it worked. And when her hair was fully dried, the new little wisps did fluff about her face, giving her a more youthful appearance.

"Terrific," she told Sabrina.

Sabrina grinned. "I'll make a sweet kid out of you yet!"

Amy winced. "Too late for that!" she said lightly.

Then the makeup. She was usually far too pale even for a Floridian. But she'd purchased a good foundation, and Sabrina knew how to perfectly apply it. And then blue eye shadow and dark eyeliner. Then finally brown contact lenses.

Together, they headed out for approval of the new look and confronted Hunter.

"Well?" she asked.

He sat back, studying her.

"Clothing?"

"Jeans and a T-shirt. Hmm. I'll wear one of my band T-shirts. Who does everyone love?"

"Oh, come on, Amy," Hunter laughed. "There's no one band everyone loves! Remember the adage, you can't please all of the people all of the time!"

She laughed. "I don't want to please anyone. I just want to attract a semimadman."

"Oh, I think you can do it!" Sabrina said.

"Do you think our man Colin is an easily seduced madman—or a narcissist greedy enough to go with the God image and cater to the Archangel?" Amy asked.

"I think he's as sane as you or me," Sabrina told her.

"At the moment that might not mean much," Hunter said.

She gave him a light punch on the arm. "Hunter. This is what we do. I'm surrounded by the best in the business—including you. This is our chance to get him."

"And I'm out of here now!" Sabrina said.

They both thanked her, grinning. When Sabrina was gone, Amy turned to Hunter again. "Seriously! This is our best chance to get him!" she repeated.

"I know, I know. And you look great. But we came into this hotel together. When I leave with you—if there are those here other than our agents keeping watch—people will know. And we can't go and see Elijah together. I'm going to leave now and let you finish getting ready. I'll call Garza. I think the man downstairs that I recognized is Rowdy Samuels. I'll let you know for sure. I'll head to the hospital ahead of you. You can see Elijah. I'll check on a few of the campaign members still being observed and then, of course—"

"You're worried about the woman from the woods on the day of the fire," Amy said.

He nodded. "I just can't fathom what they did to her to make her so…"

"Lost," Amy said. "Okay. Go. And let me know if this guy is really an agent. I'm going to do a T-shirt and denim jacket so I'll have a place for the Glock," she told him.

He nodded, rose, and looked at her. "It's pretty cool," he told her. "The dark hair with those streaks! It's like I'm out with a… hmm. Groupie! A darling little cosplaying groupie. But hmm, I really like you as you!"

He grinned and left the room. Amy hurriedly finished dressing, just guessing that even young people knew Aerosmith and choosing a T-shirt that advertised the band. Gun, handbag, clothing, and she was ready.

Hunter called.

He was right; he knew the agent downstairs, who'd been sent to keep an eye on her and Hunter—and of course, Mickey—at the hotel. But it had been cleared with the powers that be; he was to drive Amy to the hospital.

She hurried downstairs. Rowdy Samuels, also casually clad,

stood to greet her as if she was a long-lost cousin. She accepted a hug, and they left the lobby together and headed for his car.

He gave a nod to a woman who was now sitting at the little café tables just outside; she had surely been sent by Garza as well.

When they were in the car, Samuels said, "Lena Mero. Special Agent Lena Mero. Of course, none of you are there now, but we keep our eyes on anyone coming and going since even Mickey is staying there."

"Nice to know," Amy said.

"Figured Hunter would know—or suspect. And while we're all over the place working, we usually recognize one another." He grinned. "Company picnics?"

She laughed. "Right."

In no time, he had her at the hospital. When he insisted on coming in with her, she knew Mickey and Garza had made sure she was continually under guard. Not a bad thing.

They had faith in her, she knew. Otherwise, she'd be off the case.

But it never hurt to know they all had one another's backs.

She knew Hunter was there, but Special Agent Rowdy Samuels escorted her straight to Elijah's room and stood outside, talking as if he were just a friend with one of the guards who was watching over the room.

She slipped into the room.

As she had expected, Annabel was still with Elijah. She was curled up on the bed with him. They were laughing at a sitcom.

As Amy entered, Annabel quickly jumped off the bed, looking guilty.

Amy couldn't help but laugh. "It's just me, guys. It's okay!"

"What?" Elijah said.

"'Me'? Who are you?" Annabel demanded.

Amy grinned; her makeover must have been darned decent.

"Me, Special Agent Amy Larson," she told them. "I'm going to a speech."

"Of course," Elijah whispered.

"Annabel, you didn't need to move," Amy said. She couldn't help but grin. "I won't tell anyone on the two of you!"

"Still... I'll just grab the old hospital chair again."

"How are you doing?" Amy asked Elijah.

"Feeling guilty myself that I'm taking up a hospital bed. But... I'm waiting for them to move me, and I'm guessing that might be hard with all the people already working. I'm just going to do whatever they tell me. I want to stay alive!"

"And just listening and doing whatever is needed to that end is smart," Amy assured him.

"So...you're like, um, undercover?" Elijah asked.

"I'm going to try to meet Colin," Amy said. "They've been getting a few hard hits from us, so I'm assuming he may be after some new recruits."

Elijah nodded. "You're still beautiful," he assured her. "Just what he's going to want. You kind of look like a kid. An old kid. Not old—I mean like a college student."

"Good. Thanks. That's what I was trying for. What I need from you is an idea of how you attracted his attention."

"Oh," Elijah said, frowning, thoughtful. "Hmm, I'm not sure."

"You were screaming," Annabel told him.

"I wasn't with you!" he reminded her.

She shook her head and grinned. "You walked away from me screaming we needed to remember the promise of our country is true equality for all."

"Good. Thank you."

"And we both had signs at the protest," Annabel told her. "We were determined to be heard. Is Frank Hamilton really going to go through with it and run after this? I hope so!"

"I don't know," Amy told her. "But we can all hope, while also hoping he and his family are safe. Anyway, is there anything else you can think of?"

"Oh! When I met him, I was going on about the famines in the south of Africa that were the result—mostly—of the pandemic. I talked about needing to help others, being strong as Americans so we could help ourselves and others."

Amy nodded. "Thank you. I'm so glad to see you two doing so well."

"We'd do anything for you!" Annabel said.

"No, no, please, seeing you all is just great. Anyway..." She headed for the door and turned to say, "Bye for now. Stay well and sane!"

"Yeah!" Elijah said.

In the hall, she found her faithful escort was waiting for her. "That was fast, which is good. It's time, and every agent in the crowd has to play the game, go through the metal detectors, which, of course, will be off for us."

"I see, you're in the crowd, too?" she asked him.

Rowdy nodded. "It's going to be a—crowded crowd! So..."

"Let's get there."

She followed him down to his car, and they left the hospital as two casual visitors. When they reached the set area for the speech, they found the parking lot was already almost full.

"Wow!" Amy murmured.

"Yeah," Rowdy said simply. He got out of the car and went around to the back and pulled out two large cardboard signs on sticks that could be raised high.

Each read, DAC—Decency and Civility! Elect Frank Hamilton!

"Okay, so we're ready?" Rowdy asked.

"As ready as we'll ever be," she assured him.

They followed a stone trail from the parking lot to the picnic area. There was a raised dais that had been set up for the speech; Hamilton would be led out from one of the park offices just behind it.

The area in front of the dais was filled with people, many

of them young, all of them seeking to be as close as possible to the man.

Amy wasn't really accustomed to shoving through a crowd, but she and Rowdy managed to get their way near the front and then raised their placards high.

She saw Eric Dayton; he was in a hoodie, shouting in a group. She saw other agents that she knew—FDLE and FBI—also infiltrated through the crowd.

"Decency! The world has become a fight zone! Decency! Elect Hamilton!" she shouted.

People were moving close.

Closer and closer.

Someone was right next to her as Frank Hamilton appeared, and the crowd went crazy.

Hunter was there. In a vest, he was standing right by Hamilton, ready to take on anything that might be a threat to the man, including a bullet.

As Hamilton arrived and waved to the cheering crowd, she sensed someone just slightly behind her, speaking closely to her, his lips almost touching her ear.

"He's great, isn't he? I just wish… Well, I wish he knew everything! There's so much more that's happening, and he needs to know!"

She turned to the smiling young man so close at her side. She was different in appearance today, and he was also different in his appearance today. He was still clean-shaven, but now his hair was very dark, cropped from the mass of waves around his face that it had been before.

But he hadn't done much of anything to change his face.

She smiled at him in agreement.

She'd found Colin at last.

15

"My friends, welcome, and thank you from the bottom of my heart. If you saw the little video I sent out to the media, you know that I am still a determined man!" Frank Hamilton said. "We are all aware of the violence that's been going on in our state. We know about the horrible things being done to people. And I'll be honest, you must be careful. We believe in our ability to be the Americans our Founding Fathers envisioned. People who do not discriminate against others, who do not use 'witchcraft' as an excuse to execute our neighbors. But now, in this age of skewed broadcasting and social media, many who are unscrupulous have set forth to create a divided nation here. We are those who are committed to ignoring the name-calling and the bashing that sides do to one another. We are committed to talking in a civil manner and, more importantly, to listening. All too often, a fringe group gets hold of an idea or a concept, and it's that fringe group that's incredibly loud! We are capable of thinking for ourselves, capable of not being put into boxes or lanes, and capable of having different opinions on different subjects. I'm here today to tell you that it's all right to disagree with me. But I'm also here to tell you that we won't let the loud fringe groups color us against our neighbors. We won't fall into a well of hate, no matter how hard they push us!"

Hunter stood firm; he was there to see that no harm came to this man. Frank Hamilton was helping them. It was their duty—his duty—to keep him alive.

Usually, it was easy for Hunter to trust in others. They often had to work as a team. No one man or woman solved a problem; no one agent could handle the crimes of the world. Or even the crimes of a state, a city, or an area.

Usually.

Hunter knew he worked with really great people. And everyone involved in this case knew the dangers, and that no one was sure just how far it could go, but they knew how important it was that every player know their position once they were in motion.

And they were in motion.

But Hamilton had almost pleaded to get out of the rally right before his speech was to begin. The fear he kept tamped down had risen to the fore. His greatest argument had been with himself, and in the end, he had decided he had to speak—but he had asked Hunter to be with him, begged him to be part of his protection detail.

Hunter had meant to be in the crowd, ready to assist Amy at any given moment.

And there she was.

And there was Colin.

Amy had done a much better job of changing her appearance than he expected, though the man must have known he'd been mentioned by several people by now. And since he was there, he hadn't been warned about anyone looking for him.

Or he had been and he didn't care. Still, Hunter argued with himself, Colin had to know that there were abundant agents and officers crawling through the crowd. Frank Hamilton wouldn't be speaking if he wasn't being protected. He had learned the hard way just how vulnerable he was.

As it was at the moment, Colin was just standing there next to Amy. And she was playing her part to a tee, applauding Hamilton, shouting agreement to his words with others calling out in the crowd. Polite shouting because people wanted to hear the man speak.

Then Colin said something to her and Amy smiled and nodded. They were talking, chatting, and then Colin moved through the crowd again.

Amy looked right at Hunter, shaking her head slightly. She didn't want the man stopped right then.

And he knew. She had agreed to meet him somewhere after the speech. And by then, Hamilton would be off the dais, ready to be whisked back into the care of others.

She spoke quietly over the comm.

"Coffee shop, first turn after the park."

He gave her a nod. Of course, other agents had heard as well. It had worked as they had planned. Amy had appeared at the rally as the perfect recruit. Colin had arrived—not so well disguised himself. And they were to meet.

It seemed far too easy. Something was just not right.

"Great, Amy, we're right behind you," he heard over the comm. First it was Aidan, then he heard the voices of others he knew, including Eric Dayton, a good play in the crowd since Eric had spent years studying psychology with a focus on the criminal mind. Her escort from the hotel, Rowdy Samuels, was standing with the group at a distance and cheering away; she gave him a nod as well. When Amy made her move to meet with Colin, Rowdy would be right behind.

Hamilton continued to speak. He talked about fairness and equality, touching on many issues, stating his beliefs but warning those who were too much to one side of a question that the other side usually had valid arguments as well—which again meant that civil discourse was the direction in which they must head. He also reiterated they did need law and order. He also said religion could be a very good thing. But it could also be twisted, as they'd been seeing on the news. There were bad seeds everywhere. "But do we throw out the baby with the bathwater? No, my friends, we recognize the dirty water—and we let it slide down the drain. We quit wasting our time arguing, and we learn how to vet those who are in power!"

His speech received thunderous applause and he continued with, "If not people, find the person who knows how to talk. Who knows that freedom of religion means every religion, not just your own. Remember again! Many of our Founding Fathers were born just after a sad time in the history of the colonies when petty squabbles and other factors may well have influenced godly people to hang their neighbors for witchcraft. They never wanted to live through such a horror themselves. We respect one another. But my key message is that we talk, we support our law enforcement and help find ways to weed out the bad seeds! Thank you, thank you, my friends! To the land of the free and the home of the brave! And deepest thanks to our military! Remember, we are the land of the free because we are the land of the brave. Thank you again, thank you!"

Amy was saying something; Hunter could hear her voice, but the noise around her was so loud that she couldn't be understood clearly through the comm.

Even before Hamilton began to step back, the crowd was surging forward, most just wanting to touch the man who could speak with such love for people with his personal form of eloquence. Some hated him, of course. He had been labeled "wishy-washy" in a newspaper article once, and his entire headquarters had been under attack.

It was those who might not be there because they loved him so much that the agents had to watch out for.

Hamilton nodded his thanks to Hunter as others whisked

him back across the stage. He'd be returned now to his wife and child, who were waiting back at the safe house.

The local police were quickly pushing the crowd back and helping the FBI keep the crowd rounded up toward moving in a different direction away from the stage area.

"You're free to move, Hunter," he heard over his comm.

Garza. Garza himself was with Hamilton. And he was, as Garza had said, free to move.

It was time to follow Amy.

But as he made his way from his protection detail out into the crowd, he saw Amy had already moved. And he was in the tangle of the crowd himself.

There were others following. She was capable.

But something just did not jibe.

He still couldn't help but feel that it had all been too damned easy.

He wound his way determinedly through the crowd, anxious to get to the coffee shop.

Amy sat at an outside table with Colin, smiling, accepted the latte he'd purchased for her, and waited for him to sit as well.

They'd arrived well ahead of others who might have spilled from the speech wanting to stop for a quick coffee, espresso, or some other concoction. On the way, he'd introduced himself as Colin, but he did not offer his last name.

She'd decided she'd be Victoria, but she gave no last name.

Colin had spoken from behind her, right as Hamilton had been giving his speech, asking her if they shouldn't slip away quickly before the mob.

"Unless, of course, you came with friends?" he'd asked her.

"No, no, I'm good, I just hitched a ride with friends," she'd told him. "I can meet you after the speech."

And so they had met. And now he was smiling at her, sipping his coffee.

"So, you love Hamilton, right?" he asked.

"I do. And you?"

"Yeah. But…there's more, you know."

"Oh?"

She was expecting a speech about war, famine, pestilence, and disease. About the coming of the Apocalypse.

But that wasn't going to be Colin's focus at all today.

"I love the man, but I want him to concentrate more on law and order. I mean, of course, you've read or seen the news."

"I have, of course."

"All these people—dead! I mean, how come the cops and whoever haven't even begun to round up the monsters who are killing everyone. Girls, hoodwinked and drawn from their families and friends, only to find themselves being used by others— and then sometimes winding up dead! We need someone with strength. Someone with real strength, not someone who caters to criminals!"

She smiled and nodded. "What do you propose?"

"A candidate who has real power. Not just over federal crimes, but the power to come in and tell local law enforcement what to do," Colin said.

She imagined that the agents on duty for this sting were hearing everything he was saying, and they were just as surprised as she was.

She smiled, but it turned into a frown almost immediately. "Wow. You are way more up on the law than I am, but… I think we have something called 'states' rights.' I mean, wouldn't we really have to change the whole Constitution?"

"That's why we have amendments!" he told her.

"Hmm. I mean, I understand what you're saying. The recent events have been horrible."

"And they're all happening because someone out there really believes the Apocalypse is coming. Look at the past years—war, famine, and disease! Think about it, all the things happening. I mean, I'm no biblical scholar, but…hey, I did grow up going to Sunday school. Anyway, it's easy to understand that belief—"

"I did minor in history," Amy told him. "And it's sad to say, but all throughout history there has been war and famine and all kinds of bad things. The Spanish influenza in the early twentieth century, World War I, World War II—"

"And we may well be headed for World War III. That's what I mean. I love, love, love Hamilton, but someone has to get him to be fiercer on military control and on a true police force that can put down the really bad things. I mean, you know, the CIA—who the hell trusts them? They don't operate here—supposedly. The FBI. Well, those guys are jokes. Aren't they?" he asked suddenly.

"Pardon?"

"You're one of them, right?"

"No," she said, smiling because she wasn't officially FBI; she was on loan. She was FDLE. "No, I swear to you, I'm not FBI."

"Local cop?"

She grinned again. "Nope. Not a local cop."

He leaned toward her, his entire demeanor suddenly changing.

"Then what the hell are you?" he demanded.

He'd known. He'd known that the place was going to be riddled with police and agents, and he might have even chosen her, not because her disguise was so great, but because he'd known she was law enforcement.

"You have me totally confused, absolutely baffled!" she said. "I thought that we were just going to have a cup of coffee and enjoy the fact we both admire Frank Hamilton so much. I don't know what your game is—"

"Oh, come on. I do know what yours is," he said, sitting back. He looked around the coffee shop, smiling.

"All right," he said at last. "I think I can even pick out your guard! But you're not FBI. You're not a cop. You aren't CIA, are you?"

She smiled. "No."

"Then?"

"Florida Department of Law Enforcement."

"Man, then, do you suck!" he told her, crossing his arms over his chest. He smiled. "Okay, just what are you going to do? Arrest me? For what? Freedom of speech, remember. I asked a girl out for a cup of coffee. I defended law enforcement. Just what are you going to arrest me for?"

Amy had been so concentrated on Colin's words and movements, ever ready to reach for her Glock if necessary, she hadn't seen Hunter approaching from a distance.

But he was suddenly right by them at the table. "Kidnapping, rape, and murder," Hunter said flatly. "Get up. Slowly. Keep your hands where we can see them, get them behind your back."

"No! No! This is unlawful!" Colin shrieked. "Arrest and seizure under no provocation! You see this, people, witness this! I'm being—"

Others had now stepped forward, too. Aidan, along with Eric Dayton, was at the table.

Dayton spoke up, stopping him. "Oh, son, you are truly in very bad shape. I guess you haven't heard about this thing called DNA, or that we have in our care witnesses who are ready to speak against you. And if you're lucky, well, we can talk and maybe we can help... Maybe we can help you and then you can help us."

Again, the young man suddenly seemed to change. He stood dead still as he was handcuffed.

"Help you. All right. I want the death penalty off the table."

"Hey, we're just your worthless law enforcement," Amy told him sweetly. "But they'll bring in the United States Attorney General, and then we'll see what can be done."

"The death penalty must be off the table!" he ranted. "You want the Archangel? I am the Archangel. And I will help you, but I want the death penalty off the table!"

"Let's just get him booked," Amy said, rising. She hadn't touched her latte. And Colin had noticed, of course.

He began to laugh. "Victoria—or Amy, Satan's concubine, is it? Good disguise. I didn't even realize it until these guys walked up. And now… Well, don't waste that latte. There's nothing wrong with it. You see, I did nothing, said nothing, while we were seated here together."

"You just said you are the Archangel," Hunter told him.

"Because I'm terrified of you brutes!" he said. "Terrified, coerced, bullied into lying! Because you haven't got a thing on me—"

"Except, again, eyewitnesses, victims of abduction and rape, and dead people," Hunter said. "Including many tragic souls chopped to pieces and left in barrels. You truly have no respect for your fellow man."

"Only angels," Colin said.

"But which is it—you're innocent? Or you're the Archangel?" Amy asked.

He shrugged. "Depends on who is doing the talking. Attorney. I'm demanding an attorney right now. And that's my right as an American!"

Colin, their mystery man, was in custody. But now he had an attorney.

Still, he was talking. Hunter and Amy didn't need to go in with him. Garza and Mickey had taken that on themselves. They watched from the observation room. He hadn't taken on a public defender, but rather called his own attorney.

And at first, Colin denied having done anything wrong, other than talk about his beliefs and this was his God-given right as an American. He had never forced anyone to believe him.

Hunter had to hand it to their superiors in the FBI and FDLE. Both Mickey and Garza just sat and listened while he went on and on about his innocence and his rights.

"I'm afraid we do have your DNA on several rape victims," Garza said.

"Rape? Hell, no. Have I been with women? Yes! All consensual!"

"We also have your DNA on several dead people," Mickey said quietly.

"Do we?" Amy whispered to Hunter.

"No, not yet, but our man Colin doesn't know that," Hunter said. "Michael Colin Ridgeway." Once they'd taken his prints, they'd discovered his identity. He'd been arrested only once for being drunk and disorderly, but it had given them his true identity.

And apparently, he really had gone by the name Colin most of his life.

The man's parents had been killed in an automobile accident when he was twelve. A rebellious child, he'd been returned by foster family after foster family. He'd managed to keep a job at a gas station while seeking a degree in government studies from a state university.

He'd never graduated. But he'd learned enough to play the system, or so it seemed.

"I know lots of people. I'm a friendly guy. I'm a hugger. And now, with COVID officially over, I can hug all I want," Colin said.

"You said you are the Archangel," Mickey said.

"I never said anything! I was being brutalized by your people!" the man claimed.

"The café was full of witnesses. No one said the agents at the scene did anything harmful to you at all," Garza told him. "I'm afraid you will face multiple charges—state charges and federal charges. Son, it's likely you'll face execution."

"Whoa, whoa!" Colin's attorney said, speaking up. "I need to confer with my client for a minute."

"You want us to leave the room?" Mickey asked.

Colin's attorney shook his head and leaned close to whisper to Colin.

"We want the death penalty taken off the table," he said flatly after pulling back.

"That can be arranged, I believe," Garza told him.

"We want it in writing."

"Fine. Wait. We'll see to it," Mickey said.

"On both the state and the federal level!" the attorney announced.

"Got it," Garza said. He and Mickey rose, leaving the room. Colin stared into the mirror. He smiled. "I know you're back there, concubine of Satan, so, so Special Agent Amy Larson! And you don't want to believe, but it's coming!"

Amy just stared back through the one-way glass, shaking her head.

"He had a rough childhood, but if that was an excuse…"

"It is true too often," Hunter said. "But still…it's hard to fathom how much of this is really to be believed, and what is a crock for another agenda."

Mickey opened the door to the observation room.

"What do you think?" he asked.

"I don't care what he confesses to," Hunter said. "I don't think he has the capacity to pull all this off by himself."

Mickey shook his head. "We haven't asked him about Marc yet. And we have theorized that whoever did knock out Frank Hamilton's campaign headquarters and steal the kid wasn't working alone."

"But we could never find anything on the campaign workers," Amy reminded him.

"That doesn't mean they're innocent," Mickey reminded her.

"Well, that's true."

"I'm not a huge fan of the death penalty anyway," Mickey said with a shrug, "though there are people who deserve it, and he may be one of them. But we need him talking."

"Everything he says is a lie," Amy murmured.

"Not everything," Hunter said. "We just have to determine what is and what isn't."

"That's also true. I'm bringing in our profiler. Let him have a go at it, once we have the paperwork his attorney is requesting."

"A good idea," Hunter said.

"I'd thought about you and Amy giving it a go again, but I think we'd just find ourselves swimming around in circles. I did do it, I didn't do it, I'm innocent, I'm the most brilliant killer out there."

"I think you're right. And I think it will be great if he thinks Amy isn't here because she just doesn't find him all that interesting," Hunter said.

"And you may be right there," Mickey said. "He wants to taunt her—he thinks that he's getting to her when he says the things he says."

"That, or he really thinks I'm Satan's concubine," Amy said. "And that makes Hunter Satan, I think. So…"

"That would make me just a demon, I think," Hunter said. "A demon who is not that important to him."

"I believe our profiler is going to tell us that his childhood gave him something of an inferiority complex," Mickey said. "He probably doesn't believe deep down he'd be any kind of threat against any other man—but in his mind, men are innately superior to women."

Hunter grinned at Amy. "He doesn't know the women I do," he said lightly.

"And you've certainly got a point there!" Mickey said.

He left them, moving to get things done.

For a minute, Hunter and Amy just watched as Colin and his attorney whispered in the interrogation room.

Every few minutes, Colin would look to the glass and smile.

He wanted Amy to watch him.

"Let's not give him the pleasure," Amy said. "I think both

Garza and Mickey want to get what's needed—but they also want to let him stew in there awhile."

"Let's go on to the offices. I'm curious to find out just what else Sabrina might have found, and maybe there's been more on the Commonsense website or somewhere. We're missing something, something big, and I can't figure out what it is," Hunter said in disgust.

"Colin really isn't the Archangel," Amy said.

"No," Hunter agreed. "But he may know who is. And if there are obscure clues out there, Sabrina would have been the one to find them."

A dozen tech analysts were busy at their computers and screens, and they found Aidan was seated next to Sabrina. Records and pictures of Michael Colin Ridgeway were up on the screen, but Sabrina was busy pursuing something.

"What's up?" Hunter asked, approaching the two.

Sabrina let out a sigh. "This is like finding the proverbial needle in a haystack," she told them.

"We've been poring through communications regarding Frank Hamilton. And we're poring through communications that had to do with Reverend Ben's crooked church along with communications regarding the Commonsense Party website. It's enough to make a person blind or crazy or both," Aidan told them. He smiled suddenly, looking at Amy. "Good work this morning!"

"Well, I'm not so sure. He knew we were there. He planned on giving me the most innocent speech in the world. He really thought we didn't have anything on him except for suspicion, except... Well, maybe he believed we didn't have hard evidence—and that without it, we couldn't do anything."

"There are some really strange communications," Sabrina said. "And the IP addresses are all over the place, routed through a half dozen countries. It's like a crapshoot when I try something!"

"What types of things have you been getting?" Amy asked.

"Well, I'm not sure if what we see means anything or not," Sabrina said.

"Like this one," Aidan said, reading off the screen. "'Frank Hamilton is the best, just slightly missing the mark. All equality, all fairness...but we must have better control. Doesn't he see that, after all the things that have happened to him? Hamilton is the best so far, but we really need someone like him but just a little stronger!'"

"Where did that come from?"

"It came off a chat site in support of Hamilton. We're trying to trace it now."

"What else might be suspicious?" Amy asked.

"This one," Sabrina said. "'What the heck? We need to get in there and tell him what we really think. He has to take a few stands. Talking to others is great but if we're going to have a leader, he's going to need to lead!'"

"Interesting. But..." Amy began.

"But?"

"All right. I want to return to his campaign headquarters back at his house."

"Amy," Aidan said. "We've been over it and over it."

She shook her head. "I know. But I keep thinking that if I'm there... I don't know. I'm nowhere near as good as you guys are on evidence, but...something doesn't fit right. And I keep thinking that if I can get there, I can figure out what it is."

She hadn't seen Mickey come in behind her. "I want one of you two listening to Colin when he begins to talk. Listening—in the room. Catching him in lies."

"It can't be Amy. We all agreed," Hunter said.

"I want to go to Hamilton's house. Maybe he is the Archangel, manipulating this—"

"You think he risked killing his own son!" Mickey protested.

"A narcissist might do that," Hunter said thoughtfully. He looked at Amy. "But you're not going over there—"

"I'll send her with Rowdy again—he's got great fresh eyes. He can go in with no preconceived ideas. And besides the academy and being a crack shot, he's had a lot of martial arts training," Mickey said.

Amy looked at Hunter. "I need to do this," she told him. "Because if Hamilton isn't guilty, someone involved with his campaign is. And I think it might be someone who is planting all these slanted comments in various places—after bouncing them all around the world."

"All right. Amy, you do what you think may help. Hunter, you come on back down with me. And don't worry. We'll have the house/campaign headquarters covered," Mickey told them both.

Hunter nodded as Amy walked away.

There was something wrong. He had a gut feeling. He still didn't like it.

But…

Teamwork. Amy wasn't going alone. And one human archangel monster couldn't go up against well-trained agents.

And still…

Maybe she was right. Maybe her trip could provide just what it was they were missing.

He'd known something was off with Colin.

And he still felt that something was very, very wrong.

16

"They've had cops watching the place twenty-four seven," Rowdy told Amy as they arrived at Frank Hamilton's home and headquarters. "Anytime anyone comes here—a couple of people looking for a hard copy folder or other info—the computers have been studied and returned. So there's been some work done by some hearty souls. Some of his workers, a housekeeper, and Marty Benson, who seems so broken although he's trying to find all the good that he can in order to convince Frank Hamilton to stay in the race... The place hasn't been empty. But there's always been one of our federal agents at the door, watching the comings and goings since the drugged-water incident. Cops are in position out on the road that leads this way. The entries, both front and back, are on security surveillance...but—" he turned to look at her "—the cameras went down during the drugged-water incident. And to this day, we don't know how the drugs got in the water and the coffee—or who took the boy, Marc Hamilton."

"Whoever is doing this thought out every possible scenario," Amy murmured. "But there has to be something in that house, something to give us a clue as to what is going on."

"Do you think this person really believes that the Apocalypse is coming?" Rowdy asked her.

She grinned at him. "I would never swear that the Apocalypse isn't coming! But no, this whole thing has been staged to create a real horror show—but to what end, we haven't quite gotten to yet. I'm hoping that they'll get something out of our guy Colin that will lead us closer to the truth."

"You don't think it's just some fringe guy—from the right or left—pulling all this off just to get Frank Hamilton out of the race just because he's too reasonable?" Rowdy asked.

"Maybe. But now they've participated in incidents across the country—"

"Which makes it more important that someone get serious about shootings and crime around the country," Rowdy reminded her.

"That's true."

"Unless…"

She turned to him. "Unless Frank Hamilton has actually done all this himself." She paused and drew in a breath. "He could have done so in order to prove that even though we're frightened, we must carry on," she said, throwing that theory out into the open.

"So, it's occurred to you," he said. "And that's why we're here?"

Amy continued to watch his reaction closely. She liked Rowdy. She knew he wouldn't be on this assignment if he wasn't considered to be a top-notch agent. But he was also easy to talk to, easy to work with. He—along with others—had been watching her back during Hamilton's entire speech. Just searching the headquarters was hardly a dangerous situation, but she was glad to have him with her. She could concentrate on the computers in Frank Hamilton's office and on his physical files.

"You do know that federal and state forensic teams—working together—have been over and over the house," Rowdy said.

"Yes."

"Did you start your police career out in forensics?" he asked her.

She shook her head. "I'm not looking for traces, or the emails that our analysts have been over and over…"

"Then what are you looking for?" he asked.

"Something that is here. Something that will give us…anything. And I'm hoping to feel useful because I didn't want to be part of the interrogation going on with Colin. I'm sure they'll take the death penalty off the table to get him to talk, but I don't really know if anything resembling the truth is going to come out of the man. He takes such pleasure in my being there—hoping his words are tormenting me and will get a reaction from me—that I do believe they'll do better without me. But besides that, I can't help but believe there's something more to be found in this house."

"Okay, well, good luck! You can feel free to run around the house at will. There are agents outside, and I'll hold down the central living room—the campaign headquarters."

"Thanks. We'll be in the same general area. I'm going to concentrate on Hamilton's office. It's in the den just to the right of the campaign area on the first floor," she told him. Then she murmured thoughtfully, "Hmm. Then I'm going to concentrate on his bedroom. I'm not going to mess anything up and upset Aubrey when she finally gets back. But that's his personal space."

"And what better place to hide something? And here we are… It looks so…well, normal for a home. But forlorn for a campaign headquarters!" Rowdy said. "And there's our man, on duty in front where we were promised he would be."

Just as the agents had been at the safe house, this man was dressed casually. His short-sleeved tailored shirt was worn loose over his jeans. He was probably about thirty and was fit, as most young agents tended to be. He waved to them; he obviously knew Rowdy.

"Cory Zahn, he's been with the Bureau about five years, good man," Rowdy assured her.

Getting out of the car, Rowdy called out to his friend and

coworker and introduced Cory to Amy, telling him that he'd be in the central room if he was needed for anything.

Zahn was polite and nodded to Amy. "We all know about you!" he told her. "So, you're on loan. Thinking about coming to the federal side after all this?"

She smiled. "I'm not thinking anything at all until we finally get through solving this case!" she assured him. "But thank you."

They walked on in. The place looked just as it had on the day she had come with Hunter—minus the many people passed out and scattered over the floor.

"I think I'm heading upstairs first. I'll check out the bedrooms," Amy told Rowdy.

He nodded, taking up a position that gave him a clear view to the front door—and to the dining room area that led back to the kitchen and the only other entrance to the house.

"Amy!" he said as she headed to the stairs to reach the second floor.

"Yeah?"

"Hamilton was heavily drugged. So, he drugged himself?"

"Possibly. What better way to appear to be totally innocent?"

"Then again, there's the matter of his son. If you hadn't found him, and if that fire had broken out and gone wild before fire crews could get out there, that kid would have been toast."

"I'm not saying Hamilton is guilty," Amy assured him. "I'm just open to any possibility."

She continued on up the stairs, finding Marc's room first, two rooms that appeared to be guest rooms, and then the primary suite.

It was nice. There was a four-poster bed with a handsome quilted bedspread in a pattern that matched the lighter fabric of the drapes. French doors led out to a balcony that overlooked the pool and patio below. A door opened onto the bathroom. When she checked it out, she saw that it was large, attractively tiled, and offered a Jacuzzi tub as well as a shower. She looked in the medicine cabinet and then below the sink.

There was nothing in the bathroom other than the usual toiletries.

She returned to the bedroom and looked in the closet. There were all kinds of boxes there, and she drew them out and went through them one by one. Shoes, coats, sweaters, diving gear... all clothing.

There was a dressing table, and she searched that as well, certain that everything here belonged to Aubrey Hamilton. And it looked like everything did. Brushes, makeup, and a little book.

Amy brought out the book. It was Aubrey's personal schedule. Thumbing through it, Amy found little but appointments for Marc's school along with the parties he'd been invited to, appointments for hair and nail care—and for personal training. Underneath the day calendar she had written, "Must get to personal training. Must. The wife of a politician must be all together, a politician must be all together! Image can be everything."

Aubrey was strong in her determination that her husband should run. Even though it might threaten her and her son.

She put the calendar back and moved on to the dressers. The top drawer of Aubrey's dresser offered a lot of high-end panties and bras. Amy shuffled through them, not thinking that she'd find anything but determined to be thorough. She came upon a delicately wrapped parcel advertising the store that created the contents.

She started to set it down when she frowned. There was something about it that was a little too heavy.

She frowned and then decided that upsetting someone about their underwear at this time was not going to be a worry.

She ripped the bag apart.

And found, crushed between silk and satin, a phone. And lifting it, she realized it was one of the pay-as-you-go phones that could be purchased with cash just about anywhere.

A burner phone.

There was no passcode to get into it.

She began to read through the numbers, anxious then to find out just who had been making the calls—and to whom they were being made.

Michael Colin Ridgeway was out-and-out, certifiably mentally ill, Hunter thought.

Or else he was a brilliant man and an even better actor.

Even with the paperwork completed to keep him from lethal injection at both the state and federal levels, he was still going off. One minute it was all true, and he was the Archangel. Then he'd be completely calm, staring at them, almost crying to admit that he'd killed people. But it had been necessary.

Eric Dayton had glanced at Hunter several times as the two of them took a turn speaking with Colin and his attorney.

He'd give a little shake of his head.

Even the seasoned profiler wasn't sure about the man.

"I want to know where she is!" Colin said suddenly. "The concubine. You know, minion of the Archangel that I am, I could turn into something else for her! Oh…yeah," he said, smiling at Hunter. "That so annoys you! Professional people, so professional in public, but it's obvious. You are a demon, and you get to spend your nights with her. Maybe—no. No. You think you're cool, but you're not the real Antichrist. You are big, tall, studly, a dude—but you're not him, just not cool enough to be him."

"Let's get back to the information that's going to keep you off death row," Hunter said easily. The man wanted him riled.

He had no intention of losing his control.

"Where is she?" Colin asked. "I want her here. Is she behind the glass? I don't feel her. I think that I'd feel her if she was there."

"Special Agent Larson has been called away on another case," Eric told him, leaning forward. "I'm a psychologist, Mr. Ridgeway, as well as part of the Bureau. And as such, I feel it's imperative that I warn you—and your attorney—that if you don't agree with the terms of your plea bargain and follow through, the death penalty will be back on the table. And we have not just one but several women who will swear under oath that you kidnapped and raped them, and then we have bodies and DNA and…"

"We don't want more people to die!" Hunter said quietly, looking straight at Colin and leaning forward. "You're not the Archangel. You're just not. Your very rambling assures us that despite all the acts you're putting on, you're not the brains behind this thing. And get this. This person you're serving will think it's just fine if you die—"

"No! I will not die!"

"You will if you don't start telling us the truth. Were you part of the kidnapping of Marc Hamilton and drugging the water at Frank Hamilton's headquarters?"

"No. I really wasn't. I don't know anything about that," Colin swore.

"All right. Who is calling the shots? We need a name."

The man looked truly distressed. He shook his head. "I don't know. You say that he's smart—well, he is. He has been careful that no one knows his identity. He told us that we were strong, but when an angel is in human form, the flesh is very weak. If we had known, we might have given him away."

For once, Hunter believed what Colin was saying.

"Why?" Hunter asked.

Colin leaned back. "All right—no one ever knew who they were assigned to kill. I can give you names of two other people who were…are…angels. We were never assigned to kill those we knew, those with whom we'd worked to keep the Apocalypse moving. It was for a good cause. Honestly. People had to change. Those who died…they had to die. They had to suffer on earth because it's absolutely true that the world is about to implode from hate and nastiness. And that more than disease, famine, and pestilence is what will do it! War with words leads to war that kills."

Hunter glanced at Eric. Neither one of them could argue that.

He inhaled. "Technically, I didn't kill anyone. I tried once and mangled it, so I was told just to get people where the Archangel wanted them."

"Okay. Who did the physical killing?" Hunter asked.

Colin smiled. "Two people you found on the embankment. They killed the others and then the Archangel killed them. He was brilliant at cleaning up."

"How do you know that?" Hunter asked him.

"He told me."

"How?"

Colin started to laugh. "Brilliant FBI guy! Come on. Burner phones."

Colin leaned low on the table again, twisting his head at a proud angle. "I was the only one he really trusted," he said. "The Archangel wanted nothing bad to happen to me. And on this earth, I would swim in women and riches!" He sat back again, his face filled with pride.

"Because you are the pale horseman?" Hunter asked.

Colin frowned. "I..." He seemed to be stumbling suddenly. Then he sat up straight again. "I am the pale horseman. And the time of the Archangel is coming. He loves me the most, he will protect me!"

"Then why are you sitting here with us now?" Hunter asked. "Let's see...hmm, white horseman, red horseman, black horseman...all brought down! And now? He fed you up like jerky treats to a rabid pack of dogs," he added pleasantly.

The man looked troubled, shaking his head. "No, no, no. This is just... Well, when it comes, he'll get me out. I'll go to prison. I've been talking, telling you the truth. And you have to abide by my plea deal—but that's the whole point. He's going to get me out, and there will be nothing that you'll be able to do about it."

Hunter also leaned back, suddenly certain that he might be getting closer to the truth.

Hamilton? Or someone else. Someone who might want Hamilton to fail so he or she could step in, sweep elections, and then…

Seize the law of the land, and pardon all they chose.

He stood. Eric looked at him, frowning.

"Hey. Continue!" he said. "Sorry, Colin, I've got someplace I need to be, too."

Mickey caught him out in the hallway.

"I was on my way to get you. Sabrina has something—she wants to see you."

"All right. Going her way. Then I'm going to head out to the Hamilton house and see if I can help Amy. Mickey, I think someone is playing God in a way we haven't imagined. What is God? Power. So far, the Archangel has been playing with the power of life and death. But the great scheme in this whole Horseman thing is power. And how do you get power? By holding the highest office in the land."

"You think that Hamilton—"

"Or someone in his group. Let me see what Sabrina has and keep moving."

He started to walk away from Mickey, but the man called him back. "Hunter. Go carefully. You've got the last of the horsemen."

"Yeah. But it's time to stop the Apocalypse!" Hunter said.

He hurried to the tech department to find Sabrina. Again, she was working with Aidan.

"Amy found a burner phone at Hamilton's house. Forensics missed it, I'm assuming, because it was wrapped in a drawer with Mrs. Hamilton's underwear," Aidan told him. He was standing to the side behind Sabrina, who was working on her computer. "Sabrina has been tracing the number and the emails sent from it, and she's just discovered that a number of the statements—demanding more action, fiercer control—were sent from the phone."

"And it was Aubrey Hamilton's phone?" Hunter said, frowning.

"No guarantee it was her phone. But Amy found it in her drawer," Sabrina said. "Look, I can show you a few of the communications. The email on the phone traces back to a computer, too—one that we did not find at the Hamilton house. But the way that it was bounced around—country to country—the creator of the email, RighteousAmerican, might well have been at the house when the emails were sent."

"Look at this one," Aidan told him.

Hamilton, get some balls! Someone had to take control. Murderers are running rampant across the country. Shootings, mass killings. Take control man, take control! Talk is one thing, but man up and get cops out there who have the power to do something!

"I'm on my way," Hunter said. "I'll let Amy know that I'm heading out there."

He hurried down to his car, dialing Amy.

There was no answer. Of course, she was making discoveries. Finding what she was so sure had been missed.

And she was protected.

Then why the hell wasn't she answering her phone?

Sabrina was still working on all the numbers, emails, and passcodes Amy had sent to her, but she had assured Amy that she'd found information already that might help them.

So…what else?

Was it possible? Was Aubrey Hamilton trying to help her husband in an obscure way—or was she trying to sabotage everything that he was doing?

And even then, was Aubrey working with him—was he the

Archangel? Or was she working against him, working with someone else?

Or had the phone been planted? She shouldn't have been touching it. No, not true. If it had been planted, or even if Aubrey Hamilton was in some way a part of this, there would be no prints on the phone. It would have been wiped clean.

She was still digging around the room, having no clue what she was searching for or just what she might find, when she paused. There was a strange smell that seemed to be wafting up to the room.

She hurried out of the room, running down the stairs to find Rowdy.

She found him. He was on the sofa, keeled over. The smell was strong here. She drew her gun before hurrying over to him, only to have a man rise up from behind the sofa.

It took her a second to recognize him—he was wearing a gas mask.

But then she knew who it was. Marty Benson.

He, too, was carrying a gun.

And as she stared at him, he smiled and aimed his weapon at Rowdy, pressing the barrel flush to his head.

"Drop your gun. My, my, Special Agent Larson, you never can just accept anything at face value. Hell, you had your man!" Marty's voice came through the gas mask muffled and dripping with hate. "I gave you Michael Colin Ridgeway just about gift wrapped! But you couldn't just accept that. I do understand that he's truly something of a nutjob, but I also know that he has a sky-high IQ. So you should have been happy with him and… well, you got the good preacher, too. But you just had to keep digging."

"Why would I drop my gun? If I do, you're just going to kill both of us. And I didn't get a chance to see if Rowdy is even still breathing," she told him.

"He isn't dead. Neither are you. The gas won't kill. It will just keep him out long enough."

"There's another agent on the porch, you know."

"He's dreaming of better days! Oh, I just checked on him. He's going to be just fine. And Rowdy here, yeah, he's going to be just fine, too. If you drop the gun. See, here's the deal. You obey every word I say before you pass out yourself, and Rowdy lives, and the fellow dreaming on the porch lives…and all will be well."

"Right after you kill me," Amy said dryly.

He laughed. "You may not need to die. I just need to figure out if I dare keep you alive. So many of my old hangouts have been discovered now. But I still have a few. Think of it this way. You have hope."

"Why?"

"Because I think it's fun to give you hope—and you are really a pain in the ass, so… Well, letting you hope and then whatever I choose…fun!"

"Not why on hope," Amy said, exasperation in her voice. "Why the hell are you doing all this?"

"Ah, well, here. The part you didn't see. I began this journey years ago, but what you probably didn't figure was that I wanted and expected my horsemen to be caught. Or killed. Didn't matter which."

"So, so kind!" she said sarcastically.

"That's what I like about you. Facing death or worse, and you're still a wiseass!" he told her.

"Why are you doing all this? Oh, never mind. Because you do want Frank Hamilton to quit the race, and you'll swoop in and be so distressed! But you don't have a wife or a child, and you're determined that someone will fight the good fight! Except into that fight, you'll bring all the suggestions you've been getting from the people, your beloved people! Strengthen everything— laws, police, military—but have them all in your control. And it will happen because you'll be using all those people who love Frank Hamilton, who know that he is the real thing, and that he can bring people out of a divide. The ultimate power. You want to be—"

"Oh, let's not get namby-pamby on words, Special Agent Larson. I want to be king, but we don't have that kind of government anymore. And even where they have kings, those guys don't have much power. Maybe still in other countries by different names but suffice it to use the term *dictator*. That's a pretty good one. Dictator. I don't care what you want to call me, but have you ever realized that I *could* achieve that goal? Inch by inch, take a little more power, surround yourself with the right people—an archangel with his angels, saving the world when the Apocalypse is nigh!"

"Okay, I don't know who is crazier, you or Colin."

He shook his head, smiling at her. "I'm not crazy at all and you know it. It was a brilliant plan. It took time, it took recruiting the right people. And then, of course, when I'm in power, I can pardon anyone I want. Or… Well, if people become threatening in any way, it's time for them to end their earthly tenure here. I mean, you know, if you're going to sit with the angels, well, you may have to give a little here on earth."

She needed to do something. Whatever he'd filled the house with to knock Rowdy out hadn't traveled up the stairs as quickly; but she was in it now, and she could feel what it was doing to her. It was slowly creeping into her system, making her long to sit, to close her eyes, to rest, to sleep…

"I'm going to shoot you," she told him pleasantly.

"No, you're not. Because you're a Goody Two-shoes. You're not going to let this man die. You're going to do everything that I tell you to do."

She was quiet and thoughtful for a minute.

And he waited, amused.

Could he know that she had called her discovery of the phone into headquarters? Because one way or the other, the place would begin to crawl with agents soon enough.

And he was right. She wasn't going to let him shoot Rowdy to save her own life—especially when she did have the one thing that often drove the human soul.

Hope.

"Give me an idea of what you want me to do," she told him.

"Obediently follow me where I want you to go."

"Out into the Everglades, I take it."

"Deep into the Everglades. I have one place out there…such a convenient place. It's very hard to reach." He shrugged. "You see, you all have found those I've wanted you to find. I have a home that has great guard dogs. Alligators can be so useful. So you'd be an idiot to try to escape, and I just may enjoy having you around. You could be a good concubine."

"I would fight you every second!" she spit out without thinking.

"And that's okay. I do love a good fight—and winning in the end. Oh, and I will win!"

"I don't know about that. You have a lot of patsies. You've twisted the minds of many who were lost, who were hurt and desperate. But our moms always told us—you can't please all of the people all of the time. And I'm thinking maybe the majority of people will know that you're nothing like Frank Hamilton."

He grinned at that. "Oh, come on! There's another saying out there. 'Evil succeeds when good men do nothing.' And guess what? Most men—and women—don't want to be bothered to do anything. And as far as they'll all know, I'm the man who is going to stop all the evil!"

Amy shook her head. "You're wrong."

"No one knows who I am," he told her. "And when your people come today, well…they won't know it's me any more than they knew it was me when I drugged all the water in this place. Of course, I drugged my own. Just like I'll be passed out here along with Special Agent Rowdy when your friends arrive. I mean, they will, of course. But not too soon, I imagine—and they'll miss you eventually when dream-boy on the porch won't be reporting in as he's supposed to, so..."

"They will get you," Amy said softly.

"They never will. But you go ahead, and you think that. Ah, poor Agent Forrest! He'll go crazy. He'll swear he won't stop until he finds you. Poor ass really is in love! But even the deepest love fades with time. And his love will fade when he finally believes that you must be dead—which you probably will be in a bit of time because you're just incapable of stopping."

"Of stopping what?"

"Being a ball-breaking bitch," he said pleasantly. "But for now, what is it? Are you going to kill me and let Rowdy here die?"

"You know, Rowdy is great. But I could save the whole world by just shooting you here and now."

But could she? The gun seemed to weigh two tons in her hands. Her eyes... She couldn't even see him clearly. And that thing he'd talked about...

Hope!

No matter what she did here and now, Hunter and the others would figure it out. Teamwork. While Hunter had been with Colin, Sabrina and Aidan had been tracing and working information from the burner phone. Real teamwork.

Something Marty Benson would never understand.

They would know what had happened here.

"All right. No. I don't want Rowdy to die," she said. "And yes, I will work on hope. And yes, as in your terms, I am truly a ball-breaking bitch."

"One *I* will break!" he assured her.

"Well, you can live on hope, too," she told him.

He started to laugh. Then he sobered quickly. "Time to move. Give me your Glock. Now. No, I'm not going to shoot anyone. I need to get you out of here, and you know the plan. So you should obey me, and that way you both get to live for now, and I get what I want. That's a fair enough trade. I would like you leading the way. So we will go out the back, Special Agent Amy Larson, right out the back door."

"I don't know if can crawl over a fence," she told him.

"The Glock. Give me your Glock. Now."

She tried to obey him; she tried to lift her hand.

He had to walk around and take it from her.

"Get out back. The air will clear you somewhat."

She could barely move. He took the gun and began to drag her along. She hung back a moment, staring at him. "Wait! Did you kill the agent out front? He's in the air—"

"No, I didn't kill him. He's just out. A needle quickly thrust in an incredibly hard place to find is easy enough, especially when the agents all trust a good man like Marty Benson."

She could ask him to swear that it was true, but she wasn't sure if this man would ever tell the truth. And now...

Air. She desperately needed the air.

But as they reached the fence at the rear of the property, she turned back again.

"One more thing!" she said.

"What? Stop stalling! I know you're hoping that your knight in shining armor will get here and rescue you."

She stared at him and laughed, daring to take all the time she could. "Sorry, that's the old fairy tale. You're making a mistake. This ball-breaking princess doesn't need a knight in shining armor. I like one at my side, but... I'm also pretty good at fighting my own battles."

"Get your ass over the fence!" he commanded.

"I told you! There's one more thing I must know!"

"What's that?"

"Is Aubrey Hamilton involved in this? Is she with you—or did you plant the phone in her drawer in their bedroom?"

17

When Amy did not answer her phone, Hunter's next call was to Garza.

"I'm not sure yet what's going on, but either Hamilton, his wife, his campaign manager—one of them is in on this. Amy is not answering, the agent on duty isn't responding, and Rowdy isn't responding. The closest law enforcement needs to get out there now. And someone needs to get to the safe house to pick up Aubrey Hamilton and Frank Hamilton, too, and bring them both in. We're going to need to find Marty Benson, because it's one of them," he told Garza.

Garza would bring Mickey in.

"I'm heading out to the Hamilton house and headquarters now," he said. "I'll—"

"You'll need backup. Wait—"

"Garza, sir! The locals need to be there now—as in ten minutes ago!" Hunter told him.

"All right, I'm on it. Just take care. Don't do anything rash."

"Sir, I always take care," Hunter promised.

He knew, of course, that Garza was worried he'd go off protocol because of Amy. He wouldn't. Because doing it all the right way was going to be the way to save her.

And to bring an end to it all.

As he rushed out of the building, he heard someone running behind him. He almost drew his weapon.

It was Aidan.

"You may need me!" Aidan told him. "Sabrina has been reading more—she's tracing IP addresses, and despite all the boomerang nonsense going on, she's traced several of them back to Hamilton's headquarters. And that phone in Aubrey Hamilton's room... could she be involved? Would a mother risk her child?" he asked.

They'd reached the SUV.

"Get in," he told Aidan. "We've got to move. And I don't know. I'm not sure it's shocking for a true narcissist to sacrifice his own child, but Aubrey didn't strike me that way. I don't know. It could all be a setup."

"God, I'm praying our agents aren't dead!" he said, and then realized that he had spoken in front of Hunter. "Hey, no, Amy is too resilient. But—and don't forget! She was my friend before she met you!"

"I know. Sorry!"

As he drove, his phone rang. Aidan grabbed it, putting it on speaker. "Forrest and Cypress here," he said.

Mickey was on the other end. "Police will be at the headquarters as we speak. And agents are bringing the Hamilton family in."

"What about Marty Benson?"

"He's not there—he was working at the headquarters. He checked in with our man on duty."

"Thanks," Hunter said.

He drove with his siren; he seldom used it. It was only for emergencies.

This was an emergency.

But as he had requested, he saw that police officers were all but crawling all over the place; and even as he arrived, backup from the FDLE and FBI arrived as well.

One of the police officers hurried to meet them as they left their car.

"Someone let out a gas attack except… The agent on the porch was out like a light, and he's still out. EMTs are on the way. And there's an agent inside who is equally out of it, still unconscious, but both are alive. We found another man in the backyard—it's Marty Benson. I've seen him on some of the campaign posters and flyers for Frank Hamilton."

"What about Amy? Special Agent Amy Larson?" Hunter asked.

The officer shook his head. "Sir, of course, you're welcome to tear the place apart, but we've done that, and there's no one else here. No one at all."

Hunter nodded his thanks and headed into the house.

He was going to tear it apart himself, although he knew that Amy wasn't there. The Archangel had taken her.

But he was damned sure now that the Archangel was one of three people—Frank Hamilton, Aubrey Hamilton, or Marty Benson.

In the main room, he found that Rowdy was laid out on the floor with a policewoman by his side.

"He's breathing all right!" she assured Hunter quickly.

"Thanks."

"The EMTS are—"

"On the way. Thank you."

He hurried by her, determined to search every room in the house. Even though it was a large house, he could move with the speed of a bullet when he needed to. He finished with the front of the house and hesitated, heading out back.

It appeared that Marty Benson had been seated on a lawn chair when he'd been hit with whatever.

Or hit himself with it. A policeman was at his side.

"Breathing well?" Hunter asked.

"Yes, sir. His pulse is a little weak, but that's to be expected. Whatever it was that did this had dissipated by the time we got here, but I could still smell something a little sweet."

He thanked him and started to head back into the house, but something stopped him.

The EMTs arrived while he looked across the yard, and Marty Benson was retrieved from the lawn chair and taken away on a stretcher.

Hunter walked to the fence, to the area they had leaped over before when they were searching for a shack.

As he reached it, he paused, not sure whether to smile or to feel an even greater concern.

Amy had known that they would come, that they would look for her.

And she had managed to snag a piece of her jacket on the fence.

She had been forced this way. He didn't know if she'd been drugged first, or if something else had caused her to jump the fence. But the only way she would have done so was if she had been compelled to do so as a matter of life or death—her own or that of someone else.

As he waited in the yard, Aidan came upon him.

"I looked in every closet and under every bed. Amy isn't here," he said.

"I know she isn't."

Hunter showed Aidan the piece of fabric he had found.

"So she's out there. Foolish!" Aidan said. "They know we know the Everglades better than anyone. They can't hide her out there. And if Frank and Aubrey are at the safe house, and Marty Benson is out like a light, Reverend Ben and Colin are in custody...who the hell did this?"

"A liar," Hunter said. "And he—or she—knows that we're good at finding what's out there. So this is going to be something different, either something hidden or something so regular that it blends into everything else."

"There isn't anything regular out there," Aidan assured him, "just hardwood hammocks and mangrove swamps."

"But she's close!" Hunter said.

"We can't know that," Aidan said. "Both Frank and Aubrey Hamilton were at the safe house when agents went to retrieve them. And Marty Benson was attacked the same as the FBI agents. There's someone else—"

"I don't think so," Hunter said.

"How was this done, then?"

"I think I know," Hunter said. "Marty Benson. He was so, so concerned that Hamilton might quit his campaign. But who better to take it over than the ever-present and loyal and righteous campaign manager? And what better way to rule the world than make people believe that they must give up their rights if they're ever to be safe?"

"You're talking a dictator, not a president."

"Exactly. Aidan, get out there and stop the ambulance that's about to take Marty Benson. Ask the EMTs to work on him, but get a doctor out here so that we're not accused of torture or failing to provide medical care. I want that man to stay here."

"Do you think that he'll admit this to you?" Aidan asked.

"I'm going over the fence. It will take them a while to bring him around. Not that long, though. The last time there was the event here with the drugged water, Marty didn't take half as long to come around as the others. Because he dosed himself just enough to make it all look real," Hunter explained. "He had help. Reverend Ben MacDowell, I believe. MacDowell took the kid out to the woods. I'm going out there—"

"And I'm going with you."

"Great, but first—"

"Yeah, yeah, I'm on it!" Aidan said, heading back toward the house. "But—"

"I'm getting ahold of Eric Dayton. He needs to take another stab at Reverend MacDowell!" Hunter said.

He walked straight to the fence and made the call to Eric as he did so. He was certain now that he was right—on part of it, at least. Marty Benson was the great Archangel, ruling all the horsemen, heedless of what befell them. To kidnap Marc Hamilton, he had used Reverend MacDowell, not Colin because the young man was too volatile.

He was over the fence when Aidan reappeared, assuring him, "Done and done. A specialist in gas attacks and drugs is on the way out here along with a forensic team with any necessary testing equipment."

"I've got Dayton going in to see MacDowell again. He's going to lie. And that is legal when seeking to save a life!" Hunter said.

"You don't think that—"

"That Benson killed Amy already?" Hunter asked. "No. He thinks that he's better than she is, that he can force her into submission. Then he'll kill her. And he hasn't had time to manage that. But we must find her. Because he'll never tell us where she is. We can only hope that perhaps MacDowell knows more about the man's secret stashes. Or..."

"Or?"

"It was in Aubrey's room that Amy found the phone. It's almost impossible to believe that Marc's mother could have been willing to sacrifice him to the flames, but..."

"We've seen enough that is almost impossible," Aidan finished.

He was quickly over the fence. "I talked to Jimmy. No, he isn't law enforcement. But he can get the best trackers known to man to come on out here."

"That will work for me." Hunter started into the rich growth of the hardwood hammock, the wilderness that civilization encroached upon more each year.

And he shouted her name.

"Amy! Amy, if you can hear me, we're coming for you! Keep fighting!"

★ ★ ★

Amy awoke in a box.

For a moment, despite all of her training and her years in law enforcement, she panicked.

A coffin! She'd been sealed in a coffin and left to die!

She fought the panic. Panic could kill with the same ease as a bullet. And when she forced herself to calm down, she knew that the box she was in was not a coffin. And she didn't think that she could be far from the Hamilton house. Because Marty Benson would need to get back there quickly—super quickly—if he was going to pretend that he was a victim just like the others.

She'd been awake, though, breathing fresh air, walking as he directed her and then...

It had felt like a spider bite, not a mosquito bite, but a little prick...

Of course. He had hit her with a needle, just like the trusting agent who had been so diligently watching the entrance to the house.

So...

Where was she? And what was this boxlike thing?

She tried to shift and move, finally rolling over. The darkness here was complete. All she could do was feel her way around.

She knew that she was somewhere Marty Benson could return to—somewhere he could fulfill his desire to torture her.

Break her.

Not happening, Marty. I'd rather die.

Yet that idea wasn't really encouraging; the man was an expert with chemicals and drugs. He had known what he was doing to taint the water and the coffee in the Hamilton house. He had known how to give himself the appearance of being just as fragile as the others, so unknowingly victimized!

He was an expert with hallucinogens who had made so many people believe in everything he had said, and also made them believe that killing another human being was a kindness so they could sit with angels...

But she wasn't young, naive, or impressionable. Could she fight such things?

Maybe. Because maybe he hadn't knocked her out quite as well as he had planned, though...

She knew nothing of the passage of time. Still, he had been in a hurry. A hurry to get her away.

A hurry to get back.

Should she still be unconscious?

She could twist and turn. And it seemed that the box...

She wasn't in a basement. Such a thing couldn't exist since there weren't buildings out here. There were no pilings, and to the best of her knowledge, no one had started what they called a Mount Trashmore landfill with garbage.

No one could dig and build a basement out here, but...

She remembered the church and how Reverend MacDowell had seemed to disappear into thin air.

She remembered, too, that she had her penlight; she maneuvered herself around to dig it from her pocket. She was suddenly hopeful that her phone would be on her, too, but she'd left her phone at the foot of the bed in the Hamilton bedroom when she'd been so determined to get every piece of information off the burner phone she'd found to the analysts.

But she had the light. The light was something against the stygian darkness. And it showed her that no, this was no basement. It was perhaps two feet or so from top to bottom, no more. But before her...

The darkness stretched out.

And she could hope that the darkness led somewhere.

And it didn't matter.

She was not going to lie there and wait to die, no matter how powerful and godlike Marty Benson believed he had become.

★ ★ ★

"Okay, I just talked to the doc working on Marty Benson, and he believes Benson will come around in another thirty minutes or so. Rowdy and the other officer were brought into the hospital, and they're doing well but it will be a little longer. Mickey and Garza are speaking with Aubrey and Frank Hamilton now. And Eric is talking to Reverend Ben MacDowell, who apparently really was the most important man to the Archangel, no matter what Colin wants to believe."

"That's the game," Hunter said, crawling over a mangrove root. They'd come to a swamp. He couldn't see any alligators basking in the swamp, but as he kept walking, he tripped over what he thought was a root.

It wasn't.

He reached down to extricate his foot. He was dead still for a minute.

"What?" Aidan asked.

Hunter picked up the disarticulated bone that had caught him up. "What do you think this is?"

"A femur. A human femur," Aidan said. He shook his head. "Well, that's been half the man's game. When you really need to get rid of someone, feed them to the wildlife. Except that this…this has been out here a long time."

"He's been planning all this a long time. Marty Benson met Frank Hamilton and figured he was the perfect candidate for a man trying to catch on to the coattails of a rising star. He orchestrated the occults and everything that has come before this."

"And we've got him!" Aidan said.

But they didn't have Amy.

Aidan's phone rang. He answered it quickly and turned to Hunter. "The troops are on the way. Jimmy has gathered a group of guides, Mickey and Garza are sending more agents. Hunter, we will find her."

Yes, they would find her. He just prayed that…

They would find her alive! They would.

He stopped walking and frowned. There was something ahead, but it didn't look like one of the old hunter's shacks—in fact, it didn't seem to have four walls.

"Aidan—"

"I see it. Let's go."

They hurried forward, hitting water.

"It's only a few feet. Of course—"

"Yeah, yeah, I know. Snakes and the possibility of an alligator, submerged, rising. But we're much bigger than easy prey, Aidan. And it looks like there's still a food supply out here. I haven't seen a single python in this area."

He was already plunging through the shallow mangrove swamp, then rising on the other side.

"It's higher ground this side of the water," Aidan noted. "A natural crest by the swampy area. There's the...whatever it is. Lean-to?"

They'd reached whatever the wooden structure had been. There was a roof, but only three sides, no doors, just the one open side. Oddly, it was built up. Maybe not so oddly. Building a few feet above the ground helped control what wildlife could access a place. But it wasn't simply up on pilings; the ground was secured on four sides with wooden slats.

Hunter quickly mounted the few steps to the open-side entry.

There was crude, wooden, weather-beaten furniture inside, including a table and two chairs and a chest.

There was also a mat on the floor—as if sometimes someone slept there.

"Not my choice of a rustic Florida cottage," Aidan said dryly. "But we'll need that mat for whatever DNA and trace we're able to get off of it."

"Right. So..."

"It's raised a good two or three feet, but that's something that was—and is still—often done out here when building chickee huts," Aidan said. "The height helps to keep critters out. But this thing is open on one side, and that's confusing. As rustic as everything else we've seen, but..."

"I thought that these were all supposed to be torn down," Hunter said, shaking his head.

Aidan laughed. "Some have been. Some, well, it just depends on if the right person noticed they were here or not. But this one is unique. Hey, there's a trunk over there."

Hunter nodded and walked over to what looked like a large wooden trunk. He opened it; it was empty.

And bottomless. He could see the ground.

He looked at Aidan. "Reverend Benjamin MacDowell. That's how he left his place while it was being watched, and why he was long gone before we even noticed."

"Is Amy there?"

Hunter shook his head. "No, but I'm willing to bet she was." He stopped speaking and then crawled down into the hole and looked around.

Darkness.

He pulled out his penlight. The tunnel stretched out...

Into the wilderness.

But how far could it go? They were only about two feet above the wet level of the mangrove swamp.

"Hunter, if we hop in and follow it—"

"No, we need to follow from above. It heads straight out, and it must have an exit at the other end. I know Amy. She didn't just lie here waiting for rescue or death. She moved."

"If she could!" Aidan said quietly.

"She could. And we're going to find her! But we need to follow the line we can see. Straight out. We'll get to her. Or she'll get to us! Amy! Amy!"

There was no answer. Hunter hurried outside, judging the terrain and the direction of the strange tunnel.

It had to have been an escape route at one time, much like

Reverend Ben's tunnel had been. If Benson had stuffed Amy into that tunnel, he had really underestimated her.

"Hunter—"

"Come on! We'll go straight. It leads down to the mangrove swamp, northwestward of the yard, near the area where the fire was burning!"

"Amy!" Shouting her name again, Hunter was on his way, reminding himself to watch his step—he wasn't going to be much help searching with a broken leg.

"Amy!"

And then...

He wasn't sure. Was it a bird or his imagination?

But he thought he heard her, heard a voice.

Amy's voice, faint and distant.

"Hunter! Hunter, I'm here!"

The sound was so faint. Was it his imagination? His longing for everything to be all right?

Aidan appeared at his side.

"Do you hear her?"

"Hunter, there are all kinds of sounds out here, so..."

"This way!" Hunter said. "She's out— She's out here somewhere, and we're going to find her!"

Finally. She felt as if she had traveled forever, crawling in the darkness, the thin glow of her penlight showing her that the tunnel went on and on.

She began to feel that the ground around her was damper than it had been. In many places, the wood was buckling. She could see tree roots breaking through. At one point, she tried to drag one through, hoping it would break an opening for her.

It did not. She wasn't exactly a weakling, but it was going to take more strength than what she had. Not to mention that she wasn't at her best. She still felt dizzy now and then. Things began to swim before her eyes. She had to blink. To wait. To breathe. To start over again.

Finally, she reached a strange twist in the tunnel, one that allowed her to crawl up, using a tangled mangrove root to rise from her contorted crawling position and to stand at the last foot of the strange tunnellike structure, created impossibly in an area that didn't allow for anything deep before hitting the water level.

The first thing she saw through the canopy of the trees was the moon.

It had never been more beautiful, a full moon lighting the sky. And above the soft movement of the leaves and tree limbs, there were stars out.

The air remained humid, but...

There was a breeze. The most beautiful thing in the world was the breeze as it touched her cheeks.

But then she noticed her environs and she remained dead still.

She was just feet from water, from a canal that seemed to twist through the hardwood hammock. And...

Night. The time when alligators usually liked to hunt. They tended to be ambush predators, seeing prey, finding a hole or a position, and waiting for the unwary victim to come their way.

And while the moon didn't alleviate the darkness of the night, she could see several pairs of eyes, caught in the reflection of bits of light.

Not a great place to be. She wasn't cast into terror by the sight of one, but...

She was unarmed. And it always felt better to crawl around in a swampy wilderness with her Glock at her side.

She was out of the tunnel, but now she knew exactly why Marty Benson might be so sure that she wasn't going to escape. He'd be thinking that the tunnel and a return to the box where he'd left her would be preferable to being a big gator's dinner.

She was holding very still, trying to see a way around the many creatures, all in hunting mode. If she walked far enough...

Okay, admittedly, though she had grown up in the state and had respect for the creatures, she didn't completely understand their habits.

Or their hunger.

But she couldn't just stay there forever. In this area, she could also become the victim of a venomous snake.

She needed to move.

But in which direction? She was usually decent with geography and direction, but at this moment decent would not be enough.

She had no idea of what was east, west, north, or south.

And then…

She thought she heard someone call her name.

Hunter.

She smiled. She'd known he would come. And of course, Mickey would have seen to it that the entire area was crawling with agents—maybe as many as the natural predators of the area!

"Hunter! Hunter! I'm here."

There was no answer. She waited a minute and tried again. "Hunter!"

And then she heard him. He was there.

"Amy, we're on our way. Keep talking so that we can get to you!"

"There's a big pool of alligators right here. I'm at the water's edge where Benson's ridiculous tunnel let out. I mean a lot. I think he was feeding these guys to stop anyone he had captured from trying to escape. I'm babbling. You said to keep talking, but… I don't want them to notice… Okay, keep talking. Hunter! The Archangel is Marty Benson. He's been at this for years and years and…"

"I know. We figured it out."

She heard his voice, loud and clear. She turned. He was behind her, carefully balancing on a tree root, noting the glittering eyes of the hopeful alligators waiting in their ambush positions.

He reached out to her, and she threw her arms around him.

They held tight for a minute; then she saw Aidan, and she smiled and disengaged from Hunter to hug him, too.

"We knew you'd find your way out!" Aidan told her.

"I did. But now…how do we go back to the house from here?" she asked.

Hunter looked at Aidan. "We backtrack."

"Backtrack, okay…"

Aidan grinned. "I'll lead the way. Just…"

"Move quietly and without fear, and those lovely beasts will wait for something more bite-size to pass by?" she asked.

"Yeah, hopefully, that's the plan!" Hunter said.

And it was a plan. But then, they had come to her, so they knew the way back and the way out.

Finally, they came to the fence at the back of the Hamilton property. And it was there that they paused at last.

"You really need a bath!" Aidan told Amy.

She ran her fingers through her hair, feeling the mud that was caked into it.

"You think?"

"Just a suggestion," Aidan teased. "Seriously, Amy, how—"

"I'm not an idiot. I'd never have just walked out into the Everglades with Marty Benson—or anyone I didn't know and know well. But…" She paused, wincing, shaking her head. "He said he'd shoot Rowdy there and then if I didn't do as he said."

"I figured it was something like that," Hunter said. "We'll get out of here as soon as possible, but do you mind waiting here for just a few minutes?"

"What's going on?"

"Well, as you can imagine," Hunter told her, "Marty Benson played the same game, dousing himself with the gas that he had to knock out the agents. And you?"

"He wanted me to be able to walk myself—I didn't pass out until we were almost there. Then…when I woke up, I was in the tunnel," Amy told him.

"And you didn't need a knight in shining armor!" Hunter murmured.

She laughed. "Like I told him, I'm always happy to have a knight at my side." She turned to Aidan. "Two knights!"

Aidan laughed. "Hey, how about a warrior, huh? That'll work for me."

"Best warrior ever," she told him. "But, Hunter..."

"I got them to bring a doctor here—and to hold on to Marty Benson. I want to talk to him here first, see what he has to say."

"All right. But where—"

"I'm not sure. There are still agents and forensic experts in the house again. And we've got to let the agents and guides in the field know that we've got you, and we're in—"

"I'm on that!" Aidan said, pulling out his phone.

Hunter nodded at Amy. "Let's get in. I believe they'll have Benson in an ambulance out front. Let me just warn everyone inside to keep quiet, and then you can follow me. I'll go talk to him and you can join me."

Amy nodded. She gave him a minute, and then she followed with Aidan.

The front door was open, and she could see the one ambulance waiting just outside. She knew several of the agents inside the house, both FDLE and FBI. And though they were quiet, she found herself being hugged by many of them, with all the others nodding their appreciation that she was all right—if a little bit icky. Those who had hugged her were quickly knocking the muck off their clothing—or trying to do so!

She moved to the door, slipping out and to the side of the ambulance where she could hear Hunter talking.

"Where is she, Benson?" Hunter asked. "Where is Amy?"

"Oh no, oh Lord, you haven't found her?" Benson demanded.

"Where is she?" Hunter persisted.

"I...I don't know. She was here... Yes, she was here with the fellow who came to watch over her. I don't know... I don't know. I don't know anything. I was just… Well, I didn't know what was happening. I felt that I needed air, fresh air, even warm, humid air!" he murmured.

Amy could imagine the man's smile, weak and disarming, as he lied.

"There had to have been someone here… Oh God! Please tell me. Please tell me that Frank Hamilton hasn't been doing this whole thing himself. I mean, his son…his own son. But have I been a fool all this time? I don't know how this happened. I don't… I mean, I thought I was protected! An FBI agent at the door! Another in the house and Special Agent Amy Larson upstairs, and… I don't know who else could possibly have gotten in here. But I haven't understood any of this! Of course, you know, some of those chat room people have it right—you people need to have greater power and greater control under better supervision, strong supervision—"

That was it.

It was all that Amy could take. She could not wait any longer. It was time to make her appearance.

She leaped up into the ambulance. "Oh, Marty, give it a break! You're guilty as hell, and we all know it. And I don't believe you'll even have any bargaining power! Strong law enforcement, oh, Marty, we will see that you get it! Oh, strong, strong, strong—as in the death penalty!"

"No, you lying bitch! I don't know what was done to you—"

"Can it, Marty. Spare us—"

"I want my lawyer!"

"Isn't your lawyer busy defending Colin?" Amy asked sweetly. She leaned toward him, allowing mud to drip on him from her hair. "You've only got one hope for any leniency whatsoever, and that's if you answer my previous question. Was Aubrey Hamilton involved in all this in any way?"

"Involved!" he shouted. "Involved? You thought it was me? Aubrey Hamilton is the damned Archangel!"

18

There was one thing certain.

Criminals tended to be liars.

Another thing was certain—they needed to walk away from Marty Benson at that moment, to regroup, to meet with Garza and Mickey and Eric Dayton. Maybe their profiler could put a spin on this.

The question of Aubrey Hamilton was, of course, the major key. And while Hunter didn't want to believe that the strong supporter of her husband's campaign, the mom who had desperately wanted her son back, could be a human being as evil as the Archangel...

Amy wasn't giving it up.

She smiled at Marty Benson. "Well, go figure! I'm a ball-breaking bitch! But Aubrey Hamilton is the Archangel, and you've been following her dictates for years now? Is that why you saw to it that so many women were taken, abused, and then sometimes killed. Because your boss is a woman, and you're powerless against her? What a pathetic little man you are!"

Benson looked as if he wanted to say something. He was beyond furious and if he could have gone back in time, he would have shot Amy then and there. While the man was fighting to control his rage, Hunter could see the tic in the man's face.

"He's nothing, Amy," Hunter said. "Nothing at all. Let's go where someone is important enough to talk to. See you soon, Marty."

Amy stared at him, surprised and indignant at first, but apparently gathering herself together enough to know that no matter how angry she was with the man who had so brutally harmed others, who murdered people, and who ordered the murder of others, they had to ferret out the absolute truth.

"You're right. Oh, and gee, as much as I do love the Everglades, I would just as soon not be wearing quite so much of it. Let's go see the important people."

She hopped down off the back of the ambulance. Hunter nodded, indicating the doctor who had arrived at the property to treat the man. "Amy, let's check with the doc. I want to see how badly our man worked on himself."

"He was out when police arrived?"

"Yep. He knows how to play a game."

The doctor was a man of about forty-five, just beginning to gray. He was serious as he spoke to one of the EMTs, but smiled slightly as he turned to Hunter and Amy.

"Good to see you both, Agents," he assured them. "Though this has been my first out-of-the-hospital visit to treat a patient in years, I understand the complexity of the situation. And you're Special Agent Amy Larson. Truly good to see you. I heard you were lost in the woods," he told Amy.

"I was lost and found," she assured him.

"I'm very glad to see you. I'm not so sure I'd have fared at all well myself out there!"

Amy smiled. "Thank you."

"What did Marty Benson do to himself, Doc? How bad?" Hunter asked.

"He's the same as the others, but…"

"Just not as badly hit?" Hunter asked.

"He inhaled the same gas—just not so much of it," the doctor said. "I think that he's fine, but to be safe and to keep the city, county, state, and country from being sued at some point, we'll see that he's brought to detention but kept in the infirmary."

"And kept under guard," Hunter said.

"You really think that he managed to do this to himself?" the doctor asked.

"We know that he did," Amy assured him.

The doctor nodded. "Okay. And as for transport, don't worry. I've received orders that it might be like holding on to a slippery eel. I'll be riding with him until he's taken in, but an agent will be in there with me. I'm no fool and I really like living."

"Thanks," Hunter said.

Amy repeated his thanks, but the doctor was staring at her worriedly.

"Special Agent Larson. Before we leave, I understand you were drugged, knocked out as well…"

"Yes. And thank you again," Amy interrupted. "I've had plenty of time to come around, and I'm fine—I just need a shower."

"Still…let me take a quick look at you," the doctor said. He stepped forward, producing a light from his pocket, checking Amy's eyes first, then pocketing his light and taking her pulse, and drawing his stethoscope from around his neck to assure himself that her breathing was fine.

"You're good," he said.

"I have some killer insect bites, but yes, I'm good and thank you!" she told him. She looked at Hunter. "Can we get out of here?"

"Not without me!" Aidan said, stepping up. "So, do we have the Archangel?"

"According to Benson, no," Hunter said.

"What?" Aidan demanded.

"He is claiming that Aubrey Hamilton is the Archangel," Amy explained.

"Is that even possible? Wait, what am I asking?" Aidan said, shaking his head. "We've learned that just about anything is possible."

"I'm getting Amy to the hotel so she can wash off the mud of the Glades," Hunter told Aidan. "We'll report in while we drive, and then we'll get to headquarters as quickly as possible and speak with Frank and Aubrey."

"What do you think?" Aidan asked, looking at Amy. "And how—"

Amy shook her head. "Let's get to the car. I really, really, really need a shower. And come to think of it, you guys…"

"We are all a mess," Aidan said.

Amy smiled suddenly. "And thank you, both of you. I knew you wouldn't rest until you found me."

"You were doing all right on your own," Aidan told her.

"Yeah, but I'm glad you found me in one piece, and not in the belly of a bull alligator!"

"Let's go," Hunter said.

He waved to the agent in charge at the site and hurried toward his vehicle. He knew that they were right behind him. In the SUV, Amy explained that she'd found the burner phone, called in the discovery, and relayed numbers and other information from it to Sabrina. "Then I smelled it. The odor of something kind of sweet. When I hurried downstairs, I found Rowdy laid out on the couch, and then Benson popped out from behind the couch and threatened to kill him."

"The threat was in place if you didn't do what he said?" Hunter asked.

She nodded. "He's a liar," she said with determination. "He's definitely a liar, but he'll get a team of top-notch lawyers, call me a liar, and claim that the evidence I found myself points to Aubrey Hamilton."

"You don't think she might be guilty of collusion?" Aidan asked.

Amy was thoughtful for a minute. "I'm not answering that until we've had a chance to talk with Aubrey and Frank."

As she spoke, Hunter's phone rang. Mickey was on the line. "Amy, are you okay?" he asked, no anxiety apparent in his voice, but Hunter knew the man had been worried.

"Right as rain," Amy said.

"All right, well. We're having a few problems here. Frank Hamilton is growing angry. He says that we're detaining him, but I don't think he's worried about himself. He keeps insisting that his wife has been put through the wringer by all this often enough already. They have a child who should be in bed. They're angry, and he's asking that his attorney be brought in because although he's grateful, he feels he's being accused and he doesn't know why," Mickey told them.

"Has Eric been with them?" Hunter asked.

"Yes, but the faster you get in here, the better."

"All right. I'll drop Amy off as long as the hotel is covered. We don't know how many people might still be out there obeying the dictates of the Archangel. And I'll come on in."

"I don't need a shower that badly, and we do have a shower at headquarters for emergencies, sudden-notice trips, etcetera," Amy said. "Mickey, I think we can be there within the next twenty minutes."

Hunter glanced at Amy.

She looked back at him. "You can start pacifying them. I'll need no more than ten minutes. I want to… I don't know! Hunter, are we going to know if they're telling the truth? Everyone involved with this lies!"

"Amy, I think that this is it," Hunter said.

Aidan leaned forward from the back seat. "From the first cult killings until now, Amy, I believe, like Hunter—this is it. This is going to be the night we stop the Apocalypse."

Hunter put on the siren again, and they arrived within twenty minutes just as Amy had promised. She left him and Aidan when they reached headquarters, and he hurried up to Mickey's office, where the FDLE supervisor and Charles Garza were waiting together. They didn't have Frank and Aubrey in an interrogation room, but rather in a far more comfortable position in the break room, where they could be supplied with coffee and snacks, should they desire.

"I'll just be silent backup," Aidan told Hunter as he followed Hunter into the room.

"Ah, Hunter!" Garza said, rising. "Join us, please. Mr. and Mrs. Hamilton are worried about getting back to the safe house. I've assured them that we have one of our best agents, a mom herself, watching over Marc, but they are anxious to get back to their son."

Frank Hamilton stood as well. "You understand. Please, we've been through so much already—"

"Sir," Hunter said, interrupting, "you must understand. We have absolute proof that your campaign manager is the man who sabotaged your headquarters and recruited others to abduct people, to secure young women, to commit murder, and to dispose of the bodies. We believe that both Michael Colin Ridgeway and Reverend Benjamin MacDowell were 'angels,' working under him—or someone else."

Frank Hamilton stared at him, frowning.

"I...I understand that. I'm horrified, of course. I believed in Marty. He always seemed to fight so hard for what was right, and I am so sorry for the harm done to everyone. I was stupid. I was fooled. I shouldn't be in public office when I'm too stupid to see the criminals who are right under my nose. And I am so grateful for the protection that has been afforded me, but we... My wife and I are exhausted. This has been... Well, I don't know. This is what you do, but for us...oh my God! The death, the horror of all this... I am sticking to my guns. Let someone else try to make friends of those who don't want to talk, who seem to relish getting on any bandwagon to fight and—"

"Frank!" Aubrey Hamilton stood, setting a hand on his shoulder. "There are good people out there! Yes, we were taken. We were both taken—"

"Mrs. Hamilton, we need to speak with you, too," Hunter said quietly.

"Me?" Aubrey Hamilton truly appeared to be stunned.

But just as Marty Benson knew how to play a game of innocence, this woman just might know how to play that game as well. They'd learned the hard way that the "fairer" sex could be equally cruel.

Amy seemed to have impeccable timing that night. She had showered and dressed in generic black stretch pants and a matching T-shirt. Her hair was still wet, and her face was barely dry. She walked in just as Aubrey stood before Hunter with shock and denial clearly on her face.

"Mrs. Hamilton!" Amy said pleasantly. "Hi."

"Special Agent Larson—the wonderful woman who saved my son!" Aubrey said. "Please, tell me, what is going on?"

"Mrs. Hamilton," Amy said. "I'm afraid that we discovered a phone in your room at your home that has been used for all manner of communications that have to do with what has been going on."

"What?" Aubrey said, frowning. "In my room? But I thought that the house had already been swept for bugs, for anything that could explain how drugs got into our water, how... Why were you searching again?"

"What? Why?" Frank Hamilton asked. His confusion was clearly apparent on his face.

"Because we were missing something. Which, of course, turned out to be good, Mr. Hamilton, because it was at your home we discovered Marty Benson at work again, determined that he had to derail your campaign."

"Is he…is he truly this Archangel—the person behind all the horror that's been going on, not just here, but in other parts of the country?" Frank asked.

Amy glanced at Hunter and shrugged. "We know for a fact that both men we arrested—Michael Colin Ridgeway and Benjamin MacDowell—were working under the Archangel. They claim that they never knew who he was. Now, from the evidence we've gathered, Marty Benson is guilty of many, many things. But he swears that he's not the Archangel."

"Did he tell you who the Archangel is? Someone must know," Frank said.

"Well, we're very unhappy to tell you that yes, Marty Benson has pointed a finger at someone," Amy said.

"Who?" Aubrey asked.

"You," Amy said softly.

"What?" Aubrey Hamilton gasped the word and sank into a chair, staring. "Oh, come on, please, you must know that he's just striking out! How could I be guilty of… My son was at risk—you know that, Special Agent Larson! You're the one who saved him!" Aubrey cried.

"Mrs. Hamilton, please, trust me, we want to believe that there's no truth in this whatsoever, but the phone that was discovered—" Hunter began.

"It was wrapped up in your underwear. It was not easy to find, and that's why it was missed during the first go-round," Amy said.

Aubrey looked at her husband. "Frank?"

Frank Hamilton looked at his wife, and then at the group of law enforcement in front of him, waiting for his reaction.

"No!" he said. "No, it's impossible. Aubrey is always with me. She couldn't have been controlling people around the country. You caught the man. He's a liar. He was in the house, he was planting the phone, trying to make my wife look guilty."

"Possibly. We wouldn't be decent law enforcement if we didn't check everything out. The phone is with our forensic team. I'm sorry, but we have to look for fingerprints and DNA," Hunter said.

Frank Hamilton sat down by his wife.

"I never should have gotten into politics!" He shook his head. "Maybe there really is no such thing as morality out there, maybe people just want to hate people—"

"And," Amy said, taking the seat next to him, "maybe it's true that Marty Benson really is the Archangel, and he was doing all this to see that you didn't run so that he could step in and take your place. The most likely scenario is that he wants to take your place so he can rise up the ranks and seize all the power—here on earth—that he can."

"Lord Edward Acton wrote in a letter to Bishop Mandell, circa 1887," Frank Hamilton said wearily, "'Power tends to corrupt, and absolute power corrupts absolutely.'" He appeared to be dejected and disoriented. He looked up. "But Aubrey is not the Archangel! Do you hear me? That monster planted the phone in her room and—"

"My fingerprints *are* going to be on that phone," Aubrey said. She looked as stricken as her husband. "Before any of this happened, Marty gave me that phone and told me I needed to hold it for him, that he was monitoring some sites and making calls when people seemed suspicious. He said that Frank was so lax when it came to security that someone had to look after him. He was doing that, but it was safest if I watched the burner phone he used for security for him. I had no idea that he was anything but honestly in love with Frank's platform and that he wanted to do anything more than help!"

"Why didn't you just tell us that first?" Amy asked.

"Because I…I didn't want Frank to know that I was worried, that he… He is so good and he's trusting. I was never so trusting. I'm sorry, Frank, I'm so sorry!" Aubrey sobbed.

"All right, that's good to know," Mickey told her. He looked at Garza.

Hunter wasn't sure what Garza's reaction was going to be. If she were anyone else, he might have her held at least for the night.

Then again, where she was living already, she was under guard. And that night, Garza himself would see to it that she didn't go anywhere.

"We'll see you back to the safe house for tonight," Garza said. "We have major players—if not the Archangel—under arrest. And of course, don't—"

"Don't go anywhere," Frank interrupted bleakly. He looked at them. "Aubrey is not guilty! You must know that…oh God!"

He turned to his wife, who was shaking her head in misery.

"Frank, I thought… He made me worry!" Aubrey said, breaking into sobs. She looked up at Hunter. "How could you believe I would ever risk my son?" she demanded.

"As I said, we want to trust you," Hunter said simply. He looked at Garza.

"Don't worry, we do have people locked up for the night. I need sleep, these people need sleep, and we'll pick up this line of questioning again in the morning. The night shift detail will make sure none of our suspects go anywhere," Mickey said.

Of course, that included Aubrey Hamilton, even if she was being allowed to return to the safe house.

Hunter nodded to Aidan and led Amy out.

He didn't speak until they were in the SUV. "Well?"

She shook her head. "I don't know. Aubrey didn't admit that her prints would be on the phone until a few beats after she heard that it was being checked for prints and DNA. But if she really loves her husband, she might just be concerned that she had done something behind his back." She shook her head. "I still think Marty Benson is one of the slimiest creatures known to man."

"Let it go. If I had a voice, I'd sing Elsa's song from *Frozen*," he told her, trying to ease her mind some. "Hey. We have tomorrow—"

"But I thought that tonight we really were going to be done!" she said.

"We're at the finish line!" he told her. "And I don't know about you, but I am absolutely exhausted. And we'll be a hell of a lot better and more focused after some sleep."

They had just pulled into the hotel parking lot when Hunter's phone rang, and he put the call on speaker.

"Get back here!" Garza said.

"What—"

"It's Marty Benson. He pretended to be in distress right before they reached the hospital. He managed to stab our agent with a needle and then take out the terrified doctor with a right hook before slamming the driver and sending the ambulance into the embankment by the canal. He disappeared before the agents following could reach the ambulance, save the driver from drowning, and get help for the others. He's out there somewhere with a stolen Glock. He's going to be searching for the two of you. Eric Dayton has been studying everything about the man, and he believes that Benson feels strongly he must put Amy down if he's ever going to regain his power. And I know you are both capable of protecting yourselves, but God knows what he's up to. Just get back here!"

Hunter had stopped the car.

A bullet burst through the front window, slamming into the headrest just an inch from his skull.

"Down!" he shouted to Amy, but she was already out of the SUV, stooping low, drawing her replacement Glock, and ducking around seeking cover.

He slid from the vehicle himself, going instantly around to join her at the rear of the SUV. More bullets whizzed through the night. But at this hour, almost into the wee hours of the morning, there was thankfully no one else around.

"Where is he?" Amy asked softly.

"I'm trying to determine the trajectory," he told her. "It sounds as if there is more than one person out there, but all the players we know about…"

"Oh, Hunter, we'll probably be rounding up the players for the next decade!" Amy said, and she was probably right.

But if Marty Benson was doing the shooting, who was with him?

The gunfire stopped, and they heard Marty Benson call out to them. "Special Agents—the golden pair, FBI point on this mission. The good people! Well, I have a terrified young woman here—I scooped her out of the lobby, coming out drunk as a skunk. Maybe she's not so good, but she's only about twenty-two. And if I don't see you right now…she dies. Come on, Amy, we can't let her die!" he said. "Think of yourself as the Archangel now! The power of life and death for her is in your hands."

"Amy, don't!" Hunter warned. "He'll just kill her and you, and I'll be down a gun—"

"No, Hunter! We can do this. Let me go. You'll see him, you'll get a chance."

"There are two shooters out there!"

"Quick!" Marty Benson called. "She's got about five seconds!"

"Benson!" Hunter roared. "I was on the phone with headquarters when you started shooting—this place will be crawling with agents in minutes!"

"And I don't care. All I want is Amy Larson! It's a trade, Amy, come on!"

"We can do this. Watch my face!" Amy told him.

He hadn't expected her to slip away so quickly, and he wasn't sure he could have stopped her—a struggle behind the back of their SUV could have been the death knell for both of them—and for the woman he now heard sobbing softly and held by Benson. Wherever he was.

Amy walked calmly out.

Then Marty Benson appeared, rising from one of the cars parked a row in front of theirs.

And he did have a hostage. A sobbing young woman.

His stolen Glock was against her temple.

"Let her go. I'm here," Amy told him.

Hunter forced himself to remain still, but to keep his Glock aimed at the man. Of course Benson held the woman in front of him, and she was twisting and turning.

"Throw down your weapon," he said.

She lifted her Glock high, then dropped it and kicked it to the side. Not toward him, but far enough away that he wouldn't demand she push it in his direction.

"Let her go," Amy said again.

"You come here," he said.

"What? You're going to knock me out and put me in another tunnel?"

"This time I am going to give you to... Well, let's just say that I've heard you love the environment. I'll let you be a part of it, how's that?" Benson said. He started to laugh. "And with the two of you gone, good old Aubrey will never prove her innocence. So, Amy, get over here now."

"Let her go."

"And be an easy mark for Special Agent Hunter? Hell, no. Get over here first."

Amy walked to him.

Benson shouted again. "Perry! Get over here, take this one!"

Perry Carson, administrator for the site of the Commonsense Party, suddenly appeared at his side.

That was a surprise. Except...the man looked ill. And Hunter realized that he had been coerced and forced into joining Benson.

He'd been shot. His left arm was bleeding copiously.

Benson pushed the woman at him. "Hold her! Maybe you'll get to live!"

No one here was meant to live, Hunter knew. But he had to play it out and bide his time.

Perry Carson, bleeding away, sheltered the young woman in his arms. Hunter saw he was weeping.

And Marty Benson now held Amy, his Glock against her head.

Amy would have seen, of course, that Perry Carson was a victim, just as the young woman was. And he wasn't running because he knew that would be his end.

"All right, Special Agent Forrest!" Benson called, amused. "Seriously? You thought that silly woman could be the Archangel? That's the thing with people. They'll believe just about anything if you push them in a direction. Suspicion! Ah, what it can do. But it won't matter. I will disappear to begin again— my Apocalypse will come. I am the Archangel! I am the one and only, bending people to my will."

"With drugs," Amy said, shrugging. She was facing Hunter. Benson had his free arm around her, holding her back to his torso.

"Shut up!" he told her.

"You don't believe a word of that Archangel bull," Amy said.

"No, but it was a hell of a way to recruit the right people! Idiots who thought they'd have power like mine, white horse, red horse, black horse—pale horse! But above them all—the great Archangel. And I will rise again. So...let's see. The here and now. Show yourself, Special Agent. Show yourself if you want her to live!"

Watch my face! Amy had said.

She was looking at him intently. She gave him a barely perceptible nod.

And it was split-second timing.

Amy slammed an elbow with all her strength into Marty Benson's ribs.

He screamed furiously in pain, but his gun slipped, no longer aimed at her head and...

Hunter stepped out from behind the car, already taking aim. And as Benson reacted to the attack and his pain, Amy dropped low.

And Hunter fired.

He caught Marty Benson dead center in the forehead, and the man went down without another word.

Once again, dawn arrived, while they were still dealing with the aftermath of Marty Benson's escape and subsequent attack and death. Hunter knew that Amy was watching him. They were trained to know when innocent lives could be lost—and when it came to a choice between a killer and a victim and there was no choice, they had to shoot to kill.

It still bothered him. It always had. He hated to take human life, any human life. The system wasn't perfect, but he believed that the law and justice were worth seeking all the time. The courts weren't perfect, but every man should have a trial. Were there those who should be locked away permanently? Hell, yes.

Unlike Marty Benson, he had no desire to play God. People and the world were far too complicated.

The area had been roped off when the police arrived, and the medical examiner had been called. Garza and Mickey, among a slew of other agents, FDLE, and FBI, had arrived.

Eventually, the press had arrived, too. They wanted to know what had happened; they wanted to interview Hunter and Amy, but Mickey managed to fend them off, issuing a statement and assuring them that the next day he'd give a press conference.

They wanted to know—had the killing sprees across the country been stopped, had it really been the kind and handsome gentleman, swearing he was behind moderation and supporting Frank Hamilton, the mastermind of it all?

Was he dead, and with him dead, would it all end?

Hunter turned over his weapon. It was a formality in any officer shooting.

A tearful and nearly hysterical Perry Carson begged them all to believe that he'd had no choice but to accompany Benson once the man had shot him and promised the next bullet would be between his eyes.

Hunter believed him. He thought that Mickey and Garza did, too. The man had a shattered arm and his behavior during the action with Marty Benson had suggested that he'd had no choice. He had also, apparently, been a horrible shot—or a man who hadn't wanted to hit anyone.

Perry had been whisked off to the hospital, along with the young woman Benson had managed to snatch as she was returning, a "wee bit three sheets to the wind," from her night out with friends.

At last, Amy stood with Hunter and Garza and Mickey. They watched as the vehicles from the hospital and the morgue drove from the darkness and into the coming light. Aidan had come, too, along with Eric Dayton, the profiler who had known the subject enough to know that for him to regain his own feeling of superiority, he had to get rid of Amy. While the others were moving on except for the last of the forensic team, he and Aidan came over to join them as well.

"You had to do it, Hunter. There was truly no choice," Amy told him.

"A man like that?" Aidan said, shaking his head. "He'd have killed the girl he snatched and Perry once he didn't need them anymore and if he had gotten anywhere with Amy—"

"He'd have probably been sorry," Hunter tried to say lightly.

"You saved my life, Perry Carson's life, and the girl's life, Hunter."

He nodded. "I know." He smiled at her. "'Watch my face!' What you did was incredibly dangerous," he said.

"I, too, had no choice." Amy smiled. "And I knew you had my back."

"And think of the others. That man killed or ordered to be killed so many people! Think of the lives that might have been lost in the future. And it's over now. It is over, isn't it?" Aidan asked.

"The Book of Revelation—and Marty Benson's form of the Apocalypse. For our purposes, yes, it's over," Hunter said. "Benson thought it was amusing that we believed for a minute that Aubrey Hamilton might be the Archangel. He's too proud of himself for all his cleverness."

"But he was also an extreme narcissist," Eric Dayton said. "Being such a narcissist, he had to make sure you knew that it was him. He wanted you to know he was the supreme over all the others. Except, of course, those he conned—criminals and innocents—still must pay for the parts they played. Some really believed. Others just...well, they liked crime. I'm sure that now they know the Archangel isn't going to get into any form of power from which he can pardon them, they will start talking and spill everything they know." He shook his head. "Catch on the coattails, convince him you're his biggest fan—take over when he's forced to choose between family and his ideals and goals—and slowly take more and more power until... Well, that's often how a dictator rises to power."

"So that was it!" Amy murmured. "When they were talking to us, what Colin, the reverend, and others wanted was to get the death penalty off the table. They believed that Benson would come to that kind of power—pardon them and save them."

"There will be a lot of cleanups!" Garza said. He smiled suddenly. "Well, I do think the hotel is safe. Now. Hunter, there's more paperwork in the morning, you'll have mandatory sessions with a therapist—"

"I know, I know, fine. But—" Hunter began.

Garza laughed and looked at Mickey.

"But now, you really get some time off. Both of you. So figure out how you want to use it!"

Amy looked at Hunter. "Well, I was thinking that we really could use some sleep and then..."

"Then we'll work on it," he said quietly.

"Oh, this is getting sappy!" Eric Dayton teased. "I'm out of here. You two get that sleep."

He headed out. Aidan was watching them, grinning.

"Hey, I do still have connections. And we have a beautiful place in Bali."

"Bali sounds good," Amy assured him. "And we're grateful for anything that—"

"No," Aidan said. "I'm grateful for all that you've done, and that I've gotten to be a small part of stopping the Apocalypse. And taking down a monster who was making a mockery of our ancestral home."

Garza grinned at Aidan. "Think they may get to be honorary members of the Unconquered?" he asked.

"Oh, indeed. But," Aidan said, "you can't take off quite yet—I mean, not out of the state. I, um, I'd like you to be around for a few plans I've made."

"Oh?" Amy asked, smiling.

But Aidan gave her a wave as he walked away. "Later today!" he called back to them.

"All right. Later today!" Hunter said.

He put his arm around Amy. "Goodbye!" he told the others. Then, ducking under the crime tape, he led her toward the hotel.

And when they reached the room, trembling, he pulled her into his arms. They needed sleep; that was true.

But more than sleep, they needed one another.

They were off—other than tie-up paperwork, Hunter's mandatory session with a company shrink, and a few things they were determined to do themselves, they really were going to get vacations!

Amy was ready.

And in the days that followed the last event with Marty Benson, good things began to emerge, too. Perry Carson was patched up; his site for the Commonsense Party went wild with support for him—and for Frank Hamilton. Hamilton visited the man in the hospital; they became friends.

Aubrey told Amy that she and her husband had never been closer.

And Frank announced to them that although he'd been a trusting fool and they'd all nearly paid dearly, he didn't plan to change his goals—and, more importantly, and through the support of his wife and son, he was going to keep his campaign going. They meant to respect everyone, be good to everyone, and reteach the fine art of compromise over hateful discourse and name-calling. They wouldn't be stopped. They'd already learned what it was to be threatened, they would be smart, but they wouldn't be stopped.

Benjamin MacDowell and Colin learned that their Archangel was dead and somehow they began to fight desperately just to stay alive, spilling the names and locations of those who had been angel lieutenants across the country and those guilty of attempting to create such havoc that Marty Benson could rise as the true candidate for law and order.

Elijah was given probation and he and Annabel were delighted and determined to put the experience toward something good: working for Frank Hamilton.

They also learned what Aidan's big secret was…and why they needed to stay in Florida a bit.

They were to be witnesses and best man and maid of honor for a wedding; Aidan and Sabrina had decided on a quick—but perfect—wedding. Just immediate friends, coworkers, and family—and yet that meant a surprisingly big wedding!

They were going to be married on the reservation, but it proved to be a perfect combo of so much that was Florida: Miccosukee, Seminole, Hispanic, African American, and everything else that helped create the melting pot of the area.

It wasn't small, but it wasn't an "event." They were married in the open air with all their friends, family, and coworkers surrounding them, after which there was a barbecue right on the grounds.

Aidan had apologized to Amy and Hunter, saying that they'd

just decided against hiding their relationship from anyone anymore and that they'd make it legal.

And, just to keep things separated a bit, Aidan was going to
go through the hoops and ropes and become an agent while Sabrina remained in the lab.

"One hell of an agent—with all the talent and expertise you'll
be bringing to the table!" Amy had said. And looking at Hunter
she'd added, "Not to worry! I love what you're doing, and we want
the same—but we have family strewed around and I want my folks
and brother and Hunter's parents…and, naturally, you and Sabrina,
Mickey, and Garza, and so many of the people we love and work
with! Just a little planning ahead!" she told him. "But after your
wedding…could you really get us a few weeks somewhere…?"

"Beautiful and exotic?" Aidan asked. "I do have connections."

Hunter came up behind Amy and slipped his arms around her.
"Hmm, what I'd love, if it's agreeable to Amy, is just to have a
secret vacation—a real one—right back where we were. That
beautiful room that extended out into the water…and then,
maybe…Disney World!"

"Maybe you don't have to wait until after our wedding,"
Aidan said, grinning.

"What do you mean?" Hunter asked, raising an eyebrow.

"We can bring the wedding to the hotel."

Amy laughed. "I'm all into the right away!"

And so, by Aidan and Sabrina's wedding, they were back
where they had started when the first pale horse had arrived.

And it was beautiful and blissful, time just for themselves,
time to talk, to plan the wedding that they wanted, with those
they loved most in the world.

And it was a perfect and beautiful Florida day, the sky blue,
the sun shining.

The bride was gorgeous, the groom striking and handsome.
The vows were heartfelt and touching and Amy was delighted
to be a part of it.

She also took pleasure in watching Hunter before, during, and after the services. He was such a professional, such an amazing agent.

And he could still be such a simple man, a good man, enjoying friends, playing with children, laughing, smiling, and being…normal!

It was an amazingly joyous occasion.

Of course, crime wasn't going to cease—but there was good reason to be grateful that Marty Benson's version of the Apocalypse was over.

It was a day to see the best in humanity, and even though Amy liked to believe that there was incredible good to be found in human beings, the fringe was bad…and the fringe was capable of being very loud.

And as the day went on and she watched Hunter, saw him with others, saw him play with children, laugh, throw a football, and just be…Hunter, a man who could joke, entertain, and maybe even be a father, she realized she wanted something a bit different than what she thought they had needed.

That night, she whispered in his ear that she'd love a reception with everyone, and that would take some planning, but…

Instead of a big wedding, they should just get married, and then…

Have a party! A well-planned party with everyone they loved and needed and…

Hunter agreed.

And within the week, they'd acquired their license, and like proud parents, Mickey Hampton and Charles Garza stood witness, grinning throughout as if they'd planned the whole thing.

Their parents understood…

When they got to it, the wedding reception was going to be one hell of a party!

★ ★ ★ ★ ★